CROSS OF ST GEORGE

In the bitter February of 1813, with convoys from Canada and the Caribbean falling victim to American privateers, Sir Richard Bolitho returns to Halifax to pursue a war he knows cannot be won, but which neither Britain nor the United States can afford to lose. After nearly thirty years of almost continuous conflict with the old enemy, France, England and her Admiral desire only peace. But peace will not be found in the icy Canadian waters, where a young, angry nation asserts its identity, and men who share a common heritage die in close and bloody action. Nor is there peace for those who follow the Cross of St George: not for the embittered Adam, mourning the loss of his lover and his ship, nor for Rear-Admiral Valentine Keen, who remains strangely indifferent to responsibility. Nor will there be peace from those who use this struggle between nations as an instrument of personal revenge.

D1325624

CROSS OF ST GEORGE

Alexander Kent

WINDSOR SELECTION

CHIVERS PRESS
BATH

First published 1996
by
William Heinemann
This Large Print edition published by
Chivers Press
by arrangement with
Reed Consumer Books Ltd.
1997

ISBN 0 7451 5472 7

British Library Cataloguing in Publication Data available

Photoset, printed and bound in Great Britain by
REDWOOD BOOKS, Trowbridge, Wiltshire

For my Kim with love,
and with thanks for sharing
your Canada with me.

*Wherever wood can swim,
there I am sure to find this flag of England.*

Napoleon Bonaparte

CONTENTS

CONTENTS

CROSS OF ST GEORGE

CHAPTER ONE

SWORD OF HONOUR

The Royal Dockyard at Portsmouth, usually a place of noise and constant movement, was as quiet as the grave. It had been snowing steadily for two days, and the buildings, workshops, piles of timber and ships' stores which made up the clutter in every big yard had become only meaningless shapes. And it was still snowing. Even the familiar smells had been overwhelmed by the white blanket: the sharp tang of paint and tar, hemp and new sawdust, like the sounds, seemed smothered and distorted. And, muffled by the snow, the echoing report of the court-martial gun had gone almost unnoticed.

Set apart from the other buildings, the port admiral's house and offices were even more isolated than usual. From one of the tall windows, which overlooked a nearby dock, it was not even possible to see the water in the harbour.

Captain Adam Bolitho wiped the damp glass and stared down at a solitary Royal Marine, whose scarlet tunic was a stark contrast to the blinding whiteness of the backdrop. It was early afternoon; it could have been sunset. He saw his reflection in the window, and the light of the blazing log fire on the other side of the room, where his companion, a nervous lieutenant, sat perched on the edge of his chair with his hands held out to the flames. At any other time Adam Bolitho could have felt sorry for him. It was never an easy or a welcome duty to be the companion ... his mouth tightened. The *escort*, for

1

some one awaiting the convenience of a court-martial. Even though everyone had assured him that the verdict would be unquestionably in his favour.

They had convened this morning in the spacious hall adjoining the admiral's house, a place more usually the venue of receptions than a courtroom where a man's future, even his life, could be decided. Grotesquely, there had even been a few traces of the Christmas ball which had been held there recently. Adam stared at the snow. Now it was another year: January third, 1813. After what he had endured, he might have imagined that he would have grasped at a new beginning like a drowning man seizing a lifeline. But he could not. All he loved and cared for lay in 1812, with so many broken memories. He sensed the lieutenant shifting in his chair, and was aware of movement elsewhere. The court was reassembling. After a damned good meal, he thought: obviously one of the reasons for holding the proceedings here, rather than force the court to endure the discomfort of a long pull in an open boat to the flagship, somewhere out there in the snow at Spithead.

He touched his side, where the iron splinter had smashed him down. He had believed he was dying: at times, he had even wanted to die. Weeks and months had passed, and yet it was hard to accept that it was less than seven months since he had been wounded, and his beloved *Anemone* had been surrendered to the enemy, overwhelmed by the massive artillery of the U.S.S. *Unity*. Even now, the memories were blurred. The agony of the wound, the suffering of his spirit, unable to accept that he was a prisoner of war. Without a ship, without hope, someone who would soon be forgotten.

He felt little pain now; even one of the fleet

2

surgeons had praised the skill of *Unity's* French surgeon, and other doctors who had done what they could for him during his captivity.

He had escaped. Men he had barely known had risked everything to hasten his freedom, and some had died for it. And there were others, who could never be repaid for what they had done for thim.

The lieutenant said hoarsely, 'I think they've returned, sir.'

Adam acknowledged it. The man was afraid. *Of me? Of having become too intimate, if it goes against me?*

His frigate, *Anemone*, had turned to face a vastly superior enemy, out-gunned and out-manned, with many of his company sent away as prize crews. He had not acted out of arrogance, or reckless pride, but to save the convoy of three heavily laden merchantmen he had been escorting to the Bermudas. *Anemone's* challenge had given the convoy time to escape, to find safety when darkness came. He remembered *Unity's* impressive commander, Nathan Beer, who had had him moved to his own quarters, and had come to visit him as he was treated by the surgeon. Even through the mists of agony and delirium, Adam had sensed the big American's presence and concern. Beer had spoken to him more like a father to his son than like a fellow captain, and an enemy.

And now Beer was dead. Adam's uncle, Sir Richard Bolitho, had met and engaged the Americans in a brief and bloody encounter, and it had been Bolitho's turn to give comfort to his dying adversary. Bolitho believed they had been fated to meet: neither had been surprised by the conflict or its ferocity.

3

Adam had been given another frigate, *Zest*, whose captain had been killed while engaging an unknown vessel. He had been the only casualty, just as Adam had been the only survivor from *Anemone* apart from a twelve-year-old ship's boy. The others had been killed, drowned, or taken prisoner.

The only verbal evidence submitted this morning had been his own. There had been one other source of information. When *Unity* had been captured and taken into Halifax, they had found the log which Nathan Beer had been keeping at the time of *Anemone's* attack. The court had been as silent as the falling snow as the senior clerk read aloud Beer's comments concerning the fierce engagement, and the explosion aboard *Anemone* which had ended any hope of taking her as a prize. Beer had also written that he was abandoning his pursuit of the convoy due to the damage his enemy had inflicted. At the end of the report he had written, *Like father, like son.*

A few quick glances were exchanged in the court, nothing more. Most of those present were either unaware of Beer's meaning, or unwilling to remark on anything that might prejudice the outcome.

But to Adam, it had been like hearing the big American's voice in that hushed room. As if Beer was there, offering his testimony to an adversary's courage and honour.

But for Beer's log, there was little else to confirm what had truly happened. *And if I were still a prisoner? Who would be able to help? I should be remembered only as the captain who struck his colours to the enemy.* Badly wounded or not, the Articles of War left little room for leniency. You were guilty, unless proven without doubt to the contrary.

He was gripping his fingers together behind his

4

back, so hard that the pain helped to steady him. *I did not strike my colours. Then, or at any time.*

Curiously enough, he knew that two of the captains who were sitting on the board had also been court-martialled. Perhaps they had been remembering, comparing. Thinking of how it might have been, if the point of the sword had been towards them . . .

He moved away from the window and paused by a tall mirror. Perhaps this was where officers examined their appearance, to ensure it would meet with the admiral's approval. Or women . . . He stared coldly at his reflection, holding back the memory. But she was always there. Out of reach, as she had been when she was alive, but always there. He glanced at the bright gold epaulettes. *The post-captain.* How proud his uncle had been. Like everything else, his uniform was new; all his other possessions lay now in his chests on the sea-bed. Even the sword on the court-martial table was a borrowed one. He thought of the beautiful blade the City merchants had presented to him: they had owned the three ships he had saved, and were showing their gratitude. He looked away from his reflection, his eyes angry. They could afford to be grateful. So many who had fought that day would never know about it.

He said quietly, 'Your duty is all but done. I have been bad company, I fear.'

The lieutenant swallowed hard. 'I am proud to have been with you, sir. My father served under your uncle, Sir Richard Bolitho. Because of what he told me, I always wanted to enter the navy.'

Despite the tension and unreality of the moment, Adam was strangely moved.

'Never lose it. Love, loyalty, call it what you will. It

5

will sustain you.' He hesitated. 'It must.'

They both looked at the door as it opened carefully, and the Royal Marine captain in charge of the guard peered in at them.

He said, 'They are waiting, Captain Bolitho.' He seemed about to add something, encouragement, hope, who could tell. But the moment passed. He banged his heels together smartly and marched out into the corridor.

When he glanced back, Adam saw the lieutenant staring after him. Trying to fix the moment in his mind, perhaps to tell his father.

He almost smiled. He had forgotten to ask him his name.

The great room was full to capacity, although who they were and what they sought here was beyond understanding. But then, he thought, there was always a good crowd for a public hanging, too.

Adam was very aware of the distance, the click of the marine captain's heels behind him. Once he slipped. There was still powdered chalk on the polished floor, another reminder of the Christmas ball.

As he came around the last line of seated spectators to face the officers of the board, he saw his borrowed sword on the table; its hilt was toward him. He was shocked, not because he knew the verdict was a just one, but because he felt nothing. *Nothing.* As if he, like all these others, was a mere onlooker.

The president of the court, a rear-admiral, regarded him gravely.

'Captain Adam Bolitho, the verdict of this Court is that you are honourably acquitted.' He smiled briefly. 'You may be seated.'

Adam shook his head. 'No, sir. I prefer not.'

6

'Very well.' The rear-admiral opened his brief. 'The Court holds that Captain Adam Bolitho not only acquitted himself of his duty in the best tradition of the Royal Navy, but in the execution of such duty has done infinite credit to himself by a very obstinate defence against a most superior force. By placing his ship between the enemy and the vessels charged to his protection, he showed both courage and initiative of the highest order.' He raised his eyes. 'But for those qualities, it would seem unlikely that you would have succeeded, particularly in view of the fact that you had no knowledge of the declaration of war. Otherwise...' The word hung in the air. He did not need to explain further what the outcome of the court-martial would have been.

All the members of the court stood up. Some were smiling broadly, obviously relieved that it was all over.

The rear-admiral said, 'Retrieve your sword, Captain Bolitho.' He attempted to lighten it. 'I would have thought you might be wearing that fine sword of honour I have been hearing about, eh?'

Adam slid the borrowed sword into its scabbard. *Leave now. Say nothing.* But he looked at the rear-admiral and the eight captains who were his court and said, 'George Starr was my coxswain, sir. With his own hand he lit charges which speeded the end of my ship. But for him, *Anemone* would be serving in the United States navy.'

The rear-admiral nodded, his smile fading. 'I know that. I read it in your report.'

'He was a good and honest man who served me, and his country, well.' He was aware of the sudden silence, broken only by the creak of chairs as those at the back of the great room leaned forward to hear his

7

quiet, unemotional voice. 'But they hanged him for his loyalty, as if he were a common felon.'

He looked at the faces across the table, without seeing them. His outward composure was a lie, and he knew he would break down if he persisted. 'I sold the sword of honour to a collector who values such things.' He heard the murmurs of surprise behind his back. 'As for the money, I gave it to George Starr's widow. It is all she *will* receive, I imagine.'

He bowed stiffly and turned away from the table, walking between the ranks of chairs with his hand to his side as if he expected to feel the old torment. He did not even see the expressions, sympathy, understanding, and perhaps shame: he saw only the door, which was already being opened by a white-gloved marine. His own marines and seamen had died that day, a debt no sword of honour could ever repay.

There were a few people in the outer lobby. Beyond them, he saw the falling snow, so clean after what he had attempted to describe.

One, a civilian, stepped forward and held out his hand. His face seemed vaguely familiar, yet Adam knew they had never met.

The man hesitated. 'I am so sorry, Captain Bolitho. I should not detain you further after what you have just experienced.' He glanced across the room where a woman sat, gazing at them intently. 'My wife, sir.'

Adam wanted to leave. Very soon the others would be milling around him, congratulating him, praising him for what he had done, when earlier they would have watched him facing the point of the sword with equal interest. But something held him. As if some one had spoken aloud.

8

'If I can be of service, sir?'

The man was well over sixty years old, but there was an erectness, a pride in his bearing as he explained, 'My name is Hudson, Charles Hudson. You see ...' He fell silent as Adam stared at him, his composure gone.

He said, 'Richard Hudson, my first lieutenant in *Anemone*.' He tried to clear his mind. Hudson, who had slashed down the ensign with his hanger while he himself lay wounded and unable to move. Again, it was like being an onlooker, hearing others speak. *I ordered you to fight the ship*! Each despairing gasp wrenching at his wound like a branding iron. And all the while *Anemone* was dying beneath them, even as the enemy surged alongside. And Hudson's last words before Adam was lowered into a boat. *If we ever meet again....*

Adam could still hear his own answer. *As God is my witness, I will kill you, damn your eyes*!

'We had only one letter from him.' Hudson glanced again at his wife and Adam saw her nod, helping him. She looked frail, unwell. It had cost them dearly to come here.

He said, 'How is he?'

Charles Hudson did not seem to hear. 'My brother was a vice-admiral. He used his influence to have Richard appointed to your ship. When he wrote, he always spoke of you so warmly ... he was so proud to be serving with you. When I heard about your court-martial, as they dare to call it, we had to come. To see you, to thank you for what you did for Richard. He was our only son.'

Adam tensed. *Was*. 'What happened?'

'In his letter he said he wanted to find you. To explain ... something.' He dropped his head. 'He was

9

shot, attempting to escape. He was killed.'

Adam felt the room sway, like the deck of a ship. All that time, the pain and the despair, the hatred because of what had happened; and he had thought only of himself.

He said, 'I shall tell my uncle when I see him. He was known to your son.' Then he took the man's arm and led him towards his wife. 'There was nothing for Richard to explain. Now he is at peace, he will know that.'

Hudson's mother was on her feet, holding out her hand to him. Adam stooped, and kissed her cheek. It was like ice.

'Thank you.' He looked at each of them. 'Your loss is my loss also.'

He glanced round as a lieutenant coughed politely, and murmured, 'The port admiral wishes to see you, sir.'

'Can't it wait?'

The lieutenant licked his lips. 'I was told that it was important, sir. To you.'

Adam turned to say goodbye, but they had gone, as quietly and patiently as they had waited.

He felt his cheek. Her tears, or were they his own?

Then he followed the lieutenant, past people who smiled and reached out to touch his arm as he passed. He saw none of them.

He heard nothing but his own anger. *I ordered you to fight the ship.* It was something he would never forget.

*   *   *

Lady Catherine Somervell walked softly toward the window, her bare feet soundless as she glanced back

10

at the bed. She listened to his breathing. Quiet now: he was asleep, after the restlessness he had tried to conceal from her.

She realized that the night was quite still, and there was a hint of moonlight for the first time. She groped for a heavy silk shawl but paused again as he stirred on the bed, one arm resting on the sheet where she had been lying.

She looked out at the ragged clouds, moving more slowly, allowing the moon to touch the street, which shone still from the night's downpour. Across the road, which was all that separated this row of houses from the Thames, she could just discern the restless water. Like black glass in the moonlight. Even the river seemed quiet, but this was London: within hours this same road would be busy with traders on their way to market, and people setting up their stalls, rain or no rain.

She shivered, despite the thick shawl, and wondered what daylight would bring.

Little more than a month had passed since Richard Bolitho had returned home, and the guns of St Mawes battery had thundered out their salute to Falmouth's most famous son. An admiral of England, a hero and an inspiration to the men who followed his flag.

She wanted to go to him now. Not to the public figure, but to the man, *her* man, whom she loved more than life itself.

This time she could not help him. His nephew had been ordered to face a court-martial, the direct consequence of losing *Anemone* to the enemy. Richard had told her that the verdict would vindicate Adam, but she knew him so well that he could not conceal his anxiety and his doubt. His business at the

11

Admiralty had prevented him from being at Portsmouth where the court was convened; she also knew that Adam had insisted upon facing the court alone, and unaided. He knew too well how Bolitho hated favouritism, and the manipulative use of outside influence. She smiled sadly. They were so alike, more like brothers than anything else.

Vice-Admiral Graham Bethune had assured Richard that he would inform him immediately he heard anything: the fast telegraph from Portsmouth to London could bring a dispatch to the Admiralty in less than half an hour. The court had been convened yesterday morning, and as yet there had been no word. Nothing.

Had they been in Falmouth she might have distracted him, involved him in the estate's affairs, in which she had taken such an interest during his long absences at sea. But their presence had been required in London. The war with the United States, which had erupted last year, was believed to be at a turning point, and Bolitho had been summoned to the Admiralty to settle doubts, or perhaps inspire confidence. She felt the old bitterness. Was there nobody else they could send? Her man had done enough, and had too often paid the price.

She must confront it: they would soon be parted again. If only they could get back to Cornwell ... It might take all of a week, with the roads in their present state. She thought of their room at the old grey house below Pendennis Castle, the windows that faced the sea. The rides, and the walks they enjoyed so much ... She shivered again, but not from cold. What ghosts would wait for them when they took that particular walk, where the despairing Zenoria had flung herself to her death?

12

So many memories. And the other side of the coin: the envy and the gossip, even the hatred, which was more subtly revealed. Scandal, which they had both endured and surmounted. She looked at the dark hair on the pillow. *No wonder they love you. Dearest of men.*

She heard the sound of iron wheels, the first sign of life in the street. Going to fetch fish from the market, no doubt. Peace or war, the fish were always there on time.

She slipped her hand inside her gown, her fingers cold around her breast. As he had held her, and would hold her again. But not this night. They had lain without passion in one another's arms, and she had shared his anxiety.

She had felt the cruel scar on his shoulder, where a musket ball had cut him down. So many years ago, when her husband, Luis, had been killed by Barbary pirates aboard the *Navarra*. She had cursed Richard on that day, blaming him for what had happened. And then, after he had been wounded, he had been plagued by the return of an old fever, which had almost claimed his life. She had climbed into the cot with him, naked, to comfort him and hold the icy grip of the fever at bay. She could smile at the memory now. He had known nothing about it. So many years, and yet it could have been yesterday . . . .

He had changed her life, and she knew she had changed his. Something that went far beyond his demanding world of duty and danger, something only they shared, which made people turn and look at them when they were together. So many unspoken questions; something others could never understand.

She touched her skin again. *Will he always find me beautiful when he returns from another campaign,*

13

another country? I would die for him.

She reached out to close the curtains, and then stood quite still, as if she were held by something. She shook her head, angry with herself. It was nothing. She wiped the window pane with her shawl and stared at the street below, The Walk, as it was called locally. A few patches of moonlight revealed the trees, black and bare of leaves, like charred bones. Then she heard it: the rattle of wheels on the cobbles, the gentle step of a solitary horse. Moving slowly, as if uncertain of the way. A senior officer returning to his quarters at the barracks nearby after a night of cards, or, more likely, with his mistress.

She watched, and eventually a small carriage moved across a bar of moonlight: even the horse looked silver in the cold glow. Two carriage lamps were burning like bright little eyes, as if they and not the horse were finding the way.

She sighed. Probably some one who had taken too much to drink, and would be overcharged by the driver for his folly.

Her hand was still beneath her breast, and she could feel her heart beating with sudden disbelief. The carriage was veering across the road towards this house.

She stared down, barely able to breathe as the door opened and a white leg paused uncertainly on the step. The coachman was gesturing with his whip. It was like a mime. The passenger stepped down soundlessly onto the pavement. Even the gold buttons on his coat looked like pieces of silver.

And then Richard was beside her, gripping her waist, and she imagined she must have called out, although she knew she had not.

He looked down at the road. The sea-officer was

14

peering at the houses, while the coachman waited.

'From the Admiralty?' She turned toward him.

'Not at this hour, Kate.' He seemed to come to a decision. 'I'll go down. It must be a mistake.'

Catherine looked down again, but the figure by the carriage had vanished. The bang on the front door shattered the stillness like a pistol shot. She did not care. She had to be with him, now, of all times.

She waited on the stairs, the chill air exploring her legs, as Bolitho opened the door, staring at the familiar uniform, and then at the face.

Then he exclaimed, 'Catherine, it's George Avery.'

The housekeeper was here now, muttering to herself and bringing fresh candles, obviously disapproving of such goings-on.

Catherine said, 'Fetch something hot, Mrs Tate. Some cognac, too.'

George Avery, Bolitho's flag lieutenant, was sitting down as if gathering himself. Then he said, 'Honourably acquitted, Sir Richard.' He saw Catherine for the first time, and made to rise. 'My lady.'

She came down, and put her hand on his shoulder. 'Tell us. I can hardly believe it.'

Avery gazed at his filthy boots. 'I was there, Sir Richard. I thought it only right. I know what it is to face the possibility of disgrace and ruin at a court-martial.' He repeated, 'I thought it was only right. There was heavy snow on the south coast. The telegraph towers were hidden from one another. It might have taken another day for the news to reach you.'

'But you came?' Catherine saw Bolitho grip his arm.

Surprisingly, Avery grinned. 'I rode most of the

15

way. I forget how many times I changed horses. Eventually I fell in with the fellow outside, otherwise I doubt I'd have found the place.' He took the glass of cognac, and his hand shook uncontrollably. 'Probably cost me a year's pay, and I don't think I'll be able to sit down comfortably for a month!'

Bolitho walked to a window. *Honourably acquitted.* As it should be. But things did not always end as they should.

Avery finished the cognac and did not protest when Catherine refilled his glass. 'Forced a few coaches and carts off the road—' He saw Bolitho's expression and added gently, 'I was not in court, Sir Richard, but he knew I was there. Your nephew was going to see the port admiral. Someone said that he has an extended leave of absence. That is all the information I have.'

Bolitho looked at Catherine, and smiled. 'Seventy miles on dark and treacherous roads. What sort of man would do that?'

She removed the glass from Avery's nerveless fingers as he lolled against the cushions, and was asleep.

She replied quietly, 'Your sort of man, Richard. Are you at peace now?'

When they reached the bedroom they could see the river quite clearly, and there were indeed people already moving along the road. It was unlikely that anyone had noticed the sudden arrival of the carriage, or the tall sea-officer banging on the door. If they had, they would think little of it. This was Chelsea, a place that minded its own business more than most.

Together they looked at the sky. It would soon be daylight, another grey January morning. But this

16

time, with such a difference.

She held his arm around her waist and said, 'Perhaps your next visit to the Admiralty will be the last for a while.'

He felt her hair against his face. Her warmth. How they belonged.

'And then, Kate?'

'Take me home, Richard. No matter how long we must travel.'

He guided her to the bed, and she laughed as the first dogs began to bark outside.

'*Then* you can love me. In our home.'

* * *

Vice-Admiral Graham Bethune was already on his feet when Bolitho was ushered into his spacious rooms at the Admiralty, and his smile was warm and genuine.

'We are both abroad early today, Sir Richard.' His face fell slightly. 'Although I fear I have not yet had news of your nephew, Captain Bolitho. The telegraph, excellent though it may be in many ways, is no match for our English weather!'

Bolitho sat down as a servant removed his hat and cloak. He had walked only a few paces from the carriage, but the cloak was soaked with rain.

He smiled. 'Adam was honourably acquitted.' Bethune's astonishment was a pleasure to see. They had met several times since Bolitho's arrival in London, but he was still surprised that Bethune's new authority had not changed him in some way. In appearance, he had matured a good deal since his days as a midshipman in Bolitho's first command, the little sloop of war *Sparrow*. Gone was the round-faced youth, his complexion a mass of dark freckles; here was a keen-eyed, confident flag-officer who would turn any woman's head at Court, or at the many elegant functions it was now his duty to attend. Bolitho recalled Catherine's initial resentment when he had told her that Bethune was not only a younger man, but also his junior in rank. She was not the only one who was baffled by the ways of Admiralty.

He said, 'My flag lieutenant, Avery, rode all the way from Portsmouth this morning to tell me.'

Bethune nodded, his mind busy on another course. 'George Avery, yes. Sir Paul Sillitoe's nephew.' Again the boyish smile. 'I am sorry. Baron Sillitoe of Chiswick, as he is now. But I am glad to know it. It must have been hard for your nephew, losing ship and liberty at one blow. And yet you appointed him to command *Zest* at the final encounter with Commodore Beer's ships. Remarkable.' He walked to a table. 'I sent my own report, needless to say. One has little confidence in courts-martial, as we have seen many times for ourselves.'

Bolitho relaxed slightly. So Bethune had found the time to put pen to paper on Adam's behalf. He could not imagine either of his predecessors, Godschale, or particularly Hamett-Parker, even raising a finger.

Bethune glanced at the ornate clock beside a painting of a frigate in action. Bolitho knew it was his own command, when Bethune had confronted two large Spanish frigates and, despite the odds, had run one ashore and captured the other. A good beginning, which had done his career no harm at all. 'We shall take refreshment shortly.' He coughed. 'Lord Sillitoe is coming today, and I am hoping we shall learn more of the Prince Regent's views on the American conflict.' He hesitated, momentarily

18

unsure of himself. 'One thing is almost certain. You will be required to return to that campaign. What is it now, a bare four months since you engaged and defeated Commodore Beer's ships? But your opinions and your experience have been invaluable. I know it is asking too much of you.'

Bolitho realized that he was touching his left eye. Perhaps Bethune had noticed, or maybe word of the injury and the impossibility of recovery had finally reached this illustrious office.

He answered, 'I had expected it.'

Bethune observed him thoughtfully. 'I had the great pleasure of meeting Lady Somervell, Sir Richard. I know what this parting will mean to you.'

Bolitho said, 'I know you met her. She told me. There are no secrets between us, and never will be.' Catherine had also met Bethune's wife, at a reception at Sillitoe's house by the river. She had said nothing about her, but she would, when she judged that the moment was right. Perhaps Bethune had an eye for the ladies? A mistress, maybe.

He said, 'You and I are friends, is that not so?'

Bethune nodded, not understanding. 'A small word, for what it truly means.'

'I agree.' He smiled. 'Call me Richard. I feel that rank, and the past, stand in the way.'

Bethune strode to his chair, and they shook hands. 'This is a far better day than I dared hope.' He grinned, and looked very young. 'Richard.' Another glance at the clock. 'There is another matter, which I would like to discuss with you before Lord Sillitoe arrives.' He watched him for a few seconds. 'You will soon know. Rear-Admiral Valentine Keen is being appointed to a new command, which will be based in Halifax, Nova Scotia.'

19

'I had heard as much.' Full circle, he thought. Halifax, where he had left his flagship, *Indomitable*, upon his recall to England. Was it really so short a time ago? With her had been their two equally powerful prizes, Beer's U.S.S. *Unity* and the *Baltimore*, which together carried as much artillery as a ship of the line. Fate had decided the final meeting; determination and a bloody need to win had decided the outcome. After all the years he had been at sea, pictures could still stand out as starkly as ever. Allday's grief, alone among all the gasping survivors as he had carried his dead son, and had lowered him into the sea. And the dying Nathan Beer, their formidable adversary, with Bolitho's hand in his, each understanding that the meeting and its consequences had been inevitable. They had covered Beer with the American flag, and Bolitho had sent his sword to his widow in Newburyport. A place well known to men-of-war and privateers; where his own brother Hugh had once found refuge, if not peace.

Bethune said, 'Rear-Admiral Keen will hoist his flag in the frigate *Valkyrie*. Her captain, Peter Dawes, who was your second-in-command, stands to accept promotion and is eager to take another appointment.' He paused discreetly. 'His father, the admiral, suggested that the present was as good a time as any.'

So Keen was going to back to war, still in mourning for Zenoria. It was what he needed, or imagined he needed. Bolitho himself had known the haunting demands of grief, until he had found Catherine again.

'A new flag captain, then?' Even as he spoke, he knew who it would be. 'Adam?'

Bethune did not answer directly. 'You gave *Zest* to

20

him out of necessity.'

'He was the best frigate captain I had.'

Bethune continued, 'When *Zest* returned to Portsmouth she was found to be in a sorry state of repair. Over four years in commission, and after two captains—three, if you count your nephew—and several sea fights, which left her with deep and lasting damage, and without proper facilities for complete repair . . . the last battle with *Unity* was the final blow. The port admiral was instructed to explain all this to your nephew after the court's verdict was delivered. It will take months before *Zest* is ready for service again. Even then.....'

After the court's verdict. Bolitho wondered if Bethune shared the true meaning. Had the sword been pointing at Adam, he would have been fortunate to have remained in the navy, even with a ship as worn and weakened as *Zest*.

Bethune was not unaware of it. 'By which time, this war will probably be over, and your nephew, like so many others, could be rejected by the one calling he loves.' He unfolded a map without appearing to see it. 'Rear-Admiral Keen and Captain Bolitho have always been on good terms, both under your command and elsewhere. It would seem a satisfactory solution.'

Bolitho tried not to remember Adam's face as he had seen it that day in *Indomitable*, when he had given him the news of Zenoria's death. It had been like watching his heart break into pieces. How could Adam agree? Knowing that each day he would be serving alongside and under the orders of the man who had been Zenoria's husband. *The girl with moonlit eyes.* She had married Keen out of gratitude. Adam had loved her . . . loved her. But Adam, too,

21

might be grateful for an escape provided by Keen. A ship at sea, not an undermanned hulk suffering all the indignities of a naval dockyard. How could it work? How might it end?

He loved Adam like a son, always had loved him, ever since the youth had walked from Penzance to present himself to him after his mother's death. Adam had confessed his affair with Zenoria: he felt that he should have known. Catherine had seen it much earlier in Adam's face, on the day Zenoria had married Keen in the mermaid's church at Zennor.

Madness even to think about it. Keen was going to his first truly responsible command as a flag-officer. Nothing in the past could change that.

He asked, 'You really believe that the war will soon end?'

Bethune showed no surprise at this change of tack. 'Napoleon's armies are in retreat on every front. The Americans know this. Without France as an ally, they will lose their last chance of dominating North America. We shall be able to release more and more ships to harass their convoys and forestall large troop movements by sea. Last September you proved, if proof were needed, that a well-placed force of powerful frigates was far more use than sixty ships of the line.' He smiled. 'I can still recall their faces in the other room when you told their lordships that the line of battle was finished. Blasphemy, some thought, and unfortunately there are still many you have yet to convince.'

Bolitho saw him look at the clock yet again. Sillitoe was late. He knew the extent of his own influence and accepted it, knew too that people feared him. Bolitho suspected it pleased him.

Bethune was saying, 'All these years, Richard, a

22

lifetime for some. Twenty years of almost unbroken war with the French, and even before that, when we were in *Sparrow* during the American rebellion, we were fighting France as well.'

'We were all very young then, Graham. But I can understand why ordinary men and women have lost faith in victory, even now, when it is within our grasp.'

'But you never doubted it.'

Bolitho heard voices in the corridor. 'I never doubted we would win, eventually. Victory? That is something else.'

A servant opened the fine double doors and Sillitoe came unhurriedly into the room.

Catherine had described the portrait of Sillitoe's father, which she had seen at the reception in his house. Valentine Keen had been her escort on that occasion: that would have set a few tongues wagging. But as he stood there now, in slate-grey broadcloth and gleaming white silk stock, Bolitho could compare the faces as if he had been there with her. Sillitoe's father had been a slaver, 'a black ivory captain', he had called him. Baron Sillitoe of Chiswick had come far, and since the King had been declared insane his position as personal adviser to the Prince Regent had strengthened until there was very little in the political affairs of the nation he could not manipulate or direct.

He gave a curt bow. 'You look very well and refreshed, Sir Richard. I was pleased to hear of your nephew's exoneration.'

Obviously, news travelled faster among Sillitoe's spies than in the corridors of Admiralty.

Sillitoe smiled, his hooded eyes, as always, concealing his thoughts.

'He is too good a captain to waste. I trust he will accept Rear-Admiral Keen's invitation. I think he should. I believe he will.'

Bethune rang for the servant. 'You may bring refreshments, Tolan.' It gave him time to recover from his shock that Sillitoe's network was more efficient than his own.

Sillitoe turned smoothly to Bolitho.

'And how is Lady Catherine? Well, I trust, and no doubt pleased to be back in town?'

Pointless to explain that Catherine wanted only to return to a quieter life in Falmouth. But one could not be certain of this man. He who seemed to know everything probably knew that, too.

'She is happy, my lord.' He thought of her in the early hours of the morning when Avery had arrived. Happy? Yes, but concealing at the same time, and not always successfully, the deeper pain of their inevitable separation. Before Catherine, life had been very different. He had always accepted that his duty lay where his orders directed. It had to be. But his love he would leave behind, wherever she was.

Sillitoe leaned over the map. 'Crucial times, gentlemen. You will have to return to Halifax, Sir Richard—you are the only one familiar with all the pieces of the puzzle. The Prince Regent was most impressed with your report and the vessels you require.' He smiled dryly. 'Even the expense did not deter him. For more than a moment, that is.'

Bethune said, 'The First Lord has agreed that orders will be presented within the week.' He glanced meaningly at Bolitho. 'After that, Rear-Admiral Keen can take passage in the first available frigate, no matter who he selects as flag captain.'

Sillitoe walked to a window. 'Halifax. A cheerless

24

place at this time of the year, I'm told. Arrangements can be made for you to follow, Sir Richard.' He did not turn from the window. 'Perhaps the end of next month—will that suit?'

Bolitho knew that Sillitoe never made idle remarks. Was he considering Catherine at last? How she would come to terms with it. Cruel; unfair; too demanding. He could almost hear her saying it. Separation and loneliness. Less than two months, then, allowing for the uncomfortable journey to Cornwall. They must not waste a minute. Together.

He replied, 'You will find me ready, my lord.'

Sillitoe took a glass from the servant. 'Good.' His hooded eyes gave nothing away. 'Excellent.' He could have been describing the wine. 'A sentiment, Sir Richard. To your Happy Few!' So he even knew about that.

Bolitho scarcely noticed. In his mind, he saw only her, the dark eyes defiant, but protective.

Don't leave me.

CHAPTER TWO

FOR THE LOVE OF A LADY

Bryan Ferguson, the one-armed steward of the Bolitho estate, opened his tobacco jar and paused before filling his pipe. He had once believed that even the simplest task would be beyond him forever: fastening a button, shaving, eating a meal, let alone filling a pipe.

If he stopped to consider it, he was a contented man, grateful even, despite his disability. He was

25

steward to Sir Richard Bolitho and had this, his own house near the stables. One of the smaller rooms at the rear of the house was used as his estate office, not that there was much to do at this time of the year. But the rain had stopped, and they had been spared the snow that one of the postboys had mentioned.

He glanced around the kitchen, the very centre of things in the world he shared with Grace, his wife, who was the Bolitho housekeeper. On every hand were signs of her skills, preserves, all carefully labelled and sealed with wax, dried fruit, and at the other end of the room hanging flitches of smoked bacon. The smell could still make his mouth water. But it was no use. His mind was distracted from these gentle pleasures. He was too anxious on behalf of his closest and oldest friend, John Allday.

He looked now at the tankard of rum on the scrubbed table. Untouched.

He said, 'Come along, John, have your wet. It's just what you need on a cold January day.'

Allday remained by the window, his troubled thoughts like a yoke on his broad shoulders.

He said at length, 'I should have gone to London with him. Where I belong, see?'

So that was it. 'My God, John, you've not been home a dogwatch and you're fretting about Sir Richard going to London without you! You've got Unis now, a baby girl too, and the snuggest little inn this side of the Helford River. You should be enjoying it.'

Allday turned and looked at him. 'I knows it, Bryan. Course I do.'

Ferguson tamped home the tobacco, deeply troubled. It was even worse with Allday than the last time. He looked over at his friend, seeing the harsh

26

lines at the corners of his mouth, caused, he thought, by the pain in his chest where a Spanish sword had struck him down. The thick, shaggy hair was patched with grey. But his eyes were as clear as ever.

Ferguson waited for him to sit down and put his big hands around the particular pewter tankard they kept for him. Strong, scarred hands; the ignorant might think them awkward and clumsy. But Ferguson had seen them working with razor-edged knives and tools to fashion some of the most intricate ship models he had ever known. The same hands had held his child, Kate, with the gentleness of a nursemaid.

Allday asked, 'When do you reckon they'll be back, Bryan?'

Ferguson passed him the lighted taper and watched him hold it to his long clay; the smoke floated toward the chimney, and the cat lying on the hearth asleep.

'One of the squire's keepers came by and he said the roads are better than last week. Slow going for a coach and four, let alone the mail.' It was not doing any good. He said, 'I was thinking, John. It'll be thirty-one years this April since the Battle of the Saintes. It hardly seems possible, does it?'

Allday shrugged. 'I'm surprised you can remember it.'

Ferguson glanced down at his empty sleeve. 'Not a thing I could easily forget.'

Allday reached across the table and touched his arm. 'Sorry, Bryan. That was not intended.'

Ferguson smiled, and Allday took a swallow of rum. 'It means that I'll be fifty-three this year.' He saw Allday's sudden discomfort. 'Well, I've a piece of paper to prove it.' Then he asked quietly, 'How old

27

does that make you? About the same, eh?' He knew Allday was older; he had already served at sea when they had been taken together by the press gang on Pendower Beach.

Allday eyed him warily. 'Aye, something like that.' He looked at the fire, his weathered features suddenly despairing. 'I'm his cox'n, y'see. I *belongs* with him.'

Ferguson took the stone jug and poured another generous measure. 'I know you do, John. Everyone does.' He was reminded suddenly of his cramped estate office, which he had left only an hour ago when Allday had arrived unexpectedly in a carrier's cart. Despite the fusty ledgers, and the dampness of winter, it was as if she had been there just ahead of him. Lady Catherine had not been in his office since before Christmas, when she had left for London with the admiral, and yet her perfume was still there. Like jasmine. The old house was used to the comings and goings of Bolithos down over the years, he thought, and sooner or later one of them failed to return. The house accepted it: it waited, with all its dark portraits of dead Bolithos. Waited … But when Lady Catherine was away, it was different. An empty place.

He said, 'Lady Catherine perhaps most of all.'

Something in his voice made Allday turn to look at him.

'You too, eh, Bryan?'

Ferguson said, 'I've never known such a woman. I was with her when they found that girl.' He stared at his pipe. 'All broken up, she was, but her ladyship held her like a child. I shall never forget … I know you're all aback at the thought that maybe you're getting old, John, too old for the hard life of a fighting Jack. It's my guess that Sir Richard fears it, too. But

28

why am I telling you this? You know him better than anybody, man!'

Allday smiled, for the first time. 'I was that glad about Cap'n Adam keeping out of trouble at the court-martial. That'll be one thing off Sir Richard's mind.'

Ferguson grunted, smoking. A revenue cutter had slipped into Falmouth, and had brought the news with some despatches.

Allday said bluntly, 'You knew about him and that girl, Zenoria?'

'Guessed. It goes no further. Even Grace doesn't suspect.'

Allday blew out the taper. Grace was a wonderful wife to Bryan, and had saved him after he had returned home with an arm missing. But she did enjoy a good gossip. Lucky that Bryan understood her so well.

He said, 'I love my Unis more than I can say. But I'd not leave Sir Richard. Not now that it's nearly all over.'

The door opened and Grace Ferguson came into the kitchen. 'Just like two old women, you are! What about my soup?' But she looked at them fondly. 'I've just done something about they fires. That new girl Mary's willing enough, but she's got the memory of a squirrel!'

Ferguson exclaimed, 'Fires, Grace? Aren't you being a bit hasty?' But his mind was not on what he was saying. He was still turning over Allday's words. *I'd not leave Sir Richard. Not now that it's nearly all over.* He tried to brush it aside, but it would not go. What had he meant? When the war finally ended, and men paused to count the cost? Or did he fear for Sir Richard? That was nothing new. Ferguson had even heard Bolitho liken them both to a faithful dog and its master. Each fearful of leaving the other behind.

Grace looked keenly at him. 'What is it, my dear?'

He shook his head. 'Nothing.'

Allday darted a glance between them. Although separated for long periods when he was at sea, he had no closer friends.

He said, 'He thinks I'm getting old, ready to be broken up like some rotten hulk!'

She laid one hand on his thick wrist. 'That's foolish talk, you with a fine wife and a bonny baby. Old indeed!' But the smile did not touch her eyes. She knew both of them too well, and could guess what had happened.

The door opened again, and this time it was Matthew, the coachman. Like Allday, he had protested against remaining in Falmouth and entrusting Bolitho and Catherine to a common mail coach.

Ferguson was glad of the interruption. 'What's amiss, Matthew?'

Matthew grinned.

'Just heard the coach horn. Sounded it, like that other time when he was coming home!'

Ferguson said briskly, 'Drive down and fetch them from the square,' but Matthew had already gone. He had been the first to know, just as he had been the first to recognize the St Mawes salute when Bolitho had returned to Falmouth a little over a month ago.

He paused to kiss his wife on the cheek.

'What was that for?'

Ferguson glanced at Allday. *They were coming home*. He smiled. 'For making up the fires for them.' But he could not repress it. 'For so many things, Grace.' He reached for his coat. 'You can stop for a

30

meal, John?'

But Allday was preparing to leave. 'They'll not want a crowd when they gets here.' He was suddenly serious. 'But when he wants me, I'll be ready. That's it an' all about it.'

The door closed, and they looked at one another.

She said, 'Taking it badly.'

Ferguson thought of the smell of jasmine. 'So will she.'

The smart carriage with the Bolitho crest on the door clattered away across the stableyard, the wheels striking sparks from the cobbles. For several days Matthew had been anticipating this, backing the horses into position at the time when the coach from Truro could be expected to arrive outside the King's Head in Falmouth. Ferguson paused by the door. 'Fetch some of that wine they favour, Grace.'

She watched him, remembering, as if it were yesterday, when they had snatched him away in the King's ship. Bolitho's ship. And the crippled man who had returned to her. She had never put it into words before. *The man I love.*

She smiled. 'Champagne. I don't know what they see in it!'

Now that it's all nearly over. He might have told her what Allday had said, but she had gone, and he was glad that it would remain a secret between them.

Then he walked out into the cold, damp air and could smell the sea. Coming home. It was suddenly important that there should be no fuss: Allday had understood, even though he was bursting to know what was going to happen. It must be as if they had only been from Falmouth for a single day.

He looked over at the end stall and saw the big mare Tamara throwing her head up and down, the

31

white flash on her forehead very clear in the dull light.

There could be no more doubt. Ferguson walked over and rubbed her muzzle.

'She's back, my lass. And none too soon.'

Half an hour later the carriage rattled into the drive. The hero and his mistress who had scandalized the country, defying both hypocrisy and convention, were home.

* * *

Lieutenant George Avery regarded himself critically in the tailor's mirror, as he might examine a stranger. He knew very little of London, and on previous visits he had usually been on some mission to the Admiralty. The tailor's establishment was in Jermyn Street, a bustling place of shops and elegant houses, and the air, which seemed unclean after the sea, was alive with the din of carriages and hooves.

He must have walked for miles, something he always enjoyed after the restrictions of a crowded man-of-war. He smiled at his reflection; he was quite tired, unaccustomed to so much exercise.

It was strange to have money to spend, something new to him. This was prize money, earned over ten years ago when he had been second-in-command of the schooner *Jolie*, herself a French prize. He had all but forgotten about it; it had seemed unimportant in the light of his subsequent misfortunes. He had been wounded when *Jolie* was overwhelmed by a French corvette, then held as a prisoner of war in France; he had been exchanged during the brief Peace of Amiens only to face a court-martial, and to receive a reprimand for losing his ship, even though he had been too badly injured to prevent others from

32

hauling down her colours. At Adam Bolitho's court-martial he had relived every moment of his own disgrace.

He thought of the house in Chelsea, where he was still staying, and wondered if Bolitho and Catherine had reached Cornwall yet. It was difficult to accept, let alone take for granted, that they had left him to use the house as he chose. But he would have to go to Falmouth soon himself, to be with the others when Sir Richard received his final instructions. His *little crew*, as he called them. Avery thought it was dangerously close to being a family.

Arthur Crowe, the tailor, peered up to him. 'Is everything satisfactory, sir? I shall have the other garments sent to you immediately they are ready.' Polite, almost humble. Rather different from their first meeting. Crowe had seemed about to offer some critical comment on Avery's uniform, which had been made by the Falmouth tailor, Joshua Miller. *Just another impoverished luff, at thirty-five old for his rank, and therefore probably under a cloud of some sort, doomed to remain a lieutenant until dismissal or death settled the matter*. Avery had silenced the unspoken criticism by a casual mention of his admiral's name, and the fact that the Millers had been making uniforms for the Bolithos for generations.

He nodded. 'Very satisfactory.' His gaze shifted to the bright epaulette on his right shoulder. It would take some getting used to. A solitary epaulette on the right shoulder had formerly been the mark of rank for a captain, not posted, but a captain for all that. Their lordships, apparently at the insistence of the Prince Regent, had changed it. The solitary epaulette now signified the rank of lieutenant, at least until some new fashion was approved.

The room darkened, and he imagined that the sky was clouding over again. But it was a carriage, which had stopped in the street directly opposite the window: a very elegant vehicle in deep blue, with some sort of crest on the panels. A footman had climbed down and was lowering the step. It had not been lost on the tailor: he was hurrying to his door and opening it, admitting the bitter air from the street.

Curious, Avery thought, that in all the shops he had seen there appeared to be no shortages, as if war with France and the new hostilities with America were on another planet.

He watched absently as a woman emerged from the carriage. She wore a heavy, high-waisted coat almost the same colour as the paintwork, and her face was partly hidden by the deep brim of her bonnet as she looked down for the edge of the pavement.

Arthur Crowe bowed stiffly, his tape measure hanging around his neck like a badge of office.

'What a pleasure to see you again, my lady, on this fine brisk morning!'

Avery smiled privately. Crowe obviously made a point of knowing those who mattered, and those who did not.

He thought of Catherine Somervell, wondering if she had persuaded Bolitho to patronize this prosperous street.

Then he swung away, his mind reeling, the new epaulette, the shop, everything fading like fragments of a dream.

The door closed, and he barely dared to turn round.

Crowe said, 'If you are certain I can provide

34

nothing more, Mr Avery?'

Avery faced the door. The tailor was alone. Crowe asked, 'Is something wrong, sir?'

'That lady.' He made himself look, but even the carriage had gone. Another fragment. 'I thought I knew her.'

Crowe watched his assistant parcelling up the new boatcloak Avery had purchased. 'Her husband was a good customer. We were sorry to lose him, although not always an easy man to satisfy.' He seemed to realize that it was not the answer Avery had wanted. 'Lady Mildmay. The wife, or should I say, the widow, of Vice-Admiral Sir Robert Mildmay.'

It was she. Except that when he had last seen her, she had been only the wife of his captain in the old *Canopus*.

Crowe prompted, 'Was that the lady of your acquaintance?'

'I think I was mistaken.' He picked up his hat. 'Please have the other purchases delivered to the address I gave you.'

No arguments, no hesitation. Sir Richard Bolitho's name opened many doors.

He walked out into the street, glad to be moving again. Why should he care? Why did it matter so much? She had been unreachable then, when he had been stupid enough to believe it was more than just an amusing game to her, a passing flirtation.

Had she changed? He had caught a glimpse of her hair, honey-coloured; how many days, how many sleepless nights he had tried to forget it. Perhaps she had been part of the reason he had not resisted when his uncle, then Sir Paul Sillitoe, had suggested that he offer himself for the position of flag lieutenant to Sir Richard Bolitho. He had expected his application to be refused as soon as Bolitho had learned more about him. Instead, he had never forgotten that day in Falmouth, in the old house he had come to know so well, their kindness to him, the trust, and eventually the friendship which had done so much to heal the doubts and the injuries of the past. He had thought little more beyond the next voyage, the next challenge, even though it took him to the cannon's mouth yet again.

And now, this. It had been a shock. He had deluded himself. What chance would he have had? A married woman, and the wife of his own captain? It would have been like putting a pistol to his head.

Was she still as beautiful? She was two years older than himself, maybe more. She had been so alive, so vivacious. After the slur of the court-martial, and then being marooned on the old *Canopus*, he thought until the end of his service, she had been like a bright star: he had not been the only officer who had been captivated. He quickened his pace, and halted as someone said, 'Thank you, sir!'

There were two of them. Once they had been soldiers; they even wore the tattered remnants of their red coats. One was blind, and held his head at an angle as though he were trying to picture what was happening. The other had only one arm, and was clutching a hunk of bread which had obviously been handed to him by a potboy from the nearby coffee-house. It had probably been left on some one's plate.

The blind man asked, 'What is it, Ted?'

The other said, 'Bit o' bread. Don't worry. We might get lucky.'

Avery could not control his disgust. He should have been used to it, but he was not. He had once come to blows with another lieutenant who had

36

taunted him about his sensitivity.

He said sharply, 'You there!' and realized that his anger and dismay had put an uncharacteristic edge to his voice. The one-armed man even cowered, but stood protectively between the officer and his blind companion.

Avery said, 'I am sorry.' He was reminded suddenly of Adam Bolitho, and the presentation sword he had sold. 'Take this.' He thrust some money into the grimy hand. 'Have something hot to eat.'

He turned away, annoyed that such things could still move and trouble him.

He heard the blind man ask, 'Who was that, Ted?' The reply was barely audible above the clatter of wheels and harness.

'A gentleman. A true gentleman.'

How many were there like that? How many more would there be? Probably soldiers from a line regiment, maybe two of Wellington's men: shoulder to shoulder, facing French cavalry and artillery. Living from battle to battle, until luck changed sides and turned on them.

Those around him did not realize what it was like, and would never believe that either he or his admiral could still be moved by such pitiful reminders of the cost of war. Like that moment in *Indomitable's* cabin after Adam's ship had been lost, and a single survivor had been dragged from the sea by the brig *Woodpecker*, which, against orders, had returned to the scene. That survivor had been the ship's boy. Avery had watched Bolitho bring the child back to life with his compassion, even as he had endeavoured to discover what had happened to Adam.

Avery had once believed that his own suffering had left him indifferent to the fate of others. Bolitho had

37

convinced him otherwise.

Somewhere a clock chimed: St James's, Piccadilly, he thought. He had passed it without noticing it. He looked back, but the two redcoats had gone. Like ghosts, momentarily released from some forgotten field of battle.

'Why, *Mister* Avery! It *is* you.'

He stared at her, vaguely aware that she was standing in the doorway of a perfumery, with a prettily wrapped box in her arms.

It was as if the street had emptied, and, like the two ghosts, had lost all identity.

He hesitated, and removed his hat, saw her eyes move over his face, and, no doubt, he thought bitterly, the dark hair which was so thickly streaked with grey. This was the moment he had lived in his dreams, when he would sting her with sarcasm and contempt, and punish her in a way she could never forget.

She wore a fur muff on one hand, and the parcel was in danger of falling. He said abruptly, 'Let me assist you,' and took it from her; it was heavy, but he scarcely noticed. 'Is there some one who will carry this for you?'

She was gazing at him. 'I saw what you did for those poor beggars. It was kind of you.' Her eyes rested briefly on the new epaulette. 'Promotion too, I see.'

'I fear not.' She had not changed at all. Beneath the smart bonnet her hair was probably shorter, as the new fashions dictated. But her eyes were as he remembered them. Blue. Very blue.

She seemed to recall his question. 'My carriage will return for me in a moment.' Her face was full of caution now, almost uncertainty.

38

Avery said, 'I imagined that I saw you earlier. A trick of the light, I daresay. I heard that you had lost your husband.' A moment of triumph. But it was empty.

'Last year....'

'I read nothing of it in the *Gazette*, but then, I have been away from England.' He knew he sounded curt, discourteous, but he could not help it.

She said, 'It was not in battle. He had been in poor health for some time. And what of you? Are you married?'

'No,' he said.

She bit her lip. Even that little habit was painful to see. 'I believe I read somewhere that you are aide to Sir Richard Bolitho.' When he remained silent she added, 'That must be vastly exciting. I have never met him.' The slightest hesitation. 'Nor have I met the famous Lady Somervell. I feel the poorer for it.'

Avery heard the sound of wheels. So many others, but somehow he knew it was the carriage that matched her coat.

She asked suddenly, 'Are you lodging in town?'

'I have been staying in Chelsea, my lady. I shall be leaving for the West Country when I have arranged my affairs in London.'

There were two vivid spots of colour in her cheeks, which were not artificial. 'You did not always address me so formally. Had you forgotten?'

He heard the carriage slowing down. It would soon be over: the impossible dream could not harm him any more. 'I was in love with you then. You must have known that.'

Boots clattered on the pavement. 'Just the one, m' lady?'

She nodded, and watched with interest as the

39

footman took the box from Avery, noting his expression, the tawny eyes she had always remembered.

She said, 'I have reopened the house in London. We had been living at Bath. It is not the same any more.'

The footman lowered the step for her. He did not spare Avery even a glance.

She rested one hand on the carriage door. Small, well-shaped, strong.

She said, 'It is not far from here. I like to be near the centre of things.' She looked up at him, searching his face, as though considering something. 'Will you take tea with me? Tomorrow? After all this time. ...'

He watched her, thinking of when he had held her. Kissed her. The only delusions had been his own.

'I think it would be unwise, my lady. There is enough gossip and slander in this town. I'll not trouble you again.'

She was inside the carriage but had lowered the window, while the footman waited, wooden-faced, to climb up beside the coachman.

For a moment she rested her hand on his, and he found himself surprised by her apparent agitation.

'Do come.' She slipped a small card into his hand. Then she glanced quickly at the footman and whispered, 'What you said to me just now. Were you really?'

He did not smile. 'I would have died for you.'

She was still staring back at him as the dark blue carriage pulled away.

He jammed on his hat and said aloud, 'Hell's teeth, I still would!'

But the anger eluded him, and he added softly, 'Susanna.'

Yovell, Bolitho's portly secretary, waited patiently near the library desk, his ample buttocks turned toward the fire. Sharing Bolitho's life at sea as he did, Yovell knew, more than any one, the full extent of the planning and detail through which the admiral had to sift before eventually translating this paper war into written orders for his captains.

Like Bolitho's other loyal, if difficult, servant Ozzard, Yovell had a small cottage on the estate, even as Allday had lived there when home from the sea. Yovell gave a small, amused smile. That was, until Allday had suddenly become a respectable married man. Through one of the windows he saw a cat waiting expectantly for somebody to open the door. That was Allday to a letter, he thought, on the wrong side of every door. When he was at sea he worried about his wife and the inn at Fallowfield, and now there was the baby to add to his responsibilities. And when he was home, he fretted about being left on the beach when Bolitho returned to his flagship. Yovell had no such domestic problems. When he wanted to give up his present work he knew Bolitho would release him, just as he knew that many people thought him quite mad to risk his life in a man-of-war.

He watched Bolitho's strong hand leafing through the pile of papers, which he had been examining for most of the morning. He had only returned from London a week ago and had been occupied with Admiralty business for much of the time. Catherine Somervell had waved to him as she had left the house to call on Lewis Roxby, their near neighbour and 'the

41

King of Cornwall', as he was dubbed behind his back. Roxby was married to Bolitho's sister Nancy, and Yovell thought it a good thing that Catherine had family of sorts to visit while they were all away at sea.

He admired her greatly, although he knew that many men called her a whore. When the transport *Golden Plover* had been wrecked off the coast of Africa, Bolitho's woman had been with them, and had not only survived the hardships of their voyage in an open boat, but had somehow held them all together, given them heart and hope when they had no reason to expect that they would live. It had made his own suffering seem almost incidental.

Bolitho looked up at him, his face remarkably calm and rested. Two weeks on the road from London, changing coaches and horses, being diverted by floods and fallen trees: their account of it had sounded like a nightmare.

Bolitho said, 'If you would arrange for copies of these, I should like them dispatched to their lordships as soon as possible.' He stretched his arms, and thought of the letter which had been awaiting his return. From Belinda, even though there was a lawyer's hand at the helm. She needed more money, a sizeable increase in her allowance, for herself and their daughter Elizabeth. He rubbed the damaged eye. It had not troubled him very much since his return; perhaps the grey stillness of a Cornish winter was kinder than blazing sun and the sea's mirrored reflections.

Elizabeth. She would be eleven years old in a few months' time. A child he did not know, nor would he ever know her. Belinda would make certain of that. He sometimes wondered what her friends in high

42

society would think of the elegant Lady Bolitho if they knew she had connived with Catherine's husband to have her falsely charged and transported like a common thief. Catherine never spoke of it now, but she could never forget it. And like himself, she would never forgive.

Every day since their return they had tried to enjoy to the full, knowing that time did not favour them. The roads and lanes were firmer after days of a steady south-westerly, and they had ridden for miles around the estate and had visited Roxby, who remained in poor health after suffering a stroke. Poor humour, too: Roxby adored his style of living, hunting and drinking, and entertaining lavishly at his house on the adjoining estate, balancing the pleasures of a gentleman with his obligations as farmer and magistrate. He was even on intimate terms with the Prince Regent, and perhaps had been given his knighthood on the strength of that acquaintance. The advice of his doctors to rest and take things more quietly was like a sentence of death.

He thought of the long journey home on those appalling roads. Catherine had even managed to create happiness then, despite her discomfort. At one point they had been turned back by flooding, and set down at a small, shabby inn which had clearly shocked their fellow passengers, two well-dressed churchmen and their wives who were on their way to meet their bishop.

One of the women had said angrily, 'No lady should be expected to remain in such a dreadful place!' To Bolitho she had added, 'What does your wife have to say about it, I should like to know?'

Catherine had answered, 'We are not married, ma'am.' She had held his arm more tightly. 'This

43

officer is running away with me!'

They had not seen their fellow passengers again. Either they had waited for another coach, or they had slipped away in the night.

The room had been damp and slightly musty from lack of use, but the landlord, a jovial dwarf of a man, had soon got a fire going, and the supper he had presented would have satisfied even the greediest midshipman.

And with the rain on the window, and the fire's dancing shadows around them, they had sunk into the feather bed and made love with such abandon that they might well have been eloping.

There had been a short letter from Adam, saying only that he was leaving with Valentine Keen for Halifax, and asking their forgiveness for not having visited them in Falmouth.

Whenever he considered their situation his mind seemed to flinch from it. Adam and Keen. The two of them together, flag captain and admiral. *Like me and James Tyacke*. But so different. Two men who had loved the same woman, and Keen knew nothing about it. To share a secret was to share the guilt, Bolitho thought.

That same night at the inn, while they had lain exhausted by their love, Catherine had told him something else. She had taken Keen to Zennor, to the churchyard where Zenoria was buried. It was a good thirty miles from Falmouth, and they had stayed with friends of Roxby's in Redruth overnight.

She had said, 'Had we stayed anywhere else there would have been talk, more cruel gossip. I couldn't risk that—there are still too many who wish us ill.'

Then she had told him that while Keen had been alone at the grave she had spoken with the verger. He was also the gardener, and, with his brother, the local carpenter, and had confided that he made all the coffins for the village and surrounding farms.

She said, 'I thought I would ask him to see that fresh flowers were put on her grave throughout the year.'

Bolitho had held her in the firelight, feeling her sadness at the memory, and what had gone before.

Then she had said, 'He would take no payment, Richard. He told me that "a young sea captain" had already arranged it with him. After that, I went into the church, and I could see Adam's face as I saw it that day, when Val and Zenoria were married.'

What strange and perverse fate had brought Adam and Keen together? It could restore, or just as easily destroy them.

Yovell was polishing his small gold-rimmed spectacles. 'When will Mr Avery be joining us, Sir Richard?'

Bolitho eyed him thoughtfully. A man of many parts: it was rumoured that Yovell had been a schoolmaster at one time. He could well believe it. It was hard to imagine him as he had been in the boat after *Golden Plover* had gone down, his hands, unused to seamen's work, torn and bleeding on the oars, his face burned raw by the sun. But he could remember not a single word of complaint. A scholar, a man who enjoyed his Bible as another might relish a game of dice: even his casual question about the flag lieutenant held genuine interest. Perhaps they were two of a kind, both enigmatic in their fashion. George Avery was a quiet, often withdrawn man; even Sillitoe appeared not to know much about his nephew. Or care, possibly. Sillitoe's sister had been Avery's mother: of Sillitoe's brother, who had so

45

inspired Avery that he had seemed to look upon him as a father whenever they had met, Bolitho knew nothing. Sillitoe's brother had been a naval officer, and very likely had sponsored Avery for his first appointment as midshipman. Avery's own father, and austere upbringing in a religious family, had never dampened his eagerness to follow the sea. Sillitoe's brother, in the *Ganges*, had fallen at the Battle of Copenhagen, like so many on that bloody day.

There was little to do in London for a lieutenant without connections, he thought, although Catherine had hinted that there had once been a woman in Avery's life. *Only a woman could scar him so deeply.*

She was probably right.

He said, 'Mr Avery will be coming down in a week or so. Or whenever he likes.' Or perhaps Avery would leave it until the last minute. Maybe he could not bear to see others who did not hide their love from one another, when he himself had no one.

He listened to the muffled thud of hooves. 'Her ladyship is home early.'

Yovell was at the window, and shook his head. 'No, Sir Richard, it's a messenger.' He did not turn. 'Dispatches, no doubt.'

Bolitho stood, trying to prepare himself as his secretary went out to deal with it. So soon. So soon. A month more, and already they were warning him of his departure. It would have been better if they had allowed him to remain in *Indomitable*; and in the same second he knew that was a lie. To be with her, only for an hour, would have made all this worthwhile.

Yovell came back, holding the familiar canvas

envelope with its Admiralty fouled anchor, to dispel any lingering hope he might have had.

Yovell returned to the window and peered out at the trees. The cat, he noticed, had disappeared. He thought of Allday again. It was going to be difficult.

He listened to the knife slitting the envelope. The messenger was in the kitchen being given something hot to drink, no doubt full of envy for those who lived in great houses such as these. He heard Bolitho say quietly, 'It is brought forward by a week. We take passage for Halifax on February eighteenth.' When he turned from the window he thought his admiral seemed very composed: the man every one expected to see. Beyond the reach of any personal emotion.

He said, 'It is not the first time, Sir Richard.'

Bolitho seized a pen and bent over the papers on the desk. 'Give the fellow this receipt.' He stood up and held his cuff over his eye as he faced the light. 'I shall ride out to meet Lady Catherine. Tell Matthew, will you?'

Yovell hurried away, not wanting to leave, but understanding that he had to confront the prospect of separation alone. Three weeks, then an ocean, a world apart.

He closed the door quietly behind him. Perhaps cats had the right ideas about life, he thought.

*   *   *

They met by the slate wall that marked the boundary of Roxby's estate. She did not dismount until he got down and walked to her, and then she slid from the saddle and waited for him to hold her, her hair blowing out freely in the salt breeze.

'You've heard. How long?'

'Three weeks.'

She pressed her face to his so that he would not see her eyes. 'We will make it a lifetime, dearest of men. Always, always, I will be with you.' She said it without anger or bitterness. Time was too precious to waste.

He said, 'I don't want to go. I hate the thought of it.'

Through his cloak she could feel him shivering, as if he were cold or ill. She knew he was neither.

He said, 'Why must you suffer because of me, because of what I am?'

'Because I *understand*. Like your mother and all those before her. I will wait, as they did, and I will miss you more than any words can describe.' Then she did look at him, her dark eyes very steady. 'Above all, I am so very proud of you. When this is over, we shall be together, and nothing will ever force us apart again.'

He touched her face and her throat. 'It is all I want.'

He kissed her very gently, so gently that she wanted to cry.

But she was strong, too strong to allow the tears to come. She knew how much he needed her and it gave her the courage that was necessary, perhaps more now than at any other time.

'Take me home, Richard. A lifetime, remember?'

They walked in silence, the horses following companionably behind them. At the top of the rise they saw the sea, and she felt him grip her arm more tightly. As if he had come face to face with the enemy.

CHAPTER THREE

MORNING DEPARTURE

Captain Adam Bolitho tightened his boatcloak around his neck as the jolly-boat pulled out strongly into the Solent. A strange departure from Portsmouth, he thought: without the snow, everything was normal again. Noise, bustle, marching men, and many boats milling around the stairs, waiting to carry their officers out to the ships at anchor.

Except that this was not his ship. He had paused only briefly to step aboard the frigate *Zest*, to sign some papers, to take his leave as quickly as possible. The ship had fought well; without her, even *Indomitable's* formidable artillery might not have been able to beat the Yankees into submission. But that was as far as it went. He never felt that *Zest* was really his ship, nor had he attempted to make her so. His ship lay on the sea-bed, her beautiful figurehead staring into the deeper darkness, so many of her company still with her.

The midshipman in charge of the jolly-boat was very aware of his passenger's rank and reputation: even the name of Bolitho had sent a flood of rumours through the ship.

Adam looked at the chests at his feet. All new, everything, even the fighting sword he had purchased with such care. The rest lay with *Anemone*.

He glanced at his small companion. John Whitmarsh, who had been the only one saved from the sea, had served in *Anemone* for almost two years before she foundered. A mere child. He had been 'volunteered' by an uncle, if uncle he was, after the boy's father, a deep-water fisherman, had drowned off the Goodwins. John was to be his servant. Adam had never seen such pride or such gratitude when he had asked him. The boy still did not understand the lifeline had been for his captain, and not the other way round.

The midshipman said stiffly, 'There she lies, sir.'

Adam tugged down his hat. She was the *Wakeful*, a thirty-eight gun frigate, hard-worked and in constant demand like most of her breed. Now she was completing the last tasks before sailing, taking on fresh water, fruit if there was any available, and, of course, men. Even the most dedicated press gang would be hard put to find any suitable hands in a naval port.

He looked at the boy again. Not much different in spite of his smart new jacket and white trousers. Ozzard had taught him some of it; the rest he would learn quickly enough. He was bright, and if he was nervous or still suffering from his experiences and the memory of seeing his best friend, another ship's boy of the same age, drift away beyond help, he did not show it.

Adam had sent a letter to the boy's mother. Had she asked for his return, he would have put him ashore and made certain that he reached her safely. She had not acknowledged the letter. Perhaps she had moved from the area, or taken up with another 'uncle'. Either way, Adam thought his young charge had been quietly pleased about it.

He ran his eye critically over the frigate. Rigging well set up, sails neatly furled. She was smart enough. He could see the scarlet and blue of the receiving

50

party by the entry port. He knew nothing of her captain, other than that this was his first command. He found he could shut it from his mind. It was not his concern. He, like Rear-Admiral Valentine Keen, who was arriving tomorrow, was a passenger. He smiled briefly. An inconvenience.

He thought with affection of his uncle, and how close they had been after his escape from the Americans. They would all meet again in Halifax. He still did not know why he had accepted Keen's offer. Because of guilt? To allay suspicion? He knew it was neither. It was simply a feeling, like some one or something leading the way. He recalled Zennor, the quietness of the place, the hiss of the sea on the rocks beneath the cliff. Her grave. He had touched it, and had felt her spirit watching him. The little mermaid.

'Bows!' The midshipman's voice was loud. Perhaps he had taken Adam's silence for disapproval.

The bowman was on his feet, boathook poised as rudder and oars brought the boat hard round toward the main chains. The oars were tossed, showering the seamen with salt water as the boat swayed and bounced alongside.

He looked at the midshipman. 'Thank you, Mr Price. That was well done.'

The youth gaped at him, as if surprised that his name was known. He thought once more of Bolitho, all the lessons learned. *They have names.* He could almost hear his voice. *In this life we share, it is often all they do have.*

He stood up, ensuring that the new sword was safely in position on his hip. He had never forgotten Bolitho's cautionary tale of the senior officer who had fallen headlong over his sword, in full view of the

51

side party.

He glanced down at the boy. 'Ready, young John?' He knew that above his head they were all waiting: the ritual of receiving a captain on board. But this, too, was important.

Whitmarsh picked up his bag, his brown eyes unblinking as he stared at the tapering masts, the ensign curling out from the taffrail.

'Ready, sir.' He nodded firmly. 'Aye, ready.'

Adam smiled, and climbed swiftly up the side. He still wore a dressing on the jagged wound, but it was only to protect the tender scar from the pressure of his clothing.

He stepped onto the deck and removed his hat as the Royal Marines presented arms in salute. *And to remind me, so that I never forget.*

'Welcome aboard, Captain Bolitho! It is an honour!'

Adam shook his hand. Very young, and in the gleaming new epaulettes, he was like a youth playing the role of captain. He thought, *as I once did.*

The captain, whose name was Martin Hyde, led the way aft, and said almost apologetically, 'A bit crowded, I'm afraid. Rear-Admiral Keen will have my quarters, and there is an extra berth for you. I've arranged for your section to be screened off. I see you have a servant with you, so you should be comfortable enough.' He hesitated. 'I must ask this. What is the rear-admiral like? It is three thousand miles to Halifax, and he will be used to rather more luxury than I can offer, I imagine.'

Adam said, 'He is very agreeable, and a good man in every way.'

The other captain seemed relieved. 'I understand that his wife died recently. It can change one.'

52

Adam heard himself answer levelly, 'He will leave you free to direct your ship as you will.' He would have to become accustomed to it. People would always want to know.

He saw a corporal of marines pointing out something to Whitmarsh, and the boy nodding in agreement. He belonged. But just once Adam saw him glance uncertainly along the busy deck, where the guard was falling out and the hands were returning to their work.

Hyde said, 'He looks a likely lad. Young, but I'm often so desperate for bodies I'd take them from their mothers' arms if I could!'

An officer hovered nearby, obviously the first lieutenant. Hyde said, 'I am needed, Captain Bolitho. We will talk later.' He smiled, and looked even younger. 'It is a privilege to have you aboard, although after three thousand miles you may feel differently.' Then he was gone.

Overhead, the familiar sounds resumed, the twitter of bosun's calls, the 'Spithead Nightingales', the thud of bare feet, and the squeal of tackles through their blocks. *His world, but not mine.* Adam sat on a chest and stared around at the great cabin, where he would live, and attempt to accept a future with Keen.

He heard Whitmarsh walking behind him, still very careful of his shining new shoes with their bright buckles.

Adam said, 'In that chest.' He tossed him the keys. 'There's some cognac.' He watched the boy opening it. Like the others, it could have belonged to a stranger. All new. He sighed.

John Whitmarsh asked quietly, 'Be you sad, sir?'

He looked sharply at the boy. 'Remember what I told you aboard *Indomitable*, when I asked you to

53

come with me?'

He saw him screw up his eyes. 'Aye, sir. You said that when we were sad we should remember our old ship, an' our lost friends.'

Adam took the cup of cognac from his hand. 'That is so.'

The boy watched him anxiously. 'But we *will* get another ship, sir!'

The very simplicity of it moved him. 'Yes. We will, John Whitmarsh.'

He looked toward the stern windows, streaked now with salt spray like ice rime.

'But there will always be thoughts.'

The boy had not heard him, or perhaps he had spoken only to himself: he was unpacking one of the chests in an orderly fashion, as Ozzard had taught him. He was content.

Adam stood up. *And so must I be. Others depend on me. It has to be enough.*

But when he had knelt by her grave, he had known then that it was not.

* * *

George Avery paused to get his bearings, and reconsider what he was doing. When he had watched her drive away in the smart blue carriage, he should have left it right there, put it back into the past with all the other memories and bitter experiences. He had returned to Jermyn Street and prowled up and down, simply to reawaken the breathtaking sensations of that chance meeting. He had almost expected to see the same two tattered veterans begging for food, but they had receded into the day's unreality. He frowned. There had been plenty of others, though.

54

She had been right about one thing. Her house was close by; he was not even breathless from the walk. It was cold, with watery sunlight, but he had not needed the new boatcloak which he carried loosely over his arm. The house, though, was enough to chill his blood. He did not quite know what he had expected, but it was large and elegant, with a presence to match. He stopped again. He should turn and go, now. And there were several carriages outside: she was not alone. Perhaps he should have gone to the house when she had asked him, to take tea. But that invitation had been two days ago. He had looked at her little card several times since then, unable to decide what to do.

And then an Admiralty messenger had brought him the letter, and the sailing date. They would leave from Plymouth, so it was time he began the long journey to Falmouth, where Sir Richard Bolitho would be requiring his presence.

Instead, he was here.

What would she say? She might not even consent to see him. He stared at the house again, trying to remember his captain, her husband. He had assumed that Mildmay had been given the old *Canopus* as an insult, because of some past misdemeanour. Perhaps he had offended someone in high places: it was not uncommon. *That was why I was sent to her.* Taken originally as a prize from the French at the Nile, she had received such a battering and had subsequently been worked so hard that her greatest enemy was rot.

But Mildmay had left the ship while she had been in dock, and had been promoted to flag rank, with further promotion two years later. Now he was dead.

He felt his confidence, never very great, wavering. He would make an even bigger fool of himself

55

this time.

The double doors of the house were before him, although he did not recall having mounted the steps. As though he had been secretly observed, one of them swung inward, opened by a tall, rather severe-looking woman dressed from neck to toe in grey, with a bunch of keys hanging from the chatelaine at her waist.

'Yes?' Her eyes moved over him swiftly. She was probably more used to senior officers and the quality, he thought, and, surprisingly, it made him smile. It was the same assessment and dismissal that the Jermyn Street tailor had given him.

He said, 'I wish to speak to Lady Mildmay.'

The eyes moved on, looking for a carriage or some other evidence of respectability. 'She is not expecting your visit?' It was not really a question.

Avery heard music, a pianoforte, and in the sudden stillness applause, like a scattering of dry leaves.

'No, not exactly. I—'

'What is it, Mrs Pepyat? I thought I—'

Avery removed his hat. 'I am sorry, my lady.' She was standing by the great, curving staircase, one hand to the bosom of her gown, as if she had been surprised or annoyed by the intrusion.

She said, '*Mister* Avery, you keep a poor diary!' But she smiled, and walked to meet him. 'Is something amiss?'

He took the cool hand she offered and kissed the back of it. 'I am recalled, my lady. I must leave for Cornwall shortly.' The pianoforte had started to play again, and Avery said, 'I will leave. You are entertaining.'

She watched him, her blue eyes questioning. 'No, no. That is a Mr Blount—he comes from Highgate to

56

play for us, to raise money for the sailors' hospital at Greenwich.' She shrugged. 'It is an amiable way to meet old friends, or acquaintances, if you prefer...' She smiled. 'You like music, Mr Avery? It is Mozart, very fashionable, it seems.'

Avery was listening. 'Yes. His Fantasy in C Minor.' He did not see her raised brows. 'I sang in the choir, and my father's organist used to entertain us with that music afterwards.'

He must go. The formidable Mrs Pepyat obviously thought so.

'Take this gentleman's hat and cloak.' A footman darted out from nowhere, and took them from him. His line of retreat was severed.

She slipped her arm through his and guided him toward a tall doorway.

'We will sit by this pillar. See? No one has noticed a thing.'

He sat beside her. Although she had released his arm he could still feel her touch. The room was full, the women, some young, some not so young, sitting attentively, with here and there an expensively shod foot tapping in time to the music. The men were mostly older, and there were several red uniforms: senior officers putting on a brave face for society's sake, but, for the most part, obviously bored. The pianist named Blount was very small, with the frame of a youth, but his face could have been that of an old portrait, and Avery knew simply by watching him that he had completely dismissed his audience from his mind.

She leaned toward him, and Avery saw two other women turn instantly to observe them. 'There will be refreshments later. I shall have to entertain then, a little.'

She was very close, so close that he could smell her hair, her perfume, and see the rise and fall of her breasts.

'Am I as you remember, *Mister* Avery?'

She was teasing him again. Or was she.

He lowered his voice. 'Exactly as I remember.'

She turned away. The music ceased and people stood to applaud, some, he thought, out of pleasure, others with relief that it was over.

An act of charity. Avery glanced around at the rich gowns, the stylish hair arrangements, the men, smiling now as the first trays of wine appeared. How much of the collection would find its way to the sailors' hospital, he wondered, and was shocked by his own cynicism.

He remained by the pillar and took a goblet of wine from a passing footman. She was moving amongst her guests without hesitation or uncertainty. He heard her laugh, and saw two of the soldiers beaming at her.

He stepped back as a solitary naval uniform, a lady on one arm, paused to speak with Lady Mildmay before heading for the door. Escaping.

She was with him again, her eyes moving across the room. 'Are you enjoying yourself, Mr Avery?'

'That officer. I know him.'

'Vice-Admiral Bethune. Yes, he has risen like a bright star.'

It seemed to amuse her.

'And that was his wife.' She was not as he had expected. Perhaps he had been misinformed.

She was looking at him steadily. '*Not* his wife. From what we hear, one can hardly blame him. He is very attractive, if I may say so as a woman.'

Some of the others were leaving now, their duty

58

done. She asked suddenly, 'Recalled, you said? When do you return?' She turned to smile and curtsey to a big, florid-faced man and his lady. 'So good of you to come, Your Grace!' And as quickly, the smile was gone. 'Tell me.'

He shrugged. 'I am joining Sir Richard Bolitho's squadron.'

She put her hand to her breast again. Off guard, no longer so composed. 'The Americas? The war?'

He smiled. 'It is the way of sailors, madam.'

She turned again as two more women rose to leave. They smiled like old friends, but one looked directly at Avery, her eyes full of a hard curiosity.

Avery asked abruptly, 'And who was *that*?'

She closed her fingers on his arm, either ignoring or not caring for the consequences.

'That was your admiral's wife, Lady Bolitho. Did you not know?'

Avery shook his head. 'This is not my world.' He glanced at the door. 'I have things to attend to, my lady. I did not mean to disturb you. That was not my intention.' He saw the sudden doubt in her eyes.

'Do you have a carriage?'

'I can easily obtain one. I am going to Chelsea.'

Somebody called out to her but she did not appear to hear. She said, 'My carriage can take you there, and in more comfort.' She gripped his arm more tightly. 'Please.' No further pretence. 'Please stay.'

'I think we own Lady Mildmay a debt of gratitude for her charming hospitality, and the dedication with which she has always carried out her work on behalf of those less fortunate.'

She bowed low, her smile confident. The shadow between her breasts made a lie of her composure.

As she straightened again, she looked directly into

59

his eyes. 'George ... please, go tomorrow.'

It was madness. But there was the other madness, which they had all shared, the thunder of the great guns, the screams and the horror of battle. How could he explain, how extricate himself from this? But she had already vanished among the remaining guests.

Avery made his way through the house until he found the garden, which was already in twilight.

Madness, then. So be it.

*   *   *

The carriage had stopped at the crest of a slight rise, the horses stamping on the rough road, untroubled by the keen morning air.

Bolitho turned toward her, holding her hand beneath her heavy cloak, wondering how time could pass so swiftly and without mercy.

'We are almost there, Kate.'

'I know. I remember.'

They could have driven all the way from Falmouth without stopping, but had stayed the night at an inn outside Liskeard. Bolitho had been very aware of the danger of missing his ship because of a late arrival, or some accident on the road: that the tide waited for no man had been impressed upon him since he had first gone to sea at the age of twelve, or perhaps even earlier, as a child listening to his father and the local men who lived on and from the sea. Nor would he have Catherine travelling so far without some brief respite.

They had left the Turk's Head early; neither of them wanted breakfast. Even in such a small place there had been no escape from his own notoriety.

60

People had been waiting outside the inn, and had waved and called to them, wishing them luck and happiness. Catherine had responded as she always did, although their kindness must have broken her heart. It was not next week or the week after. It was today.

The other members of his 'little crew' would already be aboard: Avery, more withdrawn than usual after his sojourn in London; Yovell with his books and his Bible, untroubled as always; Ozzard, who gave nothing away; and, of course, Allday. Allday was genuinely sorry to be leaving his wife and child, but there was something more to it, pride, or a certain satisfaction because he was still needed, and had returned to what he considered his proper role in life.

He had talked with Catherine throughout the night. The ship, *Royal Enterprise*, was a fleet transport, faster than most merchant vessels, and used to carrying important passengers to any destination so ordered by their lordships. The voyage should take three weeks to a month, weather permitting: the masters of such transports were highly experienced, making the best use of prevailing winds for an untroubled passage. So there might be a hint of early spring in Cornwall by the time he rehoisted his flag above *Indomitable* in Halifax.

At least he would have James Tyacke, as well as Adam and Keen to sustain him. What would she have?

He had told her about Belinda and her need for more money. Catherine had known, or guessed.

She had exclaimed, 'Need? Self-indulgence, more likely! I'll not have that woman troubling you, Richard.'

61

When the inn had fallen quiet for the night they had held one another and talked, until desperate passion had brought them together for the last time.

They heard Matthew speaking softly with Ferguson. Ferguson had insisted on accompanying them, and would escort Catherine back to Falmouth rather than entrust her to the protection of a paid guard. He and Matthew had remained in the inn parlour yarning and drinking until they had eventually retired, Ferguson to one of the rooms, Matthew to sleep with his horses as he always did on the road.

Catherine twisted round to look at him again. 'Remember, I am always with you. I shall write often, to let you know how it looks in Falmouth, at our house.' She touched the lock of hair above his right eye; it was almost white now, and she knew he hated it. She thought the savage scar beneath it must be the cause; the rest of his hair was as black as it had been on the day she had first seen him.

She murmured, '*So proud*, Richard.' She lowered her head and her fist struck the seat. 'I will not weep. We have gone through so much, and we are so lucky. I will *not* weep.'

They had decided that they should part before he joined the ship: so different from that other time when she had climbed *Indomitable's* side and been cheered by Tyacke's sailors, many of whom had since died in that last fight with Beer's *Unity*.

But now that the time had come, it was hard to contemplate leaving her.

Reading his thoughts, she said suddenly, 'May we get out, Richard, just for a few minutes?'

They climbed down and he took her arm as her cloak billowed out in the wind. Bolitho did not need any gauge: he knew the feel of it. A sailor's wind. The *Royal Enterprise* would be tugging at her cable, eager to go. He had known it all his life, though rarely as a passenger.

And there, like a dark, twisting snake, was the Hamoaze, and beyond it, misty in the damp air, Plymouth and the Sound.

She said quietly, 'The hills of Devon, Richard. How well I know these places, because of you.'

'We have done and shared so much.'

She put her fingers on his mouth. 'Just love me, Richard. Say that you will always love me.'

They walked back to the carriage where Matthew stood by the horses, and Ferguson, shapeless in a big coachman's caped coat, sat in silence, sharing it, as he had so many times.

The door closed and they were moving again. Downhill now, with more people about, some of whom pointed at the crest on the coach, and cheered without knowing if it was occupied or empty.

Houses next, a stableyard he remembered from his time as a junior lieutenant. He held her and looked at her, knowing what it was costing, for both of them. She was beautiful, despite the shadows beneath her eyes, as he always saw her when they were separated by the ocean.

She was saying, 'I shall keep very busy, Richard. I shall help Bryan, and I will visit Nancy more often. I know she frets over Lewis. He will heed nothing the doctors tell him.'

Matthew called, 'We're here, Sir Richard.'

She clung to his arm. 'I shall walk with you to the jetty. They may not have sent a boat yet. I can keep you company.'

He touched her face, her hair. 'The boat will be

63

there. I am an admiral. Remember?'

She laughed. 'And you once forgot to tell me!'

He embraced her. Neither moved. There was no baggage: it had been sent ahead. All he had to do was get out, and walk through the gate and to the jetty. It was so simple. That was probably what they had told themselves on the way to the guillotine....

He opened the door. 'Please stay here, Kate.' He held her again, and she leaned over and kissed him. Then he stepped back and stared at the others. 'Take good care of her.' He could barely see them. 'For me.'

Matthew grinned. 'None better, sir!' But there was no smile in his eyes.

Ferguson was down on the road. He said, 'God speed, Sir Richard.'

Bolitho stood quite still; afterwards, he thought it had been as if their spirits had joined.

Then he turned on his heel and walked through the gates.

She watched, her eyes smarting, afraid to miss the moment when he would look back. He had been right: they were waiting. Uniforms blue and scarlet; formal, austere voices. Respect for her man, an admiral of England.

But he did turn, then very slowly raised his hat and bowed to her. When she looked again, he was gone.

She waited for Ferguson to climb into the carriage, and said, 'Tell Matthew to drive back along the same road.'

Ferguson replied, 'The ship'll stand well out before she changes tack, m'lady. We'll not be able to see anything.'

She sat back in the seat. 'I shall see him.' She looked at the passing cottages. 'And he will know it.'

CHAPTER FOUR

CAPTAINS

As eight bells chimed out from the forecastle belfry, Captain James Tyacke climbed through the companion and onto the broad quarterdeck. The air, like everything else, was wet, clinging, and cold, and the ship seemed hemmed in by an unmoving curtain of fog. He gripped his hands tightly behind his back and listened to the staccato beat of hammers, and the occasional squeak of blocks as some item of rigging was hauled aloft to the upper yards. When he looked up, it was uncanny: the topmasts and topgallant spars were completely cut off by the fog, as if the frigate *Indomitable* had been dismasted in some phantom engagement.

He shivered, hating the climate, too used perhaps to the African sun and the south's clear blue horizons.

He stopped by the empty hammock nettings and peered down at the water alongside. Lighters were moored there, and other boats were pulling this way and that like water-beetles, vanishing and reappearing suddenly in the mist.

This was Halifax, Nova Scotia. A busy and vital seaport, and a pleasant-looking town, from the little he had seen of it. He touched the nettings, like cold metal on this dismal day. But not for long, he told himself. Very soon this work would be completed, which, considering the winter's bitter weather and the needs of all the other men-of-war sheltering here, was a record of which to be proud. Six months had passed since they had entered harbour after the savage battle with the two American frigates. The largest prize, *Unity*, had already left for England, and would be receiving all the attention she required. She had been so badly mauled that he doubted she would have survived the long Atlantic crossing if her pumps had not been kept going throughout every watch.

He gritted his teeth to prevent them from chattering. Some captains would have donned a thick boatcloak to keep out the cold. James Tyacke did not entertain the idea. *Indomitable*'s company had to work as best they could in their usual clothing, and he did not believe that he should take advantage of his rank. It was not some facile act to impress the men. It was merely Tyacke's way.

Like the empty nettings. Ordinarily, when the hands were piped to show a leg and make ready for another working day in harbour, the hammocks were neatly stowed there, and kept in the nettings during the day: when the ship was called to battle they offered the only protection from flying splinters for the helmsmen and officers on the quarterdeck. But life was hard enough in a King's ship, Tyacke thought, and here, when the only heating throughout *Indomitable*'s impressive one hundred and eighty feet was the galley stove, wet hammocks at the end of the day would have made things even more uncomfortable.

Figures loomed and faded in the mist, officers waiting to ask him questions, others wanting final instructions before they were pulled ashore to collect the quantities of stores and supplies required by this ship of war. *My ship*. But the satisfaction would not come, and the pride he occasionally allowed himself to feel kept its distance.

66

It was March, 1813. He stared along the deck. It was impossible to believe that next month he would have been in command of *Indomitable* for two whole years. What next? Where bound, and to what end? *Indomitable* was more powerful than most of her class. Built as a third-rate, a ship of the line, she had been cut down to perform the role of a heavily-armed frigate, and as she had proved in September when she had stood alongside the U.S.S. *Unity*, she was more than a match for the superior American firepower with her forty twenty-four pounders and four eighteen-pounders, as well as the other weapons she carried.

Surrounded by busy seamen whom he could barely see, Tyacke continued his walk, his forenoon solitude respected. He smiled briefly. It had not been easy, but he had welded them into one company. They had cursed him, feared him, hated him, but that was in the past.

The lessons had been learned. He looked down at the wet deck planking. They had paid for it, too. When the mist cleared as Isaac York, the sailing-master, had claimed it would, the repairs and replaced planks and timbers would be visible despite the caulking and the tar, the fresh paint and the varnish. Men had died aplenty that day in September. Matthew Scarlett, the first lieutenant, impaled on a boarding-pike, his last scream lost in the yells and the fury, the clash of steel and the crash of gunfire. Ships fighting, men dying, many of whom had probably already been forgotten by those who had once known them. And just there ... he glanced at a newly painted shot-garland, Midshipman Deane, hardly more than a child, had been pulped into nothing by one of *Unity*'s massive balls. And all

67

the while the admiral and his tall flag lieutenant had walked the scarred deck, allowing themselves to be seen by the men who, because of press gang or patriotism, were fighting for their lives, for the ship. He smiled again. And, of course, for their captain, although he would never regard it in that light.

Tyacke had always hated the thought of serving in a major war vessel, let alone one that wore an admiral's flag. Bolitho had changed that. And strangely, in his absence, without the admiral's flag at the mainmast truck, Tyacke felt no sense of independence or freedom. Being forced to remain in harbour undergoing repairs while they awaited orders had merely increased his feeling of confinement. Tyacke loved the open sea: more than most, he needed it. He touched the right side of his face and saw it in his mind as he did when he shaved every morning. Scored away, burned, like something inhuman. How his eye had survived was a mystery.

He thought again of those who had fallen here, not least the one-legged cook named Troughton. He could recall the moment when he had assumed command of *Indomitable*, his stomach knotted with nerves as he had prepared to read himself in to the assembled company. He had forced himself to accept the stares and the pity in his previous command, the brig *Larne*. Small, intimate, with every hand dependent on the others, she had been his life. Bolitho himself had once referred to her as the loneliest command imaginable. He had understood that solitude was what Tyacke needed more than anything.

He had known that first day aboard *Indomitable* that those who had waited in the silence for him were undoubtedly more worried about their new captain's character than his disfigurement: he was, after all, the lord and master who could make or break any one of them as he chose. It had not made his ordeal easier, starting again under the eyes of strangers, in what had seemed a vast ship after *Larne*. A company of two hundred and seventy officers, seamen and Royal Marines: a world of difference.

One man had made it possible for him: Troughton. *Indomitable*'s company had watched in disbelief as their new and hideously scarred captain had embraced the man, who had been crippled by the same broadside that had burst in on Tyacke's yelling, sweating gun crews, at what they now called the Battle of the Nile. Troughton had been a young seaman then. Tyacke had always believed him dead, as most of those around him had died when his world had exploded, and left him as he was now.

Now even Troughton was gone. Tyacke had not known until two days after the fight with the Americans. He did not even know where he had come from, or if there was anyone to mourn him.

He felt a slight movement against his cheek, the wind returning. York might be proved right yet again. He was fortunate to have such a sailing-master: York had served as master's mate in this ship, and had won promotion in the only way Tyacke truly respected, through skill and experience.

So the fog would clear, and they would see the harbour once more, the ships and the town, and the well-sited central battery that would repulse any attempt, even by the most foolhardy commander, to cut out an anchored merchantman or some of the American prizes which had been brought here.

Forlorn, and in much the same condition as she had been after the battle, the American frigate

69

Baltimore was beyond recovery. Perhaps she would be used as a hulk or stores vessel. But isolated and partly aground as she was now, she was a constant reminder of the day when America's superior frigates had been challenged and beaten.

Sir Richard Bolitho would be back soon. Tyacke hesitated in his regular pacing. Suppose he was directed elsewhere? The Admiralty was never averse to changing its collective mind. In dispatches brought by the last courier brig Tyacke had been warned of Valentine Keen's impending arrival in Halifax: he would hoist his flag in *Valkyrie*, another converted two-decker like *Indomitable*, with Adam Bolitho as his flag captain. It was still hard to fathom why *he* would want to come back to these waters. Tyacke was acquainted with Keen, and had attended his wedding, but he did not consider that he knew him as a man. This would be his first command as a flag-officer: he might be out for glory. And he had recently lost both wife and child. Tyacke touched his burned face again. It could scar a man more deeply than others might realize.

He saw a guardboat pulling abeam, the armed marines straightening their backs in the sternsheets as *Indomitable* took shape above them through the thinning fog.

He returned his mind to *Valkyrie*, still invisible in the misty harbour. Peter Dawes was her present captain, and acting-commodore until Keen's arrival: he was a post-captain, young, approachable, competent. But there were limits. Dawes was an admiral's son, and it was rumoured that he would be raised to flag rank as soon as he was replaced here. Tyacke had always nursed doubts about him, and had told Bolitho openly that Dawes might prove

70

reluctant to risk his reputation and the prospect of promotion when they most needed his support. It was all written in the log now: history. They had fought and won on that terrible day. Tyacke could recall his own fury and despair: he had picked up a discarded boarding axe and had smashed it into one of *Unity*'s ladders. His own words still came in the night to mock him. *And for what?*

He knew Bolitho had warned others about the difference. This was not a foreign enemy, no matter what the flags proclaimed. Not French, or Dutchman, or Spaniard, the old and familiar adversaries. You heard the same voices as your own from these settlers in the new world, who were fighting for what they considered their freedom. Accents from the West Country and the Downs, from Norfolk and Scotland: it was like fighting your own flesh and blood. That was the vital difference in this war.

On one of his visits to *Valkyrie* Tyacke had aired his views on Bolitho's recall to London. He had not minced his words. Senseless, he had called it. Bolitho was needed here, to lead, and to exploit their hard-won victory.

He had paced the big cabin while Dawes had sat at his table, an expensive glass held in one hand. Amused? Indifferent?

Tyacke had added, 'The weather will ease soon. The Yankees will need to move. If they can't win by sea, they'll press on by land. They'll be able to bring artillery right up to the Canadian frontier.'

Dawes had shaken his head. 'I think not. Some kind of settlement will be negotiated. You really should give their lordships more credit, both for what they are and what they know.'

71

Tyacke had barely heard him. 'Our soldiers captured Detroit with the whole Yankee army defending it. Do you really think they'll not use every means to retake it, and give our soldiers a bloody nose for their trouble?'

Dawes had been suddenly impatient. 'There are great lakes to cross, rivers to navigate, forts to breach before they can do that. Do you imagine that our American cousins, the "Yankees" as you so colourfully call them, will not measure the cost of such foolhardy action?'

Apart from discussing an invitation to the local army commander-in-chief's Christmas reception, which Tyacke had declined to attend, they had scarcely spoken since.

Becoming an admiral was more important to Dawes than anything, and it was beginning to look as if doing nothing and keeping the main part of the squadron tied up in Halifax was far more attractive than behaving with any initiative that might rebound on him personally, and be seen as folly or worse.

Tyacke began to pace again. Out there, like it or not, there were enemy ships, and they were a constant threat. Dawes had only permitted local patrols, and then had detached nothing larger than a brig, claiming that Adam Bolitho's escape and vengeful attack in *Zest*, and Bolitho's personal victory would have made the Americans think again before attempting once more to harass convoys between Halifax and the West Indies. Napoleon was on the retreat: the dispatches were full of it. Tyacke swore angrily. He had been hearing that same story for so many years, from the time when Napoleon had landed his army in Egypt, and French fire had burned his face away.

It was all the more reason for the Americans to act now, and without further delay, while British forces and a whole fleet that could otherwise be released for these waters were concentrated on the old enemy, France.

And when peace came, that impossible dream, what would he do? There was nothing in England for him. He had felt like a stranger on his last visit, when he had been given *Indomitable*. Africa, then? He had been happy there. Or was that only another delusion?

He saw the first lieutenant, John Daubeny, waiting to catch his eye. Tyacke had toyed with the idea of accepting a more senior officer to replace Scarlett. Daubeny, like most of the wardroom, was young, perhaps too young for the post of senior lieutenant. Dawes had suggested that one of his own lieutenants be appointed. Tyacke grinned fiercely. That must have decided it. In any case, Daubeny had matured on that September day, like most of them. It was the navy's way. A man died or was transferred: another took his place. Like dead men's shoes after a hanging. Even the pompous Midshipman Blythe, who had been confirmed lieutenant and was now the most junior officer aboard, had proved both efficient and attentive to detail, to Tyacke's surprise, and his own division of seamen, who had known his arrogance as a midshipman, had shown him a grudging respect. They would never like him, but it was a beginning, and Tyacke was satisfied.

'Yes, Mr Daubeny?'

Daubeny touched his hat. 'We shall complete stowage today, sir.'

Tyacke grunted, picturing his ship at a distance, her trim in the water, gauging the feel of her.

He said, 'Tell my cox'n to prepare the gig when it's

73

time. I'll go around her once more. We might still have to move some of that extra powder and shot further aft.' He was not aware of the pride that had crept into his voice. 'This lady will want to fly when she finds open water again!'

Daubeny had noticed. He knew he would never be close to the captain: Tyacke kept his emotional distance, as if he were afraid to reveal his true feelings. Only with Sir Richard Bolitho had Daubeny ever seen him change, had sensed the warmth, the unspoken understanding and obvious respect of each for the other. He recalled them together, here, on this same untroubled deck. It was hard to believe that it had happened, that such chilling sights were possible. His inner voice spoke for him. *That I survived.*

He said, 'I shall be glad to see Sir Richard's flag hoisted again, sir.'

He did not even flinch when Tyacke faced him, as he had once done. How much worse it must be for him, he thought. The stares, the revulsion, and yes, the disapproval.

Surprisingly, Tyacke smiled. 'You speak for us both, Mr Daubeny!'

Tyacke turned away as York, the sailing-master, emerged from the companion, without a glance at the receding fog.

'You were right, Mr York! You have brought better weather for us!' Then he held up his hand and said sharply, 'Listen!' The hammering and the muted thuds between decks had stopped. Only six months since that last ball had smashed into the carnage of broken men. They had done well.

York studied him gravely. So many times in the last two years he had watched the captain's moods, his anguish and his defiance. He had once heard

Tyacke say of Sir Richard Bolitho, 'I would serve no other.' He could have said the same himself, of this brave, lonely man.

He said, 'Then we're ready, sir!'

Daubeny was listening, sharing it. At first he had thought he would be unable to fill Lieutenant Scarlett's shoes after he had fallen. He had even been afraid. That was yesterday. Now Scarlett was just another ghost, without substance or threat.

He stared up at the furled sails, moisture pouring from them like tropical rain. Like the ship, *the Old Indom* as the sailors called her, he was ready.

* * *

Three weeks outward bound from Portsmouth, Hampshire to Halifax, Nova Scotia, His Britannic Majesty's Ship *Wakeful* was within days of her landfall. Even Adam Bolitho, with all his hard-won experience as a frigate captain, could not recall a more violent passage. February into March, with the Atlantic using every mood and trick against them.

Although it was *Wakeful*'s young captain's first command, he had held it for two years, and two years in a frigate used almost exclusively for carrying vital dispatches to flag-officers and far-flung squadrons was equal to a lifetime in a lesser vessel. South-west and into the teeth of the Atlantic gales, with men knocked senseless by incoming seas, or in danger of being hurled from the upper yards while they kicked and fisted half-frozen canvas that could tear out a man's fingernails like pips from a lemon. Watchkeeping became a nightmare of noise and cruel discomfort; estimating their daily progress, unable even to stream the log, was based on dead reckoning, or, as the sailing-master put it, by guess and by God.

For the passengers down aft, it was uncomfortable but strangely detached from the rest of the ship and her weary company, piped again and again to the braces or aloft to reef the sails when they had only just been given a moment's rest in their messes. Simply trying to carry hot food from the swaying, pitching galley was a test of skill.

Sealed off from the life of the ship, and her daily fight against the common enemy, Adam and his new flag officer remained curiously apart. Keen spent most of his time reading his lengthy instructions from the Admiralty, or making notes as he studied various charts beneath the wildly spiralling lanterns. They burned day and night: little light penetrated the stern windows, which were either streaming with spume from a following gale, or so smeared with salt that even the rearing waves were distorted into wild and threatening creatures.

Adam could appreciate all of it. Had *Wakeful* been an ordinary fleet frigate she would likely have been short-handed, or at best manned by unskilled newcomers, snatched up by the press or offered for duty by the local assize court. This required trained seamen, who had worked together long enough to know the strength of their ship and the value of their captain. He had thought often enough, *as Anemone had been.*

Whenever he could be spared from his duties Captain Hyde had made it his business to visit them. No wonder he had not hesitated to offer his own quarters for their use: Hyde spent as many, if not more, hours on deck than any of his men.

Whenever possible Adam had sat with Keen in the cabin, and had washed down the wardroom fare with a plentiful supply of wine. To expect anything hot to drink was out of the question. The wine, however, had added no intimacy to their conversations.

Hyde must have noticed that Keen had made no impossible demands, and had not once complained of discomfort, nor had he requested a change of tack to seek out calmer waters even at the expense of losing time. It was obviously something which had surprised Hyde, in spite of Adam's first description of the admiral.

On one rare occasion when Hyde had given up the fight, and *Wakeful* had lain hove-to under storm canvas waiting for the weather to ease, Keen had seemed willing to share his confidences. Afterwards, Adam thought it might have been easier for both of them if they had been total strangers.

Keen had said, 'I cannot tell you how pleased I was to have your letter of agreement to this appointment. We have known one another for a long time, and we have shared and lost many good friends.' He had hesitated, perhaps thinking of *Hyperion*; he had been Bolitho's flag captain when the old ship had gone down, with her flag still flying. 'We have seen fine ships destroyed.' They had listened to the wind, and the sea hissing against the stern windows like a cave of serpents. 'The sea is no less a tyrant than war, I sometimes think.'

He had seemed to want to talk, and Adam had found himself studying his companion with new eyes. When Keen had been piped aboard at Portsmouth with full honours, and the port admiral to welcome him in person, Adam had felt the old hurt and resentment. Keen had worn no mark of mourning, either then or since. Nor had he mentioned Zenoria, other than to acknowledge the port admiral's meaningless murmurs of condolence.

Keen had said, 'When I was your uncle's flag captain, even though I had known him since I was a lowly midshipman, I was uncertain of the measure of confidence between us. Perhaps I did not understand the true difference between the position of flag captain, and a captain like our youthful Martin Hyde. Sir Richard showed me the way, without favour, and without overriding my own opinions merely to exercise the privileges of rank. It meant a great deal to me, and I hope I did not disappoint his trust.' He had smiled, rather sadly. 'Or his friendship, which means so much to me, and which helped to save my mind.'

He could not think of them together. Keen, always so outwardly assured, attractive to women, his hair so fair that it looked almost white against his tanned features. But ... as lovers ... He was repulsed by it.

The boy John Whitmarsh, legs braced against the movement of the deck and lower lip pouting with concentration, had carried more wine to the table.

Keen had watched him, and after he had departed had said absently, 'A pleasant youth. What shall you do with him?' He had not waited for, or perhaps expected, an answer. 'I used to plan things for my boy, Perran. I wish I had had more time to know him.'

The table had been cleared by Whitmarsh and one of the captain's messmen. He had said quietly, 'I want you to feel you can always speak your mind to me, Adam. Admiral and captain, but most of all friends. As I was, and am, with your uncle.' He had seemed uneasy, disturbed then by some thought. 'And Lady Catherine—that goes without saying.'

And then, eventually, *Wakeful* had changed

course, north-west-by-north to take full advantage of the obliging Westerlies as, close-hauled, they started on the last leg of their journey.

Of Halifax Keen had remarked, 'My father has friends there.' Again a note of bitterness had crept into his voice. 'In the way of trade, I believe.' Then, 'I just want to be doing something. Peter Dawes might have fresh information by the time we arrive.'

On another occasion, when they had been free to walk the quarterdeck, and there had even been a suggestion of sunlight on the dark, rearing crests, Keen had mentioned Adam's escape, and John Allday's son, who had risked everything to help him, only to fall in the battle with *Unity*. Keen had paused to watch some gulls skimming within inches of the sea's face, screaming a welcome. He had said, 'I remember when we were together in the boat after that damned *Golden Plover* went down.' He had spoken with such vehemence that Adam had felt him reliving it. 'Some birds flew over the boat. We were nearly finished. But for Lady Catherine I don't know what we would have done. I heard your uncle say to her, *tonight those birds will nest in Africa.*' He had looked at Adam without seeing him. 'It made all the difference. Land, I thought. We are no longer alone, without hope.'

As the miles rolled away in *Wakeful*'s lively wake, Adam had shared few other confidences with his new rear-admiral. Others might look at him and say, there is a favoured one, who has everything. In fact, his rank was all he had. And then, on that last full day when they had both been on deck, the air like knives in their faces.

'Have you ever thought of getting married, Adam? You should. This life is hard on the women, but I

79

sometimes think. . . .'

Mercifully, the masthead had yelled, 'Deck there! Land on th' weather bow!'

Hyde had joined them, beaming and rubbing his raw hands. Glad it was over, more so that he was ridding himself of his extra responsibilities.

'With good fortune we shall anchor in the forenoon tomorrow, sir.' He had been looking at the rear-admiral, but his words had been for Adam. The satisfaction of making a landfall. Even the ocean had seemed calmer, until the next challenge.

Keen had walked to the quarterdeck rail, oblivious to the idlers off-watch who were chattering, some even laughing, sharing the same elation at what they had achieved. Men against the sea.

He had said, without turning his head, 'You may hoist my flag at the mizzen at first light, Captain Hyde.' Then he did turn and face them. 'And, thank you.' But he had been looking past them, through them, as if he had been speaking to someone else.

Hyde had asked, 'May I invite you and Captain Bolitho to sup with my officers and me, sir? It is quite an occasion for us.'

Adam had seen Keen's face. Empty, like a stranger's.

'I think not, Captain Hyde. I have some papers to study before we anchor.' He made another attempt. 'My flag captain will do the honours.'

Perhaps it had been then, and only then, that the impact of his loss had really struck him.

It would have to be a new beginning, for them both.

*　　　*　　　*

Richard Bolitho walked across the cabin deck, and paused by the table where Yovell was melting wax to seal one of the many written orders he had copied.

'I think that will be an end to it for today.' The deck was rising again, the rudder-head thudding noisily as the transport *Royal Enterprise* lifted and then ploughed into another criss-cross of deep troughs. He knew Avery was watching him from the security of a chair which was lashed firmly between two ringbolts. A rough passage, even for a ship well used to such violence. It would soon be over, and still he had not reconciled himself, or confronted his doubts at the prospect of returning to a war which could never be won, but must never be lost. He was holding on, refusing to surrender, even when they were separated by an ocean.

He said, 'Well, George, we will dine directly. I am glad I have a flag lieutenant whose appetite is unimpaired by the Atlantic in ill temper!'

Avery smiled. He should be used to it, to the man, by now. But he could still be surprised by the way Bolitho seemed able to put his personal preoccupations behind him, or at least conceal them from others. *From me.* Avery had guessed what the return to duty had cost him, but when he had stepped aboard the transport at Plymouth there had been nothing to reveal the pain of parting from his mistress after so brief a reunion.

Bolitho was watching the last of the wax dripping onto the envelope like blood before Yovell set his seal upon it. He had not spared himself, but he knew very well that by the time they reached Halifax and rejoined the squadron everything might have changed, rendering their latest intelligence useless. Time and distance were the elements that determined the war at sea. Instinct, fate, experience, it was all and none of them, and ignorance was often fatal.

Avery watched the sea dashing across the thick stern windows. The ship had been more comfortable than he had expected, with a tough and disciplined company used to fast passages and taking avoiding action against suspicious sails instead of standing to fight. The Admiralty orders made that very clear to every such vessel and her master: they were to deliver their passengers or small, important cargoes at any cost. They were usually underarmed; the *Royal Enterprise* mounted only some nine-pounders and a few swivels. Speed, not glory, was her purpose.

They had had only one mishap. The ship had been struck by a violent squall as she was about to change tack. Her fore topgallant mast and yard had carried away, and one of her boats had been torn from its tier and flung over the side like a piece of flotsam. The ship's company had got down to work immediately; they were used to such hazards, but her master, a great lump of a man named Samuel Tregullon, was outraged by the incident. A Cornishman from Penzance, Tregullon was intensely proud of his ship's record, and her ability to carry out to the letter the instructions of the men at Admiralty who, in his view, had likely never set foot on a deck in their lives. To be delayed with such an important passenger in his care, and a fellow Cornishman at that, was bad enough. But as he had confided over a tankard of rum during a visit to the cabin, another transport, almost a sister ship of his own, the *Royal Herald*, had left Plymouth a few days after them, and would now reach Halifax before them.

Bolitho had commented afterwards to Avery, 'Another old Cornish rivalry. I'll lay odds that neither of them can remember how it all began.'

Bolitho had asked him about London, but he had not pressed the point, for which Avery was grateful. During the long night watches when he had lain awake, listening to the roar of the sea and the protesting groan of timbers, he had thought of little else.

He had felt no sense of triumph or revenge, as he had once believed he would. Had she been amusing herself with him? Playing with him, as she had once done? Or had he imagined that, too? A woman like her, so poised, so confident amongst people who lived in an entirely different world from his own ... Why would she risk everything if she had no deeper feeling for him?

None of the repeated questions had been answered.

He should have left her. Should never have gone to the house in the first place. He looked across at Bolitho, who was speaking warmly with Yovell, more like old friends than admiral and servant. What would he think if he knew that his wife Belinda had been there that day, obviously just as at home in that elegant and superficial world as all the others?

Yovell stood up, and grimaced as the deck swayed over again. 'Ah, they were right about me, Sir Richard. I must be mad to share the life of a sailor!'

He gathered his papers and prepared to leave, perhaps to join Allday and Ozzard before the evening meal. Allday would be feeling the separation badly, and there would be a long wait for that first letter, which Avery knew he would bring for him to read aloud. Another precious link in the little crew: Allday was a proud man, and Avery had been touched by the simplicity and dignity of his request that Avery read to him the letters from Unis that he could not read for himself.

Would Susanna ever write to him? He wanted to laugh at his own pathetic hopes. Of course she would not. Within weeks she would have forgotten him. She had money, she had beauty, and she was free. But he would think of her again tonight....

He had tried to compare his position with that of Bolitho and his mistress, although he knew it was ridiculous. There was no comparison. Apart from that one memory, what had happened was a closed door, the finish of something which had always been hopeless.

He looked up, startled, afraid that he had missed something or that Bolitho had spoken to him. But they were as before, framed against the grey stern windows, the sea already losing its menace as the fading light obscured it.

Bolitho turned and looked at him. 'Did you hear?'

Yovell steadied himself against the table. 'Another storm, Sir Richard.'

'The glass says otherwise.' He tensed. 'There. Again.'

Yovell said, 'Thunder?'

Avery was on his feet. So unlike a ship of war; too long at sea with nothing but the sea to challenge you. Day after day, week in, week out. And then the boredom and the noisy routine were forgotten.

He said, 'Gunfire, sir.'

There was a rap on the door and Allday stepped into the cabin. He moved so lightly when he wanted to, for such a big man, and one who was in more pain from his old wound than he would ever admit.

Bolitho said, 'You heard, old friend?'

Allday looked at them. 'I wasn't sure, an' then.' He

84

shook his shaggy head. 'Not a thing to lie easy on your mind, Sir Richard.'

Avery asked, 'Shall I go and speak with the master, sir?'

Bolitho glanced at the screen door. 'No. It is not our place.' He smiled at Ozzard, who had also appeared, a tray of glasses balanced in his hands. 'Not yet, in any case.'

Eventually Samuel Tregullon made his way aft, his battered hat clutched in one beefy hand like a scrap of felt.

'Beggin' yer pardon, Zur Richard, but ye'll be knowing about the guns.' He shook his head as Ozzard offered him a glass, not because he was involved with his ship but because he usually drank only neat rum. A sailor, from his clear eyes to his thick wrists and the hands that were like pieces of meat. Collier brig, Falmouth packet, one-time smuggler and now a King's man: what Bolitho's father would have described as *all spunyarn and marline spikes*.

Tregullon nodded briefly as Ozzard replaced the glass with a tankard. 'Never fear, Zur Richard. I'll get you to Halifax as I was ordered, an' take you there I will. I can outsail any felon, theirs or ours!' He grinned, his uneven teeth like a broken fence. 'I'm too old a hand to be caught aback!'

After he had gone, the distant gunfire continued for half an hour and then stopped, as if quenched by the sea itself.

The master returned, grim-faced, to say that he was resuming course and tack. It was over.

Bolitho said suddenly, 'Yours is an experienced company, Captain Tregullon. None better at this work, I think you said?'

85

Tregullon eyed him suspiciously. 'I did, Zur Richard. That I did.'

'I think we should make every effort to investigate what we have heard. At first light the sea may ease. I feel it.'

Tregullon was not convinced. 'I have my orders, zur. They comes from the lords of Admiralty. No matter how I feels about it, I am not able or willing to change those orders.' He tried to smile, but it evaded him. 'Not even for you, zur.'

Bolitho walked to the stern windows and leaned against the glass. 'The lords of Admiralty, you say?' He turned, his face in shadow, the white lock of hair above his eye like a brushstroke. 'We're all sailors here. We all know there is someone far higher who controls our lives, and listens to our despair when it pleases Him.'

Tregullon licked his lips. 'I knows that, zur. But what can I do?'

Bolitho said quietly, 'There are men out there, Captain Tregullon. In need, and likely in fear. It may already be too late, and I am well aware of the risk to your ship. To you and your company.'

'Not least to you, zur!' But there was no fight in his voice. He sighed. 'Very well. I'll do it.' He looked up angrily. 'Not for you, with all respect, zur, an' not for His Majesty, bless his soul.' He stared at his crumpled hat. 'For *me*. It has to be so.'

Bolitho and Avery ate their meal in silence: the whole ship seemed to be holding her breath. Only the creak of the rudder and the occasional thud of feet overhead gave any hint that everything had changed.

At first light, as Bolitho had expected, the wind and sea eased; and with every available telescope and lookout searching for the presence of danger

86

Tregullon shortened sail, and, arms folded, watched the darkness falling away and the sea eventually tinge with silver to mark each trough and roller.

Avery joined Bolitho on the broad quarterdeck, where he was standing in silence by the weather side, his black hair blowing unheeded in the bitter air. Once or twice Avery saw him touch his injured eye, impatient, even resentful that his concentration was interrupted.

Captain Tregullon joined him, and said gruffly, 'We tried, Zur Richard. If there was anything, we were too late.' He watched Bolitho's profile, seeking something. 'I'd best lay her on a new tack.'

He was about to shamble away when the cry came down, sharp and crisp, like the call of a hawk.

'Wreckage in th' water, sir! Lee bow!'

There was a lot of it. Planks and timber, drifting cordage and broken or upended boats, most of it charred and splintered by the fierceness of the bombardment.

Bolitho waited while the ship came into the wind, and a boat was lowered with one of the master's mates in charge.

There were a few dead, lolling as if asleep as the waves carried them by. The boat moved slowly amongst them, the bowman pulling each sodden corpse alongside with his hook and then quickly discarding it, unwilling, it seemed, to interrupt such a final journey.

Except for one. The master's mate took some time with it, and even without a glass Avery could see the dead face, the gaping wounds, all that was left of a man.

The boat returned and was hoisted inboard with a minimum of fuss. Avery heard the master pass his

87

orders for getting under way again. Heavy, unhurried: the ship, as always, coming first.

Then he came aft and waited for Bolitho to face him. 'My mate knew that dead sailor, Zur Richard. I expect we knew most of 'em.'

Bolitho said, 'She was the *Royal Herald*, was she not?'

'She was, zur. Because of our losing the t'gallant mast she overreached us. They was waiting. They knew we was coming.' Then he said in a hoarse whisper, 'It was you they was after, Zur Richard. They wanted you dead.'

Bolitho touched his thick arm. 'So it would seem. Instead, many good men died.'

Then he turned and looked at Avery, and beyond him, Allday. 'We thought we had left the war behind, my friends. Now it has come to meet us.'

There was no anger or bitterness, only sorrow. The respite was over.

CHAPTER FIVE

A FACE IN THE CROWD

Bolitho put down the empty cup and walked slowly to the tall stern window. Around and above him, *Indomitable*'s hull seemed to tremble with constant movement and purpose, so unlike the transport *Royal Enterprise*, which he had left the previous afternoon. He peered through the thick glass and saw her lying at anchor, his practised eye taking in the movement of seamen on her yards and in her upper rigging, while others hoisted fresh stores from a lighter alongside. *Royal Enterprise* would soon be off again on her next mission, with her master still brooding over the brutal destruction of the other transport which had been so well known to him and his people, and less confident now that speed was all that was required to protect them from a determined enemy.

It was halfway through the forenoon, and Bolitho had been working since first light. He had been surprised and touched by the warmth of his reception. Tyacke had come in person to collect him from *Royal Enterprise*, his eyes full of questions when Tregullon had mentioned the attack.

He glanced now around the cabin, which was so familiar in spite of his absence in England. Tyacke had done some fine work to get his ship repaired and ready for sea, for even in harbour the weather did not encourage such activities. But now there was a little weak sunlight to give an illusion of warmth. He touched the glass. It *was* an illusion.

He should be used to it. Even so, the transformation was a tribute to *Indomitable*'s captain. Even here in his cabin, these guns had roared defiance: now each one was lashed snugly behind sealed ports, trucks painted, barrels unmarked by fire and smoke.

He looked at the empty cup. The coffee was excellent, and he wondered how long his stock would last. He could imagine her going to that shop in St James's Street, Number Three, part of the new world she had opened to him. Coffee, wine, so many small luxuries, which she had known he would not have bothered to obtain for himself, nor would any one else.

Keen would be coming aboard in an hour or so: he

had sent word that he would be detained by a visit from some local military commander who wanted to discuss the improved defences and shore batteries. A casual glance at any map or chart would show the sense of that. Halifax was the only real naval base left to them on the Atlantic coast. The Americans had their pick, Boston, New York, Philadelphia, as well as scores of bays and estuaries where they could conceal an armada if they so desired.

He wondered how Adam was finding his appointment as flag captain. After the freedom of a solitary command, it might be just what he needed. Conversely, it might remain only a cruel reminder of what might have been.

He closed the canvas folder he had been studying, and considered Keen's report. A convoy of five merchantmen had been ordered to await a stronger escort off the Bermudas for their final passage to the West Indies. Until then, two brigs had been the only vessels Dawes had spared to defend them.

The convoy had never reached the Bermudas. Every ship must have been taken, or sunk. When he met Keen, he would discover his real thoughts on the matter. The disaster had happened a few days after he had hoisted his flag in *Valkyrie*; there was nothing he could have done. But what of Dawes, acting commodore until Keen's arrival? Perhaps he had had his own reasons for allowing merchantmen to venture unprotected into an area which had become a hunting ground for enemy men-of-war and privateers alike.

He had consulted Tyacke, and Tyacke had not hesitated. 'Thinking too much of keeping his house in good order. I'm told that promotion can sometimes do that to a man.' Hard and blunt, like himself.

Tyacke had even been scornful about his two new epaulettes. He had been promoted to post-captain, for rank only, the usual requirement of three years' service as captain having been waived as a mark of favour. 'I'm still the same man, Sir Richard. I think their lordships have a different set of values!' He had relented slightly. 'But I know your hand was in it, and that I do respect.'

Yes, it had surprised Bolitho that his return had, after all, been like a homecoming. And, despite what he hoped for, it was here that he belonged.

He had described the attack on *Royal Herald* and had watched Tyacke's scarred face, thoughtful, assessing each small piece of information and relating it to what he knew.

A prolonged bombardment, to catch and destroy the transport before she could find refuge in darkness. No one had heard the sound of a single shot fired in reply, not even a gesture or a final show of defiance. Nothing. It had been calculated murder. Had it been a trap set for *Royal Enterprise*? For him? Was it possible that a single mind had planned it so carefully, only to see it misfire through a fluke in the weather and an accident?

He had searched through every report Keen had gathered for him, knowing that they would be the first thing his admiral would want to see. Unless another man like Nathan Beer was abroad and at sea, unknown and undetected by the local patrols, which had been ordered to watch for any sudden ship movements, his theory seemed unlikely. But, so too was coincidence.

They wanted you dead.

Not another Nathan Beer, then. Perhaps there was no such officer with his wealth of experience and sense of honour. Beer had been a sailor first and foremost: to kill defenceless men, unable to resist, had never been his way. He wondered if his widow in Newburyport had received Beer's sword, which Bolitho himself had sent to her. Would she care? He found himself staring at the old family sword lying on its rack, where it received Allday's regular attention. Would that help Catherine, if the worst happened? He thought of the portrait she had commissioned for him. The real Catherine, she had called it. The painter had caught her exactly as she had wanted to be remembered, in the rough seaman's clothing she had worn in the open boat. Perhaps she would cherish the old sword....

The door opened slightly, shaking him from his unwelcome thoughts, and Avery peered into the cabin. The brief stay in England had affected him deeply, Bolitho thought. He had always been withdrawn: now he had become remote, troubled and introspective. Bolitho had too much respect for George Avery to pry into it, and they had shared danger too often not to know that this unspoken understanding of one another was an anchor for them both.

Avery said, 'Signal from *Valkyrie*, Sir Richard. Rear-Admiral Keen is about to come over to us.'

'Tell Captain Tyacke, will you?'

Avery said gently, 'He knows.'

Bolitho reached for his heavy uniform coat. Irrationally, he disliked wearing it when he was working in his quarters, perhaps because he sometimes believed that it influenced his decisions, and made him think more like an admiral than a man.

It was true: Tyacke did seem to know everything

92

that was happening in his ship. Maybe that was how he had overcome his resentment, fear, even, of taking command or becoming flag captain after the private world of *Larne*. The purser, James Viney, had been discharged as sick and unfit for further service at sea, and Bolitho suspected that Tyacke had guessed from the outset that Viney had been falsifying his accounts in connivance with equally dishonest chandlers. It was a common enough failing, but some captains were content to let it rest. Not James Tyacke.

He allowed his mind to stray again to the attack. Suppose it had been solely to kill him? He found that he could accept it, but the motive was something else. No single man could make so much difference. Nelson had been the only one to win an overwhelming victory by inspiration alone after he himself had fallen, mortally wounded.

Avery said abruptly, 'I meant to tell you, Sir Richard.' He glanced round, caught off-guard by the tramp of boots as the Royal Marines prepared to receive their visitor with full honours. 'It can wait.'

Bolitho sat on the corner of the table. 'I think it will not. It has been tearing you to pieces. Good or bad, a confidence often helps to share the load.'

Avery shrugged. 'I was at a reception in London.' He tried to smile. 'I was like a fish out of water.' The smile would not come. 'Your ... Lady Bolitho was there. We did not speak, of course. She would not know me.'

So that was it. Unwilling to mention it because it might disturb me. He found himself speculating on the reason for Avery's attendance.

'I would not be too certain of that, but thank you for telling me. It took courage, I think.' He picked up his hat as he heard hurrying footsteps beyond the

93

screen door. 'Especially as your admiral's mood has been far from pleasant of late!'

It was the first lieutenant, still very stiff and uneasy in his new role.

'The captain's respects, Sir Richard.' His eyes moved swiftly around the spacious cabin, seeing it quite differently from either of them, Avery imagined.

Bolitho smiled. 'Speak, Mr Daubeny. We are all agog.'

The lieutenant grinned nervously. 'Rear-Admiral Keen's barge has cast off, sir.'

'We will come up directly.'

As the door closed Bolitho asked, 'Then there was no attempt to involve you in scandal?'

'I would not have stood for it, Sir Richard.'

In spite of the deep lines on his face and the streaks of grey in his dark hair, he looked and sounded very vulnerable, like a much younger man.

Ozzard opened the door and they walked past him.

At the foot of the companion ladder, Bolitho paused and glanced at his flag lieutenant again with sudden intuition. *Or a man who was suddenly in love, and did not know what to do about it.*

When he crossed the damp quarterdeck he saw Tyacke waiting for him.

'A very smart turn-out, Captain Tyacke.'

The harsh, scarred face did not smile.

'I shall pass the word to the side-party, Sir Richard.'

Avery listened, missing nothing, thinking of the reception, the daring gowns, the arrogance. What did they know of men like these? Tyacke, with his melted face, and the courage to endure the stares, the pity and the revulsion. Or Sir Richard, who had knelt on

94

this bloodied deck to hold the dying hand of an American captain.

How *could* they know?

The boatswain's mates moistened their silver calls on their lips, side-boys waited to fend off the smart green barge, the twin lines of scarlet marines swayed slightly on the harbour current.

It is my life. There is nothing more I want.

'Royal Marines! *Present...*!' The rest was lost in the din.

Again, they were of one company.

* * *

After the long day, and the comings and goings of officers and local officials paying their respects to the admiral, and the degrees of ceremony and respect that applied to each one of them, *Indomitable* seemed quiet, and at peace. All hands had been piped down for the night, and only the watchkeepers and the scarlet-coated sentries moved on the upper decks.

Right aft in his cabin, Bolitho watched the stars, which seemed to reflect and mingle with the glittering lights of the town. Here and there a small lantern moved on the dark water: a guardboat or some messenger, or even a fisherman.

The day had been tiring. Adam and Valentine Keen had arrived together, and he had been aware of the momentary uneasiness when they had been reunited with Tyacke and Avery. Keen had brought his new flag lieutenant as well, the Honourable Lawford de Courcey, a slim young man with hair almost as fair as his admiral's. Highly recommended, Keen had said, and intelligent and eager. Ambitious, too, from the little he had said; the scion of an

95

influential family, but not a naval one. Keen had seemed pleased about it, but Bolitho had wondered if the appointment had been arranged by one of the many friends of Keen's father.

Adam had greeted him warmly, although reserved in front of the others, and Bolitho had sensed the depression he was trying to conceal. Keen, on the other hand, had been very concerned with the war, and what they might expect when the weather moderated. For the destruction of the *Royal Herald* he could offer no explanation. Most of the active American ships were in harbour, their presence carefully monitored by a chain of brigs and other, smaller commandeered vessels. Each of the latter might offer a fine chance of promotion to any young lieutenant if fortune smiled on him: such a chance had once come to Bolitho. He touched his eye, and frowned. It seemed an eternity ago.

He had walked around *Indomitable* with Tyacke, as much to be seen as to inspect the full extent of the overhaul. In her struggle with *Unity*, Tyacke's command had lost seventy officers, seamen and marines killed or wounded, a quarter of her company. Replacements had been found, taken from homeward-bound ships, and a surprising number of volunteers, Nova Scotians who had earned their living from the sea before marauding warships and privateers had denied them even that.

They would settle into *Indomitable*'s ways; but not until they were at sea, as close-knit as her original company used to be, would they know their true value.

Bolitho had seen the startled, curious eyes, those who had never met the man whose flag flew above all of them at the mainmast truck. And some of the older hands who had knuckled their foreheads, or raised a tarred fist in greeting to show that they knew the admiral, had shared the battle and its cost with him, until the enemy's flag had been dragged down through the smoke.

His total command had been christened the Leeward Squadron by Bethune, and their lordships had been more generous than he had dared to hope, giving him eight frigates and as many brigs. That did not include the heavily-armed *Valkyrie*, and *Indomitable*. In addition there were schooners, some brigantines, and two bomb vessels, the request for which the Admiralty had not even questioned. A strong, fast-moving squadron, and it would be joined by the old seventy-four gun ship of the line *Redoubtable*, which had been ordered to Antigua. With suitable intelligence gathered by the smaller patrol vessels on their endless stop-and-search missions, they should be a match for any new enemy tactics. The larger and better-armed American frigates had already proved their superiority, until *Unity* had met up with this ship. And even then ... But there was still something missing. He paced back and forth across the black and white squares of the canvas deck covering, his hair almost touching the massive beams. *Royal Herald* had been destroyed, so a ship or ships had avoided the patrols, and perhaps slipped out of harbour, taking advantage of the foul weather. It was pointless to brush it aside, or regard it as a coincidence. And if it had been a deliberate ambush gone wrong, what steps must he take? Very soon now, the Americans would have to launch a new attack. Tyacke had been convinced that it would be a military operation, straight into Canada. Once again, all the reports suggested that any such attack

97

could be contained. The British soldiers were from seasoned regiments, but Bolitho knew from bitter experience in that other American war that often too much reliance was placed upon local militia and volunteers, or on Indian scouts unused to the ways of the hard-line infantryman.

Speed was essential to the Americans. Napoleon was in retreat, and each day of the campaign he was being deserted by friends and erstwhile allies. Surely his defeat was inevitable, perhaps even sooner than strategists in London dared to hope. And when that happened ... Bolitho heard again the confidence in Bethune's voice as he had explained how a French defeat would release many more ships to join the American conflict. But until that time ... He stopped pacing and strode to the quarter gallery, and stared down at the black, swirling current.

It must have been right there in Bethune's gracious rooms at the Admiralty, and yet neither of them had seen or considered it. He looked at the reflected lights until his eye watered. The carefully worded dispatches, the lists of ships and squadrons that daily protected the vital lifelines to Wellington's armies. Ships that fed his victorious regiments, and made even the smallest advance possible. Even Sillitoe had missed it, perhaps because it had not fitted into his intricate plans and the estimates with which he advised the Prince Regent. Arrogance, over-confidence: it would not be the first time that careful strategy had been undone by those in power who had seen only what they had wanted to see.

The flaw in the pattern of things, like a face in a crowd, there, but invisible.

All they had been able to see was Napoleon's eventual defeat. After twenty years of war it had, at

98

last, seemed like the impossible landfall. He knew that Tyacke had made no attempt to conceal his disgust at Peter Dawes' handling of the squadron in his admiral's absence. Maybe Dawes was another one, blind to everything but his own advancement: promotion, which might vanish like mist if the war should suddenly end.

Bolitho considered his visitors. Keen, contained but enthusiastic at his new appointment, desperately eager to leave the past behind, to overcome his loss. Only Adam seemed unable or unwilling to forget it.

He heard something rattle behind the pantry hatch, a subtle signal from Ozzard that he was still about, in case he was required.

And what of me? So bitter at being parted from the woman he loved that he had failed to heed the instinct gained all those years ago as a frigate captain.

Maybe it was destined to end like this. He had opened the screen door without realizing that he had moved, and the marine sentry was staring at him, transfixed. Their admiral, coatless despite the damp air between decks, who had only to raise a finger to have every man running to do his bidding. What was the matter with him?

Bolitho heard a murmur of voices from the wardroom. Perhaps Avery was there. Or James Tyacke, although he was probably working alone in his cabin. He never slept for more than an hour or two at a time. Surely there was some one he could talk to?

'Something wrong, Sir Richard?'

Bolitho let his arms fall to his sides. Allday was here, watching him, his shadow moving slowly back and forth across the new paintwork, his face devoid of surprise. As if he had known.

99

'I want to talk, old friend. It's nothing ... I'm not sure.' He turned to the ramrod sentry who was still staring at him, eyes popping, as if his collar was choking him. 'At ease, Wilson. There is nothing to fear.'

The marine swallowed. 'Yessir!' As he heard the door close he wiped his face with his sleeve. His sergeant would have given him hell just for doing that. But he had been with his squad in the maintop with the other marksmen when they had thundered alongside the enemy. Only for the moment, it meant nothing. He said aloud, 'Knew me name! He knew me name!'

Ozzard had poured a tankard of rum and placed it on the table, not too close, in case Allday should take the liberty of thinking that he was his servant as well.

Allday sat on the bench seat and watched Bolitho moving restlessly about the cabin as if it were a cage.

'You remember the Saintes, old friend?'

Allday nodded. Bryan Ferguson had asked him the same thing, while they had been waiting for Bolitho and his lady to return from London.

'Aye, Sir Richard. I recalls it well.'

Bolitho ran his hand down the curved timbers as if to feel the life, the heartbeat of the ship.

'This old lady was there, although I don't remember her, nor could I imagine what she might one day mean to me. Five years old, she was then.'

Allday saw him smile. Like some one speaking of an old comrade.

'So many miles, so many people, eh?' He turned, his face composed, even sad. 'But, of course, we had another ship then. *Phalarope*.'

Allday sipped his rum, although he did not remember reaching for it. There had been many

100

moments like this, before the proud admiral's flags, the fame, and the bloody scandal. So many times. He watched him now, sharing it, very aware that he was one of the few that this man, this hero, could speak with so freely.

He would not be able to tell Unis about it, not until he was with her again. It would be out of the question to ask Lieutenant Avery to pen it for him. It would have to be later, at the right time, like the moment he had told her about his son's death. He glanced up at the closed skylight. *Just a few yards away.*

Bolitho said, 'Admiral Rodney broke the French line that day because the enemy's frigates failed to discover his intentions. Our frigates did *not* fail.'

His eyes were distant, remembering not so much the battle between the two great fleets as the slowness of their embrace, and the slaughter which had followed. He had seen too many such encounters, and he had felt like some physical assault the hostility of those at the Admiralty when he had said that the line of battle was dead. It must have sounded like blasphemy. *We'll not see another Trafalgar, I am certain of it.*

'It is every frigate captain's main concern—his duty—to discover, to observe, and to act.'

Ozzard frowned as the door opened slightly, and Avery hesitated, uncertain why he had come.

'I'm sorry, Sir Richard. I heard ... somebody said....'

Bolitho gestured to a chair. 'This time you did not have too far to come. Not like riding from Portsmouth to London!'

Avery took a goblet from Ozzard. He looked dishevelled, as if he had been trying to sleep when some instinct had roused him.

101

Allday, in the shadows, nodded. That was better. More like it.

Bolitho glanced around at them, his grey eyes keen. 'Captain Dawes did not see it, because there was nothing to see. He conserved the squadron's strength, as I so ordered, and repaired the vessels that most needed it. It was like a well-ordered plan, beyond doubt or question.'

Avery said, 'Do you believe that the outcome of the war is still undecided, sir?'

Bolitho smiled. 'We have been fighting one enemy or another for years, for some a lifetime. But always, the French were in the vanguard. Always the French.'

Allday frowned. To him one mounseer was much like another. The old Jacks could sing and brag about it when they'd had a skinful of rum, but when it came down to it, it had always been 'us' or 'them'.

'I ain't sure I follows, Sir Richard.'

'We are intent on defeating the French without further delay, so that we may bring naval reinforcements to these waters to contain the Americans. In turn, the Americans must break our line before that happens. I believe that the *Royal Herald* was destroyed by an unknown force of ships, American or French, maybe both, but under one leader, who will settle for nothing less than the destruction of our patrols and, if need be, our entire squadron.'

Captain James Tyacke was here now, his scarred face in shadow, his blue eyes fixed on Bolitho.

'In all the reports there is no mention of any American resentment at a new French presence, and yet we have missed or overlooked the most obvious fact, that war makes strange bedfellows. I believe that

102

an American of great skill and determination is the single mind behind this venture. He has shown his hand. It is up to us to find and defeat him.' He looked at each of them in turn, conscious of the strength they had given him, and of their trust.

'The face in the crowd, my friends. It was there all the time, and no one saw it.'

*   *   *

Captain Adam Bolitho walked to the quarterdeck rail and watched the afternoon working parties, each separated by craft and skill, gathered around a portion of the main deck like stall holders: no wonder it was often called the market-place. *Valkyrie* was big for a frigate, and like *Indomitable* had begun life as a small third-rate, a ship of the line.

He had met all his officers both individually and as a wardroom at a first, informal meeting. Some, like John Urquhart, the first lieutenant, were of the original company, when *Valkyrie* had been commissioned and had hoisted his uncle's flag, then a vice-admiral's, at the foremast truck. To all accounts she had been an unhappy ship, plagued with discontent and its inevitable companion of flogging at the gangway, until her last, famous battle, and the destruction of the notorious French squadron under Baratte. Her captain, Trevenen, had been proved a coward, so often the true nature of a tyrant, and had vanished overboard under mysterious circumstances.

Adam glanced up at Keen's flag, whipping out stiffly from the mizzen. Here and here, men had died. His uncle had been injured, momentarily blinded in the undamaged eye, the battle lost until Rear-

103

Admiral Herrick, who had been recovering from the amputation of his right arm, had burst on deck. Adam stared at the companion and the unmanned wheel. He could picture it as if he himself had been here. Lieutenant Urquhart had taken charge, and had proved what he could do. A quiet, serious officer, he would soon be given his own command if they were called to action.

He watched the working parties, knowing that every man jack was well aware of his presence. *The new captain.* Already known, because of his achievements in *Anemone* and because of the family name, and the admiral who was rarely out of the news. But to these men, he was simply their new superior. Nothing which had preceded him mattered, until they had learned what he was like.

The sailmaker and his mates were here, cross-legged, busy with palms and bright needles. Nothing was ever wasted, be it a sail ripped apart in a gale or the scrap that would eventually clothe a corpse for its final journey to the sea-bed. The carpenter and his crew; the boatswain making a last inspection of the new blocks and tackles above the boat tier. He saw the surgeon, George Minchin, walking alone on the larboard gangway, his face brick-red in the hard afternoon light. Another man whose story was unknown. He had been in the old *Hyperion* when she had gone down, with Keen as her captain. The navy was like a family, but there were so many missing faces now.

Adam had been on deck at first light when *Indomitable* had weighed, and sailed in company with two other frigates and a brig. She had made a fine sight, towering above the other ships with her pyramids of sails straining and hardening like

104

armoured breastplates in a sharp north-westerly. He had lifted his hat, and had known that his uncle, although unseen, would have returned their private salute. In one way, he envied Tyacke his role as Bolitho's flag captain, even as he knew it would have been the worst thing he could have attempted. This was his ship. He had to think of her as his sole responsibility, and Keen's flag made it an important one. But it would go no further. Even if he tried, he knew he would never love this ship as he had loved *Anemone.*

He thought of Keen, and the sudden energy which had surprised all those accustomed to a more leisurely chain of command. Keen had been ashore often, not merely to meet the army commanders but also to be entertained by the senior government and commercial representatives of Halifax.

Adam had accompanied him on several occasions, as a duty more than out of curiosity. One of the most important people had been Keen's father's friend, a bluff, outspoken man who could have been any age between fifty and seventy, and who had achieved his present prominence by sweat rather than influence. He laughed a good deal, but Adam had noticed that his eyes always remained completely cold, like blue German steel. His name was Benjamin Massie, and Keen had told Adam that he was well known in London for his radical ideas on the expansion of trade in America, and, equally, for his impatience at anything that might prolong the hostilities.

He was not the only person here known to Keen. Another of his father's friends had arrived earlier, with an open-handed commission from the Admiralty to examine the possibilities of increased investment in ship-building, not only for the navy, but with the immediate future in mind and with an eye to improving trade with the southern ports. *The enemy* was a term that did not find favour with Massie and his associates.

So what would happen next? Keen had arranged local patrols in a huge box-shaped zone that stretched from Boston to the south-west, and Sable Island and the Grand Banks six hundred miles in the opposite direction. A large area, yes, but not so vast that each patrol might lose contact with the other if the enemy chose to break out of port, or that Halifax-bound convoys or individual ships could be ambushed before they reached safety. Like the *Royal Herald*. A deliberate, well-planned attack with the sole intention of killing his uncle. He was not certain if Keen accepted that explanation. He had remarked, 'We will assess each sighting or conflict at its face value. We must not be dragooned into scattering and so weakening our flotillas.'

A master's mate touched his hat to him, and Adam tried to fix his name in his mind. He smiled. Next time, perhaps.

He heard a light step on the quarterdeck, and wondered why he disliked the new flag lieutenant so much when they had barely spoken. Perhaps it was because the Honourable Lawford de Courcey seemed so much at home with the sort of people they had met ashore. He knew who was important and why, who could be trusted, and who might rouse disapproval as far away as London if he were crossed or overruled. He would be perfectly at home at Court, but in the teeth of an enemy broadside? That remained to be seen.

He steeled himself. It did not matter. They would put to sea in two days' time. It was probably what

106

they all needed. *What I need.*

The flag lieutenant crossed the deck and waited to be acknowledged.

'The admiral's compliments, sir, and would you have his barge lowered.'

Adam waited. When de Courcey said nothing more, he asked, 'Why?'

De Courcey smiled. 'Rear-Admiral Keen is going ashore. Mr Massie wishes to discuss some matters. There will be a social reception also, I believe.'

'I see. *I* wish to discuss an additional patrol with the admiral.' He was angry, more with himself for rising to de Courcey's bait. 'It is what we are here for, remember?'

'If I may suggest, sir....'

Adam looked past him at the town. 'You are the admiral's aide, Mr de Courcey. Not mine.'

'The admiral would like you to accompany him, sir.'

Adam saw the officer of the watch studying the land with his telescope, and doubtless listening to the terse exchange as well.

'Mr Finlay, pipe away the admiral's barge, if you please.' He heard the shrill calls, the immediate stampede of bare feet and the bark of orders: so much a part of him, and yet he felt entirely detached from it. It was not de Courcey's fault. Adam had been a flag lieutenant himself: it had never been an easy role, even when you served a man you loved.

He turned, with some vague intention of clearing the air between them, but the fair-haired lieutenant had vanished.

Later, when he made his way aft to report that the barge was alongside, Adam found Keen dressed and ready to leave the ship.

107

He studied Adam thoughtfully, and said, 'I have not forgotten about the extra patrol, you know. We should have more news when the schooner *Reynard* returns. She was sent up to the Bay of Fundy, although I think it an unlikely place for the enemy to loiter.'

'De Courcey told you, did he, sir?'

Keen smiled. 'His duty, Adam.' He became serious again. 'Be patient with him. He will prove his worth.' He paused. 'Given the chance.'

There were thumps from the adjoining cabin, and two seamen padded past carrying what was obviously an empty chest to be stowed away.

Keen said, 'I am settling in, you see. Not a ship of the line, but she will suffice for the present ... It was suggested that I should take quarters ashore, but I think not. Speed is everything.'

Adam waited. Who had suggested it? He saw his youthful servant John Whitmarsh helping a couple of the messmen to unpack another chest.

Why cannot I be like him? Lose myself in what I do best?

There was a small, velvet-covered book on the table. He felt a sudden chill, as though awakening from a cruel dream.

Keen saw his eyes, and said, 'Poetry. My late ... It was packed in error. My sister is unused to the requirements of war.'

My late ... Keen had been unable even to speak Zenoria's name. He had seen the book that day when he had visited her in Hampshire on some pretext. When she had rejected him.

Keen said, 'Are you interested?'

He was surprised at his own calmness, the complete emptiness he felt. Like watching some one

108

else in a mirror.

'It is my intention that young Whitmarsh should learn to read. It might help, sir.'

He picked up the book, hardly daring to look at it.

Keen shrugged. 'Well, then. Some use after all.' Then, 'You will accompany me, Adam?'

He could even smile. 'Yes, sir.' He felt the soft velvet in his fingers, like skin. Like her. 'I shall fetch my sword directly.'

In his cabin, he pressed his back to the door and very slowly raised the book to his lips, amazed that his hands were so steady.

How could it be? He closed his eyes as if in prayer, and opened them again, knowing that it was the same book.

He held it with great care, all the ship noises and movements suddenly stilled, as though he were in another world.

The rose petals, pressed tightly in these pages for so long, were almost transparent, like lace or some delicate web. The wild roses he had cut for her that day in June, when they had ridden together on his birthday. When she had kissed him.

He closed the book and held it to his face for several seconds. There was no escape after all. He put the book into his chest and locked it: it was an unbelievable relief to discover that he had never wanted to escape from her memory. He straightened his back, and reached for his sword. *From Zenoria.*

CHAPTER SIX

BAD BLOOD

Standing like a perfect model above her own reflection, His Britannic Majesty's Ship *Reaper* would have held the eye of any casual onlooker, no less than a professional seaman. A twenty-six gun frigate, very typical of the breed which had entered the revolutionary war with France some twenty years earlier, *Reaper* retained the sleek lines and grace of those ships which, then as now, were always in short supply. To command such a ship was every young officer's dream: to be free of the fleet's apron strings and the whim of every admiral, his real chance to prove his ability, if necessary against impossible odds.

By today's standards *Reaper* would appear small, not much bigger than a sloop of war, and certainly no match for the newer American frigates which had already proved their superiority in armament and endurance.

On this dazzling April day *Reaper* lay almost becalmed, her sails hanging with scarcely any movement, her masthead pendant lifeless. Ahead of her, on either bow, two of her longboats, their oars rising and falling like tired wings, attempted to hold her under command, to retain steerage way until the wind returned.

She was almost at the end of her passage, twelve hundred miles from Kingston, Jamaica, which had already taken her nearly two weeks. At dusk the previous day they had crossed the thirtieth parallel, and tomorrow at first light, if the wind found them again, they would sight the colourful humps of the Bermudas.

Theirs was escort duty, the curse of every fast-moving man-of-war, necessary but tedious, retrimming sails and trying to keep station on their ponderous charges: a test of any captain's forbearance. There was only one large merchantman to deliver to the Bermudas; the rest had been safely escorted to other ports in the Leeward Islands. The heavily-laden vessel, named *Killarney*, would eventually join a strongly defended convoy whose destination was England. Many a seaman had glanced at her motionless sails and felt envy and homesickness like a fever, merely by thinking about it.

Reaper's only consort was a small, sturdy brig, *Alfriston*. Like so many of her hard-worked class, she had started life in the merchant service, until the demands of war had changed her role and her purpose. With the aid of a telescope she could just be seen, well astern of the merchantman, completely becalmed and stern-on, like a helpless moth landed on the water.

But once rid of their slow-moving charge *Reaper* would be free, so why was she different from other frigates which had risen above all the setbacks and disasters of war to become legends?

Perhaps it was her silence. Despite the fact that she carried some one hundred and fifty officers, seamen and marines within her graceful hull, she seemed without life. Only the flap of empty canvas against her spars and shrouds, and the occasional creak of the rudder broke the unnatural stillness. Her decks were clean and, like her hull, freshly painted and well-maintained. Like the other ships which had fought on that September day in 1812, there was barely a mark to reveal the damage she had suffered. Her real damage went far deeper, like guilt. Like shame.

Aft by the quarterdeck rail *Reaper's* captain stood with his arms folded, a stance he often took when he was thinking deeply. He was twenty-seven years old and already a post-captain, with a fair skin which seemed to defy the heat of the Caribbean or the sudden fury of the Atlantic. A serious face: he could have been described as handsome but for the thinness of his mouth. He was a man whom many would call fortunate, and well placed for the next phase of advancement. This had been *Reaper's* first operational cruise after completing her repairs in Halifax, and it was his first time in command of her. A necessary step, but he knew full well why he had been appointed. *Reaper's* previous captain, who had been old for his rank, a man of great experience who had left the more ordered world of the Honourable East India Company to return to service in the fleet, had fallen victim to the ruthlessness of war. *Reaper* had been raked at long range by the American's massive guns, in what was believed to have been a single broadside, although few who were there could clearly remember what had happened. *Reaper* had been almost totally dismasted, her decks buried under fallen spars and rigging, her company torn apart. Most of her officers, including her gallant captain, had died instantly; where there had been order, there had been only chaos and terror. Amongst the upended guns and splintered decks somebody, whose identity was still unclear, had hauled down the colours. Nearby, the battle had

112

continued until the American frigate *Baltimore* had drifted out of command, with many of her people either killed or wounded. Commodore Beer's flagship *Unity* had been boarded and taken by Bolitho's seamen and marines. A very close thing, but in a sea fight there is only one victor.

Reaper could probably have done nothing more; she had already been passed by and left a drifting wreck. But to those who had fought and survived that day, she was remembered only as the ship which had surrendered while the fight had still raged around her. Their lordships knew the value of even a small frigate at this decisive stage of the war, and a ship was only as strong as the man who commanded her. Haste, expediency, the need to forget, each had played a part, but even on this bright spring morning, with the sun burning down between the loosely flapping sails, the feeling was still here. Less than half of *Reaper's* people were from her original company. Many had died in the battle; others had been too badly wounded to be of any further use. Even so, to the rest of the tightly-knit squadron, *Reaper* was like an outcast, and her shame was borne by all of them.

The captain came out of his thoughts and saw the first lieutenant making his way aft, pausing here and there to speak with the working parties. They had grown up in the same town, and had entered the navy as midshipmen at almost the same time. The first lieutenant was an experienced and intelligent officer, despite his youth. If he had one failing, it was his readiness to talk with the hands, even the new, untrained landmen, as if they were on equal terms, or as equal as any one could be in a King's ship. That would have to change. *Reaper* needed to be brought to her proper state of readiness and respect, no

113

matter what it cost. His mouth twitched. There was another link. He had asked for, and obtained, the hand of the first lieutenant's sister in marriage. His next command would be decided ... He broke off as the cry came from aloft. 'Signal from *Alfriston*, sir!'

The captain snapped to one of the attentive midshipmen, 'Take a glass up yourself and see what that fool is babbling about!'

The first lieutenant had joined him. 'The lookout has no skill with flags, I'm afraid, sir.'

'He'd better mend his ways, damn him, or I'll see his backbone at the gratings! It's probably nothing, anyway.'

Somebody called a command and a few seamen ran smartly to the boat tier to execute it. The first lieutenant had grown accustomed to it. The silence, the instant obedience, everything carried out at the double. Try as he might, he could not accept it.

The captain said, 'As soon as we receive orders and rid ourselves of *Killarney*, I shall want sail and gun drill every day, until we can cut the time it takes them to do every little thing. I'll not stand for slackness. Not from any man!'

The first lieutenant watched his profile, but said nothing. Did it so change an officer who had already held a successful command? *Might it change me?*

This afternoon there would be the ritual of punishment. Two more floggings at the gangway, both severe, but one of which could have been avoided or reduced to some lesser penalty. The staccato roll of drums, the crack of the lash on a man's naked back. Again and again, until it looked as if his body had been torn open by some crazed beast....

When he had voiced his opinion about extreme

punishment, often at the instigation of some junior officer or midshipman, the captain had turned on him. 'Popularity is a myth, a deceit! Obedience and discipline are all that count, to me and to my ship!'

Perhaps when they returned to Halifax, things might improve.

Almost without thinking, he said, 'It seems likely that Sir Richard Bolitho will have hoisted his flag in Halifax again, sir.'

'Perhaps.' The captain seemed to consider it, sift it for some hidden meaning. 'A flag-officer of reputation. But it has to be said that any admiral is only as strong as his captains—and how they perform.'

The first lieutenant had never served with or under Sir Richard Bolitho, and yet, like the many he had spoken to, he felt as if he knew him personally.

The captain was smiling. 'We shall see, sir. We shall see.'

The midshipman's voice came shrilly from the masthead. 'Signal from *Alfriston*, sir! *Sail in sight to the nor' west*!' A small pause, as if the midshipman was frightened of the noise. 'Brigantine, sir.'

The captain rubbed his hands briskly, one of his rare displays of emotion. 'Not one of ours, unless the dispatches are wrong.'

He swung round as the halliards and canvas came alive, the masthead pendant lifting as if suddenly awakened.

The first lieutenant exclaimed, 'The master was right, sir! The wind is coming back!'

The captain nodded. 'Recall the boats and have them hoisted. We are well upwind of friends and stranger alike. We'll add another prize to our list, eh?' He shaded his eyes to watch the two boats casting off

115

the tow lines and pulling back toward their ship. 'Something for your sister's dowry!'

The first lieutenant was surprised at the swift change of mood. It would certainly break the monotony of this snail's pace.

He looked away as the captain added thoughtfully, 'Bring forward the punishment by an hour. It will keep them occupied, and remind them of their duty.'

Calls trilled and men ran to hoist the two dripping boats up and over the gangway while others dashed up the ratlines in readiness to make more sail, even as the slack canvas flapped and then boomed out harder to the wind. The lieutenant watched the sea's face, the black shadows of *Reaper's* masts and sails blurring like ruffled fur while the hull heeled slightly, and then more firmly to the demands of wind and rudder.

The moment every frigate officer waits for. But the elation would not come.

*   *   *

Captain James Tyacke tucked his hat beneath his arm and waited for the marine sentry to admit him. For an instant, he saw a shadow through the screen door, and was amused. The ever-vigilant Ozzard, keeping a watchful eye out for visitors to these quarters.

He found Bolitho seated at the table, some charts with written notes on them held down by two books bound in green leather, with heavily gilded spines. Tyacke recognized them as some of the collection Lady Catherine Somervell had sent aboard for the admiral. Even here, thousands of miles from England, she was never far away from this restless, sensitive man.

116

'Ah, James!' He looked up and smiled warmly. 'I was hoping that you would sup with me tonight, and leave your troubles to your lieutenants for a change.'

Tyacke looked past him at the unbroken panorama of the ocean, blue and grey, disturbed here and there by long, glassy swells. In his mind's eye he saw them all, *Indomitable* in the centre, with the two frigates *Virtue* and *Attacker* some eight miles off either beam. At dusk they would draw closer to one another, but in this formation they could scan an imposing range from horizon to horizon. Tyacke could also visualize each captain, just as he knew Bolitho would feel the strength of every ship under his flag. Keeping well up to windward like a loyal terrier, the brig *Marvel* completed this small but effective flotilla.

Bolitho said, 'I can see from your expression, James, that you had forgotten the significance of this day.'

'For the moment, Sir Richard.' There was a brief silence. 'Two years ago, I took command of this ship.' He added quietly, as if it were something private, 'The Old Indom.'

Bolitho waited for him to seat himself. It was like a signal: Ozzard was moving out of his pantry. The flag captain would be staying a while.

Tyacke said, 'We've done a lot in that time.'

Bolitho looked at the leather-bound books, remembering her at Plymouth, in the coach when they had parted. 'I sometimes wonder where it will end. Or even if we are achieving anything by waiting, always waiting, for the enemy to show his teeth.'

'It will come. I feel it. When I was in *Larne*,' for a moment he hesitated as if it was still too painful a memory to discuss, 'the slavers had the whole ocean

117

to pick and choose from. Every cargo of poor devils waiting to be shipped to the Indies and the Americas could be collected ... or dropped overboard, if they were sighted by us or another patrol. But every so often ...' He leaned forward in his chair, his scarred face suddenly clear and terrible in the reflected sunlight, 'I *knew*, like you knew about *Unity*. That sixth sense, instinct, call it what you will.'

Bolitho could feel the strength of the man, his deep pride in what he could do. Not something to be taken for granted, not a form of conceit, but true and real, like the old sword on its rack. As he had known in September, when they had walked the deck together, splinters bursting from the planking as sharp-shooters tried to mark them down, two men pacing up and down, making no attempt to conceal their ranks or their importance to those who depended upon them.

Avery, too, had walked with them that day. If he had any friend in this ship other than Bolitho himself, that friend was Tyacke. He wondered if he had confided his present preoccupation to him, and then knew he had not. Two men so different, and yet not dissimilar, each deeply reserved, driven in on himself. No, Avery would not have discussed it with Tyacke, particularly if it concerned a woman.

Unconsciously he had touched the volume of Shakespearean sonnets; she had chosen this edition with care because the print was clear, easy to read. *So far away.* Spring in the West Country. Wagtails on the beach where they had walked; swifts and jackdaws; the return of beauty and vitality to the countryside.

Tyacke watched him, not without affection. Maybe it was better to be alone, with no one to draw

118

your heart, or break it. To know no pain. Then he recalled Bolitho's woman boarding this ship, climbing the side like a sailor to the cheers of the men. It was not true. Just to have somebody, to know that she was there ... He pushed the thoughts aside: for him, they were impossible.

'I'd best go up and see the afternoon gun drill, sir.' He stood, his head brushing the deck beams. He did not appear to notice, and Bolitho knew that after *Larne, Indomitable* must seem like a palace.

He said, 'Until tonight, then.'

But Tyacke was staring at the screen door, one hand raised as if he was listening to something. They both heard measured steps, then the tap of the sentry's musket as he called, 'First lieutenant, *sir*!'

Lieutenant John Daubeny stepped into the cabin, his cheeks flushed from the salt air.

Tyacke said, 'I heard a call from the masthead. What is it?'

Bolitho felt the sudden tension. He had not heard the call himself. Tyacke had become part of the ship: he *was* the ship. In spite of his personal misgivings when he had been asked to command the flagship, they had become one.

Daubeny squinted his eyes, a habit of his when he was asked a direct or difficult question.

'Signal from *Attacker*, sir. Sail sighted to the nor' west. A brig, one of ours.' He faltered under Tyacke's intense gaze. 'They are certain of it.'

Tyacke said curtly, 'Keep me informed. Muster a good signals party, and tell Mr Carleton to be ready.'

'I have attended to it, sir.'

The door closed, and Bolitho said, 'You have them well drilled, James. This newcomer—what d'you make of her?'

119

'We're not expecting a courier, sir. Not here. Not yet.' He was pondering aloud. 'At the Bermudas, now, that would be different. A convoy is assembling there, or should be.'

Bolitho shared it, remembering how it felt. Wanting to be up there on deck, and yet aware that it might be regarded as a lack of confidence in his officers, or that they might take his presence for anxiety. He vividly recalled his own time in command, and today was no different. When the watches changed, or the hands were piped to shorten sail, his whole being protested that he should remain aloof, a man apart from the ship that served him.

The sentry called, 'First lieutenant, *sir!*'

Daubeny came back in, more flushed than ever. 'She's the *Alfriston*, sir, fourteen guns. Commander Borradaile...'

Bolitho said quickly, 'I don't know him, do I?'

Tyacke shook his head. '*Alfriston* joined the squadron while you were in England, sir.' Then, as an afterthought, 'Borradaile's a good hand. Came up the hard way.'

Bolitho was on his feet. 'Signal *Attacker*, repeat *Alfriston, close on Flag*.' He glanced out through the thick glass. 'I want him here before nightfall. I can't waste another day.'

Daubeny's face was quite untroubled now that he had shifted the responsibility to his superiors. He offered, 'She should be with the Leeward escort, sir.' His confidence wilted under their combined attention. He added, almost humbly, 'It was in orders, sir.'

Tyacke said, 'So it was, Mr Daubeny. Now tell Mr Carleton to make the signal.'

Ozzard closed the door. 'Concerning supper,

120

Sir Richard—'

'It might be delayed.' He looked at Tyacke. 'But we will take a glass now, I think.'

Tyacke sat again, his head still cocked to catch the muffled sounds from the world outside. The squeak of halliards, the voice of the signals midshipman penetratingly clear as he spelled out the signal to his men.

He said, 'You think it's bad, sir.' It was not a question.

Bolitho watched Ozzard approaching with his tray, his small figure angled against the movement of the deck without effort. The man without a past, or one so terrible that it clung to him like a graveyard spirit. So much a part of the little crew.

'I believe it may be our next move, James, albeit a foul one.'

They drank in silence.

Jacob Borradaile, the *Alfriston's* commander, was not in the least what Bolitho had been expecting. He had been on deck to observe the brig's smart performance as she had tacked this way and that, her bulging sails salmon-pink in the failing light as she had wasted no time in taking position under *Indomitable's* lee and sending a boat over the heavy swell.

Tyacke had remarked of Borradaile, *a good hand. Came up the hard way.* From him, there could be no higher praise.

As Tyacke escorted him aft into the cabin, Bolitho thought he had never seen such an untidy, awkward-looking figure. Although he must have been about the same age as Avery or Tyacke, he was like some gaunt caricature, with sprouting, badly-cut hair and deep, hollow eyes; only the ill-fitting uniform

121

revealed him to be a King's officer. However, Bolitho, who had met every imaginable kind of man both junior and senior, was immediately impressed. He entered the cabin and took his outstretched hand without hesitation or any trace of awe. A firm grip, hard, like a true sailor's.

Bolitho said, 'You have urgent news.' He saw the man's quick assessment of him, as he might examine a new recruit. 'But first, will you take a glass with me?'

Borradaile sat in the chair Ozzard had carefully prepared in advance. 'Thank 'ee, Sir Richard. Whatever you're taking yourself will suit famously.'

Bolitho nodded to Ozzard. Borradaile had a faint Kentish accent, like his old friend Thomas Herrick.

He sat on the stern bench and studied his visitor. In his fist, the fine goblet looked like a thimble.

He said, 'In your own words. I will see that you are returned to your ship before too long.'

Borradaile stared at a sealed gunport as if he expected to see the brig across the uneasy strip of water. *Alfriston* had been handled well, as if one man and not an entire trained company had been in charge. Tyacke would be thinking much the same, remembering his previous command.

Borradaile said, 'It was *Reaper*, Sir Richard. A day out from Bermuda and she broke away to chase a stranger, a small vessel—brigantine, most likely. *Alfriston* was becalmed, sea like a mill pond, an' our one remaining charge, a company ship called *Killarney*, was no better than we. But *Reaper* had the wind under her skirts and gave chase.'

Bolitho asked quietly, 'Did that surprise you, so close to your destination?'

'I don't think so.'

Bolitho said, 'Man to man. This is important. To me, maybe to all of us.'

The hollow eyes settled on him. Bolitho could almost hear his mind working, weighing the rights and wrongs of something that might end in a court-martial. Then he seemed almost visibly to make a decision.

'*Reaper*'s captain was new to the ship, his first proper patrol away from the squadron.'

'Did you know him?' Unfair maybe, but also perhaps vital.

'Of him, sir.' He paused. '*Reaper* had a reputation. Maybe he was eager to give her back something he thought she'd lost.'

The shipboard noises seemed to fade away as Borradaile related the hours that had decided *Reaper*'s fate.

'There were two frigates, sir. French-built, if I'm any judge, but wearing Yankee colours. They must have sent the brigantine as bait, an' once *Reaper* changed tack to go after it, they showed themselves.' He ticked off the points on his bony fingers. '*Reaper* had run too far down to lee'ard to be able to claw back to her station. They must have been laughin', it was so damned easy for them.'

Bolitho glanced at Tyacke; he was resting his chin on his hand, and his face was like stone.

Borradaile added, 'I could do nothin', sir. We'd barely picked up the wind again. All I could do was watch.'

Bolitho waited, afraid of breaking the picture in the man's thoughts. It was not uncommon. A young captain eager for a prize, no matter how small, and eager too to prove something to his ship's company. He knew of *Reaper*'s bitterness after the battle, when

123

her brave captain, James Hamilton, had been killed in the first broadside. It was so easy to be distracted for the few seconds needed by a skilful and dangerous enemy. *It nearly happened to me when I was so young....*

Borradaile gave a great sigh. '*Reaper* came about as soon as her captain knew what had happened. I watched it all with a big signals glass—I felt I had to. It was madness, I thought. *Reaper* stood no chance, a little sixth-rate against two big 'uns, forty guns apiece was my guess. But what could he do? What would any of us do, I asked myself.'

'Did they engage immediately?'

Borradaile shook his head, his gaunt features suddenly saddened. 'There were no shots fired. Not one. *Reaper* had run out some of her guns by then, but not all of 'em. It was then that the leading Yankee hoisted a white flag for parley and dropped a boat to go across to *Reaper*.'

Bolitho saw it all. Three ships, the others merely spectators.

'An hour, maybe more, maybe less, an' the *Reaper* lowered her flag.' He spat it out angrily. 'Without so much as a whimper!'

'Surrendered?' Tyacke leaned forward into the light. 'Not even a fight?'

Alfriston's commander seemed to truly see him for the first time, and there was compassion in the hollow eyes as they noted the full extent of his injury. 'It was mutiny,' he said.

The word hung in the damp air like something obscene, devastating.

'The next thing I knew was, a boat was sent from *Reaper* with some of the "loyal men".' He turned to Bolitho again. 'And her captain.'

Bolitho waited. It was bad, worse than he had believed possible.

Borradaile spoke very slowly. 'Just before *Reaper* left her station to give chase there were men being flogged at the gangway. I could hardly believe it.' There was disgust and revulsion in his voice, from this, a man who had come up the hardest way of all, through the ranks, to achieve his own command. A man who must have seen every kind of suffering at sea, and brutality, too, in that demanding life below decks.

'Was he dead?'

'Not then, he weren't, sir. The Yankee officers who had gone over to parley had invited *Reaper*'s people to join them. I heard from some of the men who were allowed away in the boat that it was the old cry of "dollars for shillings"—the chance of a new life, better paid and well treated under the Stars and Stripes.'

Bolitho thought of Adam's *Anemone*. Some of her people had changed sides when the flag had come down. But this was different. It was not desertion, which was bad enough: it was mutiny.

'When they agreed, the Yankee told them they could punish their captain in the way they had suffered under his command. That's what they were doing all that time. First a few of the hard men, an' then it was like a madness. They seized him up and flogged him until he was in ribbons. Two hundred, three, who could say? *Alfriston* don't rate a surgeon, but we did what we could for him, an' his senior lieutenant who was stabbed when he tried to defend him. He'll probably live, the poor devil. I'd not be in his shoes for a sack of gold!'

'And then?'

'They boarded the *Killarney* an' stood away. I waited a while and then relaid my course for the Bermudas. I landed the survivors at Hamilton and made my report to the guardship. I was ordered to find an' report to you, sir.' He glanced around the spacious cabin as if he had not noticed it before. 'They could have taken *Alfriston*, too, if they'd a mind.'

Bolitho stood up and walked to the quarter gallery. He could just see the little brig's dark silhouette, her topgallant yards still faintly pink in the dying light.

'No, Commander Borradaile. You had to be the witness, the proof that a mutiny broke out. Perhaps it was provoked, but it can never be condoned. We who command must always be aware of the dangers. And you are here. That is the other reason.'

Borradaile said. 'To bring word to you, sir? That was my thought, also.'

Bolitho asked, 'And the captain?'

'He died, sir, finally. Cursin' and ravin' to the end. His last words, were, *they'll hang for it!*'

'And so they will, if they are taken.' He crossed to the untidy figure and took his hand. 'You have done well. I shall see that it is mentioned in my dispatches.' He glanced at Tyacke. 'I'd offer you promotion, but I think you'd damn me for it first! Keep your *Alfriston*.' In his heart, he knew that Borradaile was glad to be rid of the men sent from the surrendered frigate. The shame was still there, deeper now than ever. Like a rotten apple in a barrel, it was better to be free of them.

'See Commander Borradaile over the side, James.' He watched them leave, then returned to the quarter gallery and thrust open a window. The air was surprisingly cold, and helped to steady him.

Avery, who had been present and mute throughout the discussion, observed quietly. 'A well-planned trap, a flag of truce, and mutiny provoked, if provocation were needed. And now, one of our ships under their flag.'

Bolitho faced him, his cheek wet with spray, like tears, cold tears.

'Speak out, man. Say what I know you are thinking!'

Avery lifted his shoulders in a very slight shrug. 'Justice, revenge, call it what we will, but I think I understand now what you said about the face in the crowd. To lure you into a trap, to provoke you into some reckless retaliation. It *is* you he wants.'

Bolitho listened to the trill of calls, as one captain paid his respects to another.

Avery, like Tyacke, probably shared the private conviction of the gaunt commander who had just departed: that *Reaper*'s captain had paid the just price of tyranny. He was not the first. Pray God he was the last.

He thought of the flag curling far above the deck and seemed to hear her voice. *My admiral of England.*

There was no doubt in his mind where the real responsibility would lie. Or the blame.

CHAPTER SEVEN

THE OLDEST TRICK

Adam Bolitho hesitated outside the broad, imposing house and wondered impatiently why he had come.

127

Another reception. Merchants, senior officers from the garrison, people who always seemed to know some one important and with influence. He could have made some excuse to stay aboard *Valkyrie*, but at the same time he knew he was too restless to remain in his cabin or pass an hour or so away with his lieutenants.

How Keen managed to appear unruffled by all these receptions and discussions surprised him. Adam had noticed that despite his good-natured manner and his apparent ease with this imposing people, he rarely lost his way, or allowed himself to be talked out of decisions he considered were in the best interests of his command.

Adam turned his back on the house and stared out across the great natural harbour; *chebucto*, the Indians had once called it. It impressed him as few others had done. From the glittering span of the Bedford Basin to the narrows at the far end, the harbour was teeming with ships, a forest of masts as visible proof of Halifax's growing strategic value. He had heard a general describe it as part of the British defensive square, which included England, Gibraltar and Bermuda. Cornwallis must have been as farseeing as he was shrewd when he had put his roots down here less than seventy years ago and built the first fortifications. Now, commanded by the hilltop citadel, it was further protected by Martello towers more commonly seen in Britanny or southern England, with smaller batteries to deter any enemy foolish enough to attempt a landing.

He looked towards the naval anchorage, but the house hid it from view. He had never believed that his duties as flag captain could be so frustrating. *Valkyrie* had barely ventured out of harbour, and

128

then only to meet an incoming convoy with more soldiers: if they landed many more this peninsula must surely sink under the weight. There was little news of the war. Roads on the mainland were bad, some still impassable. He glanced at the fading light across the harbour, the tiny boat lanterns moving like insects. Here, conditions were already much better. He had even felt the sun's warmth on his face on his walk from the landing stage.

He turned reluctantly away from the sea. The big double doors had opened discreetly, as if they had been waiting for his decision.

A fine old house: not 'old' by English standards, but well proportioned and vaguely foreign, the architecture perhaps influenced by the French. He handed his hat to a bobbing servant and walked towards the main reception hall. There were uniforms aplenty, mostly red, with a few green coats of the local light infantry force. The house had probably been built by some prosperous merchant, but now it was used almost exclusively by people of a world he did not know, or want to. Where men like Benjamin Massie walked a challenging path between politics and the rewards of trade. He had made no secret of his impatience with the state of war between Britain and America, calling it 'unpopular', more as if it were a personal inconvenience than a bitter conflict between nations.

Adam spoke to a footman, his eyes taking in the assembled throng, and noticing Keen's fair hair at the far end. He was with Massie. There were women present, too. That had been rare on previous occasions. Yes, he should have offered some excuse and remained on board.

'Captain Adam Bolitho!'

There was a momentary hush, more out of surprise at his lateness than from interest, he thought. At least the footman had pronounced his name correctly.

He walked down the side of the hall. There were heavy velvet curtains, and two great log fires: these houses were built with a Nova Scotia winter in mind.

'So here you are at last, Captain!' Benjamin Massie snapped his thick fingers and a tray of red wine appeared like magic. 'Thought you'd forgotten us!' He gave his loud, barking laugh, and once again Adam noticed the coldness of his eyes.

He said, 'The squadron's business, sir.'

Massie chuckled. 'That's the trouble with this place, more soldiers than labourers, more men-o'-war than cargoes! I'm told that a few years back there was five times as many brothels as banks!' He became serious instantly, as though a mask had fallen over his face. 'But it's changing. Just get this war over and we'll see some real expansion, whole new markets. And for that we'll need *ships*, and men willing to serve in them without the fear of violent death under an enemy broadside.' He winked. 'Or under the lash of some over-zealous officer, eh?'

Keen had approached them, and was listening. 'And what of my father's other friend? I thought he might meet me here.'

Adam looked at him. Keen had deliberately interrupted, to dampen down any open disagreement before it began. *Am I so obvious*?

'Oh, David St Clair?' He shook his head. 'He'll not be back for some while yet. Impetuous, that's David. You know what he's like.'

Keen shrugged. 'I have seen little of him. I liked what I knew. Shipbuilding, with backing from the Admiralty—it sounded important.'

130

'Well, since his wife died...' He touched Keen's sleeve. 'I forgot, Val. I'm sorry....'

Keen said, 'I had heard. So he is travelling alone?'

Massie grinned, his clumsy remark dismissed from his mind. 'No. He's got his daughter with him, can you imagine that? I'll lay odds he's regretting having to mark time for a woman, even if she is family!'

Adam raised his glass, but paused as he saw Keen's expression. Surprise? It was deeper than that.

'I thought she was married.'

Massie took another glass from the tray. 'Nothing came of it. The intended husband was a soldier.'

Keen nodded. 'Yes. So I heard.'

'Well, he decided to follow the drum rather than a pretty ankle!' He gave a heavy sigh. 'Then, with her mother dying so suddenly, she decided to keep David company.'

Keen looked into the nearest fire. 'That's a risk, in my view.'

Massie brushed some droplets of wine from his coat. 'There, you see? You naval and military people regard everything as a hidden danger, part of some sinister strategy!' He glanced at the clock. 'Time to eat soon. Better go and pump the bilges before I give the word.' He walked away, nodding to an occasional guest, deliberately ignoring others.

Keen said, 'You don't care much for him, do you?'

Adam watched a tall woman with bare shoulders bending to listen to her smaller companion, then she laughed and nudged him. She could not have been more blatant if she had been stark naked.

He answered, 'Or those like him, sir.' He saw a footman drawing the vast curtains, hiding the dark water of the harbour from sight. 'Men are dying every hour of the day. It has to be for something more

131

than profit, surely?' He broke off.

'Continue, Adam. Remember your uncle, and what he would say. There are no officers here. Just men.'

Adam put down his glass and said, 'Supplies, and escorts for the ships that carry them, keeping the sea-lanes open—all essential, but they will *never win a war*. We need to get to grips with them as we do with the French, and all the others we have had to fight, not just stand gloating over the prospects of trade and expansion when the bloody work is comfortably past!'

Keen said quietly, 'I wonder if you know how much like Sir Richard you are. If only ...' He looked away. 'Damnation!'

But it was not Massie: it was the flag lieutenant, de Courcey.

Adam wondered what Keen had been about to say, and why the lieutenant's arrival had disturbed his customary composure.

De Courcey exclaimed, 'I do apologize, sir, but someone came here, to this house, without any prior arrangement or excuse, and demanded to see you.' He sounded outraged. 'I sent him away with a flea in his ear, you may be sure!' His eyes moved to the footman who had taken his place on the stairs, a staff raised, ready to announce dinner. 'Most inconsiderate!'

Massie was thrusting through the throng like a plough. Keen said, 'Will you deal with it, Adam? I am the principal guest tonight, as you know.'

Adam nodded. He had not known. As he walked with de Courcey to the adjoining room, he asked sharply, 'Who is this intruder?'

'A damned ragged fellow, a scarecrow in the

132

King's coat!'

'His *name*, man.' He controlled his anger with difficulty: everything seemed able to penetrate his defences. He had seen his lieutenants watching him, obviously wondering what was troubling him.

De Courcey said offhandedly, 'Borradaile, sir. Most uncouth. I cannot imagine how he ever....'

He winced as Adam seized his arm. '*Alfriston*'s commander?' He tightened his grip so that de Courcey gasped aloud, and two passing soldiers paused with interest. 'Answer me, damn you!'

De Courcey recovered himself slightly. 'Well, yes, as a matter of fact. I thought that under the circumstances....'

Adam released him and said, 'You are a fool.' He was amazed at how calm he sounded. 'How big a fool, we shall yet discover.'

De Courcey blinked as the footman's staff tapped the stairs three times.

Adam said, 'Wait here. I may want to send word to the ship.'

From another world came the cry, 'Pray be seated, ladies and gentlemen!'

'But, sir! We are expected!'

Adam said sharply, 'Are you deaf as well?' He turned, and walked toward the main entrance.

Meanwhile, Massie and his guests were arranging themselves around the two long tables, each place setting marked with a card, each place denoting the status of each guest or the magnitude of the favour being done.

Massie said significantly, 'I've delayed grace until your young captain can spare himself from his duties.'

Keen sat on Massie's right hand. Facing him was a

woman whom he guessed was Massie's special guest. She was beautiful, self-assured, and amused by his scrutiny.

Massie said abruptly, 'Mrs Lovelace. She has a house near Bedford Basin.'

She said, 'I regret that we were not introduced earlier, Admiral Keen.' She smiled. 'It is a bad sign when even our admirals are so young!'

Adam strode between the tables and paused behind Keen's chair. An utter silence had fallen in the room.

Keen felt Adam's breath against his cheek, quick, angry. '*Alfriston*'s brought word from Sir Richard. *Reaper*'s been taken, surrendered.' All the while he was watching Keen's fine profile. 'The admiral intends to remain with the Bermuda squadron until the convoy is safely at sea.'

Keen dabbed his mouth with a napkin. 'Surrendered?' One word.

Adam nodded, seeing the woman sitting opposite for the first time. She smiled at him, and indicated the empty chair beside her.

He said, 'It was mutiny, sir.'

'I see.' Then he looked directly at Adam, his eyes very calm, and, Adam thought afterwards, very well concealing his emotions. 'I trust you have informed the ship?'

He thought of the enraged de Courcey. 'Yes, sir. They will be ready.'

Keen dropped the napkin on to his lap. 'Then *Reaper* is heading this way.' He saw the doubt in Adam's eyes. 'Trick for trick, see?' He stood up, and every face turned towards him. 'I am sorry for the interruption, ladies and gentlemen. I am certain that our host will understand.' He waited for Adam to

134

walk around the table, where a footman had drawn out the empty chair. The sound of his shoes was very loud on the polished floor, reminding him unpleasantly of that snowy day in Portsmouth, at his court-martial.

Massie cleared his throat noisily. 'We'll have grace now, Reverend!'

Adam felt the woman's slippered foot touching his, even as the prayer was being intoned. He was surprised that he could even smile about it.

Trick for trick. Keen was speaking calmly with Massie. *We Happy few*. It was as if somebody had spoken aloud. He thought of his uncle: the mark he had left on all of them.

His companion said softly, 'You say little, Captain. Should I feel insulted?'

He turned slightly to look at her. Fine, brown eyes, a mouth that was used to smiling. He glanced at her hand, which lay so near to his own at this crowded table. Married, but not to anybody here. Mistress, then?

He said, 'My apologies, ma'am. I am unused to such brilliance, even from the sea.' *Trick for trick*.

A footman loomed over them and her slipper moved away.

But she looked at him again, and said, 'We shall have to see about that, *Captain.*'

Adam glanced at their host. A slip of the tongue; was Keen remembering it even now, when outwardly he was so composed, so in control? Massie had spoken as if he had known of the mutiny. It was not a word to be used lightly. A rumour, a piece of gossip: Massie would have fingers in a lot of pies. It would mean only one thing. *Reaper* was already here.

'Are you married, Captain?'

135

'No.' It came out too abruptly, and he tried to soften it. 'It has not been my good fortune.'

She studied him thoughtfully, with delicately raised brows. 'I am surprised.'

'And you, ma'am?'

She laughed, and Adam saw Massie glance up at her. At them. She replied, 'Like a cloak, Captain. I wear it when it suits!'

Trick for trick.

*   *   *

The *Valkyrie*'s chart room was small and functional, the table barely leaving space for more than three men. Adam leaned over the chart, the brass dividers moving unhurriedly across the bearings, soundings and scribbled calculations which, to a landsman, would be meaningless.

The door was wedged open, and he could see the bright sunlight moving like a beacon, back and forth, to the frigate's easy rise and fall. They had left Halifax in company with a smaller frigate, *Taciturn*, and the brig *Doon*. They had left with mixed feelings, the prospect of hunting down *Reaper*, the only possible way of settling the score, set against the very real likelihood of directing fire on one of their own. The Americans would have had no time to replace the surrendered frigate's company, so many of them, except for the officers and professional warrant ranks, would be mutineers.

But that had been five days ago, and he had sensed Keen's uncertainty, his growing anxiety about the next decision.

One point of the dividers rested on Cape North, the tip of Nova Scotia that guarded the southernmost side of the entrance to the Gulf of St Lawrence. Across the strait lay Newfoundland, some fifty miles distant. A narrow passage, but easy enough for a determined captain who wanted to avoid capture and slip through the net. Keen would be thinking the same thing. Adam leaned closer to the chart. Two tiny islands, St Pierre and Miquelon, to the south of Newfoundland's rugged coastline, were in fact French, but at the outbreak of war had been occupied by troops from the British garrison at St John's. Keen had made no secret of his conviction that *Reaper* would be heading for these same islands. *Reaper*'s capture by the Americans would still be unknown to any of the local patrols; it would have been an obvious strategy if the enemy had intended to attack the garrison, or prey on shipping in these waters. But the brig *Doon* had investigated the area and had rejoined her two consorts with nothing to report. Beyond lay the Gulf of St Lawrence, the vital gateway to its great river, to Montreal and the lakes, to the naval base at Kingston and further still to York, the administrative, if small, capital of Upper Canada.

But the Gulf was vast, with islets and bays where any ship could shelter, and bide her time until the hunt had passed her by.

He heard shouted commands and the trill of calls. The afternoon watch was mustering aft, the air heavy with greasy smells from the galley funnel. A good measure of rum to wash it down.

He glanced at the sailing-master's log book. May third, 1813. He thought of the small velvet-covered volume in his chest, the carefully pressed fragments of the wild roses. May in England. It was like remembering a foreign country.

A shadow fell across the table: Urquhart, the first lieutenant. Adam had found him a good and competent officer, firm and fair with the hands, even with the hard men, who tested every officer for any sign of weakness. It was never easy to be both as a first lieutenant. When *Valkyrie*'s captain, Trevenen, had broken down with terror at the height of action, it had been Urquhart who had taken over and restored discipline and order. Neither Trevenen, who had vanished mysteriously on his way to face a court-martial, nor his successor, the acting-commodore Peter Dawes, had recommended Urquhart for advancement. Urquhart had never mentioned it, nor had he shown any resentment, but Adam guessed it was only because he did not yet know his new captain well enough. Adam blamed himself for that. He was unable to encourage intimacy in *Valkyrie*: even when he passed a command, he still found himself half-expecting to see other faces respond. Dead faces.

Urquhart waited patiently for his attention, and then said, 'I would like to exercise the eighteen-pounders during the afternoon watch, sir.'

Adam tossed down the dividers. 'It is about all we will be doing, it seems!'

He thought of that last night in Halifax, the lavish dinner, with their host, Massie, becoming more slurred by the minute. He thought, also, of the enticing and sensual Mrs Lovelace, laughing at Massie's crude remarks, but keeping her foot against Adam's under the table.

I should not have agreed to this post. Had he accepted it to avoid being marooned in *Zest*?

In his own heart, he knew he had acted out of a sense of obligation, perhaps some need to make reparation. Guilt....

138

Urquhart looked at the chart: he had a strong, thoughtful profile. Adam could well imagine him with a command of his own.

Urquhart said, 'It's like picking at threads, sir. She could be anywhere.'

'I know that, damn it!' He touched the lieutenant's sleeve. 'I am sorry, John. That was uncalled for.'

Urquhart eyed him warily. It was the first time the captain had called him by his first name. It had been like seeing a different person suddenly, not so much the severe stranger.

He said, 'If we run deeper into the Gulf we shall be hard put to keep together. If we had more ships, then. . . .'

A master's mate whispered around the door, 'Admiral's coming up, sir.'

Adam knew that he was speaking to Urquhart, careful to avoid his captain's eye.

He straightened his back. 'Yes. Well, we shall see.'

Keen was standing by the weather nettings when they came out of the chart room, and Adam noticed immediately that he looked strained, troubled.

Keen said, 'What time will we alter course, Captain Bolitho?'

Adam replied with equal formality, 'In two hours, sir. We shall steer nor' west.' He waited, seeing Keen's doubt, the unspoken arguments.

'Are *Taciturn* and *Doon* in sight?'

'Aye, sir. The masthead reported both of them at the change of watch. Good visibility. We should see another sail soon. Information maybe, some evidence that she was seen by some passing trader or fisherman.' He looked at Urquhart. 'It is our best hope.'

Keen said, 'We are abeam of Cape North. By

139

nightfall we shall be stretched too far to offer support to one another.'

Adam looked away. He felt a stab of resentment without knowing why. He had been up before first light, and on deck several times during the night. There were plenty of navigational hazards in these waters and the local charts were unreliable, to say the least. It was only right that *Valkyrie*'s watchkeepers should know that their captain was with them.

'From the information brought by *Alfriston*, this would seem the most likely area for independent action. Perhaps tomorrow we could decide whether or not to continue this form of search.'

Keen watched two seamen dragging new halliards along the deck. '*I* will decide. While the light is still good I shall want signals sent to *Taciturn* and *Doon*. The brig can close with us and carry my report to Halifax.' He faced Adam and added shortly, 'We will discontinue the search before dusk.'

'Halifax, sir?'

Keen studied him grimly. 'Halifax.'

He walked toward the companion way, and Adam saw the flag lieutenant waiting there to intercept him.

'Orders, sir?' Urquhart was clearly uncomfortable at having been present during the exchange, and at having sensed a barrier which he had not seen before fall so obviously between admiral and flag captain.

Adam glanced up at the streaming masthead pendant. The wind was holding steady from the south-west. It had not shifted for days; another day would make no difference. And even when they returned to Halifax, it was unlikely that there would be fresh news from Sir Richard.

He realized what Urquhart had asked. 'Carry on as before.'

He was the captain, and yet his was never the final decision. He had always known that, but Keen's curt remark had merely served to emphasize the fact. Perhaps it was because Keen had been used to ships of the line, and had served in frigates as a very junior officer. He tried to smile, to sweep it away. *With the best of teachers*. But Keen had never commanded one. It should not make any difference. But, unreasonably, it did.

As the afternoon watch drew to a close, Keen came on deck again.

'I think it is time to make the signal.' He watched the small figure of John Whitmarsh walking aft, some clean shirts folded over one arm, and smiled unexpectedly. 'To be his age again, eh, Adam?'

The sudden informality, *just men*, was disconcerting. 'Aye, sir. But I think I could manage without some of the past.'

Keen made up his mind. 'You probably think I am giving up too easily. You think we should waste days, weeks even, pursuing what may be a lost cause.'

Adam said, 'I still believe we should continue, sir.'

Keen shrugged. The bridge between them was gone. 'It is my decision. Make the signal!'

Adam saw de Courcey hurrying toward Midshipman Rickman and the prepared hoists of bunting. Back to Halifax, then. Receptions and balls: a ship going stale at her anchorage.

'Deck there! *Taciturn*'s hoisted a signal!'

Adam saw another midshipman reaching for a telescope.

'Aloft, Mr Warren! Lively there!'

He knew Urquhart was watching him. He would never offer his own opinion, or mention what he had seen and heard. Adam shaded his eyes and stared at

141

the sun, like red gold now. But there was still time. If only....

The midshipman's young voice echoed down from the main-top. 'From *Taciturn*, sir! *Enemy in sight to the nor' east!*' Even at that distance and above the drumming chorus of canvas and rigging, Adam could hear his excitement.

Heading for the strait they had just left. Another hour, and they would have missed them. What sort of enemy, that *Taciturn* was so certain?

Warren shouted down again. 'She's *Reaper*, sir!'

Urquhart forgot himself. 'Hell's teeth! You were right, sir!'

Keen had reappeared. 'What is it? Are they sure?'

Adam said, 'Certain, sir.'

'They'll run for it.' He sounded unconvinced. 'Try and lose us in the Gulf.'

Adam beckoned to Urquhart. 'Get the t' gallants on her!'

He glanced up at the flag whipping out from the mizzen truck. 'This ship could outpace *Reaper*, no matter what she tried!' He was surprised at his own voice. Pride, where there had been only acceptance; triumph, when he had so recently felt bitterness at Keen's dismissal of his proposals.

Calls squealed and the deck shook to the rush of bare feet as men ran to obey them. He was aware of their excitement, the relief that something was happening, and awe, when some of the new hands looked aloft to see the topgallant sails bursting from their yards, their canvas already hard to the steady wind.

Adam took a glass and rested it on Midshipman Rickman's shoulder. First *Taciturn*; the brig *Doon* was still not in sight from the deck. And then ... He tensed, his back chilled despite the lingering warmth of the sun. A thin plume of pale canvas: *Reaper*. Not running, and yet they must have sighted them. Three ships on a converging tack. *Reaper*'s men might fight to the death; they would face it in any case after the brief formality of a court-martial. They would have known the penalty for mutiny from the instant they had hauled down the flag. He licked his dry lips. *And murdered their captain* ....

Keen spoke for him. 'They dare not fight!'

Adam turned to Urquhart. 'Beat to quarters, if you please. Then clear for action.' He walked to the taffrail and then back again, his mind grappling with the sudden change of fortune. A show of defiance? A bloody gesture? It would be all of that. *Taciturn* alone outgunned the smaller *Reaper*: *Valkyrie* could blow her out of the water without even getting to close quarters.

Keen said, 'She's holding her course.' He held out his arms as his servant appeared beside him to clip on his sword.

'Cleared for action, sir!'

Adam stared at the first lieutenant. He had barely heard the rattle of drums, the stampede of seamen and marines to their stations, and now all was still again, each long gun fully crewed, the decks sanded, the scarlet coats of the marines visible at the hammock nettings and high in the fighting tops. They had learned well under Peter Dawes, or perhaps it was all due to the impassive Urquhart.

Keen said, 'Make to *Taciturn, close on Flag.*' He turned away as de Courcey urged the signals party to greater efforts. The flags soared aloft.

'Acknowledged, sir!'

Of the brig *Doon* there was no sign, but her

143

masthead lookouts would be watching, probably glad they were well clear of it.

'*Reaper's* showing her teeth!'

Without a glass there was no apparent change, but when Adam propped his on the midshipman's shoulder he could see the line of protruding guns along the other vessel's side.

Keen said, 'When you are ready, Captain Bolitho.' They looked at each other like strangers.

Adam shouted, 'Just like the drill, Mr Urquhart!' He saw some of the nearest men turn to grin at him. 'Load and run out!'

'*Open the ports*!' A whistle shrilled from Monteith, the fourth lieutenant, and with a chorus of yells the seamen threw themselves on their tackles and hauled their guns up and through the open ports. With the wind across the quarter, their task was easier. If they changed tack, or lost the wind-gage, it would be different: uphill all the way, as the old gun captains warned.

Adam turned as young Whitmarsh walked unhurriedly between the crouching gun crews and watchful marines, Adam's new hanger held in his hands like a talisman. Adam looked around at the others on the quarterdeck. George Starr, his old coxswain, should be here, Hudson, who had also died, and other faces, so painfully clear that he was caught off-guard.

He waited for the boy to clip on his hanger and said, 'Below with you, my lad! No heroics today!' He saw the dismay on his face and added gently, 'You need no reminding either, do you?'

Keen was beside him. 'What can they hope to achieve?'

Adam saw the telescopes being trained on the

144

distant *Taciturn*, heard de Courcey's smooth voice reading out a signal. Then he lowered his glass, his mind suddenly blank. 'They have hostages, sir.'

'So that is what they intend. To sail directly past us, knowing we will not fire!' He seemed to consider it, with disbelief. 'Would they do that?'

'It may be a bluff, sir.' But he knew it was not. It was all the enemy had left. With this wind they would be within range in less than half an hour.

Keen said, 'It would be murder!'

Adam watched him, feeling his anger and revulsion. *His decision*, just as he had insisted earlier.

When Adam remained silent, Keen exclaimed, 'For God's sake, what should I do?'

Adam touched the hilt of his new hanger, the one he had chosen with such care in the old sword cutler's shop in the Strand.

'Men will die in any case if we fight, sir. But to lose *Reaper* now would be an even greater tragedy.'

Keen seemed to sigh. 'Signal *Taciturn* to take station astern of Flag.'

The signal was acknowledged, and Adam watched the leading frigate's sails in momentary confusion as she began to come about as ordered. He could feel both pity and admiration for Keen. He was not going to leave the first encounter to one of his captains. As Richard Bolitho had so often said, here was where the responsibility began and ended, like the flag at the mizzen-truck. *Final*.

He had forgotten about Midshipman Warren, who was still in the maintop.

'Deck, there!' Then shock, disbelief. 'There are prisoners on *Reaper*'s deck, sir!' There was a pause. 'Women, too!'

Keen said sharply, 'D' you still think they're bluffing?'

It was like a nightmare, Adam thought. *Reaper* would suffer the same fate yet again; she would be raked as she had been by the Americans, before she could even get within range.

Urquhart had gone to his station by the mainmast, his sword laid across one shoulder as if he were about to perform a ceremony.

Adam gripped the quarterdeck rail. He did not need to be told what would happen when these long eighteen-pounders, double-shotted as ordered, thundered out at the oncoming ship.

He knew that some of the gun crews were peering aft at him, and wanted to shout at them. *There is no decision to be made. They must not escape.*

He heard de Courcey say, 'Two women, sir. The rest look like sailors.' Even he sounded dazed, unable to accept what he saw.

Adam raised his voice. 'On the uproll, Mr Urquhart! As you bear!' Urquhart knew what to do: they all did. But they had to be held together, and commanded, no matter what they believed.

'Take in the t' gallants!' High overhead, men moved like monkeys, detached from the tension and apprehension on the deck below.

Adam turned to the sailing-master. 'Stand by to bring her up two points, Mr Ritchie. Then we will fire.'

Keen was in the shrouds, oblivious to the spray and risk; he was holding the midshipman's big telescope, his fair hair whipping in the wind.

Like that day at the church in Zennor ... Val and Zenoria ... He closed his eyes as Keen said harshly, 'One of the hostages is David St Clair! His daughter must be with him!'

146

He thrust the memories aside; this was no place for them. He heard Keen say, 'No bluff, then.' He climbed down to the deck and faced him.

Adam said, 'Stand by!' He forced himself to look at the oncoming frigate, leaning over to expose her bright copper, her gilded figurehead with the upraised scythe suddenly clear and terrible.

Each gun captain would be staring aft at the solitary figure by the rail, looking to a captain whom they knew only by reputation. But every man knew what he would see when *Valkyrie* altered course, and the target filled each port. Here, a man cleared his throat; another turned to wipe the sweat from his eyes.

Suppose they refused to fire on men like themselves?

Adam felt the anger pound through him. They were not like them. *I must not think of it!*

He drew his hanger and raised it shoulder-high.

Dear God, what are we doing?

'Alter course, Mr Ritchie!'

He swung round as the uneven roar of cannon fire rolled and echoed across the short, white-tipped waves.

With disbelief he saw *Reaper*'s guns recoiling in a broken broadside, in pairs or singly, until at last only one fired from the bow.

There were leaping patches of foam now; the taller water-spouts of the heavier guns churned up the sea's face and faded almost as suddenly. A full broadside, fired into oblivion.

Keen said, 'They would not fire on us!' He looked at those nearest him. 'Because they knew we would destroy them!'

Adam said, 'The bluff failed.' He saw some of the

147

gun crews staring at each other; two seamen even reached across their eighteen-pounder to shake hands. It was no victory, but at least it was not bloody murder, either.

'Signal her to heave to! Stand by, boarding parties!'

Adam called, 'Be ready to fire. We will take nothing for granted!'

He touched his hat to Keen. 'I'd like to go across myself, sir.'

Keen gazed past him as something like a great sigh came from the watching seamen and marines.

'She's struck her colours, thank God.'

Richie, the old sailing-master, wiped his lips with the back of his hand. 'Poor old girl. She's taken all she can, I reckon!'

Adam looked at him. A toughened, unsentimental professional, but in his simple way he had said it all.

Keen said, 'Take good care of St Clair and his daughter. The ordeal must have been dreadful for them.'

Adam saw the boats being swayed up and over the larboard gangway: Urquhart had taught them well. The guns would still be able to fire if necessary, without being hampered by their presence.

'I will, sir.' He stared across at the other ship, her sails flapping as she came into the wind. Another minute and it would have ended differently. As it was ... He recalled the sailing-master's words, like an epitaph. For a ship, not for those who had betrayed her.

*　　　　*　　　　*

Keeping in line abreast, *Valkyrie*'s boats pulled

148

steadily toward the other frigate. Tension remained high. If *Reaper*'s captors decided to resist, they might still be able to make sail and escape, or attempt it.

Adam looked over at the other boats. His captain of marines, Loftus, was very conspicuous in his scarlet tunic, an easy target for any marksman, nor would his own own epaulettes have gone unnoticed. He found himself smiling slightly. Gulliver, the sixth lieutenant, glanced quickly at him, perhaps taking comfort in what he saw.

He said, 'This will even the score, sir!'

He spoke like a veteran. He was about twenty years old.

'*Reaper*, ahoy! We are coming aboard! Throw down your weapons!'

Adam touched the pistol beneath his coat. This was the moment. Some hothead, a man with nothing to lose, might use it as a last chance. Boat by boat they went alongside, and he was conscious of a strange sense of loneliness with *Valkyrie* hidden by this pitching hull. *No chances.* But would Keen order his flagship to open fire with so many of his own men on board?

It was uncanny. Like a dead ship. They scrambled up and over the gangway, weapons held ready, while from the opposite end of the vessel some of the marines were already swarming onto the forecastle. They had even swung round a swivel, and had trained it on the silent figures lining the gun deck.

His men parted to let their captain through, seeing the ship through different eyes now that she had struck. The guns which had fired blindly into the open water moved restlessly, unloaded and abandoned, rammers and sponges lying where they had been dropped. Adam walked aft to the big

149

double wheel, where two of his men had taken control. The hostages, released and apparently unharmed, were grouped around the mizzen mast, while along the gundeck the seamen seemed to have separated into two distinct groups, the mutineers and the American prize crew.

There were two American lieutenants waiting for him.

'Are there any more officers aboard?'

The senior of the two shook his head. 'The ship is yours, Captain Bolitho.'

Adam concealed his surprise. 'Mr Gulliver, take your party and search the ship.' He added sharply as the lieutenant hurried away, 'If any one resists, kill him!'

So they knew who he was. He said, 'What were you hoping to do, Lieutenant?'

The tall officer shrugged. 'My name is Robert Neill, Captain. *Reaper* is a prize of war. They surrendered.'

'And *you* are a prisoner of war. Your men, also,' He paused. 'Captain Loftus, take charge of the others. You know what to do.' To Neill he said, 'You offered British seamen a chance to mutiny. In fact, you and your captain incited it.'

The man named Neill sighed. 'I have nothing to add.'

He watched the two officers hand their swords to a marine. 'You will be well treated.' He hesitated, hating the silence, the smell of fear. 'As I was.'

Then, with a nod to Loftus, he turned and walked toward the waiting hostages.

One, a silver-haired man with an alert, youthful face, stepped forward, ignoring the raised bayonet of a marine.

150

'My name is David St Clair.' He reached out his hand. 'This is my daughter, Gilia. Your arrival was a miracle, sir. A miracle!'

Adam glanced at the young woman. She was warmly dressed for travel, her eyes steady and defiant, as if this were the ordeal rather than its relief.

He said, 'I have little time, Mr St Clair. I am to transfer you to my ship, *Valkyrie*, before it becomes too dark.'

St Clair stared at him. 'I know that name!' He held his daughter's arm. 'Valentine Keen's ship, you recall it!' But she was observing *Valkyrie's* seamen and marines, as if sensing the friction between them and their prisoners.

Adam said, 'His flagship. I am his flag captain.'

St Clair said smoothly, 'Of course. He is promoted now.'

Adam said, 'How were you taken, sir?'

'We were on passage in the schooner *Crystal*, out of Halifax, bound for the St Lawrence. Admiralty business.' He seemed to become aware of Adam's impatience and continued, 'These others are her crew. The woman is the master's wife, who was aboard with him.'

'I was told of your business here, sir. I thought it dangerous, at the time.' He glanced at the girl again. 'I was proved right, it seems.'

A boatswain's mate was waiting, trying to catch his eye.

'What is it, Laker?'

The man seemed surprised that his new captain should know his name. 'The two Yankee officers, sir....'

'Send them over to the ship. Their own men, too. Lively now!'

151

His eyes moved to the gangway where one of the guns was still abandoned on its tackles. There was a great stain on the planking, like black tar. It must be blood. Perhaps it marked the place where they had flogged their captain without mercy.

He called, 'And run up our colours!' It was a small enough gesture, amid so much shame.

One of the American lieutenants paused with his escort. 'Tell me one thing, Captain. *Would* you have fired, hostages or not?'

Adam swung away. 'Take them across.'

St Clair's daughter said quietly, 'I wondered that myself, Captain.' She was shivering now, despite her warm clothing, the shock and realization of what had happened cutting away her reserve.

St Clair put his arm around her, and said. 'The guns were loaded and ready. At the last minute some of the men, her original people, I believe, fired them to show their intentions.'

Adam said, 'The American lieutenant, Neill, is probably asking himself the same question that he put to me.' He looked the girl directly in the eyes. 'In war, there are few easy choices.'

'Boat's ready, sir!'

'Have you any baggage to be taken across?'

St Clair guided his daughter to the side, where a boatswain's chair had been rigged for her.

'None. There was no time. Afterwards, they destroyed the *Crystal*. There was an explosion of some kind.'

Adam looked around the deserted deck, at his own men, who were waiting to get *Reaper* under way again. They would probably have preferred to send her to the bottom. *And so would I.*

He walked to the side, and ensured that the girl was

152

securely seated.

'You will be more comfortable in the flagship, ma'am. We shall be returning to Halifax.'

Some of *Reaper's* original company, urged ungently by Loftus's marines, were already being taken below, to be secured for the remainder of the passage.

She murmured, 'What will become of them?'

Adam said curtly, 'They will hang.'

She studied him, as if searching his face for something. 'Had they fired on your ship we would all be dead, is that not so?' When Adam remained silent, she persisted, 'Surely that must be taken into consideration.'

Adam turned suddenly. 'That man! Come here!'

The seaman, still wearing a crumpled, red-checkered shirt, came over immediately and knuckled his forehead. 'Sir?'

'I know you!'

'Aye, Cap'n Bolitho. I was a maintopman in *Anemone* two years back. You put me ashore when I was took sick o' fever.'

Memory came, and with it the names of the past. 'Ramsay, what in *hell's* name happened, man?' He had forgotten the girl, who was listening intently, her father, the others, everything but this one, familiar face. There was no fear in it, but it was the face of a man already condemned, a man who had known the nearness of death in the past, and had accepted it.

'It ain't my place, Cap'n Bolitho. Not with you. That's all over, done with.' He came to a decision, and very deliberately dragged his shirt over his head. Then he said, 'No disrespect to you, miss. But for you, I think we would have fired.' Then he turned his back, allowing the fading sunlight to fall across

153

his skin.

Adam said, '*Why?*' He heard the girl give a strangled sob. It must seem far worse to her.

The seaman named Ramsay had been so cruelly flogged that his body was barely human. Some of the torn flesh had not yet healed.

He pulled his shirt on again. 'Because he enjoyed it.'

'I am sorry, Ramsay.' He touched his arm impulsively, knowing that Lieutenant Gulliver was watching him with disbelief. 'I will do what I can for you.'

When he looked again, the man was gone. There was no hope, and he would know it. And yet those few words had meant so much, to both of them.

Gulliver said uneasily, 'Ready, sir.'

But before the boatswain's chair was swung out to be lowered into the waiting boat, Adam said to St Clair's daughter, 'Sometimes, there are no choices whatsoever.'

'Lower away! Easy, lads!'

Then he straightened his back and turned to face the others. He was the captain again.

CHAPTER EIGHT

TOO MUCH TO LOSE

Richard Bolitho leaned away from the bright sunshine that lanced through *Indomitable's* cabin windows to rest his head against the chair's high back. It was deep and comfortable, a *bergère*, which Catherine had sent on board when this ship had first

154

hoisted his flag. Yovell, his secretary, sat at the table, while Lieutenant Avery stood by the stern bench watching two of the ship's boats pulling back from the brig *Alfriston*, which had met up with them at dawn.

Tyacke had made it his business to send across some fresh fruit. Having commanded a small brig himself, he would have appreciated its value to her hard-worked company.

There had been a burst of cheering when *Alfriston* had hove-to to pass across her dispatches, which was quickly quelled by officers on watch who had been very aware of their admiral's open skylight, and perhaps the importance of the news *Alfriston* might have brought to him.

Tyacke had come aft, bringing the heavy canvas satchel himself.

When Bolitho asked about the cheering, he had replied impassively, '*Reaper*'s been retaken, Sir Richard.'

He glanced now at the heavy pile of dispatches on the table. The entire report of the search for, and capture of, *Reaper* was there, written in Keen's own hand rather than that of a secretary. Did he lack confidence in his own actions, or in those who supported him, he wondered. It remained a private document, and yet, despite the seals and the secrecy, *Indomitable*'s people had known its contents, or had guessed what had happened. Such intuition was uncanny, but not unusual.

He listened to the creak of tackles and the twitter of a bosun's call as the next net full of stores was hoisted outboard before being lowered into a boat for *Alfriston*. It was difficult to look at the vast blue expanse of ocean beyond the windows. His eye was

155

painful, and he had wanted to rub it, even though he had been warned against disturbing it. He must accept that it was getting worse.

He tried to concentrate on Keen's careful appraisal of *Reaper's* discovery and capture. He had missed out nothing, even his own despair when he had seen the hostages paraded on her deck, a human barricade against *Valkyrie's* guns. He had generously praised Adam's part in it, and his handling of the captured sailors, American and mutineers alike.

But his mind rebelled against the intrusion of duty. In the bag sent over with Keen's dispatch had been some letters, one from Catherine, the first since they had parted in Plymouth some three months ago. He had held it to his face, had seen Yovell's discreet glance, had caught the faint reminder of her perfume.

Avery said, 'The last boat's casting off, Sir Richard.' He sounded tense, on edge. Perhaps he, too, had been hoping for a letter, although Bolitho had never known him to receive one. Like Tyacke, his only world seemed to be here.

Bolitho turned once more to Keen's lengthy report, rereading the information concerning David St Clair and his daughter, who had been prisoners aboard *Reaper*. Taken from a schooner, but surely no accidental encounter? St Clair was under Admiralty contract, and Keen had mentioned that he had been intending to visit the naval dockyard at Kingston and also a ship-building site at York, where a thirty-gun man-of-war was close to completion. The final work on the vessel had apparently been delayed by a dispute with the Provincial Marine, under whose control she would eventually be. St Clair, well used to dealing with bureaucracy, had been hoping to speed things to a satisfactory conclusion. Captains in the fleet might find it difficult to regard such a relatively small vessel as a matter of great importance, but as Keen had learned from St Clair, when in commission the new vessel would be the biggest and most powerful on the lakes. No American craft would be able to stand against her: the lakes would be held under the White Ensign. But should the Americans attack and seize her, completed or not, the effect would be disastrous. It would mean the end of Upper Canada as a British province. Just one ship; and the Americans would have known of her existence from the moment her keel had been laid. In the light of this, St Clair's capture appeared even less of a casual misfortune. His mission had also been known: he had had to be removed. Bolitho thought of the savage gunfire, the pathetic wreckage of the *Royal Herald*. Or killed.

He said to Yovell, 'Have our bag sent over to *Alfriston*. She'll be impatient to get under way again.' He thought of the brig's gaunt commander, and wondered what his feelings had been when he had heard of *Reaper*'s capture, and that her only defiance had been fired deliberately into open water.

Ozzard peered through the other door. 'Captain's coming, sir.'

Tyacke entered and glanced at the littered papers on Bolitho's table. Bolitho thought he was probably like *Alfriston*'s commander, eager to move.

Without effort he could picture his ships on this great, empty ocean: two hundred miles south-west of the Bermudas, the other frigates *Virtue* and *Attacker* mere slivers of light on opposite horizons. Perhaps if they had not waited, the Americans would have attacked the assembled convoy, their powerful frigates destroying it or beating it into submission, no

157

matter what the escorting men-of-war might have attempted.

A mistake, a waste of time? Or had the Americans outguessed them yet again? The enemy's intelligence sources were without parallel. To know about St Clair and to see his involvement as a direct threat to some greater plan matched the impudent way they had seized *Reaper* and turned the advantage into a shame, news of which would ring throughout the fleet in spite of, or even because of, the punishments which would be meted out to the men who had mutinied against their captain, and against the Crown.

The convoy was well away, and would be standing out into the Atlantic. Their speed would be that of the slowest merchantman, a misery for the escorting frigates and brigs. But safe, in a few days' time.

Before they had left Bermuda, Avery had gone ashore to visit *Reaper's* first lieutenant at a military hospital in Hamilton. Bolitho himself would have liked to have spoken to the *Reaper*'s only surviving officer, who had been with his captain until the incident's macabre and brutal conclusion, but *Reaper* had been one of his own squadron. He could not become personally involved with men whose warrants he might be called upon to sign.

Reaper's captain had been a tyrant and a sadist, terms which Bolitho would never use without great consideration. He had been moved from another command to make *Reaper* into an efficient and reliable fighting ship once more, and to restore her reputation. But early in his tenure another side of his nature had revealed itself. Perhaps he had, in fact, been moved from that other command because of his own brutality. Any captain sailing alone had to keep the balance between discipline and tyranny firmly in his mind. Only the afterguard, with its thin ranks of Royal Marines, stood between him and open rebellion. And even if provoked, it could never be condoned.

Tyacke said, 'Orders, Sir Richard?'

Bolitho turned away from the glare and saw that Yovell and Avery had left the cabin. It seemed a mutual awareness of his desire to confer privately with his flag captain: a loyalty which never failed to move him.

'I want your views, James. Return to Halifax and discover what is happening? Or remain here, and so weaken our squadron?'

Tyacke rubbed the scarred side of his face. He had seen the letter handed to Bolitho and been surprised by his own envy. *If only* ... He thought of the wine which Catherine Somervell had sent him, like the deep green leather chair in which Bolitho was sitting, her gifts, and her abiding presence in this cabin. With a woman like that....

Bolitho asked, 'What is it, James? You know me well enough to speak out.'

Tyacke dismissed the thoughts, glad that they could not be known.

'I believe the Yankees—' he smiled awkwardly, recalling Dawes, 'the Americans will need to move very soon. Maybe they've already made a beginning. Rear-Admiral Keen's information about the shipbuilder, this man St Clair, points to it. Once we have more ships, as their lordships say we will when Bonaparte is finally beaten, they'll face a blockade of their entire coastline. Trade, supplies, ships, unable to move.' He paused, and seemed to come to a decision. 'I've spoken to Isaac York, and he insists that this weather will hold.' Again he offered a small,

159

attractive smile, which even his disfigurement could not diminish. 'And my new purser *assures* me that we are well supplied for another month. The pips might squeak a bit, but we can manage.'

'Remain on this patrol? Is that what you are telling me?'

'Look, sir, if you were some high an' mighty Yankee with good ships, albeit Frogs, at your disposal, what would you do?'

Bolitho nodded, considering it. He could even see the unknown ships in his mind, as clearly as the hollow-eyed Commander Borradaile had seen them through his telescope. Big, well-armed, free of all authority but their own.

'I'd take advantage of this south-westerly and go for the convoy, even at this stage. A long way, and a risk if you are facing the unknown. But I don't think it is unknown to our man.'

There were muffled cheers on deck, and he left the chair to walk to the stern windows. 'There goes *Alfriston*, James.'

Tyacke watched him, with affection and concern. Every time he thought he knew this man he found there was something more to learn. He noticed that Bolitho was shading his left eye, and saw the sadness and introspection in the profile against the light. Thinking of his letter in that same little brig, and the endless miles and transfers from ship to ship before Catherine Somervell would open and read it. Perhaps thinking, too, of his own independence as a very young commander, when each day was a challenge, but not a burden. A proud man, and a sensitive one, a man Tyacke had seen holding the hand of a dying enemy in *Indomitable*'s last and greatest battle. Who had tried to comfort his coxswain when Allday's son

160

had been killed in that same fight. He cared, and those who knew him loved him for it. The others were content with the legend. And yet his would be the responsibility for sending *Reaper*'s seamen to choke from a yardarm. Tyacke had only known *Reaper*'s captain by reputation. It had been enough.

Bolitho turned from the sea. 'I agree with you, James. We will remain on station.' He walked back to the table and spread his hands on the open dispatches. 'Another day or so. After that, time and distance can become a handicap.' He smiled. 'Even to our enemy.'

Tyacke picked up his hat. 'I'll make the necessary signals to our consorts when we alter course at two bells, sir.'

Bolitho sat down again and rested his head against the warm green leather. He thought of May in Cornwall, the tide of pure colour, thousands of bluebells, the sea sparkling . . . It would soon be June. He felt his fingers tighten on the arms of the chair she had had made for him. So long. So long. . . .

The familiar sounds faded; the sunlight no longer tormented him as wind and rudder guided this great ship like a bridle.

Then, and only then, did he take the letter from his coat. He held it to his face again, to his mouth, as she would have done.

Then he opened it with great care, always with the same uncertainty, even fear.

My dearest Beloved Richard. . . .

She was with him. Nothing had changed. The fear was gone.

161

had been called * that while lights flickered and those who were firmly to lead that for it. The others were

Bolitho turned from the sea.

*   *   *

Lieutenant George Avery wedged his feet against his sea-chest and stared up at the deckhead in his tiny, screened cabin. Feet moved occasionally on the wet planking as men hastened to take in the slack of some running rigging.

Outside it was pitch black, with plenty of stars but no moon. He toyed with the idea of going on deck but knew he would be in the way, or worse, those on watch might think that he had been sent to report on their progress. He glanced at his gently swaying cot and rejected it. Where was the point? He would not be able to sleep, or at least, not for long. Then his doubts would come to torment him. He considered the wardroom, but knew there would be somebody there, like himself unable to sleep, or looking for a partner for a game of cards. Like the dead Scarlett, *Indomitable*'s first lieutenant when she had ceased to be a private ship and had first worn Bolitho's flag. He had wanted so much to have a command of his own, and outwardly had been a good officer, but he was being driven quietly mad by his mounting debts, his inability to stop gambling, and his desperate need to win. Avery had seen David Merrick, the acting captain of marines, sitting in the wardroom earlier, a book open on his lap to deter conversation, but his eyes unmoving. His superior, du Cann, had died that day with Scarlett and many others, but promotion seemed to have brought him no pleasure.

He thought of *Alfriston*, and the letter he had seen resting between the leaves of a book on Bolitho's table. Envy? It went deeper than that. He had even been denied the odd pleasure it gave him to read one of Allday's letters aloud: there had been none for him

162

from Unis, and Avery knew he was troubled, confused by a separation he had been unable to accept. Avery had seen him, too, that afternoon, motionless on the deck, alone despite the bustling hands around him. He was standing at the place where his son had died, maybe trying to see the sense of it all.

He glanced at his small cupboard, thinking of the good cognac he kept there. If he had a drink now, he would not stop.

More feet rushed overhead. The ship was altering course very slightly, the shrouds drumming in a muffled tattoo. And tomorrow—what then? It had been late afternoon when the brig *Marvel* had closed with the flagship. She had sighted two ships to the north, steering east, as far as her commander could tell. He had turned away rather than run up a hoist of signals, and he had acted wisely. Any small vessel would have run for it, if the two ships were the enemy.

But overnight all could change. It could be a waste of time: the ships might have changed tack completely, or *Marvel*'s lookouts might have been mistaken, seeing only what they expected to see, as was often the case in these hit-and-run tactics.

He recalled Bolitho when they had last met, strengthened or troubled by his letter from Catherine, it was not possible to say. He had spoken unexpectedly of his childhood at Falmouth, and his awe of his father, Captain James Bolitho. He had said that he had never doubted or questioned his vocation as a sea-officer, although Avery thought privately that he was more uncertain now than at any other time.

Of the two reported ships he had said, 'If they *are* the enemy, it is unlikely that they will know of

163

Reaper's recapture. Yet. If they are truly after the convoy from Bermuda, then I think they will come at us. They are becoming too used to success. This may be one gamble too many.'

He could have been speaking of somebody else, or some report he had read in his dispatches or in the *Gazette*. Avery had looked around the spacious cabin, the tethered guns on either side, the books, and the fine wine cooler with the Bolitho motto on the top. The same place which had been blasted and blackened in that action, where men had fought and died, and survival had seemed like an accident or a miracle. If he returned to it now, he thought he would probably find Bolitho still sitting in the leather chair, reading one of his books, his fingers occasionally brushing against the letter which he would open again before he turned in.

He ran his fingers through his hair and allowed the thought and the memory to intrude. As if she had suddenly appeared in this tiny hutch, the only place he could truly be alone.

Suppose they had not met? He shook his head as if to deny it. That had only been partly the cause. *I am thirty-five years old. A lieutenant without prospects, beyond serving this man for whom I care more than I would have believed humanly possible.* The same Lieutenant Scarlett, during one of their many heated exchanges, had suggested that he was waiting only for the reward of promotion, for a command of his own, no matter how small. And once, that might have been true. There had seemed no other course, no hope for someone of his station; even the lingering stain of his court-martial would not have been forgotten in the high offices of admiralty.

I am not a round-eyed midshipman, or a young

lieutenant with the world still for the asking. I should have stopped there. Stopped, and forgotten her ... She was probably laughing about it at this very moment. Just as he knew it would break his heart, if he really believed that she was.

I should have known. A sea-officer who had proved his courage in battle, and in his bitter struggle to live after being wounded. But when it came to women he was a child, an innocent.

But it would not disperse. He was still there, and it was like a dream, something so vivid and unplanned. Something inevitable.

The house had been almost empty; the full staff were only expected to arrive after Rear-Admiral Sir Robert Mildmay's residence in Bath was finally closed and sold.

She had been so calm, amused, he thought, by his concern for her reputation, assuring him that the formidable housekeeper was completely loyal and discreet, and the cook, the only other person residing in the house, was all but deaf. He had often recalled that description, *loyal* and *discreet*. Did it have a double meaning? That her affairs were numerous? He rubbed his forehead. That she might be entertaining some other man even at this moment?

He heard footsteps outside, the click of Captain Merrick's boots. He would be going around his sentries, inspecting places deep in the lightless hull where guards were mounted day and night. Another man with a private torment: unable to sleep, afraid of what dreams might bring. Avery smiled grimly. As well he might.

He opened the shutter of his solitary lantern very slightly, but instead of the small flame he saw the great fire, half red, and half white ash. She had led

165

him by the hand across the room. 'It will be cold tonight.'

He had attempted to touch her, to take her arm, but she had moved away, her eyes in shadow while she had watched him. 'There is some wine on the table. It would be pleasant, don't you think?' She had reached for the tongs beside a basket of logs.

'Let me.' They had knelt together, watching the sparks going up the chimney like fireflies.

She had said, 'I must go. I have things to do.' She had not looked at him. Later, he had realized that she had been unable to.

The house had been like a tomb, the room facing away from the street and the occasional noise of carriage wheels.

Avery had had no experience with women, except for one brief incident with a French lady who had visited sick and wounded prisoners of war. There had been no affection, only need, an urgency which had left him feeling used and vaguely degraded.

He was still unable to believe what had happened in London.

She had appeared on the edge of the shadows, her body all in white, her feet bare on the carpet, the feet alone touched by the flickering firelight.

'Here I am, *Mister* Avery!' She had laughed softly, and when he had got up from the fire, 'You spoke to me of your love.' She had held out her arms. 'Show me.'

He had held her, gently at first, then more firmly as he had felt the curve of her spine under his hand, and had realized that beneath the flimsy gown she was naked.

Then, for the first time, he had felt her shivering, although her body was warm, even hot. He had tried

166

to kiss her, but she had pressed her face into his shoulder, and repeated, '*Show me.*'

He had seized the gown, and in seconds had her in his arms again, unable to stop himself, even if his senses had permitted it. He had carried her to the great bed and had knelt over her, touching her, exploring her, kissing her from her her throat to her thigh. He had seen her raise her head to watch him as he threw off his clothes, her hair like living gold in the light. Then she had laid back again, her arms spread out as if crucified.

'*Show me!*' She had resisted when he had gripped her wrists, and had twisted from side to side, her body arched as he had forced her down, and down, finding her, unable to wait, unwilling to restrain his desire.

She had been ready, and had drawn him to her, passionate, tender, experienced, enclosing him deeply in her body until they were both spent.

She had murmured, 'That was love, Mister Avery.'

'I must leave, Susanna.' It was the first time he had called her by name.

'First, some wine.' She had lifted up on one elbow, making no attempt to cover herself. Nor did she resist when he touched her again; she reached out to provoke and arouse him once more, and he had known then that he could not leave her. At dawn's first intrusion they had finally tasted the wine, and had crouched again by the fire, now all but dead in the faint grey light.

The rest had become blurred, unreal. Fumbling into his clothes again while she had stood watching him, quite naked but for his cocked hat. Then he had embraced her once more, unable to find the words, his mind and body still reeling from the impossible dream, which had become reality.

She had whispered, 'I promised you a carriage.'

He had pressed her hair against his chin. 'I shall be all right. I could possibly fly to Chelsea!'

The moment of parting had been painful, almost embarrassing.

'I am sorry if I hurt you, Susanna ... I am ... clumsy.'

She had smiled. 'You are a man. A real man.'

He might have said. 'Please write to me.' But he could not honestly say that he had. The door had closed, and he had made his way down the stairs to the street doors, where someone had placed and lighted a fresh stand of candles for his departure. *Loyal* and *discreet*.

There was a tap at the screen door, startling him, and he found Ozzard standing outside, a small tray beneath his arm. For a moment Avery though he must have been reliving it all aloud, and that Ozzard had heard him.

Ozzard said only, 'Sir Richard's compliments, sir, and he'd like to see you aft.'

'Of course.' Avery closed the door and groped for a comb. Did Ozzard never sleep either?

He sat down again and grinned ruefully. She would be laughing, maybe, but remembering too.

Perhaps he had been a worse fool than he knew. But he would never forget.

He smiled. *Mister Avery*.

*   *   *

Captain James Tyacke stepped into the stern cabin and looked around at the familiar faces, his eyes accepting the light with surprising ease after the blackness of the quarterdeck, where little more than a

168

tiny compass lamp pierced the night.

Bolitho was standing at the table, with his hands spread on a chart, Avery by his elbow, while the plump and scholarly Yovell sat at a smaller table, his pen poised over some papers. Ozzard moved only occasionally to refill their cups with coffee but remained, as usual, silent, merely shifting from one foot to the other to betray any agitation he might feel.

And framed against the great span of thick glass windows was Allday, a drawn sword in one hand, while he moved a cloth slowly up and down the blade as Tyacke had seen him do so often. Bolitho's oak: only death would separate them.

Tyacke shut it from his mind. 'All the hands have been fed, Sir Richard. I've been around the ship to have a quiet word with my people.'

He could not have slept much, Bolitho thought, but he was ready now, even if his admiral were to be proved wrong. He had even considered that possibility. The ship's company had been roused early, but they had not yet cleared for action. There was nothing worse for morale than the anti-climax of discovering that the enemy had outguessed or outmanoeuvred them, and the sea was empty.

My people. That was also typical of Tyacke. He was referring to the ship's backbone of professionals, his warrant officers, all skilled and experienced men like Isaac York, the sailingmaster, Harry Duff, the gunner, and Sam Hockenhull, the squat boatswain. Men who had come up the hard way, like *Alfriston*'s untidy commander.

Set against them, the lieutenants were amateurs. Even Daubeny, the first lieutenant, was still young for his position, which would not have come his way so soon but for the death of his predecessor. But that one fierce battle eight months ago had given him a maturity that seemed to surprise him more than anybody. As for the others, the most junior was Blythe, only just promoted from the midshipmen's berth. He was bigheaded and very sure of himself, but even Tyacke had overcome his dislike of him to say that he was improving. Slightly.

And Laroche, the piggy-faced third lieutenant, who had once received the rough edge of Tyacke's tongue when he had been in charge of a press gang, also lacked experience except for their encounter with *Unity*.

Tyacke was saying, 'The new hands have settled down quite well, sir. As for the Nova Scotians who volunteered, I'm glad they're with us and not the enemy!'

Bolitho stared down at the chart, the soundings and calculations between his hands. Ships meeting, the mind of an enemy, all meaningless if there was nothing when daylight came.

York had been right about the wind. It was even and steady from the south-west, and the ship, under reduced canvas, was lying well to it; when he had been on deck he had watched the spray bursting like phantoms along the lee side and up through the beakhead with its snarling lion.

Avery asked, 'Will they fight or run, Sir Richard?' He saw the alertness in the grey eyes that lifted to him; there was no hint of fatigue or doubt. Bolitho had shaved, and Avery wondered what he and Allday had discussed while the big coxswain had used his razor as easily as if it were broad daylight.

His shirt was loosely fastened, and Avery had seen the glint of silver when he had stooped over the chart. The locket he always wore.

170

Bolitho shrugged. 'Fight. If they have not already gone about and headed for port somewhere, they will have little choice, I think.' He looked up at the deckhead beams. 'The wind is an ally today.'

Avery watched, at peace now in this company, the consequences of what daylight might bring somehow secondary. He heard the drumming vibration of rigging, the occasional squeal of blocks, and imagined the ship leaning over to the wind, knowing that Bolitho was seeing it also, even as they spoke.

Tyacke would consider the situation rather differently, perhaps, but with the same end in mind. How many times had this ship lived through moments like this? She was thirty-six years old, and her battle honours read like history itself: the Chesapeake, The Saintes, the Nile, and Copenhagen. So many men, so much pain. He thought of Tyacke's fiercely contained pride for the ship he had not wanted. *And she had never been beaten.*

Bolitho said suddenly, 'Your assistant, George—Mr Midshipman Carleton. Doing well, isn't he?'

Avery glanced quickly at Tyacke, who gave the merest hint of a smile, but no more.

'Yes, sir, he is very good with his signals crew. He hopes to be offered promotion. He is seventeen.' The question had disconcerted him: he never really knew what Bolitho might toss his way, or why.

Tyacke said, 'He's a damned sight quieter than Mr Blythe ever was.'

Bolitho felt them relaxing, except Ozzard. He was waiting to hear, to *know*. He would go below, as deep as possible into the hull, when the first shots were fired. He should be ashore, Bolitho thought, away from this life. And yet, he knew that he had nowhere to go, no one who waited for him. Even when they were in Cornwall, and Ozzard lived in his cottage on the estate, he remained profoundly alone.

Bolitho said, 'I want young Carleton aloft.' He tugged out his watch and flicked open the guard.

Tyacke read his thoughts. 'Less than an hour, sir.'

Bolitho glanced at his empty cup, and heard Ozzard say tentatively, 'I could make another pot, Sir Richard.'

'I think it may have to wait.' He turned his head as somewhere, almost drowned out by the muffled hiss of the sea, he heard a man laugh. Such a small thing, but he thought of the wretched *Reaper*: there had been no laughter there. He remembered as if it were yesterday the evening when Tyacke had taken the lordly Midshipman Blythe below deck to visit the crowded seamen's and marines' messes, to show him what he had called 'the strength of a ship'. That had been before the battle. The same strength had prevailed then. He thought of Allday's grief. At a cost....

He said, 'If we fight, we will give of our best.' For a moment it was like hearing someone else's voice. 'But we must never forget those who depend on us, because they have no other choice.'

Tyacke reached for his hat. 'I'll have the galley fire doused in good time, Sir Richard.'

But Bolitho was looking at Avery. 'Go and speak with your Mr Carleton.' He closed his watch, but was still holding it. 'You may pass the word now, James. It will be warm enough today.'

As Ozzard gathered up the cups and the others left the cabin, Bolitho looked over at Allday.

'Well, old friend. Why here, you must be thinking, a tiny mark on this great ocean. Are we destined to fight?'

Allday held out the old sword and ran his eye along the edge.

'Like all them other times, Sir Richard. It was meant to be. That's it an' all about it.' Then he grinned, almost his old self again. 'We'll win, no matter what.' He paused, and the defiant humour was gone. 'Y' see, Sir Richard, we've both got too much to lose.' He slid the blade back into its scabbard. 'God help them that tries to take it away!'

* * *

Bolitho walked to the quarterdeck rail and gripped it while he peered up at the towering mainmast with its iron-hard canvas. He was shivering, not because of the cold morning air, but with the instinctive awareness of danger that could still surprise him after a lifetime at sea. The sails were paler now, but there was no horizon, and the only movement he recognized through the thick criss-cross of rigging and flapping canvas seemed to float above the ship, keeping pace with her like a solitary sea bird. It was his flag, the Cross of St George, which flew day and night while he was in command. He thought of her letter in the pocket of his coat, and imagined he could hear her voice. *My admiral of England.*

He could still taste the bitterness of coffee on his tongue, and wondered why he had not forced himself to eat. Tension, uncertainty perhaps. But fear? He smiled. Perhaps he could no longer recognize that emotion.

Figures moved all around him, each one careful not to intrude upon his solitude. He could see Isaac York, a head taller than his mates, his slate-coloured

173

hair blowing in the wind: a good man and a strong one. Bolitho knew that he had even tried to help Scarlett when the extent of his debts had become known. The white breeches of the lieutenants and midshipmen stood out in the lingering darkness, and he guessed that they were preparing themselves for what might happen today, each in his own fashion.

He moved to the compass box and glanced at the tilting card. North-east by north, with the wind still firm across the larboard quarter. Men were working high overhead, feeling for frayed cordage or jammed blocks with the sureness of true seamen.

Tyacke was down on the lee side, his lean figure framed against the pale water creaming back from the bows. One long arm moved to emphasize a point, and he could imagine Daubeny concentrating on every word. They were chalk and cheese, but the mixture seemed to work: Tyacke had a peculiar gift of being able to communicate his requirements to his subordinates without unnecessary anger or sarcasm. At first they had been afraid of him, and repulsed by the hideous scars: eventually they had all overcome such things, and had become a company of which to be proud.

He heard a midshipman whisper to his friend and saw them look up, and he shaded his eyes and stared with them at his flag, the red cross suddenly hard and bright, touched by the first light of dawn.

'*Deck there!*' Carleton's voice was clear and very loud: he was using a speaking-trumpet. 'Sail on the larboard bow!' A pause, and Bolitho could picture the young midshipman asking the masthead lookout his opinion. Tyacke was always careful with his choice of 'eyes': they were invariably experienced sailors, many of whom had grown older with the

174

ships they were serving, or fighting.

Carleton called again, 'She's *Attacker*, sir!' He sounded almost disappointed that it was not a first sighting of the enemy. The other frigate was one of the smaller sixth-rates, and mounted only twenty-six guns. Bolitho frowned. The same as *Reaper*. But she was not like *Reaper*. In his mind's eye he could see *Attacker*'s captain, George Morrison, a tough northerner from Tyneside. But no sadist: his punishment book was one of the cleanest in the squadron.

Avery said quietly, 'He must sight *Virtue* soon, sir.'

Bolitho looked at him, and saw the new light driving the shadows from his face.

'Perhaps. We may have become separated in the night. Not for long.'

He knew Allday was close by: he must be standing almost where his son had fallen that day.

He pushed the thought away. This was now. *Attacker* was on her proper station, or soon would be, once she had sighted the flagship. The other frigate, *Virtue*, carried thirty-six guns. Her captain was Roger M' Cullom, in character a little like Dampier, who had been *Zest*'s captain before Adam had taken command. Devil-may-care and popular, but inclined to be reckless. Whether to impress his men or for his own benefit, it was still a dangerous and, as Dampier had discovered, sometimes a fatal flaw.

Sam Hockenhull the boatswain had come aft to speak with the first lieutenant. Bolitho noticed that he was careful to avoid contact with Allday, who still blamed him for sending his son to join the afterguard on the day he had died. The quarterdeck and poop were always ripe targets for enemy sharp-shooters and the deadly swivel guns in close combat: command and authority began and were easily ended here. It was nobody's fault, and Hockenhull probably felt badly about it, although nothing had been said.

Bolitho sensed the restlessness among the waiting seamen. The leading edge of tension and apprehension had passed. They might be relieved later, when there was time to think on it. Now they would feel cheated that the sea was empty. As though they had been misled.

And here was the sun at last, giving a bronze edge to the horizon. Bolitho saw *Attacker*'s topsails for the first time, the faint touch of colour from her streaming masthead pendant.

Someone gasped with alarm as a muffled bang echoed across the sea's jagged whitecaps. One shot, the sound going on and on for seconds, as if in a mine or a long tunnel.

Tyacke was beside him immediately. 'Signal, Sir Richard. It's *Virtue*. She's sighted 'em!'

Bolitho said, 'Make more sail. Then as soon as. ...'

Carleton's voice came down from the masthead again. 'Deck there! Two sail in sight to the nor' east!'

There were more far-off shots, in earnest this time.

Tyacke's strong voice controlled the sudden uncertainty around him. 'Hands aloft, Mr Daubeny! Get the royals on her!' To York he called, 'Weather-helm, let her fall off two points!' He rubbed his hands. 'Now we'll see her fly, lads!'

More shots, sporadic but determined. Two ships, perhaps more. Tyacke was looking toward him again.

Bolitho said, 'When you are ready, Captain Tyacke.' Then he looked up as the royals thundered

176

from their yards, adding their power to the straining masts and rigging.

'Beat to quarters, Mr Daubeny! Then clear for action, if you please!'

Daubeny was staring at him. Reliving the past, trying to face the future.

The marine drummers were already below the poop, and at a signal from their sergeant they began to beat out the familiar rattle, the sounds soon lost in the answering rush of feet as idlers and off-watch hands divided into teams, each of which knew precisely what was expected of them. Bolitho stood quite still, aware of the order and purpose around him, gained by months of drills and exercises, and Tyacke's own forceful example.

The cabin beneath his feet would be stripped bare like the rest of the ship, screens torn down, all privacy gone, until the vessel was open from bow to stern. A ship of war.

'Cleared for action, sir!' Daubeny turned back to his captain.

Tyacke nodded. 'That was well done.' Then, formally, he touched his hat to his admiral. '*Virtue* is engaging without support, Sir Richard.'

Bolitho said nothing. M'Cullom was not the kind to wait. It would be ship to ship, evening old scores, a seizing of the initiative like any frigate captain. Carleton's voice came down like an intrusion.

'Third sail in sight, sir! There's smoke!'

Bolitho said, 'Go aloft, George. Discover what you can.'

Avery glanced at him even as he hurried to the shrouds. Afterwards, he was to recall the pain in his eyes, as if he already knew.

More gunfire, and Bolitho saw the smoke for the

177

first time, like a stain on the shark-blue water. He could feel the deck lifting and then shuddering down as *Indomitable* thrust her fourteen hundred tons into each oncoming roller. Even the yards appeared to be bending like giant bows, every sail full, each shroud and stay bar-taut under her great pyramid of sails.

'Load, sir?' Tyacke's eyes were everywhere, even aloft, where a man had almost lost his hold as he was securing one of the nets which had been spread to protect the gun crews from falling spars.

Bolitho glanced at the masthead pendant. Like an arrow. The enemy could not outpace this ship, nor did they have the time to beat back into the wind. M'Cullom must have seen all this, and set it against the risk. The odds.

'Yes. Load, but do not run out. *Virtue* has given us time. Let us use it!'

Avery called down suddenly, '*Virtue* has lost a topmast, sir! There are two frigates engaging her!' The rest was lost in an angry growl from the gun crews as they paused to peer up at the mainmast, their legs braced on the freshly sanded deck, their expressions shocked, but free of fear. This was different. *Virtue* was one of their own.

Bolitho looked away. *My men.*

More explosions, and then Avery returned to the quarterdeck.

'She can't hope to last much longer, sir.'

'I know.' He spoke sharply, angry with himself at the cost, which was already too high. 'Make to *Attacker, Close on the Flag.*' As Avery shouted for the signal party, he added, 'Then hoist *Close Action!*'

So easily said. He felt for the locket under his shirt. *May Fate always guide you.*

A tiny mark on this great ocean, he had said

to Allday.

He turned and started along the full length of the ship, past each unmoving gun crew, the lieutenants at the foot of each mast, then beyond the lion, with its upraised paws ready to strike.

The sea was cleaner, and a darker blue now, the sky empty of cloud in the first frail sunlight.

He gripped the sword at his side and tried to feel something, some emotion. No place now for any *perhaps* or *maybe*. Like all those other times, this was the moment. *Now*.

And there lay the enemy.

CHAPTER NINE

A FLAG CAPTAIN

Bolitho waited for the bows to rear across another broken roller, then raised the telescope to his eye. The sea was glinting in a million mirrors, the horizon hard and sharp like something solid.

He moved the glass very slowly until he had found the embattled ships, changing shape in a swirling pall of gunsmoke.

Avery said, '*Attacker*'s on station, sir.' He sounded unwilling to disturb Bolitho's concentration.

On station. It seemed only minutes since the signal had been acknowledged; perhaps everything had been frozen in time, with only the three distant ships a reality.

Virtue was still fighting hard, engaging the enemy on either beam, her broadsides regular and well timed despite the ripped and ragged sails, and the gaps in her rigging and spars which revealed the true measure of her damage.

Two big frigates. He could see the Stars and Stripes curling from the leader's gaff, the stabbing tongues of orange flame along her side as her battery fired, and fired again.

The nearest enemy ship was breaking off the action, her smoke rolling down across her adversary as if to swamp her, her sails flapping in disorder but without confusion, as she began to alter course. She was coming fully about. Bolitho searched his feelings: there was neither satisfaction nor even anxiety. To fight, not to run, to grasp what wind she could and use it.

Had she tried to break free and stand away, *Indomitable* would have outsailed her, and raked her at least twice before the other captain had been made to face an inevitable defeat.

What Adam would have done. He smiled faintly, bleakly. *What I would do.*

He called to one of the midshipmen. 'Over here, Mr Blisset!' He waited for the youth to join him, and then rested the telescope on his shoulder. He saw the midshipman grin and wink to one of his friends. *See me? I am helping the admiral!*

Bolitho forgot him and all those around him as he watched a tiny cluster of coloured flags break from the other frigate. She was still engaging the defiant *Virtue*, and the pockmarks in her own sails showed that it was not all going in the enemy's favour.

He rubbed his left eye with his sleeve, angry at the interruption. The signal was being acknowledged, so the engaging vessel was the senior of the two. Almost certainly the same captain who had bluffed *Reaper* into surrender and worse. Who had intended to go after the convoy as he had probably done with others. Had they been his guns, too, which had smashed the transport *Royal Herald* into oblivion? *The face in the crowd.*

Someone shouted, '*Virtue*'s mizzen is going!'

And Isaac York's angry retort. 'We can see that, Mr Essex!'

Bolitho trained the glass still further. He could feel the youth's shoulder quivering: excitement, fear, it could be both.

The frigate was almost bows-on, leaning over as her yards were hauled round to hold her on the opposite tack. So close now, five miles or thereabouts. She would soon be on a converging course. Tyacke must have anticipated it, had put himself in the other captain's place when he had ordered York to let *Indomitable* fall off two points. Either way, they would hold the wind-gage. It would be a swift, and possibly decisive, embrace.

The enemy frigate was trying to head further into the wind, but her flapping canvas filled again while she held her present course.

Bolitho heard Tyacke say, almost to himself, '*Got you!*'

'*Royal Marines, stand to!*' That was Merrick. A good officer, but one who had always been dominated by du Cann, who had been torn to bloody shreds by a swivel even as he had led his marines onto the American's deck. Was Merrick hearing his voice even now, as he ordered his men to their stations?

He moved the glass again, his lips dry as he saw *Virtue*'s blurred shape falling downwind, obviously out of command, her steering gone, her remaining sails whipping in the wind like ragged banners.

Tyacke again. 'Starboard battery, Mr Daubeny!

181

Open the ports!'

A whistle shrilled, and Bolitho imagined the portlids lifting like baleful eyes along their spray-dappled side.

'*Run out!*'

Bolitho lowered the glass and murmured a word of thanks to the midshipman. He saw Avery watching him, and said, 'The senior captain is holding off for the present.'

Tyacke joined him and exclaimed angrily, 'To let another do his work for him, the bastard!'

There was a puff of smoke from the approaching frigate, and seconds later a ball slapped down beyond *Indomitable*'s thrusting jib-boom. Bolitho said, 'You may shorten sail, Captain Tyacke.' He could have been speaking to a stranger.

Tyacke was shouting to his lieutenants, while high above the tilting deck the topmen were already kicking and fisting the wild canvas under control, yelling to one another as they had done so often during their endless drills and contests, mast against mast. Bolitho straightened his back. It was always the same: the big maincourse brailed up to lessen the risk of fire, but leaving the crouching gun crews and the barebacked seamen at the braces and halliards feeling exposed and vulnerable.

He stared at the drifting *Virtue*. If she survived this day, it would take months to repair and refit her. Many of her people would not see that, or any other day.

But her flag still flew, hoisted with pathetic jauntiness to an undamaged yard, and through the smoke he could see some of her seamen climbing on to the shattered gangways to cheer and gesture as *Indomitable* surged towards them.

Avery tore his eyes away from the other ship and looked toward Bolitho as he said, 'See? They can still cheer!' He pressed one hand to his eye, but Avery had seen the emotion and the pain.

Tyacke leaned on the rail as if to control his ship singlehanded.

'On the uproll, Mr Daubeny!' He drew his sword and lifted it, until the first lieutenant had turned towards him. 'When you are ready, Mr York!'

York raised a hand in acknowledgment. 'Helm a-lee! Hold her steady there!'

Responding to the quarter-wind, *Indomitable* turned slightly and without effort, her long jib-boom slicing above the other ships like a giant's lance.

'Steady she is, sir! Nor' by east!'

'*Fire!*'

Controlled, gun by gun, the broadside thundered out from bow to quarter, the sound so loud after the distant sea-fight that some of the seamen almost lost their grip on the braces as they hauled with all their strength to drag the yards round, to harness the wind. The oncoming frigate had been waiting, to draw closer, or to anticipate Tyacke's first move. By a second or an hour, it was already too late, even before it had begun.

Bolitho watched *Indomitable*'s double-shotted broadside smashing into the other ship, and imagined that he saw her stagger as if she had run aground. He saw great holes in the sails, the wind already exploring them and tearing them apart. Severed rigging and shrouds dangled over her side, and more than one gunport had been left empty, blinded, its cannon running free to cause more havoc inboard.

'*Stop your vents! Sponge out! Load! Run out!*'

183

Even as the enemy fired, the gun crews threw themselves into their work in a barely controlled frenzy.

Gun captains peered aft where Tyacke stood watching the other frigate. Perhaps he could exclude all else but the moment and his duty; he certainly did not seem to notice as one of the packed hammocks was torn apart by a jagged splinter a few yards from his body.

Bolitho felt the hull jerk as some of the other frigate's iron found its mark. The range was closing fast; he could even see men running to retrim the yards, and an officer waving his sword, before Tyacke's arm came down and the guns hurled themselves inboard on their tackles once more. Through the black shrouds and stays the American frigate looked as if she would run headlong into *Indomitable*'s side, but it was an illusion of battle, and the sea churned between the two ships was as bright as before.

Bolitho snatched up a glass and walked to the opposite side, expecting to see the senior American frigate running into the fight, with only the smaller *Attacker* standing in her way. He stared with disbelief as he realized that she had already gone about, and was making more sail even as he watched.

Avery said hoarsely, 'Not bluffing this time, sir!'

There was a wild cheer as the frigate's foremast began to fall. He imagined he could hear the terrible sounds of splintering wood and tearing rigging, although his ears were still deaf from the last broadside. So slow, so very slow. He even thought he could see the final hesitation before shrouds and stays snapped under the weight, and the whole mast, complete with yards, top and sails, thundered down alongside, dragging the vessel round like some giant sea-anchor.

He watched the range closing fast, the American frigate turning clumsily while some of her men ran to cut the mast adrift, their axes like bright stars in the smoky sunshine.

Daubeny called, 'All loaded, sir!'

Tyacke did not seem to hear. He was watching the other ship as she drifted helplessly to the thrust of wind and current.

The American officer was still waving his sword, and the huge Stars and Stripes streamed as proudly as before.

'*Strike, damn you*!' But Tyacke's voice held no anger or hatred; it was more a plea, one captain to another.

Two of the enemy's guns recoiled in their ports and Bolitho saw more packed hammocks blasted from their nettings, and seamen reeling from their weapons while one of their number was cut in half by a ball, his legs kneeling in grotesque independence.

Tyacke stared at Bolitho. Nothing was said. The sudden silence was almost more painful than the explosions.

Bolitho glanced at the enemy ship, and saw that some of her seamen who had been running seconds earlier to hack away the dragging wreckage had stopped as if stricken, unable to move. But here and there a musket flashed, and he knew that her invisible marksmen could not be cheated for much longer.

He nodded. 'As you bear!'

The sword fell, and in one shattering roar the starboard battery fired into the drifting smoke.

Daubeny yelled, '*Reload!*'

Stooping like old men, the gun crews sponged out

185

the hot guns and rammed home the fresh charges and shining black balls from the garlands. At one of the ports the men hauled their gun back, oblivious even to the sliced corpse and the blood that soaked their trousers like paint. A fight they could understand; even the pain and fear that kept it close company were part of it, something expected. But a drifting ship, unable to steer and with most of her guns either unmanned or out of action, was something different.

A lone voice shouted, 'Strike, you bloody bastard! Strike, for Jesus' sake!' Above the wind in the rigging, it sounded like a scream.

Tyacke said, 'So be it.' He dropped his sword and the guns exploded, the vivid tongues of flame appearing to reach and touch the target.

The smoke funnelled downwind, and men stood away from their guns, their eyes red-rimmed in smoke-grimed faces, sweat cutting stripes across their bodies.

Bolitho watched coldly. A ship which could not win, and which would not surrender. Where the working party had been gathered there was only splintered timber and a few corpses, tossed aside with brutal indifference. Men and pieces of men, and from her scuppers there were tiny threads of scarlet, as if the ship herself was bleeding to death. Daubeny had removed his hat, probably without knowing what he had done. But he stared aft again, his face like stone as he called, 'All loaded, sir!'

Tyacke turned toward the three figures by the weather rail: Bolitho, Avery close beside him, and Allday a few paces away, his naked cutlass resting on the deck.

One more broadside would finish her completely, with so much damage below deck that she might even burst into flames, deadly to any vessel that came near her. Fire was the greatest fear of every sailor, in both war and peace.

Bolitho felt the numbness. The ache. They were waiting. Justice; revenge; the completeness of defeat.

His was the final responsibility. When he looked for the other American ship, he could barely find her beyond the smoke. But waiting, watching to see what he would do. *Testing me again.*

'Very well, Captain Tyacke!' He knew that some of the seamen and marines were staring at him, with disbelief, perhaps even disgust. But the gun captains were responding, answering the only discipline they understood. The trigger-lines were pulled taut, each man staring across his muzzle, the helpless target filling every open port.

Tyacke raised his sword. Remembering that moment at the Nile when hell had burst into his life and had left its mark as a permanent reminder? Or seeing just another enemy, a fragment of a war which had outlived so many, friends and foes alike?

There was a sudden burst of shouting and Bolitho shaded his eyes to watch the solitary figure on the enemy's torn and bloodied quarterdeck. No sword this time, and one arm hanging broken, or even missing in the dangling sleeve.

Very deliberately and without even turning towards *Indomitable*, he tugged at the halliards, and almost fell as the big Stars and Stripes spiralled down into the smoke.

Avery said in a tight voice, 'He had no choice.'

Bolitho glanced at him. Like Tyacke, another memory? Of his own little schooner surrendering to the enemy, while he lay wounded and helpless?

He said, 'He had every choice. Men died for no

good purpose. Remember what I told you. *They* have no choice at all.'

He looked in Allday's direction. 'Bravely, old friend?'

Allday lifted the cutlass and balanced the blade on one hand.

'It gets harder, Sir Richard.' Then he grinned, and Bolitho thought that even the sunshine was dim by comparison. 'Aye, set bravely!'

Tyacke was watching the other vessel, the brief savagery of action already being crowded aside by the immediate needs of command.

'Boarding parties, Mr Daubeny! The marines will go across when the ship is secured! Pass the word for the surgeon and let me know the bill—we'll see the cost of this morning's show of courage!'

Indomitable was responding, the carpenter and his crew already below, hammers and squeaking tackles marking their progress through the lower hull.

Then Tyacke sheathed his sword, and saw the youngest midshipman observing him closely, although his eyes were still blurred with shock. Tyacke looked steadily back at him, giving himself time to consider what had so nearly happened.

He barely knew the midshipman, who had been sent out from England as a replacement for young Deane. His eyes moved unwillingly to one of the quarterdeck guns. Right there, as others had just fallen.

'Well, Mr Campbell, what did you learn from all this?'

The boy, who was only twelve years old, hesitated under Tyacke's gaze, unused as yet to the scars, and the man who bore them.

In a small voice he answered, 'We *won*, sir.'

Tyacke walked past him and touched his shoulder, something he did not often do. He was more surprised than the midshipman at the contact.

'*They lost*, Mr Campbell. It is not always the same thing!'

Bolitho was waiting for him. 'She's not much of a prize, James. But her loss will be felt elsewhere!'

Tyacke smiled. Bolitho did not wish to speak of it, either.

He said, 'No chance of a chase now, Sir Richard. We have others to care for.'

Bolitho stared at the dark blue water, and the other American frigate, which was already several miles clear.

'I can wait.' He tensed. Someone was crying out in agony as others attempted to move him. 'They did well.'

He saw Ozzard's small figure picking his way through the discarded tackles and rammers by the guns. So much a part of it, and yet able to distance himself from all the sights and sounds around him. He was carrying a bottle, wrapped in a surprisingly clean cloth.

Tyacke was still beside him, although aware of those on every hand who were demanding his attention.

'They're lucky, Sir Richard.'

Bolitho watched Ozzard preparing a clean goblet, oblivious to everything but the job in hand.

'Some may not agree, James.'

Tyacke said abruptly, '*Trust*, sir.' One word, but it seemed to hang there even as he walked away for the final act with a vanquished enemy.

Bolitho raised the goblet to his lips as the shadow of the enemy's topmast laid its patterns on the deck

189

beside him. He saw some of the bloodied seamen pause to watch him; a few grinned when they caught his eye, others merely stared, needing to recognize something. To remember, perhaps, or to tell somebody later, who might want to know about it. He found himself touching the locket beneath his shirt. She would understand what it meant to him. Just that one word, so simply put.

*   *   *

While the sun climbed higher in the clear sky to raise a misty haze on either horizon, *Indomitable's* company worked with scarcely a pause to cleanse their ship of the scars and stains of battle. The air was heady with rum, and it was hoped that a meal would be ready by noon. To the ordinary sailor, strong drink and a full belly were considered a cure for almost everything.

Below the sounds of repair and the disciplined activity, on *Indomitable's* orlop deck the contrast was stark. Beneath the ship's waterline, it was a hushed place that never saw daylight, nor would it until she was broken up. Through the ship's length it was a place for stores and spare timber, rigging and fresh water, and in the carefully guarded magazines, powder and shot. Here was the purser's store, with slop clothing and tobacco, food, and wine for the wardroom, and in the same darkness, broken here and there by clusters of lanterns, some of *Indomitable's* company, midshipmen and other junior warrant officers, lived, slept, and by the light of flickering glims studied and dreamed of promotion.

It was also a place where men were brought to

survive or to die, as their wounds and injuries dictated.

Bolitho ducked low between each massive deck beam and waited for his eyes to accept the harsh change from sunlight to this gloom, from the relief and high spirits of the victors, to the men down here who might not live to see the sun again.

Because of their opening broadsides and Tyacke's superior ship-handling at close quarters, *Indomitable's* casualties, her bill, had been mercifully light. He knew from long experience that that was no consolation to the unlucky ones down on the orlop. Some were lying, or propped against the great curved timbers of the hull, bandaged, or staring at the little group around the makeshift table where the surgeon and his assistants, the lob-lolly boys, worked on their patients: their victims, the old Jacks called them.

Bolitho could hear Allday's painful breathing, and did not know why he had chosen to accompany him. He must be grateful that his son had been spared this final indignity and despair.

They were holding a man down on the table, his nakedness still revealing the powder stains of battle, his face and neck sweating as he almost choked on the rum which was being poured down his throat before the leather strap was put between his teeth. The surgeon's apron was dark with blood. No wonder they called them butchers.

But Philip Beauclerk was not typical of the uncaring, hardened surgeons who were usually found throughout the fleet. He was young and highly skilled, and had volunteered with a group of other surgeons to serve in ships of war, where it was known that conditions and the crude treatment of wounds often killed more men than the enemy. After his present commission Beauclerk would return to the College of Surgeons in London, where, with his colleagues, he would contribute his knowledge to a practical guide, which might help to ease the suffering of men like these.

Beauclerk had done well during the fight with the U.S.S. *Unity*, and had offered great support to Adam Bolitho when he had been brought aboard after his escape from prison. He had a composed and serious face, and the palest and steadiest eyes Bolitho had ever seen. He recalled the moment when Beauclerk had mentioned his finest tutor, Sir Piers Blachford, who had been researching the same conditions himself aboard *Hyperion*. Bolitho saw him even now, his tall, heron-like figure striding between decks, asking questions, talking to anyone he chose, a severe man, but possessing great qualities of courage and compassion, which had made even the hardest seamen respect him. Blachford had been in *Hyperion* to her last day, when she had finally given up the fight and gone down, with Bolitho's flag still flying. Many had gone down with her: they could be in no better company. And they still sang about his old ship, *How Hyperion Cleared the Way*. It always brought a cheer in the taverns and the pleasure gardens, even though those who cheered her name rarely had any idea what it was like. What *this* was like.

For a few seconds Beauclerk looked up, his eyes like chips of glass in the light of the swinging lanterns. He was a very private man, no easy thing to achieve in a crowded warship. He had known for some time of Bolitho's damaged eye, and that it had been Blachford who had told him that there was no hope for it. But he had said nothing.

The wounded seaman was quieter now,

192

whimpering to himself, not seeing the knife in Beauclerk's hand, the saw held ready by an assistant.

'You are welcome here, Sir Richard.' He watched him, assessing him. 'We are nearly done.' Then, as the seaman twisted his face toward the admiral, he gave a brief shake of his head.

Bolitho was deeply moved, and wondered if this was why he had come. This man might die: at best, he would be one more cripple thrown on the beach. His leg had been crushed, no doubt by a recoiling gun.

Tyacke's words still haunted him, from that September day when so many others had fallen. *And for what?* An enemy frigate taken, but so badly damaged that it was unlikely she would survive a sudden squall, let alone fight in the line. *Virtue* had also been severely mauled, and had lost twenty of her men. Surprisingly, her captain, the devil-may-care M' Cullom, had survived without a scratch. This time.

Indomitable had lost only four men killed, and some fifteen wounded. Bolitho moved to the table and took the man's wrist, the surgeon's mate stepping aside, staring at Beauclerk as if for an explanation.

Bolitho closed his fingers around the man's thick wrist, and said gently, 'Easy, now.' He glanced at Beauclerk and saw his lips form the name. 'You did well, Parker.' He raised his voice very slightly and looked beyond, into the shadows, knowing that others were listening to his empty words. 'And that applies to you all!'

He felt the wrist start to shake. It was not a movement, but a mere sensation, like something running through him, out of control. It was terror.

Beauclerk nodded to his assistants and they seized

193

the leg, their eyes averted as the knife came down and cut deeply. Beauclerk showed no hesitation, no outward emotion, as his patient arched his back and tried to scream through the strap. Then the saw. It seemed endless, but Bolitho knew only a matter of seconds had passed. It was followed by a sickening thud as they dropped the leg into the 'wings and limbs' tub. Now the needle, the fingers bright and bloody in the swaying lantern light. Beauclerk glanced at Bolitho's hand on the man's wrist, the admiral's gold lace against the smoke-grimed skin.

Somebody murmured, 'No good, sir. Lost him.'

Beauclerk stood back. 'Take him.' He turned to watch as the dead seaman was dragged from the table. 'It's never easy.'

Bolitho heard Allday clearing his throat. Seeing it all again, as if it were his own son, floating away, eventually sinking into the depths. *And for what?*

He stared at the table, the pools of blood, the urine, the evidence of pain. There was no dignity here in death, no answer to the question.

He walked back toward the ladder and heard Beauclerk ask, 'Why did he come?' and did not linger to hear the reply. Beauclerk saw the instant guard in Allday's eyes and added, quite gently, 'You know him better than any man. I should like to understand.'

''Cause he blames himself.' He recalled his own words when the American flag had come down. 'It gets harder, see?'

'Yes. I think I do.' He wiped his bloody hands. 'Thank you.' He frowned as two of the injured men raised a hoarse cheer. 'That will not help him, either.' But Allday had gone.

When he returned to London it would all be so
194

different. His experience might help others one day: it would certainly assist him in his chosen career. He looked around, recalling the admiral's austere face after that other battle, as it must have been after all those which had preceded it. And the day his nephew had been brought aboard. More like two brothers, he thought. Like love.

He smiled, knowing that if they saw it, his assistants might think him callous. London or not, nothing would ever be the same.

* * *

The captain's quarters in *Indomitable* were no longer as spacious as they had been during her life as a two-decker, but after his previous command of the brig *Larne* James Tyacke still found them palatial. Although cleared for action like the rest of the ship, they had remained undamaged by the swift bombardment, as they were on the larboard and disengaged side.

Bolitho sat in the proffered chair and listened to the muffled thuds and dragging sounds from his own stern cabin, as screens were replaced and the smoke stains were washed away, until the next time.

Tyacke said, 'We got off very lightly, Sir Richard.'

Bolitho took a glass of cognac from Tyacke's coxswain, Fairbrother. He looked after his captain without fuss or fancy, and seemed a man pleased with his role, and the fact that his captain called him by his first name, Eli.

He gazed around the cabin; it was neat but spartan, with nothing to reveal any hint of the character of the man who lived and slept here. Only the big sea-chest was familiar, and he knew it was the

195

one in which Tyacke used to carry the silk gown he had bought for the girl he intended to marry. She had refused him after his terrible injury at the Nile. How long he had carried the gown was unknown, but he had given it to Catherine to wear when he had found them after their ordeal in *Golden Plover*'s longboat. Bolitho knew she had sent it back to Tyacke when they had reached England, beautifully cleaned and pressed, in case there should be another woman in the future. It was probably in the chest at this moment, a reminder of the rejection he had suffered.

Tyacke said, 'I've made a full report. The prize is nothing much.' He paused. 'Not after we'd finished with her. She had over fifty killed, and twice as many wounded. She was carrying a lot of extra hands, for prize crews, no doubt. If they'd managed to board us...' He shrugged. 'A different story, maybe.'

He studied Bolitho curiously, having heard about his visit to the orlop and that he had restrained one of the badly wounded as the surgeon had taken off his leg. He thought with a mental shudder of Beauclerk's pale eyes. A cold fish, like the rest of his breed.

Bolitho said, 'She was the U.S.S. *Success*, formerly the French *Dryade*.' He looked up at Tyacke, and felt his scrutiny like something physical. 'Her captain was killed.'

'Aye. It was like a slaughterhouse. Our gun captains have learned well.' There was the pride again, which even the horror he had described could not diminish.

He held his goblet to the light and said, 'When I became your flag captain, it was an even greater challenge than I had expected.' He gave his faint, attractive smile. 'And I knew I was going into deep water from the start. It wasn't just the size of the ship,

196

and my responsibility to all her people, but also my role within the squadron. I had been so used to a small command—a seclusion which, looking back, I know I myself created. And then, under your flag, there were the other ships, and the whims and weaknesses of their captains.'

Bolitho said nothing. It was one of those rare moments of confidence, something he did not wish to interrupt, a mutual trust which had made itself felt between them from the very beginning, when they had first met in Tyacke's schooner *Miranda*.

Tyacke said abruptly, 'I started keeping my own log book. I discovered that a flag captain should never rely on memory alone. And when your nephew was brought aboard wounded, after his escape from that Yankee prison, I made notes on everything he told me.' He glanced at a sealed gunport as if he could see the American prize riding under *Indomitable's* lee. Victors and vanquished were working together aboard her to fit a jury rig, which, with luck and fair sailing, might take her to Halifax.

'There was a lieutenant aboard the *Success*. A young man, so badly hurt by splinters that I wondered what was keeping him alive.' He cleared his throat, as if embarrassed by the emotion his voice revealed. 'I talked with him for a while. He was in great pain. There was nothing anyone could do.'

Bolitho saw it with a poignant clarity, as if he had been there with them. This strong, remote man sitting with an enemy, perhaps the only one truly able to share his suffering.

'In some ways he reminded me of your nephew, sir. I thought it was the battle, being beaten, knowing he was paying with his life. But it wasn't that. He simply could not believe that their other ship had cut and

197

run—had left them to fight alone.'

There were whispering voices outside the door, officers needing advice or instructions. Tyacke would know of their presence, but nothing would move him until he was ready.

He said, 'The lieutenant's name was Brice, Mark Brice. He had prepared a letter to be dispatched should the worst happen.' He was momentarily bitter. 'I've warned others about that kind of maudlin sentiment. It's ... it's asking for death.'

'Brice?' Bolitho felt a chill of recognition run through him, as though he were hearing Adam's own voice as he had described it to him. 'It was a Captain Joseph Brice who invited Adam to change sides when he was captured.'

Tyacke said, 'Yes. He was that captain's son. An address in Salem.'

'And the letter?'

'The usual, sir. Duty and love of country, not a lot of value when you're dead.' He picked up a small book from the table. 'Still, I'm glad I wrote it down.'

'And the other ship, James? Is that what's troubling you?'

Tyacke shrugged heavily. 'Well, I learned quite a bit from them. She's the U.S.S. *Retribution*, another ex-Frenchman, *Le Gladiateur*. Forty guns, maybe more.' Then he said, 'There's no doubt in my mind that these were the ships that took *Reaper*.' He glared at the door. 'I shall have to go, sir. Please make use of these quarters until yours are ready.'

He hesitated by the door, as though grappling with something. 'You were once a flag captain yourself, sir?'

Bolitho smiled. 'Yes. A very long time ago, in a three-decker. *Euryalus*, one hundred guns. I learned a

198

great deal in her.' He waited, knowing there was more.

Tyacke said, 'The American lieutenant had heard about it. Your time in *Euryalus*, I mean.'

'But that was all of seventeen years ago, James. This lieutenant, Brice, would hardly have been old enough....'

Tyacke said bluntly, '*Retribution*'s captain told him. About you, about *Euryalus*. But he died before he could tell me anything more.'

He opened the door a few inches. 'Wait!' There were a few murmurings from beyond, and then he added sharply, 'Well, do it, or I'll find somebody else better suited.' He turned toward Bolitho again. '*Retribution*'s captain is named Aherne.' He hesitated. 'That's all I know.'

Bolitho was on his feet, without realizing that he had left the chair. The big three-decker *Euryalus* had seemed the final step to flag rank, and he had carried even more responsibility than was usual for a flag captain. His admiral, Rear-Admiral Sir Charles Thelwall, had been old for his rank; he was dying, and he knew it. But England was facing heavy odds, with France and Spain confident of an early invasion. It had been in *Euryalus* that he had first met Catherine...

Tyacke's coxswain held out the bottle. 'Another, Sir Richard?'

Bolitho saw Tyacke's unconcealed surprise when he accepted. He said slowly, 'Dangerous times, James.' He was thinking aloud. 'We were ordered to Ireland. A French squadron was reported ready to support an uprising. Had it come about, the balance might have shifted against England there and then. There was even worse to follow ... the great mutinies
199

in the fleet at the Nore and Spithead. Dangerous times, indeed.'

'And Ireland, sir?'

'There were a few battles. I think the strain of the responsibility finally killed Sir Charles Thelwall. A fine man, a gentle man. I much admired him.' He faced Tyacke, his eyes suddenly hard. 'And of course there was the inevitable aftermath of recrimination and punishment meted out to those who had conspired against the King. It proved nothing, it solved nothing. One of those hanged for treason was a patriot called Daniel Aherne, the scapegoat who became a martyr.' He picked up his glass, and found that it was empty. 'So, James, we have found the missing face: Rory Aherne. I knew he had gone to America, but that is all I know. Seventeen years. A long time to nurture hatred.'

Tyacke said, 'How can we be sure?'

'I am certain, James. Coincidence, fate, who knows?' He smiled briefly. '*Retribution*, eh? A good choice.'

He thought suddenly of Catherine's words to him, when they had first been thrown together. *Men are made for war, and you are no exception.*

That was then, but can we ever change?

Aloud he said, 'Call me when we get under way, James. And thank you.'

Tyacke paused. 'Sir?'

'For being a flag captain, James. That, and so much more.'

200

CHAPTER TEN

TIME AND DISTANCE

Sir Wilfred Lafargue put down the empty cup and walked to one of the tall windows of his spacious office. For such a heavily-built man he moved with remarkable agility, as if the young, eager lawyer was still there, a prisoner of his own success. Lafargue had once been described as handsome, but now, in his late fifties, he was showing signs of good living and other excesses which even his expensively cut coat and breeches could not disguise.

The coffee was good: eventually, he might send for more. But he was content for the moment to stand looking out of this window, one of his favourites, across the City of London, where, despite more buildings than ever before, there were still many restful parks and ornamental gardens. This was Lincoln's Inn, one of the centres of English law, and the prestigious address of many legal practices which served a world of both power and money.

This particular house, for instance, had once been the London residence of a famous general, who had met an ignominious death by fever in the West Indies. Now it held the offices of the legal firm which bore his family name, and of which Lafargue was the senior partner.

He idly watched some carriages as they rattled past on their way to Fleet Street. It was a fine day, with clear blue sky above the spires and impressive buildings. From the far window he would be able to see St Paul's, or at least the dome of the cathedral; it

201

was a sight that always pleased him. Like the centre of things, in his world.

He considered the visitor who was waiting to see him. His staff had been busy on her behalf, but this would be his first meeting with the lady in question, Lady Catherine Somervell. When he had mentioned the appointment to his wife she had been sharp, even angry, as if it offended her personally in some way.

He smiled. But then, how could she understand?

Now he would see for himself what the notorious viscountess was really like. She was certainly one of the most discussed women of the day: if only a tenth of it was true, he would soon discover her strength and her weakness. She had risen above it all, the scandal and the secret slander. The fact that her last husband had died mysteriously in a duel had been conveniently forgotten. He smiled more broadly. *Not by me.*

He turned with irritation as a door opened slightly, and his senior clerk peered in at him.

'What is it, Spicer?' The offices revolved around the senior clerk, a dedicated man who missed no detail in all the legal papers and documents that passed through his hands. He was also very dull.

Spicer said, 'Lady Somervell is about to leave, Sir Wilfred.' He spoke without expression. When the Prime Minister, Spencer Perceval, had been assassinated by some lunatic at the House of Commons the previous year, he had announced it in much the same fashion, as if it was a comment on the weather.

Lafargue snapped, 'What do you mean, leaving? That lady has an appointment with me!'

Spicer was unmoved. 'That was nearly half an hour ago, Sir Wilfred.'

202

Lafargue contained himself with an effort. It was his practice to keep clients waiting, no matter how high or low they stood on the social scale.

It was a bad beginning. He said curtly, 'Bring her in.'

He sat at his vast desk and watched the other door. Everything was in its place, a chair directly opposite him, an impressive background of leather volumes from floor to ceiling behind. Sound, reliable, like the City itself. Like a bank.

He rose slowly as the doors were opened and Lady Catherine Somervell entered the room. It was far too large for an office but Lafargue liked it for that reason: it often intimidated visitors who had to walk almost its full length to reach the chair by the desk.

For the first time in his experience, the effect was completely reversed.

She was taller than he had expected, and walked without hesitation or uncertainty, her dark eyes never leaving his face. She was dressed all in green, and carrying a broad-brimmed straw hat with a matching ribbon. Lafargue was intelligent enough to appreciate that his clumsy ploy of allowing her to wait could never impress a woman like this.

'Please be seated, Lady Somervell.' He watched the easy way she sat in the straight-backed chair, confident, but wary. Defiant, perhaps. 'I regret the delay. Some difficulty arose at the last minute.'

Her dark eyes moved only briefly to the empty coffee cup.

'Of course.'

Lafargue sat down again and touched some papers on his desk. It was hard not to stare at her. She was beautiful: there was no other possible description. Her hair, so dark that it might have been black, was

203

piled above her ears, so that her throat and neck seemed strangely unprotected. Provocative. High cheekbones, and now the merest hint of a smile as she said, 'So what news may I expect?'

Catherine had seen the assessing glance. She had seen many such before. This illustrious lawyer, recommended by Sillitoe when she had asked for his advice, was no different, in spite of the grand setting and the air of showmanship. Sillitoe had remarked, 'Like most lawyers, his worth and his honesty will be measured by the weight of his bill!'

Lafargue said, 'You have seen all the details of your late husband's affairs.' He coughed politely. 'Your pardon. Your previous husband, I mean. His business ventures prospered even during the war between Great Britain and Spain. It was his surviving son's wish that you receive that which was always intended for your own use.' His eyes flicked down to the papers. 'Claudio Luis Pareja was his son by his first marriage.'

She said, 'Yes.' She ignored the unspoken question: he would know, in any case. When Luis had asked her to marry him he had been more than twice her age, and even his son, Claudio, had been older than she. She had been afraid, desperate, lost, when the small, amiable Luis had taken her as his bride. It had not been love as she now knew it to be, but the man's kindness, his need of her, had been like a door opening for her to step through. She had been a mere girl, and he had given her vision and opportunity, and she had learned the manners and graces of the people he knew or did business with.

He had died when Richard Bolitho's ship had taken control of the vessel in which they had been passengers, on their way to Luis's estate in Minorca.

She had known afterwards that she loved Richard, but she had lost him. Until Antigua, when he had sailed into English Harbour with his flag flying above the old *Hyperion*.

She could feel the lawyer's eyes exploring her, although when she looked at him directly he was examining his papers again.

She said, 'So I am a very rich woman?'

'At the stroke of a pen, my lady.' He was intrigued that she had shown neither surprise nor triumph, not since they had first exchanged letters. A beautiful widow, envied, wealthy: the temptation would be a great one for many men. He thought of Sir Richard Bolitho, the hero, whom even common sailors seemed to admire. He glanced at her again. Her skin was brown like a country woman's, like her hands and wrists. He speculated on their life together when they were not separated by the ocean, and the war.

The thought made him remark, 'I have heard that things are moving at last in North America.'

'What is that?' She stared at him, one hand moving to her breast. How quickly it could happen. Like a shadow, a threat.

He said, 'We received word that the Americans attacked York, crossed the lake in force and burned the government buildings there.'

'When?' One word, like a stone falling into a still pond.

'Oh, some six weeks ago, apparently. News is very slow to reach us.'

She stared at the window, at the fresh leaves visible beyond it. Six weeks. The end of April. Richard might have been there: he would be involved, in any case. She asked quietly, 'Anything else?'

He cleared his throat. Her unexpected anxiety had

encouraged him: perhaps she was vulnerable after all.

'Some story of a mutiny in one of our ships. Poor devils, one can hardly blame them.' He paused. 'But there are limits, and we *are* at war.'

'What ship?' She knew he was enjoying her concern in some way. It did not matter. Nothing else did. Not the money, unexpected gift though it was from poor Luis, dead these many years. She asked more sharply, 'Can you remember?'

He pursed his lips. '*Reaper.* Yes, that was it. Do you know her?'

'One of Sir Richard's squadron. Her captain was killed last year. I do not know her, beyond that.' How could he understand? Mutiny ... She had watched Richard's face when he had described it, and what it cost the guilty and the innocent alike. He had been involved in the great naval mutinies, which had stunned the entire country at a time when the enemy was expected to invade. Some had believed it was the first fire of the same revolution which had brought the Terror to France.

How Richard would hate and loathe such an outbreak in his own command. Would blame himself for not having been there when the seeds were sown.

A total responsibility. And a punishment to him, also.

Lafargue said, 'Now, the other matter we discussed. The lease of the property has become available.' He watched her hand at her breast, the glittering pendant moving to betray the heightened pulse. 'The owner of the lease, an earl impoverished by bad luck or over-confidence at the tables, was more than willing to exchange deeds. Expensive property, madam. And occupied.'

He knew; of course he knew. She said, 'By Lady

Bolitho.' She glanced down at the ruby ring on her hand, which he had given her in the church at Zennor on the day Valentine Keen had married Zenoria. It wrenched at her heart. They would all be waiting for her in Falmouth: the admiral's lady, or whore, as the mood dictated. 'It was my decision. I intend to lower the cost of the lease.' She looked up suddenly, and Lafargue saw the other woman in her eyes, the woman who had braved the sea in an open boat after shipwreck, who had captured the hearts of all who knew her. Now, in her face, he could see that everything he had heard of her was true.

She added, 'And I intend that she shall know it!'

Lafargue rang a small bell, and his senior clerk, with one other, appeared as if by magic.

He stood up and watched Spicer preparing the documents, a fresh pen already placed by her hand. He looked at the ring, assessing the cost: it was of rubies and diamonds, like the pendant she wore, which was in the shape of a fan. He thought of his wife and wondered how, or even if, he would describe his day to her.

Spicer said, 'Here and here, my lady.'

She signed her name quickly, recalling the small, untidy lawyer's office in Truro, which had handled the Bolitho affairs for generations. Chairs filled with files and dog-eared documents, far too dusty to ever have been used. Not surprisingly, it had been the portly Yovell who had guided her there when she had told him what she had heard from Seville. From Spain, where she had left childhood behind.

Untidy, yes, but she had been received there as if she had always belonged. As John Allday would have described it, *one of the family*.

Lafargue said, 'We are accustomed to such

transactions, my lady. A head so beautiful should never be troubled by affairs of business.'

She looked up at him, and smiled. 'Thank you, Sir Wilfred. I value your skills as a lawyer. Flattery I can have at any time from a Billingsgate porter!'

She stood, and waited while Lafargue took her hand, and after a small hesitation held it to his lips.

'It has been an honour, my lady.'

She nodded to the two clerks, and saw the smile on the impassive features of the one named Spicer. It was a day he would remember, for whatever reasons of his own.

Lafargue made a last attempt. 'I noticed that you arrived in Lord Sillitoe's carriage, my lady...' He almost flinched as the dark eyes turned toward him.

'How observant of you, Sir Wilfred.'

He walked beside her to the double doors. 'An influential man.'

She regarded herself in a tall mirror in passing. Her next visit was to the Admiralty, and she wondered if Bethune would eventually tell her about the attack on York and the mutiny.

'With respect, my lady, I think that even Lord Sillitoe would regard you as a challenge.'

She faced the lawyer again, her heart suddenly heavy. Wanting not to be alone: wanting Bolitho, needing him.

'I have found that a challenge can so easily become an obstacle, Sir Wilfred. One which may need to be removed. Wouldn't you agree?'

Back at his favourite window, Sir Wilfred Lafargue saw the liveried coachman hurry to open the carriage door for her. One of Sillitoe's hard men, he thought, more like a prize-fighter than a servant. He saw her pause to watch a clutter of sparrows drinking from a horse-trough's overflow. Distance hid her expression, but he knew she did not see or care for the passers-by who glanced at her.

He tried to arrange his impressions rationally, as he might marshal facts and arguments in a law suit, or with an opposing brief. But all he could find was envy.

*   *   *

The Old Hyperion inn at Fallowfield was crowded on this warm June evening, mostly with workers from the surrounding farms, enjoying the companionship of their friends after a long day in the fields. Some sat outside at the scrubbed trestle tables, and the air was so still that the smoke from their long pipes hung in an unmoving canopy. Even the banks of tall foxgloves barely quivered, and beyond the darkening trees the Helford River gleamed in the fading light like polished pewter.

Inside the inn every door and window stood open, but the older customers, as was their habit year round, gathered by the great fireplace, although it was empty but for a tub of flowers.

Unis Allday glanced from her parlour door and was satisfied with what she saw. Familiar faces, thatchers from Fallowfield, and the carpenter and his mate who were still working on the local church, where she and John Allday had been married. She repressed a sigh, and turned to the cot where their child, little Kate, lay sleeping. She touched the cot: another reminder of the big, shambling sailor who was so far away. He had even made the cot with his own hands.

She heard her brother, another John, laughing at

209

something as he drew and carried tankards of ale. A one-legged former soldier of the 31st Foot, he lived in a tiny cottage nearby. Without his company and support, she did not know how she would have managed. She had had no letter from Allday. Over four months had passed since he had walked through that door to take passage to Canada, with the admiral he served and loved like no other. Lady Catherine would be feeling much the same loneliness, she thought, with her own man on the other side of the ocean, even though she had travelled far and wide herself. Unis smiled. She had never been further than her native Devon before coming to live in Cornwall, and although she had settled in well, she knew that to the local people she would always be a foreigner. She had been attacked on the coast road on her way here, by men who had attempted to rob and assault her. John Allday had saved her that day. She could even talk about it now, but not to many. She touched some flowers on the table. The stillness, the warm, unmoving air was making her restless. If only he was back. She tested the idea. For good and always. . . .

She looked once more at the sleeping child, and then walked out to join her brother.

He said, 'Good business today, love. Picking up.' He watched an unwavering candleflame. 'There'll be a few ships' masters cursing and swearing if they have to lie becalmed all night in Falmouth Bay. It'll mean they'll have to pay another day's wages!'

She said, 'What about the war, John? Out there, I mean.'

He said, 'Soon be over, I expect. Once the Iron Duke forces the French to surrender, the Yankees'll lose the stomach for a war on their own.'

'You do think that?' She remembered John

210

Allday's face when he had finally told her about his son, and how he had died in the fight with the Americans. Was it only last year? When he had come home and had taken their child, so tiny in his big hands, and she had told him she would not be able to carry another, would never give him another son.

His reply was still stark in her mind. *She'll do me fine. A son can break your heart.* She had guessed then, but had said nothing until he was ready to tell her.

'Someone's on the road.' He looked toward the window, and was not aware of the sudden fear in her eyes.

She heard the sound of a single horse, and saw the men around the empty grate pause in their conversation to stare at the open door. A horse usually meant authority out this way, so close to Rosemullion Head. The coastguard, or revenue men, or some of the dragoons from Truro, searching for deserters or hunting down footpads.

The horse clattered across the cobbles and they heard someone hurrying to assist the rider. Her brother said, 'That's Lady Catherine. I'd know her big mare anywhere.'

He smiled as his sister straightened her apron and her hair, as she always did.

'I'd heard she was back from London. Luke said he saw her.'

She came through the door, her dark hair almost touching the low beam. She seemed startled that there were so many customers, as if she were hardly aware of the time of day.

Some of the men stood up, or shuffled as though they would make the effort, and one or two voices called, ''Evenin' to 'ee, m'lady.'

211

She held out her hand. 'Please sit down. I am sorry....'

Unis reached her, and guided her to the small parlour. 'You shouldn't be out alone on this road, m' lady. 'Twill be dark soon. 'Tisn't safe these days.'

Catherine sat and pulled off her gloves. 'Tamara knows the way. I am always safe.' She took Unis's hand impulsively. 'I needed to come. To be with a friend. And you are that, Unis.'

Unis nodded, shocked by the quiet desperation in her voice. It did not seem possible. The admiral's lady, a woman of courage as well as beauty, accepted even here where scandal, like sin, could be condemned openly every Sunday in church and chapel....

'None stronger, m' lady.'

Catherine stood, and crossed to the cot. 'Young Kate,' she said, and reached down to adjust the covering. Unis watched, and was oddly moved.

'Shall I make some tea, or maybe coffee? An' I'll see that someone rides with you when you go back to Falmouth. Five miles can be a long way on your own.'

Catherine barely heard her. She had rested very little since her return from London. There had been no letter waiting from Richard: anything might be happening. She had ridden to the adjoining estate to visit his sister, Nancy, and found Lewis Roxby very ill. Despite the stroke he had suffered, he had taken little heed of his doctors' warnings. Without his hunting and his entertaining, and his hectic life as landowner, magistrate and squire, he could neither see nor accept any future as an invalid. Nancy had known: she had seen it in her eyes. Lewis was not merely ill this time; he was dying.

Catherine had sat with him, holding his hand while he had lain propped up in his bed, his head high enough for him to see the trees, and his stone folly, which was almost completed. His face had been grey, his grip without strength. But from time to time he had turned his head to look at her, as if to reassure her that the old Lewis Roxby was still there.

She had told him about London, but had not mentioned the unexpected settlement with which Luis's estate had endowed her. Nor had she told him about her visit to Richard's town house. The lawyer, Lafargue, had sent word to Belinda of her intended arrival, but her visiting card had been returned at the door, torn in two halves. But Belinda knew now that the house where she lavishly entertained, and lived in a style to which she had been unaccustomed before her marriage, was the property of the woman she hated. It would change nothing between them, but it might prevent her asking for more money. She would never admit to her circle of friends that she was living in a house owned by the one she had openly called a prostitute.

She heard herself say, 'Something a little stronger, Unis. Some brandy, if you have any.'

Unis hurried to a cupboard. Was it possible, that there was no one else she could turn to now that Sir Richard was away? Perhaps Bryan Ferguson and his wife at the big grey house were too close, painful reminders of those others who were absent: Bolitho's 'little crew', as she had heard John call them.

Catherine took the glass, wondering where the brandy had come from. Truro, or run ashore along this rocky and treacherous coast by freetraders in the dark of the moon?

Beyond the door, the conversation and laughter

213

had resumed. It was something to relate to their wives when they finally reached their own homes.

Unis said gently, 'When ... I mean ... if Sir Lewis gives up the fight ... what will become of all that he's worked for? Just the son of a local farmer, they tells me, and now look at him. A friend of the Prince himself, owner of all that land—will his son not take over?'

Now look at him. A grey, tired face. Every breath an effort.

'I believe that his son is making a name for himself in the City of London. Lewis wanted it. He was so proud of him, and of his daughter. There will be many changes, no matter what happens.'

She sat for some time in silence, thinking of the visit to the Admiralty, which had been her final task in London. Bethune had greeted her warmly, professing surprise at her arrival, and had offered to take her to a reception somewhere, and introduce her to some of his particular friends. She had declined. Even as she had sat in that familiar office, watching him, listening to him, she had sensed his genuine interest in her, the undeniable charm which might lead him into serious trouble if he became careless or over-confident in his affairs. He had been unable to give her any information about the war in North America, although she had suspected that he knew more than he was saying. On her last night in Chelsea she had lain awake on the bed, almost naked in the bright moonlight across the Thames, and had considered what might have happened if she had pleaded with Bethune to use all his influence, and his obvious affection and admiration for Richard, to enable him to be brought back to England. She had had little doubt what the price would have been. She

214

had felt the sudden tears scalding her eyes. Could she have gone through with it? Given herself to another, whom instinct told her would have been kindness itself? She knew she could not have done it. There were no secrets between herself and Richard, so how could she have pretended with the man she loved?

To think that she could even consider such a bargain disgusted her. They called her a whore. Perhaps they were right.

Nor had she been able to tell Lewis what had happened after she had left Belinda's house. In the square, she had seen the child walking with her governess. If the place had been crowded with a hundred children, she would still have known it was Elizabeth, Richard's daughter. The same chestnut hair as her mother, the poise and confidence, so assured for one so young. She was eleven years old, and yet a woman.

'May I speak with you?' She had immediately sensed the governess's hostility, but she had been totally unprepared when Elizabeth had turned to look up at her. That had been the greatest shock of all. Her eyes were Richard's.

She had said calmly, 'I am sorry. I do not know you, ma'am.' She had turned away, and walked on ahead of her companion.

What could I have expected? Hoped for? But all she could think of was the child's eyes. Her contempt.

She stood up, listening. 'I must leave. My horse....'

Unis saw her brother in the doorway. 'What is it, John?'

But he was looking at the beautiful woman, her long riding habit torn in places where she had ridden carelessly, too close to the hedgerows.

215

'The church. The bell's tolling.' Then, as though making a decision, 'I can't allow you to ride at this hour, m' lady.'

She appeared not to hear him. 'I must go. I promised Nancy.'

She walked to the open window, and listened. The bell. An end of something. The beginning of what?

John had returned. 'One of the keepers is here, m' lady. He'll ride with you.' He hesitated, and looked at his sister as if appealing to her. 'Please. Sir Richard would insist, if he were here.'

She held out her hands to them. '*I know.*'

Some envied her, others hated her, and one at least feared her after her visit to the lawyer. She must not give way now. *But without him I am nothing, have nothing.*

She said, 'I needed to be with friends, you see. *Needed* to be.'

Tamara was already outside the door, eager to leave.

Sir Lewis Roxby, Knight of the Hanoverian Guelphic Order and friend of the Prince Regent, was dead. She remembered his many bluff kindnesses, and particularly the day when, together, they had found Zenoria Keen's body.

The King of Cornwall. So would he always remain.

CHAPTER ELEVEN

A WARNING

Richard Bolitho and Rear-Admiral Valentine Keen stood side by side and stared out across the crowded anchorage of Halifax harbour.

The sun was strong, the air warmer than for a long time, and after the restricted confines of a frigate, even one as large as *Indomitable*, Bolitho was very conscious of the land, and the peculiar feeling that he did not belong here. The house was the headquarters of the general officer commanding the garrisons and defence of Nova Scotia, and below the wooden verandah soldiers were marching back and forth, drilling in platoons, front ranks kneeling to take aim at an imaginary enemy while the second ranks prepared to march through them and repeat the process: manoeuvres the army had perfected over the years, which had eventually turned the tables on Napoleon.

But Bolitho was looking at the anchored frigate directly opposite. Even without a telescope, he could see the damage and the piles of broken timber and rigging on her decks. She still flew the Stars and Stripes, but the White Ensign was hoisted above it as a symbol of victory. She was the U.S.S. *Chesapeake*, which had been brought to action by His Britannic Majesty's ship *Shannon*. The fight had been brief but decisive, and both captains had been wounded, the American mortally.

Keen said, 'A welcome victory. *Shannon* towed her prize into Halifax on the sixth. Couldn't have happened at a better time, with all our other setbacks.'

Bolitho had already heard something of the engagement. *Shannon's* captain, Philip Bowes Vere Broke, was both experienced and successful, and had been cruising up and down outside Boston, where *Chesapeake* lay at anchor. It was rumoured that he had been grieving over the loss of so many of his

217

contemporaries to the superior American frigates. He had sent a challenge into Boston in the best tradition of chivalry, requesting that Captain Lawrence of the *Chesapeake* should come out and 'try the fortunes of their respective flags.' If Broke had had one advantage over his American adversary, it was his dedication to and insistence upon gunnery and teamwork. He had even invented and fitted sights to all his main armament. It had won the day, but nobody had shown more distress than Broke himself when Lawrence had succumbed to his wounds.

Now, lying just beyond her like a guilty shadow, was the smaller frigate *Reaper*. A guardboat was moored alongside, and her upper deck was marked with tiny scarlet figures where Royal Marine sentries kept watch over the imprisoned mutineers.

Keen glanced at him, seeing the strain on his profile as he lifted his face to the sun.

'It is good to be of one company again.'

Bolitho smiled. 'Only for the moment, Val. We shall have to be on the move again shortly.' He shaded his eyes to look across at *Indomitable*, where Tyacke was taking on fresh water and supplies while final repairs were carried out. It was Tyacke's reason, or rather his excuse, for not accompanying him to this meeting.

He heard Avery talking quietly with Keen's flag lieutenant, the Honourable Lawford de Courcey. They would have little or nothing in common, he thought, and he had gathered that Adam did not care much for him, either. It was just as well. There was no room for complacency here, even amongst friends. They needed an edge, a purpose, like the old sword at his side.

218

There had been letters awaiting his return to Halifax, both from Catherine: he could feel them now in his coat. He would read them as soon as he could, then again later, and more slowly. But there was always the first anxiety, like a fear, that she would have changed towards him. She would be lonely beyond measure.

He turned away from the sun as he heard de Courcey greeting someone, and then another voice, a woman's.

Keen touched his arm. 'I should like you to meet Miss Gilia St Clair. I sent you word of her presence aboard *Reaper*.'

So easily said, but Bolitho had already gone through Keen's carefully worded report on *Reaper's* surrender, and the discharge of her guns into empty sea. He felt that Keen and Adam had disagreed about something at the time. It might reveal itself later.

His shoe caught on something as he turned, and he saw Avery's vague outline move towards him. Troubled; but protective of him, as always.

It was so dark after the brilliant sunlight and the dazzling reflections from the harbour that the room could have been curtained off.

Keen was saying, 'I wish to present Sir Richard Bolitho. He commands our squadron.'

It was not to impress: it was genuine pride. Val, as he had always been, before Zenoria's death, before Zenoria. Perhaps Catherine was correct in her belief that he would easily recover from his loss.

The woman was younger than he had expected, in her late twenties, he thought. He had an impression of a pleasant, oval face and light brown hair; the eyes were level and serious.

Bolitho took her hand. It was very firm; he could

219

easily imagine her with her father aboard the stricken *Reaper*, watching *Valkyrie* running out her powerful broadside.

She said, 'I am sorry to intrude, but my father is here. I had hoped I could discover....'

Keen said, 'He is with the general. I'm sure it is quite all right for you to stay.' He gave his youthful grin. 'I will take full responsibility!'

She said, 'I wanted to know about York. My father was going there to assist with the completion of a ship.'

Bolitho listened in silence. Her father's plans were not the source of her concern.

Keen said, 'I expect you will be returning to England sooner rather than later, Miss St Clair?'

She shook her head. 'I would like to remain here, with my father.'

The door opened, and an urbane lieutenant almost bowed himself into the room.

'The General's apologies, Sir Richard. The delay was unintentional.' He seemed to see the girl for the first time. 'I am not certain....'

Bolitho said, 'She is with us.'

The adjoining room was large and crammed with heavy furniture, a soldier's room, with two vast paintings of battles on the walls. Bolitho did not recognize the uniforms. A different war, a forgotten army.

The general seized his hand. 'Delighted, Sir Richard. Knew your father. Fine man. In India. He'd be damned proud of you!' He spoke in short, loud bursts, like mountain artillery, Bolitho thought.

Other faces. David St Clair: good handshake, firm and hard. And there was another soldier present, tall, very assured, with the unemotional bearing of

220

a professional.

He bowed slightly. 'Captain Charles Pierton, of the Eighth Regiment of Foot.' He paused, and said with a certain pride, 'The King's Regiment.'

Bolitho saw the girl's hands gripped together in her lap. Waiting with a curious defiance which succeeded only in making her appear suddenly vulnerable.

David St Clair said quickly, 'Are you feeling well, my dear?'

She did not answer him. 'May I ask you something, Captain Pierton?'

Pierton glanced quizzically at the general, who gave a brief nod. 'Of course, Miss St Clair.'

'You were at York when the Americans attacked. My father and I would have been there too, had circumstances not dictated otherwise.'

Her father leaned forward in his chair. 'The thirty-gun ship *Sir Isaac Brock* was burned on the slipway before the Americans could take her. I would have been too late in any case.'

Bolitho knew that she did not even hear him.

'Do you know Captain Anthony Loring, of your regiment, sir?'

The soldier looked back at her steadily. 'Yes, of course. He commanded the second company.' He turned to Bolitho and the other naval officers. 'Ours was the only professional force at York. We had the militia and the York Volunteers, and a company of the Royal Newfoundland Regiment.' He glanced at the girl again. 'And about one hundred Mississauga and Chippewa Indians.'

Bolitho noted how easily the names rolled off his tongue: he was a seasoned campaigner, although this vast, untamed country was a far cry from Spain or France. But the others would know all these facts. It

221

was merely an explanation for the girl's benefit, as if he thought it was owed to her.

He continued in the same grave, precise manner. 'The defences at Fort York were poor. My commanding officer believed that eventually the navy would be able to send more vessels to the lakes, to hold off the Americans until larger men-of-war were constructed. There were some seventeen hundred American soldiers that day, almost all of them regulars and well-trained. We had to gain time, to evacuate the fort and finally to burn the *Sir Isaac Brock*.'

She stood, and walked to the window. 'Please continue.'

Pierton said quietly, 'Captain Loring took his men to the lower shore where the Americans were landing. He gallantly led a bayonet charge and dispersed them. For a time. He was wounded, and died shortly afterwards. I am sorry. A good number of our men fell that day.'

Keen said, 'I think you might be more comfortable in another room, Miss St Clair.'

Bolitho saw her shake her head, heedless of her hair, which had fallen loosely across her shoulder.

She asked, 'Did he speak of me, Captain Pierton?'

Pierton looked at the general, and hesitated. 'We were hard pressed, Miss St Clair.'

She persisted. '*Ever*?'

Pierton replied, 'He was a very private person. A different company, you understand.'

She left the window and crossed over to him, then she put her hand on his arm. 'That was a kind thing to say. I should not have asked.' She gripped the scarlet sleeve, unaware of everyone else. 'I am so glad that you are safe.'

222

The general coughed noisily. 'Sending him to England on the first packet. God knows if they'll learn anything from what happened.'

The door closed quietly. She had gone.

Captain Pierton exclaimed, '*Damn!*' He looked at the general. 'My apologies, sir, but I forgot to give her something. Perhaps it would be better to send it with his other effects to Ridge ... our regimental agent in Charing Cross.'

Bolitho watched as he took a miniature painting from his tunic and laid it on the table. Charing Cross: like the casual mention of the Indians fighting with the army, it seemed so alien here. Another world.

Keen said, 'May I?'

He held the miniature to the sunlight and studied it. 'A good likeness. Very good.'

A small tragedy of war, Bolitho thought. She had sent or given him the miniature, even though the unknown Loring had decided not to encourage a more intimate relationship. She must have been hoping to see him again when her father visited York, perhaps fearing what she might discover. Now it was too late. Her father probably knew more than he would ever disclose.

Keen said, 'Well, sir, I think it should be returned to her. If it were me...' He did not go on.

Thinking of Zenoria? Sharing the same sense of loss?

The general frowned. 'Perhaps you're right.' He glanced at the clock. 'Time to stop now, gentlemen. I have a very acceptable claret, and I believe we should sample it. After that....'

Bolitho stood near the window, studying the captured American, *Chesapeake*, and the *Reaper* beyond.

He asked, 'And what of York, Captain Pierton? Is it secure?'

'Unfortunately, no, Sir Richard. My regiment withdrew in good order to Kingston, which is now doubly important if we are to withstand another attack. If the Americans had gone for Kingston in the first place. . . .'

'Well?'

The general answered for him. 'We would have lost Upper Canada.'

Two servants had appeared with trays of glasses. Keen murmured, 'I shall not be a moment, Sir Richard.'

Bolitho turned as Avery joined him by the window. 'We shall not wait longer than necessary.' He was concerned at the expression in the tawny eyes: they were deeply introspective, and yet, in some strange way, at peace. 'What is it? Another secret, George?'

Avery faced him, making up his mind. Perhaps he had been struggling with it all the way from the ship to this place of stamping boots and shouted orders.

He said, 'I received a letter, sir. A letter.'

Bolitho twisted round and grasped his wrist. 'A letter? Do you mean. . . .'

Avery smiled, rather shyly, and his face was that of a much younger man.

'Yes, sir. From a lady.'

Outside, in the sun-dappled passageway, Keen sat beside the girl on one of the heavy leather couches.

He watched her as she turned the miniature over in her hands, recalling the calm acceptance in her face when he had given it to her. Resignation? Or something far deeper?

'It was good of you. I did not know. . . .'

He saw her mouth quiver, and said, 'While I

224

command here at Halifax, if there is anything I can do to serve you, anything you require. . . .'

She looked up into his face. 'I will be with my father, at the Massie residence. They are . . . old friends.' She lowered her eyes. 'Of a sort.' She looked at the miniature again. 'I was younger then.'

Keen said, 'It is . . .' He faltered. 'You are very brave, and very beautiful.' He tried to smile, to break the tension within himself. 'Please do not be offended. That is the very last thing I intend.'

She was watching him, her eyes steady once more. 'You must have thought me a fool, an innocent in a world I know not. The sort of thing to bring a few laughs in the mess when you are all together as men.' She thrust out her hand, impetuous, but sharing his uncertainty. 'Keep this, if you like. It is of no further use to me.' But the careless mood would not remain. She watched him take the miniature, his lashes pale against his sunburned skin as he gazed down at it. 'And . . . take care. I shall think of you.'

She walked away along the passage, the sun greeting her at every window. She did not look back.

He said, 'I shall depend on it.'

He walked slowly back toward the general's room. Of course, it could not happen. It could not, not again. But it had.

* * *

Adam Bolitho paused with one foot on the high step and looked up at the shop. With the sun hot across his shoulders and the sky intensely blue above the rooftops, it was hard to remember the same street obscured by great banks of snow.

He pushed open the door and smiled to himself as a

225

bell jingled to announce his entrance. It was a small but elegant place which he thought would fit well into London or Exeter.

As if to some signal, a dozen or so clocks began to chime the hour, tall clocks and small, ornate timepieces for mantel or drawing room, clocks with moving figures, phases of the moon, and one with a fine square-rigger which actually dipped and lifted to each stroke of the pendulum. Each one pleased and intrigued him, and he was walking from one to another examining them when a short man in a dark coat came through a doorway by the counter. His eyes instantly and professionally examined the uniform, the bright gold epaulettes and short, curved hanger.

'And how may I be of service, Captain?'

'I require a watch. I was told....'

The man pulled out a long tray. 'Each of those is tested and reliable. Not new and untried, but of excellent repute. Old friends.'

Adam thought of the ship he had just left at anchor: ready for sea. It was impossible not to be aware of the captured American frigate *Chesapeake* in the harbour, which he had seen from *Valkyrie*'s gig. A truly beautiful ship: he could even accept that at one time he would have wanted no finer command. But the emotion would not return: the loss of *Anemone* had been like having part of himself die. She had been escorted into Halifax by her victorious opponent *Shannon* on the sixth of June. *My birthday.* The day he had been kissed by Zenoria on the cliff track; when he had cut the wild roses with his knife for her. So young. And yet so aware.

He glanced at the array of watches. It was not vanity: he needed one now that his own had disappeared, lost or stolen when he had been wounded and transferred to the U.S.S. *Unity*. They might as well have left him to die.

The shopkeeper took his silence as lack of interest. 'This is a very good piece, sir. Open-faced with duplex escapement, one of James McCabe's famous breed. Made in 1806, but still quite perfect.'

Adam picked it up. Who had carried it before, he wondered. Most of the watches here had probably belonged to army or sea officers. Or their widows....

He found himself thinking with increasing bitterness of Keen's interest in David St Clair's daughter Gilia. At first he had thought it was merely pity for the girl; Keen might even have been making comparisons with Zenoria, whom he had rescued from a convict transport. She had carried the mark of a whip across her back as a constant and cruel reminder, the mark of Satan, she had called it. He was being unfair to Keen, more so perhaps because of his own guilt, which never left him. That, willing or otherwise, Zenoria had been his lover.

He asked suddenly, 'What about that one?'

The man gave him an approving smile. 'You are an excellent judge as well as a brave frigate captain, sir!'

Adam had become accustomed to it. Here in Halifax, despite the heavy military presence and the comparative nearness of the enemy, security was a myth. Everyone knew who you were, what ship, where bound, and probably a whole lot more. He had mentioned it with some concern to Keen, who had said only, 'I think we give them too much credit, Adam.'

An indefinable coolness had come between them. Because of Adam's threat to fire on the *Reaper*, hostages or not, or was it something of his own

227

making or imagination, born of that abiding sense of guilt?

He took the watch, and it rested in his palm. It was heavy, the case rubbed smooth by handling over the years.

The man said, 'A rare piece, Captain. Note the cylinder escapement, the fine, clear face.' He sighed. 'Mudge and Dutton, 1770. A good deal older than yourself, I daresay.'

Adam was studying the guard, the engraving well worn but still clear and vital in the dusty sunlight. A mermaid.

The shopkeeper added, 'Not the kind of workmanship one finds very often these days, I fear.'

Adam held it to his ear. Recalling her face that day in Plymouth, when he had picked up her fallen glove and returned it to her. Her hand on his arm when they had walked together in the port admiral's garden. The last time he had seen her.

'What is the story of this watch?'

The little man polished his glasses. 'It came into the shop a long while ago. It belonged to a seafaring gentleman like yourself, sir ... I believe he needed the money. I could find out, perhaps.'

'No.' Adam closed the guard very carefully. 'I will take it.'

'It is a mite expensive, but ...' He smiled, pleased that the watch had gone to a suitable owner. 'I know you are a very successful frigate captain, sir. It is right and proper that you should have it!' He waited, but the responding smile was not forthcoming. 'I should clean it before you take it. I can send it by hand to *Valkyrie* if you would prefer. I understand that you are not sailing until the day after tomorrow?'

Adam looked away. He had only just been told

himself by Keen before he had come ashore.

'Thank you, but I shall take it now.' He slipped it into his pocket, haunted by her face once more. The local people of Zennor still insisted that the church where she and Keen had been married had been visited by a mermaid.

The bell jingled again and the shopkeeper glanced around, irritated by the intrusion. He met all kinds of people here: Halifax was becoming the most important sea port, and certainly the safest, set as it was at the crossroads of war. With the army to defend it and the navy to protect and supply it, there were many who regarded it as the new gateway to a continent. But this young, dark-haired captain was very different from the others. Alone, completely alone, alive to something which he would allow no one else to share.

He said, 'I am sorry, Mrs Lovelace, but your clock is still misbehaving. A few days more, perhaps.'

But she was looking at Adam. 'Well, Captain Bolitho, this is a pleasant surprise. I trust you are well? And how is your handsome young admiral?'

Adam bowed to her. She was dressed in dark red silk, with a matching bonnet to shade her eyes from the sun. The same direct way of looking at him, the slightly mocking smile, as if she were used to teasing people. Men.

He said, 'Rear-Admiral Keen is well, ma'am.'

She was quick to notice the slight edge to his reply.

'You have been shopping, I see.' She held out her hand. 'Will you show me?'

He knew that the shopkeeper was observing them with interest. No doubt he knew her well, and her reputation would make a fine piece of gossip. He was surprised to find that he had actually taken out his

229

watch to show her.

'I needed one, Mrs Lovelace. I like it.' He saw her studying the engraved mermaid.

'I would have bought something younger for you, Captain Bolitho. But if it's what you want, and it takes your fancy...' She glanced out at the street. 'I must go. I have friends to entertain later.' She looked at him directly again, her eyes suddenly very still and serious. 'You know where I live, I think.'

He answered, 'On the Bedford Basin. I remember.'

For a second or two her composure and her humour were gone. She gripped his arm, and said, 'Be careful. Promise me that. I know of your reputation, and a little of your background. I think perhaps you do not care for your own life any more.' When he would have spoken she silenced him, as effectively as if she had laid a finger on his lips. 'Say nothing. Only do as I ask, and be very careful. Promise me.' Then she looked at him again: the invitation was very plain. 'When you come back, please call on me.'

He said coolly, 'What about your husband, ma'am? I think he may well object.'

She laughed, but the first vivid confidence did not return. 'He is never here. Trade is his life, his whole world!' She played with the ribbon of her bonnet. 'But he is no trouble.'

He recalled their host, Benjamin Massie, that night when the brig *Alfriston* had brought the news of *Reaper's* mutiny and capture. Massie's mistress then, and perhaps the mistress of others as well.

'I wish you well, ma'am.' He recovered his hat from a chair, and said to the shopkeeper, 'When I check my ship's affairs against my watch, I shall remember you and this shop.'

230

She was waiting on the steps. 'Remember what I have said to you.' She studied his face, as if seeking something in it. 'You have lost that which you can never rediscover. You must accept that.' She touched the gold lace on his lapel. 'Life must still be lived.'

She turned away, and as Adam stepped aside to avoid a mounted trooper, she vanished.

He walked back toward the boat jetty. *Be very careful*. He quickened his pace as he caught sight of the water and the great array of masts and spars, like a forest. Whatever action they took, it would be Keen's decision: he had made that more than clear. But why did it hurt so much?

He thought suddenly of his uncle, and wished he could be with him. They could always talk; he would always listen. He had even confessed his affair with Zenoria to him.

He saw the stairs and *Valkyrie*'s gig moored alongside. Midshipman Rickman, a lively fifteen-year-old, was speaking with two young women who were doing little to hide their profession from the grinning boat's crew.

Rickman straightened his hat and the gig's crew came to attention when they saw their captain approaching. The two girls moved away, but not very far.

Adam said, 'Back to the ship, if you please, Mr Rickman. I see that you were not wasting your time?'

Two blotches of scarlet appeared on the youth's unshaven cheeks, and Adam climbed quickly into the boat. *If only you knew.*

He glanced toward the captured American frigate and the other, *Success*, which *Indomitable*'s broadsides had overwhelmed in minutes, recalling the young lieutenant who had died of his wounds, son

231

of the Captain Joseph Brice who had interviewed him during his captivity. A sick but dignified officer, who had treated him with a courtesy reminiscent of Nathan Beer. He wondered if Brice knew, and would blame himself for guiding his son into the navy.

Face to face, blade to blade with men who spoke the same language but who had freely chosen another country ... Perhaps it was better to have an enemy you could hate. In war, it was necessary to hate without questioning why.

'Oars *up!*'

He stood and reached for the hand rope. He had barely noticed the return journey to *Valkyrie*.

He saw the flag lieutenant hovering by the entry port, waiting to catch his eye. He raised his hat to the quarterdeck, and smiled.

It was, of course, easier to hate some more than others.

*   *   *

Rear-Admiral Valentine Keen turned away from *Valkyrie*'s stern windows as Adam, followed by the flag lieutenant, entered the great cabin.

'I came as soon as I could, sir. I was ashore.'

Keen said gently, 'It is no great matter. You should have more leisure.' He glanced at the flag lieutenant. 'Thank you, Lawford. You may carry on with the signals we discussed.'

The door closed, reluctantly, Adam thought. 'More news, sir?'

Keen seemed unsettled. 'Not exactly. But the plans have changed. *Success* is to leave for Antigua. I have spoken with the Dock Master, and I can see we have no choice in the matter. Halifax is crammed with vessels needing overhaul and repair, and *Success* was in a very poor condition after her clash with *Indomitable*—as much due to severe rot as to Captain Tyacke's gunnery, I suspect.'

Adam waited. Keen was trying to make light of it. *Success* was badly damaged, yes, but would sail well enough after work was completed on her rigging. But Antigua, two thousand miles away, and in the hurricane season ... It was taking a chance.

'There is another big convoy due within a week, or so, supplies and equipment for the army, nothing unusual in that. Sir Richard intends to take *Indomitable* and two others of the squadron to escort them on the final approach. There is a possibility that the Americans might attack and attempt to scatter or sink some of them.' He regarded him calmly. '*Success* must have a strong consort.' He glanced around the cabin. 'This ship is large enough to fight off any foolhardy privateer who might want to take her.' He smiled thinly. 'And fast enough to get back to Halifax, in case of more trouble.'

Adam walked to the table, and hesitated as he saw the miniature lying beside Keen's open log book. It took him completely by surprise, and he scarcely heard Keen say, 'I am required to remain here. I command in Halifax. The rest of our ships may be needed elsewhere.'

He could not take his eyes from the miniature, recognizing the subject at once. The smile, which had been painted for some one else to cherish, to keep.

Keen said abruptly, 'It will be nothing to you, Adam. Certain other commanders, I would have to consider more carefully. *Success* will be safer in English Harbour. At best, she can be used as a guardship, and at worst, her spars and weapons will

233

be put to good use there. What do you say?'

Adam faced him, angry that he could not accept it, that he himself had no right to refuse.

'I think it's too risky, sir.'

Keen seemed surprised. '*You*, Adam? You talk of risk? To the world at large it will merely be the departure of two big frigates, and even if enemy intelligence discovers their destination, what then? It will be too late to act upon it, surely.'

Adam touched the heavy watch in his pocket, remembering the small shop, the peaceful chorus of clocks, the owner's matter-of-fact mention of *Valkyrie*, almost to the time of her departure.

He said bluntly, 'There is no security here, sir. I shall be away for a month. Anything could happen in that time.'

Keen smiled, perhaps relieved. 'The war will keep, Adam. I trust you with this mission because I want you to carry orders to the captain in charge at Antigua. A difficult man in many ways. He needs to be reminded of the fleet's requirements there.'

He saw Adam's eyes move to the miniature once more. 'An endearing young lady. Courageous, too.' He paused. 'I know what you are thinking. My loss is hard to believe, harder still to accept.'

Adam clenched his fists so tightly that the bones ached. *You don't understand. How can you forget her? Betray her?*

He said, 'I will make all the arrangements, sir. I'll pick a prize crew from spare hands at the base.'

'Who will you put in charge of *Success*?'

Adam contained his anger with an almost physical effort. 'John Urquhart, sir. A good first lieutenant—I'm surprised he hasn't been chosen for promotion, or even a command.'

234

The door opened an inch, and de Courcey coughed politely.

Keen said sharply, 'What is it?'

'Your barge is ready, sir.'

'Thank you.' Keen picked up the miniature, and after a moment's hesitation placed it in a drawer and turned the key. 'I shall be aboard later. I'll send a word.' He looked at him steadily. 'The day after tomorrow, then.'

Adam thrust his hat beneath his arm. 'I'll see you over the side, sir.'

Keen nodded to two midshipmen who sprang out of his way by the companion ladder. 'I'd be obliged if you would take my flag lieutenant with you when you sail. Good experience. See how the professionals do things.' He seemed about to say something else, but changed his mind.

As the barge pulled away from *Valkyrie*'s shadow, Adam saw the first lieutenant walking across the quarterdeck in deep conversation with Ritchie, the sailing-master.

They eyed him as he approached, and Adam was again reminded that he did not truly know these men, just as he accepted that it was his own fault.

'Come forrard with me, Mr Urquhart.' To the master he added, 'You've been told, I take it.'

'Aye, sir. The Leeward Islands again. Bad time o' year.' But Adam was already out of earshot, striding along the starboard gangway with Urquhart in step beside him. Below, men working at the gun tackles or flaking down unwanted cordage paused only briefly to glance up at them.

Adam halted on the forecastle deck and rested one foot on a crouching carronade, the 'smasher', as the Jacks called them. Opposite them lay the captured

235

Success, and although her side and upperworks still bore the scars of *Indomitable*'s iron, her masts were set up, with men working on the yards to secure each new sail. They had done well to achieve so much in so short a time. And beyond her, the beautiful *Chesapeake*, and *Reaper* swinging, untroubled, to her cable. Did ships know or care who handled, or betrayed, or loved them?

Urquhart said, 'If the weather stays friendly, we'll not have much trouble, sir.'

Adam leaned over the rail, past one great catted anchor to the imposing gilded figurehead: one of Odin's faithful servants, a stern-faced maiden in breastplate and horned helmet, one hand raised as if to welcome her dead hero to Valhalla. It was not beautiful. He tried to thrust the thought aside. Not like *Anemone*. But through the smoke and the din of war, it would certainly impress an enemy.

'I want you to take charge of *Success*. You will have a prize crew, but only enough hands to work the ship. Her fighting ability has not yet been determined.'

He watched the lieutenant's face, strong, intelligent, but still wary of his captain. Not afraid, but unsure.

'Now hear me, Mr Urquhart, and keep what I ask of you to yourself. If I hear one word from elsewhere it will lie at your door, understood?'

Urquhart nodded, his eyes very calm. 'You can rely on that.'

Adam touched his arm. 'I rely on *you*.'

He thought suddenly of the miniature of Gilia St Clair. Her smile, which Keen had appropriated as his own.

'Now, this is what you must do.'

236

But even as he spoke, his mind still clung to it. Perhaps Keen was right. After the battle, losing his ship and the agony of imprisonment, there was always a chance of becoming crippled by caution.

When he had finished explaining what he required, Urquhart said, 'May I ask you, sir, have you never feared being killed?'

Adam smiled a little, and turned his back on the figurehead.

'No.' He saw John Whitmarsh walking along the deck beside one of the new midshipmen, who was about his own age. They both seemed to sense his eyes upon them and paused to peer up into the sun at the shadows on the forecastle. The midshipman touched his hat; Whitmarsh raised one hand in a gesture which was not quite a wave.

Urquhart remarked, 'You certainly have a way with youngsters, sir.'

Adam looked at him, the smile gone. 'Your question, John. It is true to say that I have ... died ... many times. Does that suit?'

It was probably the closest they had ever been.

CHAPTER TWELVE

CODE OF CONDUCT

Lieutenant George Avery leaned back in his chair and put one foot on his sea-chest as if to test the ship's movement. In the opposite corner of the small, screened cabin Allday sat on another chest, his big hands clasped together, frowning, as he tried to remember exactly what Avery had read to him.

Avery could see it as if he had left England only yesterday, and not the five months ago it was in fact. The inn at Fallowfield by the Helford River, the long walks in the countryside, untroubled by conversation with people who only spoke because they were cooped up with you in a man-of-war. Good food, time to think. To remember....

He thought now of his own letter, and wondered why he had told the admiral about her. More surprising still, that Bolitho had seemed genuinely pleased about it, although doubtless he thought his flag lieutenant was hoping for too much. *A kiss and a promise.* He could not imagine what Bolitho might have said if he had told him all that had happened on that single night in London. The mystery, the wildness, and the peace, when they had lain together, exhausted. For his own part, stunned that it could have been real.

His thoughts came back to Allday, and he said, 'So there you are. Your little Kate is doing well. I must buy her something before we leave Halifax.'

Allday did not look up. 'So small, she was. No bigger than a rabbit. Now she's walking, you say?'

'Unis says.' He smiled. 'And I'll lay odds that she fell over a few times before she got her proper sea-legs.'

Allday shook his head. 'I would have liked to see it, them first steps. I never seen anything like that afore.' He seemed troubled, rather than happy. 'I should've been there.'

Avery was moved by what he saw. Perhaps it would be useless to point out that Bolitho had offered to leave him ashore, secure in his own home, after years of honourable service. It would be an insult. He recalled Catherine's obvious relief that Allday was

238

staying with her man. Maybe she sensed that his 'oak' had never been more needed.

Avery listened to the regular groan of timbers as *Indomitable* thrust through a criss-cross of Atlantic rollers. They should have made contact with the Halifax-bound convoy yesterday, but even the friendly Trades could not always be relied upon. This was a war of supply and demand, and it was always the navy who supplied. No wonder men were driven to despair by separation and hardships which few landsmen could ever appreciate.

He heard the clatter of dishes from the wardroom, somebody laughing too loudly at some bawdy joke already heard too often. He glanced at the white screen. And beyond there, right aft, the admiral would be thinking and planning, no doubt with the scholarly Yovell waiting to record and copy instructions and orders for each of the captains, from flagship to brig, from schooner to bomb ketch. Faces he had come to know, men he had come to understand. All except the one who would be uppermost in his mind, the dead captain of *Reaper*. Bolitho would regard the mutiny as something personal, and the captain's tyranny a flaw that should have been removed before it was too late.

Justice, discipline, revenge. It could not be ignored.

And what of Keen, perhaps the last of the original Happy Few? Was his new interest in Gilia St Clair merely a passing thing? Avery thought of the woman in his arms, his need of her. He was no one to judge Keen.

He looked up as familiar footsteps moved across the quarterdeck. Tyacke, visiting the watchkeepers before darkness closed around them and their two consorts. If the convoy failed to appear at first light, what then? They were some five hundred miles from the nearest land. A decision would have to be made. *But not by me.* Nor even by Tyacke. It would fall, as always, to that same man in his cabin aft. The admiral.

He had not mentioned the letter to Tyacke: Tyacke would probably know. But Avery respected his privacy, and had come to like him greatly, more than he would believed possible after their first stormy confrontation at Plymouth more than two years ago. Tyacke had never received a letter from anyone. Did he ever look for one, ever dare to hope for such a precious link with home?

He handed Unis's letter to Allday, and hoped that he had read it in the manner he had intended. Allday, a man who could recognize any hoist of signals by their colours or their timing, whom he had watched patiently instructing some hapless landman or baffled midshipman in the art of splicing and ropework, who could carve a ship model so fine that even the most critical Jack would nod admiringly, could not read. Nor could he write. It seemed cruel, unfair.

There was a tap on the door and Ozzard looked in. 'Sir Richard's compliments, sir. Would you care to lay aft for a glass?' He purposefully ignored Allday.

Avery nodded. He had been expecting the invitation, and hoping that it would come.

Ozzard added sharply, 'You too, of course. If you're not too busy.'

Avery watched. Another precious fragment: Ozzard's rudeness matched only by Allday's awakening grin. He could have killed the little man with his elbow. They knew each other's strength,

240

weakness too, in all likelihood. Maybe they even knew his.

His thoughts dwelled again on the letter in his pocket. Perhaps she had written it out of pity, or embarrassment at what had happened. She could never realize in ten thousand years what that one letter had meant to him. Just a few sentences, simple sentiments, and wishes for his future. She had ended, *Your affectionate friend, Susanna.*

That was all. He straightened his coat and opened the door for Allday. It was everything.

But Avery was a practical man. Susanna, Lady Mildmay, an admiral's widow, would not remain alone for long. Perhaps could not. She had rich friends, and he had seen for himself the confidence, born of experience, she had displayed at the reception attended by Bolitho's wife and by Vice-Admiral Bethune. He could recall her laughter when he had mistaken Bethune's mistress for his wife. *Is that all I could hope for?*

Susanna was available now. She would soon forget that night in London with her lowly lieutenant. At the same time, he was already composing the letter he would write to her, the first he had written to anyone but his sister. There was no one else now.

He walked aft towards the spiralling lantern, the rigid Royal Marine sentry outside the screen doors.

Allday murmured, 'I wonder what Sir Richard wants.'

Avery paused, hearing the ship, and the ocean all around them.

He answered simply, 'He needs us. I know very well what that means.'

*   *   *

It was cold on the quarterdeck, with only the smallest hint of the daylight which would soon show itself and open up the sea.

Bolitho gripped the quarterdeck rail, feeling the wind on his face and in his hair, his boatcloak giving him anonymity for a while longer.

It was a time of day he had always found fascinating as a captain in his own ship. A vessel coming alive beneath his feet, dark figures moving like ghosts, most of them so used to their duties that they performed them without conscious thought even in complete darkness. The morning watch went about their affairs, while the watch below cleaned the messdecks and stowed away the hammocks in the nettings, with barely an order being passed. Bolitho could smell the stench of the galley funnel; the cook must surely use axle-grease for his wares. But sailors had strong stomachs. They needed them.

He heard the officer-of-the-watch speaking with his midshipman in brusque, clipped tones. Laroche was a keen gambler who had felt the rough edge of Lieutenant Scarlett's tongue the very day Scarlett had been killed in the fight with the U.S.S. *Unity*.

It would be six in the morning soon, and Tyacke would come on deck. It was his custom, although he had impressed on all his officers that they were to call him at any time, day or night, if they were disturbed by any situation. Bolitho had heard him say to one lieutenant, 'Better for me to lose my temper than to lose my ship!'

If you doubt, speak out. His father had said it many times.

He found he was walking along the weather side, his shoes avoiding ring-bolts and tackles without effort. Catherine was troubled; it was made more apparent by her determination to hide it from him in her letters. Roxby was very ill, although Bolitho had seen that for himself before he had left England, and he thought it a good thing that his sister felt able to share her worries and hopes with Catherine, when their lives had been so different from one another.

Catherine had told him about the Spanish inheritance from her late husband, Luis Pareja. All those years ago, another world, a different ship; they had both been younger then. How could either of them have known what would happen? He could recall her exactly as she had been at their first meeting, the same fiery courage he had seen after the *Golden Plover* had gone down.

She was concerned about the money. He had mentioned it to Yovell, who seemed to understand all the complications, and had accompanied Catherine to the old firm of lawyers in Truro, to ensure that 'she was not snared by legal roguery', as he had put it.

Yovell had been frank, but discreet. 'Lady Catherine will become rich, sir. Perhaps very rich.' He had gauged Bolitho's expression, a little surprised that the prospect of wealth should disquiet him, but also proud that Bolitho had confided in him and no other.

But suppose ... Bolitho paused in his pacing to watch the first glow of light, almost timid as it painted a small seam between sky and ocean. He heard a voice whisper, 'Cap'n's comin' up, sir!' and a few seconds later Laroche's pompous acknowledgement of Tyacke's presence. 'Good morning, sir. Course east by north. Wind's veered a little.'

Tyacke said nothing. Bolitho saw it all as if it were indeed broad daylight. Tyacke would examine the compass and study the small wind-vane that aided the helmsmen until they could see the sails and the masthead pendant: he would already have scanned the log book on his way here. A new day. How would it be? An empty sea, a friend, an enemy?

He crossed to the weather side and touched his hat. 'You're about early, Sir Richard.' To any one else, it would have seemed a question.

Bolitho said, 'Like you, James, I need to feel the day, and try to sense what it might bring.'

Tyacke saw that his shirt was touched with pink, as the light found and explored the ship.

'We should sight the others directly, sir. *Taciturn* will be well up to wind'rd, and the brig *Doon* closing astern. As soon as we can see them I'll make a signal.' He was thinking of the convoy they were expecting to meet: there would be hell to pay if they did not. Any escort duty was tedious and an enormous strain, especially for frigates like *Indomitable* and her consort *Taciturn*. They were built for speed, not for the sickening motion under the reefed topsails necessary to hold station on their ponderous charges. He sniffed the air. 'That damned galley—it stinks! I must have a word with the purser.'

Bolitho stared aloft, shading his eye. The topgallant yards were pale now, the sails taut and hard-braced to hold the uncooperative wind.

More figures had appeared: Daubney the first lieutenant, already pointing out tasks for the forenoon watch to Hockenhull the boatswain. Tyacke touched his hat again and strode away to speak with his senior lieutenant, as though he were eager to get started.

Bolitho remained where he was while men hurried past him. Some might glance toward his cloaked

244

figure, but when they realized that it was the admiral they would stay clear. He sighed faintly. At least they were not afraid of him. But to be a captain again … *Your own ship*. Like Adam. …

He thought of him now, still at Halifax, or with Keen making a sweep along the American coast where a hundred ships like *Unity* or *Chesapeake* could be concealed. Boston, New Bedford, New York, Philadelphia. They could be anywhere.

It had to be stopped, finished before it became another draining, endless war. America had no allies as such, but would soon find them if Britain was perceived to be failing. If only. …

He looked up, caught off guard as the lookout's voice penetrated the noises of sea and canvas.

'Deck there! Sail on larboard bow!' The barest pause. ''Tis *Taciturn*, on station!'

Tyacke said, 'She's seen us and hoisted a light. They have their wits about them.' He looked abeam as a fish leaped from the glassy rollers to avoid an early predator.

Laroche said in his newly affected drawl, 'We should sight *Doon* next, then.'

Tyacke jabbed his hand forward. 'Well, I hope the lookout's eyesight is better than yours. That fore staysail is flapping about like a washerwoman's apron!'

Laroche called to a boatswain's mate, suitably crushed.

And quite suddenly, there they were, their upper sails and rigging holding the first sunshine, their flags and pendants like pieces of painted metal.

Tyacke said nothing. The convoy was safe.

Bolitho took a telescope, but clung to the sight before he raised it. Big and ponderous they might be, yet in this pure, keen light they had a kind of majesty. He thought back to The Saintes, as he often did at times like this, recalling the first sight of the French fleet. A young officer had written to his mother afterwards, comparing them with the armoured knights at Agincourt.

He asked, 'How many?'

Tyacke again. 'Seven, sir. Or so it said in the instruction.' He repeated, 'Seven,' and Bolitho thought he was wondering if their cargoes were worthwhile or necessary.

Carleton, the signals midshipman, had arrived with his men. He looked fresh and alert, and had probably eaten a huge breakfast, no matter what the galley smelled like. Bolitho nodded to him, remembering when a ship's rat fed on breadcrumbs from the galley had been a midshipman's delicacy. They had said it tasted like rabbit. They had lied.

Tyacke checked the compass again, impatient to make contact with the senior ship of the escort and then lay his own ship on a new tack for their return to Halifax.

Carleton called, 'There is a frigate closing, sir, larboard bow.' He was peering at the bright hoist of flags, but Tyacke said, 'I know her. She's *Wakeful...*' Like an echo, Carleton called dutifully, '*Wakeful*, thirty-eight, Captain Martin Hyde.'

Bolitho turned. The ship which had brought Keen and Adam out from England, after which the *Royal Herald* had been pounded into a coffin for her company. Mistaken identity. Or a brutal extension of an old hatred?

Carleton cleared his throat. 'She has a passenger for *Indomitable*, sir.'

'*What?*' Tyacke sounded outraged. 'By whose order?'

246

Carleton tried again, spelling out the hoist of flags with extra care.

'Senior officer for duties in Halifax, sir.'

Tyacke said doubtfully, 'That must have been a potful to spell out.' Then, surprisingly, he smiled at the tall midshipman. 'That was well done. Now acknowledge.' He glanced at Bolitho, who had discarded his cloak and was facing into the frail sunlight.

Bolitho shook his head. 'No, James, I do not know who.' He turned and looked at him, his eyes bleak. 'But I think I know why.'

Wakeful was coming about, and a boat was already being swayed up and over the gangway in readiness for lowering. A smart, well-handled ship. The unknown senior officer would have been making comparisons. Bolitho raised the glass again and saw the way falling off the other ship, the scars of wind and sea on her lithe hull. A solitary command, the only kind to have. He said, 'Have the side manned, James. A boatswain's chair too, although I doubt if it will be needed.'

Allday was here, Ozzard, too, with his dress coat, clucking irritably over the admiral's casual appearance.

Allday clipped on the old sword, and murmured, 'Squalls, Sir Richard?'

Bolitho looked at him gravely. He of all people would remember, and understand. 'I fear so, old friend. There are still enemies within our own ranks, it seems.'

He saw the marines stamping to the entry port, picking up their dressing, their bayonets gleaming like silver. Showing a mark of respect, a salute to yet

247

another important visitor. Equally, they would not question an order to place him in front of a firing-squad.

Avery hurried from the companion hatch, but hesitated as Tyacke looked over at him and shook his head very slightly in warning.

Indomitable was hove-to, her seamen obviously glad of something to break the monotony of work and drill.

Wakeful's gig came alongside, rolling steeply in the undertow. Bolitho walked to the rail and stared down, saw the passenger rise from the sternsheets and reach for the guiderope, disdaining the assistance of a lieutenant, and ignoring the dangling chair as Bolitho had known he would.

Coming to judge the *Reaper*'s mutineers. How could it be that they should meet like this, on a small pencilled cross on Isaac York's chart? And whose hand would have made this choice, unless it were guided by malice, and perhaps personal envy?

He made himself watch as the figure climbing the side missed a stair and almost fell. But he was climbing again, each movement an effort. As it would be for any man with only one arm.

The colour-sergeant growled, 'Royal Marines ... *Ready!*' more to cover his own surprise at the time it was taking the visitor to appear at the entry port than out of necessity.

The cocked hat and then the rear-admiral's epaulettes appeared finally in the port, and Bolitho strode forward to meet him.

'Guard of honour! *Present arms!*'

The din of the drill, the squeal of calls and the strident rattle of drums drowned out his spoken welcome.

248

They faced one another, the visitor with his hat raised in his left hand, his hair quite grey against the deep blue of the ocean behind him. But his eyes were the same, a more intense blue even than Tyacke's.

The noise faded, and Bolitho exclaimed, 'Thomas! You, of all people!'

Rear-Admiral Thomas Herrick replaced his hat and took the proffered hand. 'Sir Richard.' Then he smiled, and for those few seconds Bolitho saw the face of his oldest friend.

Tyacke stood nearby, watching impassively; he knew most of the story, and the rest he could fathom for himself

He waited to be presented. But he saw only an executioner.

*　　　*　　　*

Herrick hesitated inside the great cabin as if, for a moment, he was uncertain why he had come. He glanced around, acknowledging Ozzard with his tray, remembering him. As usual on such occasions, Ozzard revealed neither surprise nor curiosity, no matter what he might be thinking.

Bolitho said, 'Here, Thomas. Try this chair.'

Herrick lowered himself with a grunt into the high-backed *bergre* and thrust out his legs. He said, 'This is more like it.'

Bolitho said, 'Did you find *Wakeful* a mite small?'

Herrick smiled slightly. 'No, not at all. But her captain, Hyde—a bright young fellow with an even brighter future, I shouldn't wonder—he wanted to *entertain* me. Humour me. I don't need it. Never did.'

Bolitho studied him. Herrick was a year or so younger than himself, but he looked old, tired, and not only because of his grey hair and the deep lines of strain around his mouth. They would be the result of his amputated arm. It had been a close thing.

Ozzard padded nearer and waited.

Bolitho said, 'A drink, perhaps.' There was a thud on deck. 'Your gear is being brought aboard.'

Herrick looked at his legs, stained and wet from his climb up the ship's tumblehome. 'I can't order you to take me to Halifax.'

'It is a pleasure, Thomas. There is so much I need to hear.'

Herrick looked across at Ozzard. 'Some ginger beer, if you have any?'

Ozzard did not blink. 'Of course, sir.'

Herrick sighed. 'I saw that rascal Allday when I came aboard. He doesn't change much.'

'He's a proud father now, Thomas. A little girl. In truth, he shouldn't be here.'

Herrick took the tall glass. 'None of us should.' He examined Bolitho as he sat in another chair. 'You look well. I'm glad.' Then, almost angrily, 'You know why I'm here? The whole damned fleet seems to!'

'The mutiny. *Reaper* was retaken. It was all in my report.'

'I can't discuss it. Not until I've carried out my own investigation.'

'And then?'

Herrick shrugged, and winced. His pain was very evident. The steep climb up *Indomitable*'s side would have done him no good.

'Court of inquiry. The rest you know. We've seen enough mutinies in our time, eh?'

'I know. Adam captured *Reaper*, by the way.'

'So I hear.' He nodded. 'He'd need no urging.'

Calls shrilled overhead and feet thudded across the planking. Tyacke was under sail, changing tack now that the way was clear.

Bolitho said, 'I must read my dispatches. I'll not be long.'

'I can tell you some of it. We heard just before we weighed anchor. Wellington has won a great victory over the French at Vitoria, their last main stronghold in Spain, I understand. They are in retreat.' His face was closed, distant. 'All these years we've prayed and waited for this, clung to it when all else seemed lost.' He held out the empty glass. 'And now it's happened, I can't feel anything, anything at all.'

Bolitho watched him with an indefinable sadness. They had seen and done so much together: blazing sun and screaming gales, blockade and patrols off countless shores, ships lost, good men killed, and more still would die before the last trumpet sounded.

'And you, Thomas? What have you been doing?'

He nodded to Ozzard and took the refilled glass. 'The *scraps*. Visiting dockyards, inspecting coastal defences, anything no one else wanted to do. I was even offered a two-year contract as governor of the new sailors' hospital. *Two years*. It was all they could find.'

'And what of this investigation, Thomas?'

'Do you remember John Cotgrave? He was the Judge Advocate at *my* court-martial. He sits at the top of the legal tree where the Admiralty's concerned. It was his idea.'

Bolitho waited, only the taste of cognac on his tongue to remind him that he had taken a drink. There was no bitterness in Herrick's tone, not even resignation. It was as if he had lost everything, and believed in nothing, least of all the life he had once

251

loved so dearly.

'They want no long drawn-out drama, no fuss. All they want is a verdict to show that justice is upheld.' He gave the thin smile again. 'Has a familiar tune, don't you think?'

He looked towards the stern windows, and the sea beyond. 'As for me, I sold the house in Kent. It was too big, anyway. It was so empty, so desolate without...' He hesitated. 'Without Dulcie.'

'What will you do, Thomas?'

'After this? I shall quit the navy. I don't want to be another relic, an old salt-horse who doesn't want to hear when he is surplus to *their lordships'* requirements!'

There was a tap at the door, and as the sentry had remained silent Bolitho knew that it was Tyacke.

He entered the cabin and said, 'On our new course, Sir Richard. *Taciturn* and *Doon* will remain with the convoy as you ordered. The wind's freshening, but it'll suit me.'

Herrick said, 'You sound pleased with her, Captain Tyacke.'

Tyacke stood beneath one of the lanterns.

'She's the fastest sailer I've ever known, sir.' He turned the scarred side of his face towards him, perhaps deliberately. 'I hope you will be comfortable on board, sir.'

Bolitho said, 'Will you sup with us this evening, James?'

Tyacke looked at him, and his eyes spoke for him. 'I must ask your forgiveness, sir, but I have some extra duties to attend to. At some other time, I would be honoured.'

The door closed, and Herrick said, 'When I've left the ship, he means.' Bolitho began to protest. 'I do

252

understand. A ship, a King's ship no less, has mutinied against rightful authority. At any time in war it is a crime beyond comparison, and now when we face a new enemy, with the additional temptation of better pay and more humane treatment, it is all the more dangerous. I will doubtless hear that the uprising was caused by a captain's brutality ... sadism ... I have seen it all before, in my early days as a lieutenant.'

He was speaking of *Phalarope*, without mentioning her name, although it was as if he had shouted it aloud.

'Some will say that the choice of captain was faulty, that it was favouritism, or the need to remove him from his previous appointment—that too is not uncommon. So what do we say? That because of these "mistakes" it was a just solution to dip the colours to an enemy, to mutiny, and to cause the death of that captain, be he saint or damned sinner? There can be no excuse. There never was.' He leaned forward and glanced around the shadowed cabin, but Ozzard had vanished. They were alone. 'I am your friend, although at times I have not shown it. But I know you of old, Richard, and could guess what you might do, even if you have not yet considered it. You would risk everything, throw it all away on a point of honour and, may I say it, decency. You would speak up for those mutineers, no matter what it cost. I tell you now, Richard, it would cost you everything. They would destroy you. They would not merely be victims of their own folly—they would be martyrs. Bloody saints, if some had their way!'

He paused: he seemed wearied suddenly. 'But you do have many friends. What you have done and have
253

tried to do will not be forgotten. Even that damned upstart Bethune confided that he feared for your reputation. So much envy, so much deceit.'

Bolitho walked past the big chair and laid his hand for a moment on the stooped shoulder.

'Thank you for telling me, Thomas. I want a victory, I crave it, and I know what this has cost you.' He saw his reflection in the salt-smeared glass as the ship fell off another point or so. 'I know how you feel.' He sensed the wariness. 'How I would feel if anything happened to separate me from Catherine. But duty is one thing, Thomas ... it has guided my feet since I first went to sea at the age of twelve ... and justice is something else.' He walked around, and saw the same stubborn, closed face, the determination which had first brought them together in *Phalarope*. 'In battle I hate to see men die for no purpose, when they have no say and no choice at all in the matter. And I'll not turn my back on other men who have been wronged, driven to despair, and already condemned by others who are equally guilty, but not charged.'

Herrick remained very calm. 'I am not surprised.' He made to rise. 'Do we still sup this evening?'

Bolitho smiled: it came without effort this time. They were not enemies; the past could not die. 'I had hoped for that, Thomas. Make full use of these quarters.' He picked up the dispatches and added, 'I promise you that nobody will attempt to entertain you!'

Outside the cabin he found Allday loitering by an open gunport. He had simply happened to be there, in case.

He asked, 'How was it, Sir Richard? Bad?'

Bolitho smiled. 'He has not changed much,

old friend.'

Allday said, 'Then it *is* bad.'

Bolitho knew that Tyacke and Avery would be waiting, united even more strongly because of something which was beyond their control.

Allday said harshly, 'They'll hang for it. I'll shed no tears for 'em. I hates their kind. *Vermin.*'

Bolitho looked at him, moved by his anger. Allday had been a pressed man, taken the same day as Bryan Ferguson. So what had instilled in them both such an abiding sense of loyalty, and such courage?

It was no help to understand that Herrick knew the answer. So did Tyacke. *Trust.*

CHAPTER THIRTEEN

'LET THEM NEVER FORGET'

John Urquhart, *Valkyrie*'s first lieutenant, paused in the entry port to recover his breath while he stared across at the captured American frigate *Success*. The wind was rising very slightly, but enough to make her plunge and stagger while the small prize crew fought to keep her under command.

He regarded the orderly, almost placid scene on the quarterdeck of this ship, in which he had served for four years, noting the curious but respectful eyes of the midshipmen, reminding him, if it were necessary, of his own crumpled and untidy appearance; then he glanced up at the sky, pale blue, washed-out and, like the ocean, almost misty in the unwavering sunshine.

He saw Adam Bolitho speaking with Ritchie, the

sailing-master. Ritchie had been badly wounded in the first clash with the U.S.S. *Unity*, when the admiral had been almost blinded by flying splinters, and the previous captain's nerve had broken.

A day he would never forget. Neither would Ritchie, cut down by metal fragments: it was a wonder he had lived. Always a strong, tireless sailing-master of the old school, he was still trying not to show his pain and refusing to recognize his terrible limp, as if in the end it would somehow cure itself.

Urquhart touched his hat to the quarterdeck. There were countless men like Ritchie on the streets of any sea port in England.

Adam Bolitho smiled. 'Hard pull, was it?'

Urquhart nodded. Three days since they had quit Halifax, with only about five hundred miles to log for it. With the perverse winds and the prospect of storms, it was not the time of year for any one to be complacent, least of all the captain. But while Urquhart had been away from *Valkyrie* aboard the battered prize, the captain seemed to have changed in some way, and was quite cheerful.

Urquhart said, 'I've had the pumps going watch by watch, sir. She's built well enough, like most French ships, but the rot is something else. The old *Indom* gave her more than her share, I'd say!'

Adam said, 'We'll let *Success* fall off a point or so. That should ease the strain.' He stared abeam at the sea's face, set in a moving pattern of blue and pale green; it had an almost milky appearance, broken now and then by a lingering blast of wind, a north-easterly, which could make every sail strain and thunder like a roll of drums. The sea here looked almost shallow and the drifting gulf weed intensified the effect. He smiled. But there were three thousand

256

fathoms beneath the keel hereabouts, or so they said, although no one could know.

He watched the other frigate's sails lifting and puffing in the same passing squall. 'We'll take her in tow tomorrow, Mr Urquhart. It may slow us even more, but at least we'll stay in company.' He saw Urquhart's eyes move beyond his shoulder and heard the flag lieutenant's brisk footsteps on the deck. De Courcey had kept out of his way, and had in fact probably been instructed to do so by Keen. But would he learn anything on this passage? His future seemed already assured.

De Courcey touched his hat, with a cool glance at Urquhart's dishevelled appearance. 'Is all well?' He looked at Adam. 'Isn't it taking longer than expected, sir?'

Adam gestured across the nettings. 'Yonder lies the enemy, Mr de Courcey. America. In fact, Mr Ritchie insists that we are due east of Chesapeake Bay itself. I have to believe him, of course.'

Urquhart saw the sailing-master's quick, conspiratorial grin. It was more than that. It was pleasure that the captain could now joke with him. They had all known that Captain Adam Bolitho was one of the most successful frigate captains in the fleet, and the nephew of England's most respected, and loved, sailor, but it had been impossible to know him as a man. Urquhart also saw and was amused by the flag lieutenant's sudden alarm as he peered abeam, as if he expected to actually see the coastline.

Adam said, 'Two hundred miles, Mr de Courcey.' He glanced up as the masthead pendant cracked out like a long whip.

Urquhart wondered if he missed the sight of a rear-admiral's flag at the mizzen truck, or was he

257

savouring this independence, limited though it would be?

The previous day, the lookouts had sighted two small sail to the south-west. They had been unable to leave the damaged *Success* to give chase, so the strangers might have been anything, coasters willing to risk the British patrols if only to earn their keep, or enemy scouts. If the captain was troubled by it, he was disguising it well.

De Courcey said suddenly, 'Only two hundred miles, sir? I thought we were heading closer to the Bermudas.'

Adam smiled and touched his arm lightly, something else Urquhart had not seen him do before.

'The nor' easterlies are friendly, Mr de Courcey, but to whom, I wonder?' He turned to Urquhart, excluding the others. his face calm, assured. 'We'll pass a tow at first light. After that...' He did not continue.

Urquhart watched him walk away to speak with the sailing-master again. So certain. But how could he be? Why should he be? He considered the previous two captains, the intolerant and sarcastic Trevenen, who had broken in the face of real danger, and had vanished overboard without trace, and Captain Peter Dawes, the acting-commodore, who had been unable to think beyond promotion. Any fault would reflect badly on a first lieutenant, and Urquhart had intended never to fully trust a captain again, for his own sake. No one else would care what became of him.

De Courcey remarked, 'I wonder what he truly thinks?' When Urquhart remained silent, he went on, 'Works all of us like a man possessed, and then when he has a spare minute, he sits down aft, teaching that boy servant of his to write!' He laughed shortly. 'If that is what he is really doing!'

Urquhart said quietly, 'It is rumoured that Captain Bolitho is very skilled with both blade and pistol, Mr de Courcey. I suggest you do nothing to foster or encourage scandal. It could be the end of you, in more ways than one.'

Adam came back, his face in a small frown. 'May I ask you to take a meal with me, John? I doubt if *Success*'s fare is any sounder than her timbers!'

Urquhart smiled without reservation. 'I would be grateful, sir. But are you certain?' He looked up at the pendant, then at the real strength the two helmsmen were using against the kick of the wheel.

'Yes, I am sure of it. They need the wind, the advantage of it. For us to fight with only the land at our backs, first light will be soon enough.' He looked at him keenly. 'If I'm wrong, we shall be no worse off.'

For only a second, Urquhart saw the face he had just evoked for de Courcey. He could well imagine those same eyes, calm and unblinking along the barrel of a pistol in some quiet clearing at dawn, or testing the edge of his favourite sword. And quite suddenly, he was glad of it.

Adam said, almost casually, 'When this is over and we are back about our rightful affairs, I intend to put you forward for promotion.'

Urquhart was taken aback. 'But, sir—I don't think—I am satisfied to serve you...' He got no further.

Adam said, 'That's enough,' and shook his arm a little for emphasis. 'Never say that, John. Never even think it.' He looked up at the sky and the quivering belly of the main topsail. 'My uncle once described

259

his first command as the greatest gift. But it is much more than that.' His eyes hardened. 'Which is why I mistrust those who betray such a privilege.' Then he seemed to shake off the mood. 'At noon, then. Today is Friday, is it not?' He smiled, and Urquhart wondered why there was no woman in his life. 'Tonight the toast will be, a willing foe and enough sea room. A perfect sentiment!'

That evening the wind rose again, and backed to northeast-by-north. Urquhart was pulled once more to the *Success*, and was drenched in spray before he was halfway across.

Somehow, he did not care. The stage was set. And he was ready.

* * *

Captain Adam Bolitho walked across the black and white checkered deck covering and stared through the tall stern windows. The wind had eased a good deal overnight, but still made its presence felt in short, fierce gusts, dashing the spray high over the ship until it pattered from the dripping sails like rain.

He saw the murky outline of the other frigate, her shape distorted by the caked salt on the glass, her bearing so extreme that she appeared out of control, adrift.

It had been hard work to pass the tow across at first light, requiring tough, experienced seamanship, or as Evan Jones, the boatswain, had been heard to remark, 'All brute force and bloody ignorance!' But they had done it. Now, yawing drunkenly to each gust of wind, the *Success* fought her tow like a beast being led to slaughter.

He heard eight bells chime from the forecastle and

260

made himself leave the windows. He glanced around the big cabin. Keen's quarters: he had almost expected to see him here at the table where he had placed his own chart within easy reach, so that Ritchie or the lieutenants should not be able to watch his concern as one more hour passed. He leaned on the table, the American coastline under one palm. He had seen his uncle do this, holding the sea in his hands, translating ideas into action. *In so many ways we are very alike. But in others. . . .*

He straightened his back and looked up at the skylight as somebody laughed. Urquhart had kept his word. Others might suspect his intentions, but nobody knew. And they could still laugh. It was said that when Trevenen had been in command, any sound had been offensive to him. Laughter would be like insubordination or worse.

He thought of the book of poems which Keen had given him, here in this very cabin, with, he believed, few memories of the girl who had owned it, and not knowing the pain it had aroused. And here, he had seen the miniature that Gilia St Clair had intended another to keep and cherish.

More voices came down from the quarterdeck and for a moment he thought he heard a lookout. But it was only another working party, splicing, stitching, repairing: a sailor's lot.

The door opened and the boy John Whitmarsh stood looking in at him.

Adam asked, 'What is it?'

The boy said, 'You've not touched your breakfast, Cap'n. Coffee's cold, too.'

Adam sat in one of Keen's chairs and said, 'No matter.'

'I can fetch some fresh coffee, sir.' He looked at the

261

chart and said gravely, 'Cape Breton to . . .' He hesitated, his lips moving as he studied the heavy print at the top of the chart. 'To Delaware Bay.' He turned and stared at him, his eyes shining. 'I *read* it, sir! Just like you said I would!'

Adam walked into the other cabin, unable to watch the boy's excitement and pleasure. 'Come here, John Whitmarsh.' He opened his chest and withdrew a parcel. 'D' you know the date of today?'

The boy shook his head. 'It be Saturday, sir.'

Adam held out the parcel. 'July twenty-first. I could not very well forget it. It was the day I was posted.' He tried to smile. 'It was also listed in *Anemone*'s log as the date when you were volunteered. Your birthday.' The boy was still staring at him, and he said roughly, 'Here, take it. It's yours.'

The boy opened the parcel as if it were dangerous to touch, then gasped as he saw the finely made dirk and polished scabbard. 'For me, sir?'

'Yes. Wear it. You are thirteen years old. Not an easy passage, eh?'

John Whitmarsh was still staring at it. 'Mine.' It was all he said, or could say.

Adam swung round and saw the second lieutenant, William Dyer, staring in from the passageway.

Dyer seemed to be a reliable officer and Urquhart had spoken well of him, but it was too good a piece of gossip to miss. What he had just witnessed would soon be all over the wardroom. The captain giving gifts to a cabin boy. Losing his grip.

Adam quietly said, 'Well, Mr Dyer?' They could think what they damned well pleased. He had known few acts of kindness when he himself had been that age. He could scarcely remember his mother, except

262

for her constant love, and even now he did not understand how she could have given herself like a common whore in order to support her son, whose father had not known of his existence.

Dyer said, 'The master sends his respects, sir, and he is anxious about our present course. We will have to change tack shortly for the next leg—a hard enough task, even without that great drag on the tow-line.'

Adam said, 'The master thinks that, does he? And what do you think?'

Dyer flushed. 'I thought it better coming from me, sir. In Mr Urquhart's place, I felt it was my duty to bring his unease to your notice myself.'

Adam walked back to the chart. 'You did well.' Had Urquhart seen the folly of his idea? For folly was what it would be. 'You deserve an answer. So does Mr Ritchie.'

Dyer gaped as Adam swung round and shouted, 'The sky-light, John Whitmarsh! Open the skylight!'

The boy climbed on a chair to reach it, his new dirk still clutched in one hand.

Adam heard the wind gusting against the hull and imagined it ruffling the sea's face, like a breeze on a field of standing corn. The cry came again. *Two sail to th' nor' east!'*

Adam said sharply, 'That is the answer, Mr Dyer. The enemy was not asleep, it seems.' To the boy he said, 'Fetch my sword, if you please. We shall both be properly presented today.'

Then he laughed aloud, as if it were some secret joke. 'July twenty-first, 1813! It will be another day to remember!'

Dyer exclaimed, 'The enemy, sir? How can it be certain?'

'You doubt me?'

'But, but ... if they intend to attack us they will hold the wind-gage. All the advantages will be theirs!' He did not seem able to stop. 'Without the tow we might stand a chance....'

Adam saw the boy returning with his captain's hanger. 'All in good time, Mr Dyer. Tell Mr Warren to hoist Flag Seven for *Success* to recognize. Then pipe all hands aft. I wish to address them.'

Dyer asked in a small voice, 'Will we fight, sir?'

Adam looked around the cabin, perhaps for the last time. He forced himself to wait, to feel doubt, or worse, a fear he had not known before *Anemone* had been lost.

He said, 'Be assured, Mr Dyer, we shall win this day.' But Dyer had already hurried away.

He raised his arms so that the boy could clip on his sword, as his coxswain, George Starr, had used to do: Starr, who had been hanged for what he had done aboard *Anemone* after her flag had come down. Without knowing that he spoke aloud, he repeated, 'We shall *win* this day.'

He glanced once more at the open skylight, and smiled. A very close thing. Then he walked out of the cabin, the boy following his shadow without hesitation.

*   *   *

Midshipman Francis Lovie lowered his telescope and wiped his streaming face with the back of his hand.

'*Flag Seven*, sir!'

Urquhart eyed him grimly. It had come as he expected, but it was still a shock. The captain's private signal.

264

He took the telescope from Lovie's hands and trained it towards the other ship. His ship. Where he had been trusted, even liked by some when he had stood between *Valkyrie's* company and a tyrant of a captain. As it must have been in *Reaper*, and in too many other ships. Adam Bolitho's words seemed to intrude through all his doubts and uncertainties. *I mistrust those who betray such a privilege.* He watched the familiar figures leap into the lens, men he knew so well: Lieutenant Dyer, and beside him the most junior lieutenant, Charles Gulliver, not long ago a midshipman like the one who was sharing this dangerous task with him. Lovie was seventeen, and Urquhart liked to believe that he himself had played his part in making him what he was. Lovie was ready to sit his examination for lieutenant.

He moved the glass slightly, feeling the warm spray on his mouth and hair. Ritchie was there, listening intently with his master's mates close by, Barlow, the new lieutenant of marines, his face as scarlet as his tunic in the misty sunlight. Beyond them the mass of sailors, some of whom he knew and trusted, and others whom he accepted would never change, the hard men who saw all authority as a deadly enemy. But fight? Yes, they would do that well enough.

And there was the captain, his back towards him, his shoulders shining and wet as if he did not care, did not feel anything beyond his instinct, which had not failed him.

Lovie asked, 'What will the captain tell them, sir?'

Urquhart did not look at him. 'What I will tell *you*, Mr Lovie. We will stand by the tow, and break it when we are so ordered.'

Lovie watched his profile. Urquhart was the only first lieutenant he had ever known, and secretly he

265

hoped that he himself would be as good, if he ever got the chance.

He said, 'The fuse you laid, sir. You've known all this time.'

Urquhart watched the image in the glass. Men cheering: but for the wind they would have heard the sound from here.

'Guessed would be closer to the truth. I thought it was a last resort to prevent the prize being retaken.' He lowered the glass and regarded him intently. 'And then, suddenly I understood. Captain Bolitho *knew*, and had already decided what he must do.'

Lovie frowned. 'But there's two of them, sir. Suppose....'

Urquhart smiled. 'Aye, suppose—that one word, which never appears in dispatches.' He recalled Adam Bolitho's face when he had first come aboard and had read himself in: a sensitive, guarded face, which betrayed little of what it must have cost him to lose a ship, be a prisoner of war, and endure the ritual of a court-martial. When, very rarely, he allowed himself to relax, as he had yesterday when they had shared a meal, Urquhart had glimpsed the man behind the mask. In some ways, still a prisoner. Of something, or someone.

Urquhart said, 'You stand fast and watch the tow. Call me immediately if anything happens.' He was about to add something humourous, but changed his mind abruptly and headed for the companion way. Knowledge came like a blow in the face, something he could not forget or ignore. Lovie was standing where he had left him, perhaps dreaming of the day when he, too, would wear a lieutenant's rank.

Urquhart clattered down the ladder and stood for a few minutes in the shadows to compose himself. It was not the first time this had happened, and he had heard others, more experienced, speak of it. But in his heart he knew that Midshipman Lovie would not be alive by the end of the day.

A gunner's mate was watching him, a slow match moving in his fist like a solitary evil eye.

'All ready, Jago?' It was something to say. The gunner's mate was a true seaman, which was why he had picked him in the first place. Trevenen had had him flogged for some trivial offence and Urquhart had clashed with the captain about it. The rift had cost him dearly; he knew that now. Even Dawes had never mentioned the possibility of promotion to him. But his efforts had earned him Jago's trust, and something far stronger, although he would carry the scars of that unjustified flogging to the grave.

Jago grinned. 'Just give the word, sir!'

No question, no doubts. Perhaps it was better to be like that.

He looked up the ladder, to a patch of pale blue sky. 'The boats will be warped alongside. The rest is up to us.'

He walked on through the ship, where many men had once worked and lived, hoped too. Men who spoke the same language, but whose common heritage had become like an unbroken reef between nations at war.

Urquhart listened to the creak of the tiller, and the lonely clank of a single pump.

It was almost done. The ship was already dead.

*   *   *

Ritchie called, 'Course is south south-east, sir. Steady as she goes.'

267

Adam walked a few paces to the rail and back again. It seemed strangely still and quiet after the tapping drums had beaten *Valkyrie's* seamen and marines to quarters. He had felt the sudden unnerving excitement, and after that, the cheering. It had been unexpected, and overwhelming. These men were still strangers for the most part, because he had kept them so, but their huzzas had been infectious, and he had seen Ritchie forgetting himself so far as to shake hands with George Minchin, the surgeon, who had made a rare appearance on deck to listen to the captain speaking. Minchin was a butcher of the old orlop tradition, but in spite of his brutal trade and his dependence on rum, he had saved more lives than he had lost, and had won the praise of the great surgeon, Sir Piers Blachford, when he had been aboard *Hyperion*.

Lieutenant Dyer said, 'The enemy are on the same bearing, sir.'

Adam had seen them briefly, two frigates, the same ones or others unknown to him. Perhaps it did not matter. But he knew that it did.

He glanced astern and pictured the two ships as he had last seen them. Their captains would have marked *Valkyrie's* every change of course, no matter how small. They would expect them to cast off the tow: any captain would, unless he wanted to sacrifice his ship without a fight.

Suppose they did not swallow the ruse? He might lose Urquhart and his prize crew, to be forced to leave them, if only to save his own command.

Run? He beckoned to the signals midshipman. 'Mr Warren! Get aloft with your glass and tell me what you see.' He turned, and watched de Courcey walking stiffly to the lee side as if to study some marines, who were climbing to the maintop with more ammunition for the swivel there. He had removed his epaulette and the twist of gold lace that proclaimed him to be admiral's flag lieutenant, perhaps in the hope of offering a less tempting target if the enemy drew close enough.

Adam heard the midshipman yell, 'The rear ship wears a broad-pendant, sir!'

He breathed out slowly. A commodore then, like Nathan Beer . . . He dismissed the thought. No, not at all like the impressive Beer. He must forget him. It was not merely foolish to show admiration for an enemy, it was also dangerous. If this was the man his uncle suspected, there could be no admiration. Out of personal hatred, he had already tried to avenge himself on Sir Richard Bolitho by any means he could invent, and Adam was almost convinced that it was the same mind which had planned to use him as bait to tempt his uncle into a rescue attempt. He often thought of that bare but strangely beautiful room, where he had been interrogated by the American captain, Brice. Perhaps Brice would recall that meeting when he received news of his son's death.

Hatred was the key, if it was in fact Rory Aherne, whose father had been hanged for treason in Ireland. An incident long forgotten in the confusion and pain of many years of war, but he had not forgotten: nor would he forgive. Perhaps it had given this unknown Aherne a purpose, and allowed him to achieve a measure of fame which might otherwise have escaped him. A renegade, a privateer, who had found a place in America's young but aggressive navy. Some might sing his praises for a while, but renegades were never fully trusted. Like John Paul Jones, the Scot who had found glory and respect in battles against England.

Nevertheless, he had never been offered another command, famous or not.

He frowned. *Like my father....*

There was a dull bang, which echoed around the ship as if the sound were trapped in a cave. The solitary ball ripped abeam of the *Success* before splashing down in a cloud of spray.

Somebody said, 'Bow-chaser.'

Dyer remarked, 'First shot.'

Adam took out his watch and opened the guard, remembering the dim shop, the ticking clocks, the silvery chorus of chimes. He did not glance at the mermaid, trying not to think of her or hear her voice. *Not now.* She would understand, and forgive him.

He said, 'Note it in the log, Mr Ritchie. The date and the time. I fear that only *you* will know the place!'

Ritchie grinned, as Adam had known he would. Was it so easy to make men smile, even in the face of death?

He closed the watch with a snap and returned it to his pocket.

'Leading ship is changing tack, sir. I think she intends to close with the prize!'

The lieutenant sounded surprised. Baffled. Adam had tried to explain, when the lower deck had been cleared and the hands piped aft. All night long the two American frigates had beaten and clawed their way into the teeth of the wind. *All night long*: determined, confident that they would take and hold the wind-gage, so that *Valkyrie* could either stand and fight against the odds, or become the quarry in a stern-chase, to be pounded into submission at long range or finally driven aground.

They had not cheered out of any sense of duty: they had seen and done too much already to need to prove

270

themselves. Perhaps they had cheered simply because he had told them, and they knew, just this once, what they were doing, and why.

He strode to the shrouds and climbed into the ratlines, his legs soaked with spray as he levelled his telescope at a point beyond Urquhart's temporary command.

There she was. A big frigate, thirty-eight guns at least, French-built like *Success*. Before the glass misted over, he saw hurrying figures massing along the enemy's gangway. *Success* was under tow, her guns still secured and unmanned. The whole of Halifax had probably heard about it, and there were many other ears only too ready to listen.

He returned to the deck. 'Make the signal, Mr Warren. *Cast off!*'

He could see the upper yards of the enemy frigate criss-crossing with those of *Success*, but knew that they were not yet close, let alone alongside. There were a few shots: marksmen in the tops testing the range, seeking a kill like hounds after a wounded stag.

Success seemed to suddenly grow in size and length as the tow broke free and she yawed around, her few sails in wild disorder to the wind.

Adam clenched his fists against his thighs. *Come on. Come on.* It was taking too long. They would be up to her in minutes, but still might sheer away if they suspected anything.

Warren said hoarsely, 'One boat pulling away, sir!'

Adam nodded, his eyes stinging but unable to blink. Urquhart's boat would be next, and soon. Or not at all.

More shots, and he saw the gleam of sunlight on steel as the boarders prepared to hack their way

271

aboard the drifting prize. He tried to shut it from his thoughts. he shouted, 'Stand by to come about, Mr Ritchie! Mr Monteith, more hands on the weather braces there!' He saw the gun captains crouched low and ready, while they waited for the next order.

He felt rather than saw de Courcey by the quarterdeck rail, speaking rapidly to himself, as though he were praying. The enemy's yards were being hauled round, to lessen the impact when the two hulls ground together.

Adam saw the boat pulling away from both ships, fear giving them the strength and the purpose.

Somebody said quietly, 'The first lieutenant's left it too late.'

He snapped, 'Hold your bloody noise, damn you!' and barely recognized his own voice.

Ritchie saw it first: all the years at sea in many different conditions, matching his eye against sun and star, wind and current. A man who, even without a sextant, could probably find his way back to Plymouth.

'Smoke, sir!' He glared round at his mates. 'By Jesus, *he done it!*'

The explosion was like a fiery wind, so great that despite the thousands of fathoms of sea beneath them, it felt as if they had run aground on solid rock.

Then the flames, leaping from hatches and through fiery holes that opened in the decks like craters, the wind exploring and driving them until her sails became blackened rags and her rigging was spitting sparks. The fires spread rapidly to the American grappled alongside, where jubilant figures had been cheering and waving their weapons only seconds before.

Adam raised his fist.

'For *you*, George Starr, and *you*, John Bankart. *Let them never forget!*'

'There's the other boat now, sir!' Dyer sounded shocked by what he was seeing, the very savagery of it.

Ritchie called, 'Standing by, sir!'

Adam raised the telescope, and then said, 'Belay that, Mr Ritchie.'

He had seen the first lieutenant at the tiller, the remaining seamen lying back on their looms, no doubt staring at the exploding flames which had almost consumed them. Beside Urquhart lay the midshipman, Lovie, staring at the smoke and the sky, and seeing neither.

To those around him Adam said, 'We'll pick them up first—we have the time we need. I'll not lose John Urquhart now.'

The two frigates were completely ablaze, and appeared to be leaning toward one another in a final embrace. *Success*'s bilge had been blown out in the first explosion, and grappled to her attacker, she was taking the American with her to the bottom.

A few men were splashing about in the water; others floated away, already dead or dying from their burns. From a corner of his eye Adam saw Urquhart's small boat drifting clear of *Valkyrie's* side. It was empty: only the midshipman's coat with its white patches lay in the sternsheets to mark the price of courage.

He hardened himself to it, and tried to exclude the sounds of ships breaking up, guns tearing adrift and thundering through the flames and choking smoke, where even now a few demented souls would be stumbling and falling, calling for help when there was none to respond.

Midshipman Warren called, 'The other ship's standing away, sir!' Adam looked at him and saw the tears on his cheeks. All this horror, but he was able to think only of his friend, Lovie.

Ritchie cleared his throat. 'Give chase, sir?'

Adam looked at the upturned faces. 'I think not, Mr Ritchie. Back the mizzen tops'l while we recover the other boat.' He could not see the American ship with the commodore's broad-pendant: it was lost in the smoke, or the painful obscurity of his own vision.

'Two down, one to go. I think we can rest on a promise.'

He saw Urquhart coming slowly toward him. Two members of a gun's crew stood to touch his arm as he passed. He paused only to say something to Adam's servant, Whitmarsh, who, despite orders, had been on deck throughout. He would be remembering, too. Perhaps this was also vengeance for him.

Adam stretched out his hand. 'I am relieved that you did not leave it too late.'

Urquhart looked at him gravely. 'Almost.' His handshake was firm, thankful. 'I'm afraid I lost Mr Lovie. I liked him. Very much.'

Adam thought of one of his own midshipmen, who had died on that other day. It was pointless, destructive to have friends, to encourage others to form friendships which would only end in death.

When he looked again, *Success* and the American were gone. There was only a great haze of smoke, like steam from a volcano, as if the ocean itself were burning in the deep, and wreckage, men and pieces of men.

He walked to the opposite side and wondered why he had not known. To hate was not enough.

CHAPTER FOURTEEN

VERDICT

Rear-Admiral Thomas Herrick stood squarely by the quarter-deck rail, his chin sunk in his neckcloth, and only his eyes moving while *Indomitable*, under reduced sail, glided slowly toward her anchorage.

'So this is Halifax.' His eyes followed the running figures of the extra hands who were answering the boatswain's hoarse shout. Only then did he turn his head and glance at the captain on the opposite side of the deck. Tyacke was studying the landmarks, the nearest ships, anchored or otherwise, his hands behind him as if he were unconcerned.

Herrick said, 'A good ship's company, Sir Richard. Better than most. Your Captain Tyacke would be hard to replace, I'm thinking.'

Bolitho said, 'Yes,' sorry that they were soon to be parted, and also saddened on behalf of the man he had once known so well. He had offered Herrick the full use of the ship while she was in Halifax, and typically, Herrick had refused. He would take the accommodation he had been offered. It was as if it was painful for him simply to see and feel a ship working around him again.

York, the sailing-master, called, 'Ready when you are, sir!'

Tyacke nodded, without turning. 'Wear ship, if you please!'

'Man the lee braces there! Hands wear ship!' The calls shrilled and more men scampered to add their weight to haul the yards around. 'Tops'l sheets!'

Two fishermen stood in their heavy dory to wave as they passed through *Indomitable's* shadow.

Bolitho saw one of the midshipmen waving back, then freeze as he found the captain's eyes on him.

'Tops'l clew lines! Roundly there—take that man's name, Mr Craigie!'

Bolitho had already noticed that *Valkyrie* was not at her usual anchorage, nor was the American ship *Success*. He was not surprised that the latter had been moved. The harbour, large though it was, seemed to be bursting with ships, men-of-war, merchantmen and transport vessels of every type and size.

'Helm a' lee!'

Slowly, as though recalling her earlier life as a ship of the line, *Indomitable* turned into the light wind, the panorama of houses and rough hillside gliding past her jib-boom, as if the land and not the ship was moving.

'*Let go!*'

The great anchor dropped into the water, spray dashing as high as the beakhead and its crouching lion while the ship came obediently to rest.

'I'll have the gig take you ashore, Thomas. I can send my flag lieutenant with you until you are ready....'

The bright blue eyes studied him for a moment. 'I can manage, thank you.' Then he held out his remaining hand, his body visibly adjusting to the movement, as if still unaccustomed to the loss. 'I can see why you have never quit the sea for some high office ashore or in the Admiralty. I would be the same, if they had allowed it.' He spoke with the same curious lack of bitterness. 'I'll wager you'd find no Happy Few in that damned place!'

Bolitho took his hand in both of his own. 'There

276

are not too many left, I'm afraid, Thomas.'

They both looked along the deck, the busy seamen, the marines waiting by the entry port, the first lieutenant leaning out from the forecastle to check the lie of the cable. *Even here*, Bolitho thought. Charles Keverne had been his first lieutenant in the three-decker *Euryalus*, when he had been a flag captain himself. A reliable officer despite a hasty temper, with the dark good looks which had won him a lovely wife. About twelve years ago, as a captain, Keverne had commanded this same ship, when she had been a third-rate. Together they had fought in the Baltic. Once again, *Indomitable* had triumphed, but Keverne had fallen there.

Herrick watched his sea-chest and bags being carried on deck. The gig was already hoisted out: the contact was almost severed.

Herrick paused by the ladder, and Bolitho saw the Royal Marine colour-sergeant give a quick signal to his officer.

Herrick was fighting with something. Stubborn, strong-willed, intransigent, but loyal, always loyal above everything.

'What is it, Thomas?'

Herrick did not look at him. 'I was wrong to regard your feeling for Lady Somervell so ill. I was so full of grief for my Dulcie that I was blind to all else. I tried to tell her in a letter....'

'I know. She was very moved by it. And so was I.'

Herrick shook his head. 'But I can see now, don't you understand? What you've done for the navy, for England, no less—and yet still you drive yourself.' He reached out and seized Bolitho's arm. 'Go while you can, Richard. Take your Catherine and be grateful. Let some one else carry this goddamned

277

burden, this war that nobody wants, except those who intend to profit from it! *It is not our war*, Richard. Just this once, accept it!'

Bolitho could feel the strength of the man in the grip of the solitary hand. No wonder he had forced himself to climb the ship's side, to prove what he could do, and who he was.

'Thank you for saying that, Thomas. I shall tell Catherine when I write to her next.'

Herrick walked beside him to the entry port. His bags and sea-chest had vanished. He saw Allday waiting, and said, 'Take care, you rascal.' He stared past him at the land. 'I was sorry to hear about your son. But your daughter will give you much happiness.'

Allday looked at Bolitho. It was as if he had known what Herrick had just said, had felt the very urgency of the plea.

'He won't listen to me, Mr Herrick. Never does!'

Herrick held out his hand to Tyacke. 'She does you credit, Captain Tyacke. You have suffered for what you have earned, but I envy you, for all that.' He turned toward Bolitho and removed his hat. 'You, Captain, and one other.'

The calls shrilled and the marines' bayonets flashed in the bright sunlight.

When Bolitho looked down once more, the gig was already backing water from the side. He watched until it was lost beyond an anchored brigantine. Then he smiled. Typically, again, Herrick did not look back.

Tyacke fell into step beside him. 'Well, I don't envy him *his* job, Sir Richard. It's *Reaper's* captain who should be on trial. I've run better slavers up to the mainyard before now!'

Bolitho said, 'He may surprise us, but I agree. His is a thankless task.' But the force of Herrick's words refused to leave him, and he could not imagine what it must have cost him to speak them.

Tyacke said suddenly, 'This victory you mentioned, Sir Richard. Some place in Spain, you said?'

It was said to be Wellington's greatest triumph over the French so far. The war could not last much longer, surely.

Bolitho replied, 'They speak of months, not years any more, James. I have learned not to hope too much. And yet...' He watched the courier schooner *Reynard* speeding toward the harbour mouth, her ensign dipping in salute as she passed abeam of his flagship. A small, lively command for the young lieutenant who was her lord and master. Like *Miranda*, the schooner which had been Tyacke's first command; he would be thinking of it now, and of their own first wary meeting. What they had now become to one another.

He said abruptly, 'Well, James, the war is still with us here, so I *shall* have to accept it!'

*　　　*　　　*

Bolitho stood by a window and watched his flag lieutenant walking along the stone-flagged terrace, carrying his hat in the warm sunshine. In the background, the anchorage was so crowded that it was hardly possible to see *Indomitable*. But for his flag curling in the wind, she might have been any one of them.

Valentine Keen was saying, 'I decided to send *Valkyrie* to Antigua. She was the only ship powerful

279

enough to escort the prize and frighten off any over-eager enemy.'

In the glass Bolitho saw Keen's reflected arm wave across the litter of papers and dispatches which the schooner *Reynard* had delivered to him. Bolitho had sensed a moment's uneasiness when the schooner had sailed smartly abeam as he had been speaking to Tyacke: *Reynard's* youthful commander had known then that Keen was here, otherwise he would have made his report on board *Indomitable*.

'*Valkyrie* met with two American frigates. It is all here in Adam's report, which he passed to *Reynard* when they happened to meet at sea.'

'And one was destroyed, Val. *Valkyrie* suffered no losses but for a midshipman. Remarkable.'

'Yes, they picked up a few survivors, not many, apparently, and discovered that the ship that went down with *Success* was the U.S.S. *Condor*. A Captain Ridley was in command, killed, with most of his people, it seems.'

'And the other frigate was the *Retribution*.'

Keen did not seem to hear him. 'I did not intend that either *Valkyrie* or the prize should be put at unnecessary risk. Had I been aboard, I would have made certain that a more open course was observed. Captain Bolitho was too near to the enemy coast.'

'Two hundred miles, you say?' He turned from the glare, his eye suddenly painful. 'You and I have trailed our coats a good deal nearer than that, in our time!'

'I think it was deliberate.' Keen faced him across the table.

'I know he is your nephew, and I am the first to appreciate that. But I think it was an impetuous and dangerous course of action. We could have lost both ships.'

Bolitho said, 'As it was, Val, we exchanged a broken-down prize which would have taken months or perhaps years to overhaul and refit, for one of a group which has been a thorn in our side since our return to Halifax. Your place was here, while you were waiting to receive the latest convoy. You made the right decision, and it was yours to make. And as the one in command, Adam had no choice but to act as he did. I would expect that of any of my captains. You must know that.'

Keen recovered himself with an effort. 'The survivors also confirmed your belief that Captain, now Commodore Rory Aherne was in command of the group.' He banged his hand down on the papers, and anger put an edge to his voice. 'He might have taken my flagship!'

'And Adam—where is he now?'

Keen plucked his shirt away from his skin. 'He had orders for the Captain in Charge at Antigua. He will return here when he has carried out my instructions.'

'Remember when you were my flag captain, Val. Trust extends in two directions. It has to be the strongest link in the chain of command.'

Keen stared at him. 'I have never forgotten that. I owe everything to you ... and Catherine.' He smiled, ruefully, Bolitho thought, and said, 'And to Adam, I know that!' He touched his pocket, and Bolitho wondered if he carried the miniature there. So that was it. This was, after all, Benjamin Massie's house, and the St Clairs would be staying here also. It was not difficult to guess what had come between Keen and his flag captain. *The girl with moonlit eyes.*

In fairness, it might prove to be the best thing that could happen to Keen. As Catherine had predicted

... A brave and defiant young woman, one strong enough to help Keen in his future. And able to stand up against his father, he thought grimly.

Adam would not regard it in that light at all.

'And what of the latest intelligence, Val?'

Keen took two goblets from a cupboard. 'The Americans have brought two more frigates to Boston. I ordered *Chivalrous* and the brig *Weazle* to patrol outside the port. If they come out....'

Bolitho said, 'I think they will. And soon.' He looked up, and asked, 'And York—is there any more news?'

Keen shrugged. 'Very little. It takes so long to reach here. But David St Clair told me that weapons and supplies were stored there for our ships on the lakes. They might have seized or destroyed them. Either way, it will make our vessels less able to control Lake Erie, which St Clair insists is the vital key to the whole area.'

'And tell me about *Miss* St Clair.' He saw Keen start, so that some of the claret he was about to pour pattered onto the table. He added gently, 'I shall not pry, Val. I am a friend; remember that, too.'

Keen filled the two goblets. 'I admire her greatly. I have told her as much.' He faced him again. 'Perhaps I delude myself.' He gave his boyish smile, which Bolitho had seen from his youth to this moment, and seemed relieved that he had at last spoken openly about it.

Bolitho thought of Adam's despair, his agony when he had read Catherine's letter, breaking the news of Zenoria's lonely and terrible death. But he said, 'Thank you for sharing it with me. I wish you good fortune, Val. You deserve it.' He returned the smile, touched by Keen's obvious relief. 'I mean it.

You cannot be an admiral all of the time!'

Keen said suddenly, 'I am told that Rear-Admiral Herrick is here. Transferred to *Indomitable* when you made your rendezvous with the convoy.' He did not attempt to soften his tone.

'I know there was no love lost between you, Val. He does not relish this mission, let me assure you.'

Keen said shortly, 'The right man for the task, I think. He has known what it is to sit on both sides of the table at a court-martial!'

'That is past, Val. It has to be.'

Keen persisted, 'But what can he do? Ninety men, British sailors. Hang them or flog them? The crime was done, the penalty is already decided. It has always been so.'

Bolitho moved to the window again, and saw Avery speaking with Gilia St Clair.

Without turning he asked, 'When you met up with *Reaper*, and before she struck to you, did you believe that Adam would order the guns to fire on them?' He waited a few seconds. 'Hostages or not?'

'I . . . am not certain.'

Bolitho saw the girl throw back her head and laugh at something Avery had said. Caught up in a war, and now in something more personal. She had talked with Adam: she would have known, or guessed, how near death might have been that day.

He walked away from the window, turning his back on the light. 'The schooner *Crystal* in which the St Clairs were on passage when *Reaper* captured them—who owned her?'

'I believe it was Benjamin Massie. You have a very good memory for names.'

Bolitho put down the glass, thankful for the

sunlight behind him, hiding his face and his thoughts.

'It's getting better all the while, Val!'

*   *   *

Richard Bolitho stepped on to the jetty stairs and waited for Tyacke and his flag lieutenant to follow him. Across the heads of the barge crew Allday was watching him, sharing it all with him, even if he probably saw things differently.

Bolitho said to him, 'I'm not certain how long we shall be.'

Allday squinted into the hard light. 'We'll be here, Sir Richard.'

They walked up to the roadway in silence, and Bolitho noted that the air felt cooler despite the sun. It was September: could the year be passing so quickly?

He thought of the letter he had received from Catherine, telling him of Roxby's final hours, and describing the funeral in detail so that he felt he had been there with her. Quite a grand affair, as was appropriate for a knight of the Hanoverian Guelphic Order: Roxby had been well liked by his own set of people, respected by all those who worked for him, and feared by many others who had crossed his path in his other role as magistrate. He had a been a fair man, but he would have had little patience with today's happenings. Even in the barge Bolitho had sensed the tension, the oarsmen avoiding his eyes, Avery staring abeam at the anchored *Reaper*, and Tyacke quite detached from it all, more withdrawn than he had been for many months.

He raised his hat to a troop of soldiers as they clattered past on perfectly matched horses, their young ensign raising his sabre with a flourish at the sight of an admiral's uniform.

All these soldiers. When would they be called upon to fight, or was the die already cast? Tyacke, like David St Clair, had been right about the Americans and their determination to take and hold the lakes. They had made another raid on York, and had burned supply sheds and military equipment which had been abandoned when the British army had retreated to Kingston three months ago. The need to wrest control of Lake Erie from the Americans was vital, to protect the line of water communications and keep open the army's only supply route, without which they would be forced into further retreat, and perhaps even surrender.

He saw the barracks gates ahead of them, and realized with pleasure that he was not out of breath.

The guard had turned out of them, with bayonets glinting as they walked into the main building. A corporal opened the doors for them, and Bolitho saw his eyes move briefly to Tyacke's disfigured face, and then just as hastily away. He knew that Tyacke had noticed, and wondered if that was why he was so unusually remote. He was intensely aware of the stares, the pity, and the revulsion: he was never allowed to forget, and Bolitho knew that that was why he avoided going ashore whenever possible.

More doors and clicking heels, and then they entered a large, spartan room containing a table and two rows of chairs. Keen and Adam were already present, as was the languid de Courcey. A dusty-looking civilian clerk sat at one end of the table, a major of the Royal Marines at the other. Despite the room's bare austerity, it already had the atmosphere of an official court.

They shook hands, more like strangers than

friends. Bolitho had seen very little of Adam since his return from Antigua, but had written to congratulate him on his destruction of the prize and her attacker, with the loss of only one man. It was hard to tell what Adam really thought about it.

The other door was opened and Rear-Admiral Thomas Herrick walked straight to the table and sat down, his eyes moving briefly across their faces, his own impassive, with nothing to reveal the strain under which he had placed himself with his personally conducted enquiry into the loss and recapture of His Britannic Majesty's frigate *Reaper*.

Bolitho knew that Herrick had read all the statements, including that taken by Avery from *Reaper's* badly injured first lieutenant at Hamilton, and Adam's account of the recapture from the Americans when *Reaper's* guns had been discharged into the sea. Herrick had also spoken with David St Clair, and very likely with St Clair's daughter. Bolitho recalled the moment at the general's house when the youthful captain of the King's Regiment had handed the girl's miniature over to Keen. This latest attack on York had occasioned no more casualties, as the British army had not returned to the burned-out fort, but she must have thought of it, all the same: the man she had loved, and had believed had cared deeply for her, lying up there somewhere with his dead soldiers. The Americans had quit York after only three days; perhaps the stores and weapons they had hoped to find were already gone, or had been destroyed during the first attack. Compared with many other battles, the action was not one of the most significant, but in proportion it was certainly one of the bloodiest; and the full consequences were still to be measured.

Herrick looked up from his file of papers.

'This is an official court of enquiry into the loss and recapture of His Britannic Majesty's Ship *Reaper*, intelligence of which I am authorized and ordered to summarize for the Lords of Admiralty, for their guidance and final approval.'

He waited for the clerk to pass him another sheet of paper.

'We are all very well aware of the consequences of bad example, and of poor leadership. It is often too simple to be wise after an event which has already done so much wrong and caused so much damage.' For only a moment, his blue eyes rested on Bolitho. 'In all these years of war, against one foe or another, we have won many victories. However, we have never won the freedom to question or challenge what we did, or why we were so ordered.' He almost smiled. 'And I fear we never will, in our lifetimes.'

He looked down again. 'We require no reminding of the absolute need for order and discipline at all times. Without them, we are a shambles, a disgrace to the fleet in which we serve.' His shoulder moved, and the empty sleeve swayed slightly; he did not appear to notice. 'It is a lesson which any captain forgets at his peril.'

Bolitho glanced at his companions. Keen and Adam had both been his midshipmen, and had learned the hazards and the rewards on their way up the ladder of promotion. De Courcey was listening intently, but his expression was devoid of understanding. James Tyacke was leaning back in the shadows as if to conceal his face, but his hands, which rested in his lap, were very tense, locked together as if he, too, were preparing for the inevitable. Like those others who would be waiting:

287

some ninety souls, whose suffering under a sadistic captain would soon be obliterated in the name of justice.

He saw Adam gazing at him with unblinking eyes, his face drawn, as if he were in pain. But Bolitho knew it was a deeper pain even than the body's wounds: he was reliving the loss of his ship, the flag coming down while he lay where he had fallen on that bloody day. Remembering those who had fought and died at his bidding. Men who, as Herrick had rightly said, had never known the freedom to question or challenge what they were ordered to do.

He thought Adam must be remembering their many long conversations, each gaining from the other's experience. He was headstrong and impetuous, but his love had never been in doubt, caring always for the man who would be called upon to sign the warrants for those condemned to be hanged, or at best flogged into something inhuman.

Bolitho touched the locket beneath the fresh shirt he wore, and thought he saw understanding in Adam's face.

Herrick was saying, 'The Americans are, fortunately, a nation of magpies. They are slow to throw away items which may be of historic interest at some later time.'

He gestured to the clerk, and waited while he opened a large, canvas-covered volume.

Herrick continued, without expression, '*Reaper's* punishment book. It tells me more than five hundred written reports and dying declarations. This captain was not long in command and on his first active service as such, and yet this book reads like a chapter from Hell itself.'

Bolitho could almost feel Tyacke's sudden tension.

Wanting to speak out. But Herrick knew for himself what quarterdeck tyranny could be: Bolitho had become his captain in *Phalarope* all those years ago only because the previous captain had been removed. Another tyrant.

'To go back to that day, gentlemen. The mutiny, which we now know was both inspired and encouraged by the Americans who boarded that unhappy ship. There were ringleaders, of course, but without American aid and a ready presence, who could swear to the truth of what would have happened?' He peered at his papers, as he must have done every day since his arrival in Halifax. 'Vengeance is a terrible disease, but in this case it was probably inevitable. We know that *Reaper's* captain died as a result of the flogging he received that day.' He looked up sharply, his eyes hard. 'I have known common seamen die even under a *legal* flogging. We must not allow the deed to overshadow or dispel the cause.'

Two army officers strode past the closed doors, their noisy laughter dying instantly when they realized what was happening within. Herrick frowned. 'These observations are in my personal report, which will be presented to their lordships.' His eyes shifted to Bolitho. 'When I am gone from here.'

The frigate *Wakeful* had been taking on stores and water as he had been pulled ashore. Her work done on this station, she would be speeding back to England for fresh orders. Herrick would be taking passage in her again. Being 'entertained'.

Herrick glanced at a tumbler of water, but apparently rejected the idea. 'My considered conclusion in this miserable affair is that the two ringleaders, Alick Nisbet, Master-at-Arms, and Harry Ramsay, maintopman and able-bodied seaman, are detained, with a recommendation for the maximum penalty.'

Bolitho saw Adam clenching his fists until the knuckles were drained of blood beneath the tanned skin. He had heard about the man Ramsay, once of *Anemone*, whose mutilated back was living proof of the ship's punishment book. The other man was a surprise: the master-at-arms was the symbol of discipline and, when necessary, punishment aboard any King's ship, and he was usually hated for it.

And now the rest. He wanted to stand up and speak on behalf of the men he did not even know, but it would have damaged whatever frail hope they might still have.

Herrick continued, 'My further instruction is that all the other seamen and landmen involved be returned to their duties forthwith. They have suffered enough, and yet, when called, they would not, could not fire upon ships of this navy, no matter what the refusal would have cost them.'

Tyacke exclaimed, 'Hell's teeth! They'll crucify him when he gets back to London!' He turned and looked at Bolitho, his eyes revealing a rare emotion. 'I would never have believed it!'

Herrick said with no change of expression, 'I will insist that a new captain be appointed to *Reaper* without delay.' He glanced at Bolitho, then at Keen. 'That responsibility must be yours.'

Keen stood. 'My flag captain has already suggested such an officer for promotion, sir. Lieutenant John Urquhart.' He paused. 'I will support it, sir.'

Herrick said, 'Can you manage without him?'

Keen looked at Adam, who made a gesture of agreement, and said, 'We will, sir.'

Herrick beckoned to the clerk and the major of marines.

'Sign after my signature.' He straightened his back, and winced. 'It is done.' Then he said shortly, 'I wish to speak to Sir Richard Bolitho. Alone.'

It seemed an age before the others had filed out, and the room was silent.

Bolitho said, 'You did that for me, Thomas.'

Herrick said, 'I would relish a glass—a wet, as that rascal Allday calls it.' Then he looked up at him, searching for something, and finding it. 'I have nothing to lose, Richard. My flag will never fly again after this last passage. Maybe we shall meet again, but I think not. The navy is a family—you have often said as much. Once released from it, you become ordinary, like a ship laid up.'

A horse clattered noisily across the yard by the gates reminding Bolitho poignantly of Catherine and her Tamara. How would he tell her, describe to her all that Herrick had said, and had thrown away. . . .

Herrick walked to the doors, his shoulder angled stiffly, his face clearly showing the pain of his wound. He said, '*You* have everything to lose, as would all those godforsaken souls who depend on you, and those like you.' He added bitterly, 'Though I've yet to meet one!'

An invisible hand opened the doors, and Bolitho saw Avery waiting for him, his tawny eyes moving between them, trying to understand.

'We have had a messenger from the lookout, Sir Richard. The brig *Weazle* is entering harbour. She has signalled that the American vessels have left Boston with others from New York. They are steering north-east.'

Bolitho said quietly. 'So they're coming out. Pass the word to Captain Tyacke, George. I shall be aboard as soon as I can.' Avery hurried away, but stopped uncertainly and stared back at them.

Herrick said, 'Listen! Cheering! How could they know already?'

They walked down the steps together, while the cheering rolled across the harbour like one great voice.

Bolitho said, 'They always know, Thomas. The family, remember?'

Herrick looked back toward the barracks, his eyes suddenly, deeply fatigued.

'Take good care, Richard.' He touched his sleeve. 'I shall raise a glass to you when that young puppy hauls anchor for England!'

At the jetty they found Allday standing at the tiller of the admiral's barge with the crew grouped on the stairs, grinning hugely. Their places had been taken by officers, three of them captains, including Adam.

Herrick held out his hand to Tyacke. 'Your work, I presume, sir?'

Tyacke did not smile. 'All we could do at such short notice.'

Bolitho followed him down the stairs, recalling Tyacke's words. *They'll crucify him.* But Herrick would have his way. Perhaps the 'damned little upstart' Bethune had used his influence. He would know the man he had served as a midshipman better than many, and perhaps had attempted to help by subtle means.

Allday had seen Herrick's face and said awkwardly, 'I don't get too many chances to tell the officers what to do, an' that's no error!' Then he said,

292

'Good luck, Mr Herrick.' Just for those seconds they were back on board *Phalarope*, young lieutenant and pressed man.

The barge pulled away, the stroke surprisingly smart and regular. As they wended between the anchored men-of-war the cheering escorted them, some of it from *Reaper* herself. And this time Herrick did look back, although it was doubtful if he could see anything.

Bolitho turned away, and saw that Keen was speaking quietly with Gilia St Clair. And suddenly, he was glad for them.

'Call a boat, James. Sailing orders.'

Tyacke was gazing impassively after the barge. 'Aye, Sir Richard. But first....'

Bolitho smiled, but shared the unspoken sadness. 'A wet. So be it.'

CHAPTER FIFTEEN

NO DIN OF WAR

Richard Bolitho flattened the chart very carefully on his table and opened a pair of brass dividers. He could feel the others watching him, Avery standing by the stern windows, Yovell seated comfortably in a chair, paper and pens within easy reach as always.

Bolitho said, 'Two days, and we've sighted nothing.' He studied the chart again, imagining his ships as they might appear to a cruising sea bird: five frigates sailing in line abreast, with *Indomitable*, the flagship, in the centre. The extended line of frigates, half of his entire force, could scan a great expanse of ocean in this formation. The sky was clear, with only a few streaks of pale cloud, the sea a darker blue in the cool sunlight.

He thought of the solitary patrolling frigate, *Chivalrous*, which had sent the brig *Weazle* to Halifax with the news that the Americans were on the move again. In his mind's eye he could see *Chivalrous's* captain, Isaac Lloyd, an experienced officer, twenty-eight years old. He would be trying to keep the enemy in view, but would have sense enough not to be trapped into engaging them.

Two days, so where were they? In the approaches to Halifax, or out further still towards St John's in Newfoundland? He had discussed various possibilities with Tyacke and York. When he had suggested the Bay of Fundy to the north-west of Nova Scotia, York had been adamant.

'Unlikely, sir. The bay has the world's highest tides, twice a day for good measure. If I was the Yankee commander I wouldn't want to get trapped in the middle of that!'

Bolitho had been warned of the situation in the Bay of Fundy. His Admiralty Instructions had already stated that the tides could rise and fall as much as fifty feet and more, with the added risk to smaller vessels of fierce tidal bores. No place to risk a frigate, even the large Americans. Or *Indomitable*.

He thought of Herrick, on his way now across the Atlantic to throw his findings in someone's face at the Admiralty. Had he been glad to leave, after all? Or deep inside, was the old, tenacious Herrick still hating what amounted to a dismissal from the only life he knew?

It had obviously had a great effect on Tyacke. He had been more withdrawn than ever after Herrick had been taken out to the frigate which was to carry him back to England.

He tossed the dividers onto the chart. Perhaps this was all a waste of time, or worse, another ruse to draw them away from something more important.

He walked to the stern windows, and felt the ship lifting and leaning beneath him. That, too, he could see in his mind, *Indomitable* close-hauled on the larboard tack, the wind holding from the south-east as it had for most of the time since they had weighed anchor. Adam was openly fretting at having been left at Halifax, but *Valkyrie* was their second most powerful frigate: Keen might need her.

Adam had not hesitated in recommending his first lieutenant for promotion to the questionable command of *Reaper*. A challenge for any man, but Adam had said bluntly, 'I'd have taken her myself, had I been free to do so.' Were things between him and Val so strained?

Avery said gently, 'We could have missed them overnight, Sir Richard.'

'If they were looking for us, I think not.' Bolitho dismissed the thoughts, and recalled himself to the matter at hand. 'Ask Mr York to let me see his notes again, will you?'

The cabin was tilting over once more, and the brass dividers clattered onto the deck. Yovell tried to lean down to recover them, but the angle was so extreme that he sank back in his chair and mopped his face with a bright red handkerchief. But lively or not, the *Old Indom* was riding it well. As York had remarked with his usual cheerful confidence, 'Like a baldheaded barque she is, Sir Richard. Stiff in any wind and stiff when she's not!'

Yovell said suddenly, 'You could describe me as a

295

civilian, could you not, Sir Richard? Despite the warlike surroundings, and our way of life, I am not truly bound to the niceties and traditions of sea-officers?'

Bolitho smiled at him. He never changed. Not even in that wretched longboat, when his hands had been raw and bleeding from pulling on an oar with the others. With Catherine.

'I hope you remain so.'

Yovell frowned, then polished his small gold-rimmed spectacles, something he often did when he was pondering a problem.

'Mr Avery is your flag lieutenant—he stands between you and the captain and serves both.' He breathed on his spectacles again. 'He is loyal to both. He would never speak behind the captain's back, because you are friends. It would seem like a betrayal of trust, and the association which has grown between them.' He smiled gently. 'Between all of us, if I may say so, Sir Richard.'

There was complete silence from the pantry. Ozzard would be there, listening.

'If it troubles you, then tell me. I felt something was amiss myself.' He turned towards the sea again. Yovell's remark had touched him more than he cared to accept, reminding him uncomfortably of Herrick's comments on the Happy Few. In truth, there were not many left now. Keverne, who had once commanded this ship; Charles Farquhar, once a midshipman like Bethune, who had been killed aboard his own command at Corfu. And dear Francis Inch, eager, horse-faced, married to such a pretty woman at Weymouth. Her name was Hannah ... He recalled it with effort. And so many others. John Neale. Browne, with an 'e', and Avery's

296

predecessor, Stephen Jenour. So many. *Too many*. And all dead.

He turned from the light as Yovell said quietly, 'Captain Tyacke received a letter in Halifax. It was in the bag delivered by the schooner *Reynard*.'

'Bad news?'

Yovell replaced his spectacles with care. 'I am told that it had travelled far. As is often the way with the fleet's mail.'

Bolitho stared at him. Of course. Tyacke never received letters. Like Avery, until he had been sent one by his lady in London. It was so typical of Avery to remain silent, even if he knew the cause of Tyacke's withdrawal. He would understand. Just as he had understood Adam's anguish at having been a prisoner of war.

'Is it all over the ship?'

'Only the flag lieutenant knows, sir.'

Bolitho touched his eyelid, and recalled the gown Catherine had been given when *Larne* finally found them. When she had returned it to Tyacke, she had expressed the wish that it might be worn by someone worthy of him. . . .

He clenched his fist. Surely not the same woman? It could not be; why, after so long, and after the cruel way she had rejected him, and his disfigured face? But in his heart, he knew that it was.

He saw Catherine, as clearly as if he had looked at her locket. They had no secrets. He knew of her visits to London, and that she occasionally consulted Sillitoe for his advice on investing the money from Spain; he trusted her completely, as she trusted him. But what if . . . He thought of Tyacke's silence and reticence, the reawakened pain that must be hidden. What if . . . Catherine needed to be loved, just as she needed to return love.

'If I spoke out of turn, Sir Richard. . . .'

Bolitho said, 'You did not. It is good to be reminded sometimes of things that truly matter, and those who are out of reach.'

Yovell was reassured, and glad that he had spoken out. As a civilian.

The other door opened and Ozzard padded into the cabin, a coffee pot in his hands.

'Is that the last of it, Ozzard?'

Ozzard glanced severely at the pot. 'No, Sir Richard. Two weeks more, at most. After that. . . .'

Avery returned to the cabin, and Bolitho saw him waiting while he took a cup from the tray, gauging the moment when the ship staggered through a confusion of broken crests. Ozzard had poured a cup for the flag lieutenant, almost grudgingly. What did he think about; what occupied his mind in all the months and years he had been at sea? A man who had obliterated his past, but, like Yovell, an educated one, who could read classical works, and had the handwriting of a scholar. It seemed as if he wanted no future, either.

Bolitho took the notes Avery had brought, and said, 'One more day. We might fall in with a courier from Halifax. Rear-Admiral Keen may have more news.'

Avery asked, 'These American ships, sir—will they wish to challenge us?'

'Whatever they intend, George, I shall need every trick we can muster. Just as I will need all of my officers to be at their best, if fight we must.'

Avery glanced at Yovell, and lowered his voice. 'You know about the captain's letter, sir?'

'Yes. Now I do, and I appreciate and respect your

feelings, and your reluctance to discuss it.' He paused. 'However, James Tyacke is not only the captain of my flagship, he *is* the ship, no matter how he might dispute that!'

'Yes. I am sorry, Sir Richard. I thought—'

'Don't be sorry. Loyalty comes in many guises.'

They looked at the door as the sentry called, 'First lieutenant, *Sir*!'

Lieutenant John Daubeny stepped into the cabin, his slim figure angled in the entrance like that of a drunken sailor.

'The captain's respects, Sir Richard. *Taciturn* has signalled. Sail in sight to the nor' west.'

Avery remarked quietly, 'She'll have a hard beat to reach us, sir.'

'One of ours, you believe?'

Avery nodded. '*Chivalrous*. Must be her. She'd soon turn and run with the wind otherwise.'

Bolitho smiled unconsciously at his judgment. 'I agree. My compliments to the captain, Mr Daubeny. Make a signal. *General*. To be repeated to all our ships. *Close on Flag*.'

He could see them, tiny dabs of colour as the flags broke from their yards, to be repeated to the next vessel even though she might barely be in sight. The chain of command, the overall responsibility. Daubeny waited, noting everything, to go in the next letter to his mother.

Bolitho glanced up at the skylight. Tyacke with his ship. A man alone, perhaps now more than ever.

'I shall come up at seven bells, Mr Daubeny.'

But the first lieutenant had gone, the signal already hoisted.

He touched the locket beneath his shirt.

Stay close, dear Kate. Don't leave me. They met

with the thirty-gun frigate *Chivalrous* in late afternoon, *Indomitable* and her consorts having made more sail to hasten the rendezvous. It would also ensure that Captain Isaac Lloyd could board the flagship with time to return to his own command before nightfall, or in case the wind freshened enough to prevent the use of a boat.

Lloyd was only twenty-eight but had the face of an older, more seasoned officer, with dark, steady eyes and pointed features that gave him the demeanour of a watchful fox. He used the chart in Bolitho's cabin, his finger jabbing at the various positions which York had already estimated.

'Six of them all told. I could scarce believe my eyes, Sir Richard. Probably all frigates, including a couple of large ones.' He jabbed the chart again. 'I signalled *Weazle* to make all haste to Halifax, but I fully expected the Yankees to try and put a stop to it.' He gave a short, barking laugh: a fox indeed, Bolitho thought. 'It was as if we did not exist. They continued to the nor' east, cool as you please. I decided to harry the rearmost one, so I set me royals and t' gallants and chased them. That changed things. A few signals were exchanged, and then the rearmost frigate opened fire with her chasers. I had to admit, Sir Richard, it was damn' good shootin'.'

Bolitho sensed Tyacke beside him, listening, perhaps considering how he might have reacted in Lloyd's shoes. Yovell was writing busily and did not raise his head. Avery was holding some of York's notes, although he was not reading, and his face was set in a frown.

Lloyd said, 'It got a bit too warm, and I reduced sail. Not before that damn Yankee had brought down a spar and punched my forecourse full of holes.

300

I thought that maybe he'd been ordered to fall back and engage *Chivalrous*. I would have accepted that, I think. But I says to meself, no, he don't intend to fight, not now, anyways.'

Bolitho said, 'Why?'

'Well, Sir Richard, he had all the time he needed, and he could see I had no other ship to support me. I knew he would have put his boats in the water, had he meant to show his mettle.' He grinned. 'He may have carried more guns than my ship, but with all those boats stowed on deck we could have cut down half his men with their splinters in the first broadside!'

Tyacke roused himself from his silent contemplation and said abruptly, 'Boats? How many?'

Lloyd shrugged, and glanced through the smeared windows as if to reassure himself that his ship was still riding under *Indomitable's* lee.

'Double the usual amount, I'd say. My first lieutenant insisted that the next ship in the American's line was likewise equipped.'

Avery said, 'Moving to a new base?'

Tyacke said bluntly, 'There is no other base, unless they take one of ours.' When Lloyd would have said something, Tyacke held up one hand. 'I was thinking. Remembering, while you were speaking just now. When it was decided that the slavetrade was not quite respectable, unbefitting civilized powers, their lordships thought fit to send frigates to stamp it out. Faster, better-armed, trained companies, and yet...' He turned and looked directly at Bolitho. 'They could never catch them. The slavers used small vessels, cruel, stinking hulls where men and women lived and died in their own filth, or were pitched to the sharks if a King's ship happened to stumble

301

on them.'

Bolitho remained silent, feeling it, sharing it. Tyacke was reliving his time in *Larne*. The slavers had come to fear him: *the devil with half a face.*

Tyacke continued in the same unemotional tone, 'All along that damnable coast, where the rivers came out to the Atlantic, the Congo, the Niger and the Gaboon, the slavers would lie close inshore, where no man-of-war of any consequence would dare to venture. Which was why they evaded capture and their just deserts for so long.' He glanced at the young captain, who did not avoid his eyes. 'I think you fell in with something you were not supposed to see.' He moved to the chart and laid his hand on it. 'For once, I think our Mr York was wrong. Mistaken. They didn't give chase, Captain Lloyd, because they could not. They *dared* not.' He looked at Bolitho. 'Those boats, sir. So many of them. Not for picking up slaves like those cruel scum used to do, but to put an invading army ashore.'

Bolitho felt the shock and the truth of his words like a cup of icy water in his face.

'They're carrying soldiers, as they did on the lakes, except that these are larger vessels, with something bigger in prospect at the end of it!'

He thought of the army captain who had survived the first attack on York, and of the reports which had filtered through with information of a second attack three months later. Perhaps Lake Erie had already fallen to the Americans? If so, the British army would be cut off, even from retreat. The young captain had described the Americans at York as being well-trained regulars.

Bolitho said, 'If these ships entered the Bay of Fundy but turned north, and not towards Nova

302

Scotia, they could disembark soldiers who could force their way inland, knowing that supplies and reinforcements would be waiting for them once they reached the St Lawrence. It would seal off all the frontier districts of Upper Canada, like ferrets in a sack!'

He gripped Lloyd's hand warmly in farewell. 'You did not fight the American, Captain Lloyd, but the news you have carried to me may yet bring us a victory. I shall ensure that you receive proper recognition. Our Nel would have put it better. He always insisted that the Fighting Instructions were not a substitute for a captain's initiative.'

Tyacke said roughly, 'I'll see you over the side, Captain Lloyd.'

As the door closed, Avery said, 'Is it possible, sir?'

Bolitho half-smiled. 'Do you really mean, is it likely? I think it is too important to ignore, or to wait for a miracle.' He listened to the trill of calls as the fox-like captain went down to his gig.

Tyacke returned, and waited in silence while Bolitho instructed his secretary to send a brief dispatch to Halifax.

'We shall alter course before nightfall, James, and steer due north. Make the necessary signals.' He saw the concern in the clear eyes that watched him, from the burned remains of the face. 'I know the risks, James. We all do. It was there for all of us to see, but only you recognized it. Your loneliest command was not wasted. Nor will it be.' He wondered if Tyacke had been going over it all again. The letter, the girl he might scarcely remember, or not wish to remember. One day he might share it; at the same time, Bolitho knew that he would not.

'Do you think your man Aherne is with them?'

303

'I am not certain, but I think it possible that he may have fallen out of favour with his superiors, like John Paul Jones.' *Like my own brother*.

Tyacke was about to leave, but turned when Bolitho said with sudden bitterness, 'Neither side can win this war, just as neither can afford to lose it. So let us play our part as best we can ... And then, in God's mercy, let us go home!'

*   *   *

They stood crowded together around York's chart-table, their shadows joining in a slow dance while the lanterns swung above them.

More like conspirators than King's men, Bolitho thought. It was pitch black outside the hull, early dark as he had known it would be, the ship unusually noisy as she rolled in a steep swell. There was no land closer than seventy miles, Nova Scotia's Cape Sable to the north-east, but after the great depths to which they had become accustomed they sensed its presence. Felt it.

Bolitho glanced at their faces in the swaying light. Tyacke, his profile very calm, the burns hidden in shadow. It was possible to see him as the woman had once done: the unscarred side of his face was strongly boned and handsome. On his other side the master was measuring his bearings with some dividers, his expression one of doubt.

Avery was crammed into the small space too, with Daubeny the first lieutenant bobbing his head beneath the heavy beams as he tried to see over their shoulders.

York said, 'In broad daylight it's bad enough, sir. The entrance to the bay, allowing for shallows and sandbars, is about twenty-five miles, less, mebbee. We'd not be able to hold our formation, and if they are ready and waiting...' He did not go on.

Tyacke was still grappling with his original idea. 'They can't go in and attack anything in the dark, Isaac. They'd need to take soundings for most of the bay. The boats could be separated, swamped even, if the worst happened.'

York persisted, 'The whole of that coastline is used by small vessels, fishermen mostly. A lot of the folk who made their homes in New Brunswick after the American rebellion were loyalists. They've no love for the Yankees, but...' He glanced at Bolitho. 'Against trained soldiers, what could they do?'

Bolitho said, 'And if they have already carried out a landing, those ships might be waiting for us to appear like ducks in a waterfowler's sights. But it takes time—it always does. Lowering boats, packing men and weapons into them, more than likely in the dark, and with some of the soldiers half sick from the passage ... Marines, now, that would be different.' He rubbed his chin, aware of its roughness: one of Allday's shaves then, if there was time. He said, 'Our captains know how to perform. We have exercised working together, although not with Mr York's unwelcoming bay in mind!' He saw them smile, as he had known they would. It was like being driven, or perhaps led. Hearing somebody else speak, somehow finding the faith and confidence to inspire others. 'And we must admit, the plan, if that is what they have in mind, is a brilliant one. Seasoned soldiers could march and fight their way northwards and meet with their other regiments on the St Lawrence. What is that, three hundred miles? I can remember as a boy when the 46th Regiment of Foot marched all

305

the way from Devon to Scotland. And doubtless back again.'

York asked uneasily, 'Was there more trouble up north then, sir?'

Bolitho smiled. 'No, it was the King's birthday. It was his wish!'

York grinned. 'Oh, well, that's different, sir!'

Bolitho picked up the dividers from the chart. 'The enemy know the risks as well as we do. We shall remain in company as best we can. Each captain will have his best lookouts aloft, but they cannot work miracles. By dawn we shall be in position, *here.*' The points of the dividers came down like a harpoon. 'We may become scattered overnight, but we must take that chance.'

Tyacke studied him in silence. *You will take it*, his expression said. Bolitho said, 'If I were the enemy commander I would send in my landing parties, and perhaps release one of my smaller ships as close inshore as possible to offer covering fire if need be. That would even the odds.' He put down the dividers very carefully. 'A little.'

Tyacke said, 'If we're wrong, sir....'

'If *I* am wrong, then we will return to Halifax. At least they will be prepared there for any sudden attack.' He thought of Keen when he had spoken of St Clair's daughter: he might become a vice-admiral sooner than his highest hopes, if the enemy had outwitted this makeshift plan.

He saw Avery bending over the table to scribble some notes in his little book, and for a second their eyes met. Did Avery know that his admiral was barely able to see the markings on the a chart without covering his damaged eye? He felt the sudden despair lift from his spirit, like a dawn mist rising from the

306

water. Of course they knew, but it had become a bond, a strength, which they willingly shared with him. Again he seemed to hear Herrick's words. *We Happy Few. Dear God, don't let me fail them now.*

Then he said quietly, 'Thank you, gentlemen. Please carry on with your duties. Captain Tyacke?'

Tyacke was touching his scars; perhaps he no longer noticed that he was doing it.

'I would like to have the people fed before the morning watch, sir. Then, if you agree, we will clear for action.' He might have been smiling, but his face was in shadow again. 'No drums, no din of war.'

Bolitho said lightly, 'No *Portsmouth Lass*, either?' The same thought returned. Like conspirators. Or assassins.

Tyacke twisted round. 'Mr Daubeny, do not strain your ears any further! I want all officers and senior warrant officers in the wardroom as soon as is convenient.' He added, almost as an afterthought, 'We had better assemble our young gentlemen as well on this occasion. They may learn something from it.'

York left with Daubeny, probably to confer with his master's mates. It would keep them busy, and a lack of sleep was nothing new to sailors.

Avery had also departed, understanding better than most that Tyacke wished to be alone with Bolitho. Not as the officer, but as a friend. Bolitho had almost guessed what his flag captain was going to say, but it still came as a shock.

'If we meet with the enemy, and now that I have weighed the odds for and against, I think we shall, I would ask a favour.'

'What is it, James?'

'If I should fall.' He shook his head. 'Please, hear me. I have written, two letters. I would rest easy and with a free mind to fight this ship if I knew...' He was silent for a moment. 'One is for your lady, sir, and the other for somebody I once knew ... thought I knew ... some fifteen years back, when I was a young luff like Mr Know-it-all Blythe.'

Bolitho touched his arm, with great affection. It was the closest to the man he had ever been.

He said, 'We shall both take care tomorrow, James. I am depending on you.'

Tyacke studied the well-used chart. 'Tomorrow, then.'

Later, as he made his way aft to his quarters, Bolitho heard the buzz of voices from the wardroom, rarely so crowded even in harbour. Two of the messmen were crouching down, listening at the door as closely as they dared. There was laughter too, as there must have been before greater events in history: Quiberon Bay, The Saintes, or the Nile.

Allday was with Ozzard in the pantry, as he had known he would be. He followed Bolitho past the sentry and into the dimly lit cabin, with the sea like black glass beyond the windows. Apart from the ship's own noises, it was already quiet. Tyacke would be speaking to his officers, just as he would eventually go around the messdecks and show himself to the men who depended on him. Not to tell them why it was so, but how it must be done. But the ship already knew. Like *Sparrow* and *Phalarope*, and *Hyperion* most of all.

Allday asked, 'Will Mr Avery be coming aft, Sir Richard?'

Bolitho waved him to a chair. 'Rest easy, old friend. He'll find a minute to pen a letter for you.'

Allday grinned, the concern and the pain falling away. 'I'd take it kindly, Sir Richard. I've never been much for book-learnin' an' the like.'

Bolitho heard Ozzard's quiet step. 'Just as well for the rest of us, I daresay. So let us drink to those we care about, while we can. But we'll wait for the flag lieutenant.' He looked away. Avery had probably already written a letter of his own, to the unknown woman in London. Perhaps it was only a dream, a lost hope. But it was an anchor, one which was needed by them all.

He walked to the gun barometer and tapped it automatically, recalling Tyacke's acceptance of what must be done, his confidence in his ship. And of his words. 'If I should fall . . .' The same words, the same voice which had spoken for all of them.

Avery entered the cabin even as the sentry shouted his arrival.

Bolitho said, 'Did it go well, George?'

Avery looked at Ozzard and his tray of glasses.

'Something I heard my father say, a long time ago. That the gods never concern themselves with the protection of the innocent, only with the punishment of the guilty.' He took a glass from the unsmiling Ozzard. 'I never thought I would hear it again under these circumstances.'

Bolitho waited while Allday lurched to his feet to join them.

Tomorrow, then.

Thinking of Herrick, perhaps. Of all of them.

He raised his glass. 'We Happy Few!'

They would like that.

CHAPTER SIXTEEN

LEE SHORE

Lieutenant George Avery gripped the weather shrouds and then paused to stare up at the foremast. Like most of the ship's company, he had been on deck for over an hour, and yet his eyes were still not accustomed to the enfolding darkness. He could see the pale outline of the hard-braced topsail, but beyond it nothing save an occasional star as it flitted through long banners of cloud. He shivered; it was cold, and his clothing felt damp and clinging, and there was something else also, a kind of light-headedness, a sense of elation, which he thought had gone forever. Those days when he had been in the small schooner *Jolie*, cutting out equally small prizes from the French coast, sometimes under the noses of a shore battery ... Wild, reckless times. He almost laughed into the damp air. It was madness, as it had been madness then.

He swung himself out and wedged his foot onto the first ratline, then, slowly and carefully, he began to climb, the big signals telescope hanging across his shoulder like a poacher's gun. Up and up, the shrouds vibrating beneath his grip, the tarred cordage as sharp and cold as ice. He was not afraid of heights, but he respected them: it was one of the first things he could remember when he had been appointed midshipman under his uncle's sponsorship. The seamen, who had been rough and independent although they had shown him kindness, would rush up the ratlines barefooted, the skin so calloused and hardened that they scorned the wearing of shoes, which they would keep for special occasions.

He stopped to regain his breath, and felt his body being pressed against the quivering rigging while the invisible ship beneath him leaned over to a sudden gust of wind. Like cold hands, holding him.

Even though he could see nothing below him but the unchanging outline of the upper deck, sharpened occasionally when a burst of spray cascaded over the gangways or through the beakhead, he could imagine the others standing as he had left them. So different from the usual nerve-wrenching thrill when the drums rattled and beat the hands to quarters, the orderly chaos when a ship was cleared for action from bow to stern: screens torn down, tiny hutches of cabins where the officers found their only privacy transformed into just another part of a gundeck, furniture, personal items and sea-chests dragged or winched into the lower hull, below the waterline, where the surgeon and his assistants would be preparing, remaining separate from the noise before battle: their work would come to them. On this occasion clearing for action had been an almost leisurely affair, men moving amongst familiar tackle and rigging as if it were broad daylight.

As ordered, the hands had been given a hot meal in separate watches, and only then was the galley fire doused, the last measure of rum drained.

Tyacke had remained by the quarterdeck rail, while officers and messengers had flowed around him, like extensions of the man himself. York with his master's mates, Daubeny, the first lieutenant, with a junior midshipman always trotting at his heels like a pet dog. And right aft by the companion way where he had walked with Sir Richard, Avery could see that in his mind also. Where the command of any ship or squadron began or ended. He smiled as he recalled what Allday had said of it. 'Aft, the most honour, Forward, the better man!' Bolitho had been holding his watch closely against the compass light, and had said, 'Go aloft, George. Take a good glass with you. I need to know instantly. You will be my eyes today.'

It still saddened him. Did those words, too, have a hidden meaning?

And Allday again, taking his hat and sword from him. 'They'll be here when you needs 'em, Mr Avery. Don't want our flag lieutenant gettin' all tangled up in the futtock shrouds, now, do we?'

He had written the letter Allday had requested. Like the man, it had been warmly affectionate, and yet, after all he had seen and suffered, so simple and unworldly. Avery had almost been able to see Unis opening and reading it, calling her ex-soldier brother to tell him about it. Holding it up to the child.

He shook his head, thrusting the thoughts aside, and started to climb again. Long before any of their letters reached England, they might all be dead.

The foremast's fighting top loomed above him, reminding him of Allday's joke about the futtock shrouds. Nimble-footed topmen could scramble out and around the top without interruption, those on the leeward side hanging out, suspended, with nothing but the sea beneath them. The fighting top was a square platform protected by a low barricade, behind which marksmen could take aim at targets on an enemy's deck. It matched the tops on the other masts, above which the shrouds and stays reached up to the next of the upper yards, and beyond.

The foremast was perhaps the most important and

complicated in the ship. It carried not only the bigger course and topsails, but was connected and rigged to the bowsprit, and the smaller, vital jib and staysails. Each time a ship attempted to come about and turn across the eye of the wind, the small jib sails would act like a spur or brake to prevent her floundering to a standstill, taken all aback with her sails flattened uselessly against the masts, unable to pay off in either direction. At the height of close action, the inability to manoeuvre could mean the death of a ship.

He thought of Tyacke and York and men like them, the true professionals. How many people ashore would ever understand the strength and prowess of such fine sailors, when they saw a King's ship beating down-channel under a full press of sail?

He dragged himself between the shrouds and took the easier way into the foretop by way of a small opening, the 'lubber's hole', as the old Jacks derisively termed it.

There were four Royal Marines here, their white crossbelts and the corporal's chevrons on one man's sleeve visible against the outer darkness.

'Mornin', sir! Fine day for a stroll!'

Avery unslung the telescope and smiled. That was another thing about being a flag lieutenant, neither fish nor fowl, like an outsider who had come amongst them: he was not an officer in charge of a mast or a division of guns, nor a symbol of discipline or punishment. So he was accepted. Tolerated.

He said, 'Do you think it will be light soon?'

The corporal leaned against a mounted swivel gun. It was already depressed, and covered with a piece of canvas to protect the priming from the damp air. Ready for instant use.

He replied, ''Alf hour, sir. Near as a priest's promise!'

313

They all laughed, as if this were only another, normal day.

Avery stared at the flapping jib and imagined the crouching lion beneath it. What if the sea was empty when daylight came? He searched his feelings. Would he be relieved, grateful?

He thought of the intensity in Bolitho's voice, the way he and Tyacke had conferred and planned. He shivered suddenly. No, the sea would not be empty of ships. *How can I be certain?* Then he thought, *Because of what we are, what he has made us.*

He tried to focus his thoughts on England. London, that busy street with its bright carriages and haughty footmen, and one carriage in particular ... She was lovely. She would not wait, and waste her life.

And yet, they had shared something deeper, however briefly. Surely there was a chance, a hope beyond this cold dawn?

The corporal said carefully, 'I sometimes wonders what he's like, sir. The admiral, I mean.' He faltered, thinking he had gone too far. 'It's just that we sees him an' you walkin' the deck sometimes, and then there was the day when 'is lady come aboard at Falmouth.' He put his hand on his companion's shoulder. 'Me an' Ted was there. I'd never 'ave believed it, see?'

Avery did see. Replacing Catherine's shoes and remarking on the tar on her stocking after her climb up this ship's side. The flag breaking out, and then the cheers. Work them, drive them, break them; but these same men had seen, and remembered.

He said, 'He *is* that man, Corporal. Just as she is that lady.' He could almost hear Tyacke's words. *I would serve no other.*

One of the other marines, encouraged by his corporal, asked, 'What will us do when th' war's over an' done with?'

Avery stared up at the great rectangle of sail, and felt the raw salt on his mouth.

'I pray to God that I shall be able to choose something for myself.'

The corporal grunted. 'I'll get me other stripe an' stay in the Royals. Good victuals an' plenty of rum, an' a hard fight when you're needed! It'll do me!'

A voice echoed down from the crosstrees. 'First light a-comin', sir!'

The corporal grinned. 'Old Jacob up there, he's a wild one, sir!'

Avery thought of Tyacke's description of the seaman named Jacob, the best lookout in the squadron. Once a saddle-maker, a highly skilled trade, he had found his wife in the arms of another man, and had killed both of them. The Assizes had offered him the choice of the gibbet or the navy. He had outlived many others with no such notoriety.

Avery withdrew the big telescope from its case, while the marines made a space for him and even found him something to kneel on.

One of them put his hand on the swivel gun and chuckled. 'Don't you go bumpin' into old Betsy 'ere, sir. You might set 'er off by accident, an' blow the 'ead off our poor sergeant. That'd be a true shame, wouldn't it, lads?' They all laughed. Four marines on a windswept perch in the middle of nowhere. They had probably no idea where they were, or where bound tomorrow.

Avery knelt, and felt the low barricade shivering under the great weight of spars and canvas, and all the miles of rigging that ruled the lives of such men as these. *Of one company.*

He held his breath and trained the glass with great care, but saw only cloud and darkness. Old Jacob on his lofty lookout would see it first.

He was shivering again, unable to stop.

''Ere, sir.' A hand reached out from somewhere. 'Nelson's blood!'

Avery took it gratefully. It was against all regulations: they knew it, and so did he.

The corporal murmured, 'To wish us luck, eh, lads?'

Avery swallowed, and felt the rum driving out the cold. The fear. He stared out again. *You will be my eyes today.* As if he were right beside him.

And suddenly, there they were. The enemy. Captain James Tyacke watched the shadowy figures of Hockenhull, the boatswain, and a party of seamen as they hauled on lines and secured them to bollards. Every one of *Indomitable*'s boats was in the water, towing astern like a single unyieldy sea anchor, and although he could scarcely see them, he knew that the nets were already spread across the gundeck. The scene was set.

Tyacke searched his feelings for doubt. Had there been any? But if so, they were gone as soon as the old lookout's doleful voice had called down from the foremast crosstrees. Avery would be peering through his glass, searching for details, numbers, the strength of the enemy.

York remarked, 'Wind's falling away, sir. Steady enough, though.'

Tyacke glanced over at Bolitho's tall figure framed against the pale barrier of packed hammocks, and saw him nod. It was time: it had to be. But the wind was everything.

He said sharply, 'Shake out the second reef, Mr Daubeny! Set fores'l and driver!' To himself he added, *where are our damned ships?* They might have become scattered during the breezy night; better that than risk a collision, now of all times. He heard the first lieutenant's tame midshipman repeating his instructions in a shrill voice, edged with uncertainty at the prospect of something unknown to him.

He considered his other lieutenants, and frowned. Boys in the King's uniform. Even Daubeny was young for his responsibilities. The words repeated themselves in his mind. *If I fall ...* It would be Daubeny's skill, or lack of it, that would determine their success or failure.

He heard Allday murmur something and Bolitho's quick laugh, and was surprised that it could still move him. Steady him, like the iron hoops around each great mast, holding them together.

The marines had laid down their weapons, and had manned the mizzen braces as the driver filled and cracked to the wind.

He knew that Isaac York was hovering nearby, wanting to speak to him, to pass the time as friends usually did before an action. Just in case. But he could not waste time in conversation now. He needed to be alive and alert to everything, from the men at the big double wheel to the ship's youngest midshipman, who was about to turn the half-hour glass beside the compass box.

He saw his own coxswain, Fairbrother, peering down at the boats under tow.

'Worried, Eli?' He saw him grin. He was no Allday, but he was doing his best.

'They'll all need a lick o' paint when we picks 'em

up, sir.'

But Tyacke had turned away, his eyes assessing the nearest guns, the crews, some bare-backed despite the cold wind, standing around them, waiting for the first orders. Decks sanded to prevent men slipping, in spray or perhaps in blood. Rammers, sponges, and worms, the tools of their trade, close to hand.

Lieutenant Laroche drawled, 'Here comes the flag lieutenant.'

Avery climbed the ladder to the quarterdeck, and Allday handed him his hat and sword.

He said, 'Six sail right enough, Sir Richard. I think the tide's on the ebb.'

York muttered, 'It would be.'

'I think one of the frigates is towing *all* the boats, sir. It's too far and too dark to be sure.'

Tyacke said, 'Makes sense. It would hold them all together. Keep 'em fresh and ready for landing.'

Bolitho said, 'We can't wait. Alter course now.' He looked at Tyacke, and afterwards he imagined he had seen him smile, even though his features were in shadow. 'As soon as we sight our ships, signal them to *attack at will*. This is no time for a line of battle!' Avery recalled the consternation at the Admiralty when Bolitho had voiced his opinions on the fleet's future.

Tyacke called, 'Alter course two points. Steer north-east by north!' He knew what Bolitho had seen in his mind, how they had discussed it, even with nothing more to go on than Captain Lloyd's sighting report and his own interpretation of the extra boats carried by the enemy. Tyacke gave a crooked grin. *Slavers, indeed.*

Men were already hauling at the braces, their bodies angled almost to the deck while they heaved

318

the great yards round, muscle and bone striving against wind and rudder.

Tyacke saw Daubeny urging a few spare hands to add their weight to the braces. But even with the Nova Scotian volunteers, they were still short-handed, a legacy of *Indomitable*'s savage fight against Beer's *Unity*. Tyacke straightened his hat. It was unnerving when he considered that that was a year ago.

Bolitho joined him by the rail. 'The enemy have the numbers and the superior artillery, and will readily use both.' He folded his arms, and could have been discussing the weather. 'But he is on a lee shore and knows it. Being a sailor, I am sure he was never consulted about the choice of landing places!' He laughed, and added, 'So *we* must be sharp about it.'

Tyacke leaned over to consult the compass as the helmsman called, 'Nor' east by north, sir! Full an' bye!'

Tyacke peered up at each sail, watchful and critical as his ship leaned over comfortably on the starboard tack. Then he cupped his hands and shouted, 'Check the forebrace, Mr Protheroe! Now belay!' He said almost to himself, 'He's only a boy, dammit!'

But Bolitho had heard him. 'We were all that, James. Young lions!'

'*Chivalrous* is in sight, sir! Larboard quarter!'

Just an array of pale canvas riding high into the dull clouds. How did he know? But Tyacke did not question the lookout: he knew, and that was all there was to it. The others would be in sight soon. He saw the first feeble light exploring the shrouds and shaking topsails. So would the enemy.

The wind was still fresh, strong enough, for the moment anyway. There would be no land in sight until the sun came out, and even then ... But you could feel it all the same. Like a presence, a barrier reaching out to rid the approaches of all ships, no matter what flag they paraded.

Tyacke touched his face, and did not notice Bolitho turn his head towards him. So different now, out in the open, to see and to be seen. Not like the choking confines of the lower gundeck on that day at the Nile, when he had almost died, and afterwards had wanted to die.

He thought of the letter in his strongbox, and the one he had written in reply. Why had he done it? After all the pain and the despair, the brutal realization that the one being he had ever cared for had rejected him, *why?* Against that, it was still hard to believe that she had written to him. He remembered the hospital at Haslar in Hampshire, full of officers, survivors from one battle or another. Everyone else who had worked there had pretended to be so normal, so calm, so unmoved by the pervasive suffering. It had almost driven him crazy. That had been the last time he had seen her. She had visited the hospital, and he now realized that she must have been sickened by some of the sights she had seen. Hopeful, anxious faces, the disfigured, the burned, the limbless, and others who had been blinded. It must have been a nightmare for her, although all he had felt at the time had been pity. For himself.

She had been his only hope, all he had clung to after the battle, when he had been so savagely wounded in the old *Majestic*. Old, he thought bitterly: she had been almost new. He touched the worn rail, laid his hand on it, and again was unaware of Bolitho's concern. *Not like this old lady.* Her captain had died there at the Nile, and *Majestic*'s first lieutenant had taken over the ship, and the fight. A young man. He touched his face again. *Like Daubeny.*

She had been so young ... He almost spoke her name aloud. *Marion.* Eventually she had married a man much older than herself, a safe, kindly auctioneer who had given her a nice house by Portsdown Hill, from where you could sometimes see the Solent, and the sails on the horizon. He had tortured himself with it many times. The house was not very far from Portsmouth, and the hospital where he had wanted to die.

They had had two children, a boy and a girl. *They should have been mine.* And now her husband was dead, and she had written to him after reading something about the squadron in the newsheet, and the fact that he was now Sir Richard Bolitho's flag captain.

It had been a letter written with great care, and without excuse or compromise: a mature letter. She had asked for his understanding, not for his forgiveness. She would value a letter from him, very much. *Marion.* He thought, as he had thought so often, of the gown he had bought for her before Nelson had led them to the Nile, and the way that Sir Richard's lovely Catherine had given the same gown grace and meaning after they had lifted her from that sun-blistered boat. Had she perhaps given him back the hope that had been crushed by hatred and bitterness?

'Deck there! Sail in sight to the nor' east!'

Tyacke snatched a glass from the rack and strode up to the weather side, training it across the deck and through the taut rigging. A glimpse of sunshine, without warmth. Waters blue and grey . . . He held his breath, able to ignore the marines and seamen who were watching him. One, two, three ships, sails filling and then flapping in an attempt to contain the wind. The other ships were not yet visible.

We have the advantage this time. But with the wind as it was, their roles could quite easily change.

He lowered the glass and looked at Bolitho. 'I think we should hold our course, Sir Richard.'

Just a nod. Like a handshake. 'I agree. Signal *Chivalrous* to *close on Flag.*' He smiled unexpectedly, his teeth white in his tanned face. 'Then hoist the one for *Close Action.*' The smile seemed to evade him. 'And keep it flying!'

Tyacke saw his quick glance at Allday. Something else they shared. A lifeline.

'*Chivalrous* has acknowledged, sir.'

'Very good.'

Bolitho joined him again. 'We will engage the towing vessel first.' He looked past Tyacke at the other frigate's misty sails, so clean in the first frail light. 'Load when you are ready, James.' The grey eyes rested on his face. 'Those soldiers must not be allowed to land.'

'I'll pass the word. Double-shotted, and grape for good measure.' He spoke without emotion. 'But when we come about we shall have to face the others, unless our ships give us support.'

Bolitho touched his arm and said, '*They will come*, James. I am certain of it.'

He turned as Ozzard, half-crouching as if he had expected to find an enemy engaged alongside, stepped from the companion way. He was carrying the admiral's gold-laced hat, holding it out as if it were something precious.

Tyacke said urgently, 'Is this wise, Sir Richard? Those Yankee sharp-shooters will be all about today!'

Bolitho handed his plain sea-going hat to Ozzard, and after the slightest hesitation pulled the new one onto his spray-damp hair.

'Go below, Ozzard. And thank you.' He saw the little man bob gratefully, with no words to make his true feelings known. Then Bolitho said calmly, 'It is probably madness, but that is the way of it. Sane endeavour is not for us today, James.' He touched his eye and stared at the reflected glare. 'But a victory it must be!'

The rest was drowned out by the shrill of whistles and the squeak of blocks, as the great guns were cast off from their breechings and their crews prepared to load.

He knew that some of the afterguard had seen him put on his new hat, the one he and Catherine had bought together in St James's Street: he had forgotten to tell her of his promotion, and she had loved him for it. A few of the seamen raised a cheer, and he touched his hat to them. But Tyacke had seen the anguish on Allday's rugged face, and knew what the gesture had cost him.

Tyacke walked away, watching the familiar preparations without truly seeing them. Aloud he said, 'And a victory you shall have, no matter what!'

*　　　*　　　*

Bolitho walked to the taffrail where Allday was shading his eyes to peer astern.

Like feathers on the shimmering horizon, two more ships of the squadron had appeared, their captains no doubt relieved that the dawn had brought them together again. The smaller of the two frigates would be *Wildfire*, of twenty-eight guns. Bolitho imagined her captain, a dark-featured man, bellowing orders to his topmen to make more sail, as much as she could carry. Morgan Price, as craggy and as Welsh as his name, had never needed a speaking trumpet, even in the middle of a gale.

Allday said, 'That's more like it, Sir Richard.'

Bolitho glanced at him. Allday had not been concerned about the other ships. Like some of the others on the quarterdeck, he had been watching the cluster of boats falling further and further astern, drifting to a canvas sea anchor, to be recovered after the action. It was a necessary precaution before fighting, to avoid the risk of additional wounds being caused by splinters. But to Allday, like all sailors, the boats represented a final chance of survival if the worst happened. Just as their presence on deck would tempt terrified men to forget both loyalty and discipline, and use them as an escape.

Bolitho said, 'Fetch me a glass, will you?'

When Allday had gone to select a suitable telescope, he stared at the distant frigate. Then he covered his undamaged eye, and waited for the pale topsails to mist over or fade away altogether. They did not. The drops the surgeon had provided were doing some good, even if they had a sting like a nettle when first applied. Brightness, colour; even the sea's face had displayed its individual crests and troughs.

Allday was waiting with the telescope. 'Set bravely, Sir Richard?'

Bolitho said gently, 'You worry too much.'

Allday laughed, relieved, satisfied.

'Over here, Mr Essex!'

Bolitho waited for the midshipman to reach him, and said, 'Now we shall see!'

He rested the heavy glass on the youth's shoulder and carefully trained it across the starboard bow. A fine clear morning had emerged from the cloud and chilling wind: winter would come early here. He felt the young midshipman's shoulder shiver slightly. Cold; excitement; it was certainly not fear. Not yet. He was a lively, intelligent youth, and even he would be thinking of the day when he would be ready for examination and promotion. Another boy in an officer's uniform.

Three ships at least, the rest not yet in sight. Almost bows-on, their sails angled over as they tacked steeply across the wind. Far beyond them was a purple blur, like a fallen cloud. He pictured York's chart, his round handwriting in the log. Grand Manan Island, the guardian at the entrance to the Bay. The American would be doubly aware of the dangers here: being on a lee shore, with shallows as an extra menace once the tide was on the turn.

He stiffened and waited for the midshipman's breathing to steady; or perhaps he was holding his breath, very aware of his special responsibility.

A fourth ship, a shaft of new sunlight separating her from the others, bringing her starkly to life in the powerful lens.

He knew Tyacke and York were watching him, weighing the odds.

Bolitho said, 'The fourth ship has the boats under tow. The flag lieutenant was not mistaken.' He heard Avery laugh as Tyacke remarked, 'That makes a fair change, sir!'

Bolitho closed the glass with a snap and looked down at the midshipman. He had freckles, as

Bethune had once had. He thought of Herrick's assessment. *The upstart.*

'Thank you, Mr Essex.' He walked to the rail again. 'Bring her up closer to the wind, James. I intend to attack the towing ship before she can slip the boats. Filled or empty, it makes no difference now. We can stop them landing, and within the hour it will be too late.'

Tyacke beckoned to the first lieutenant. 'Stand by to alter course.' A questioning glance at the sailing-master. 'What say *you*, Isaac?'

York squinted his eyes to stare up at the driver and the mizzen topsail beyond it. 'Nor' east by east.' He shook his head as the driver's peak with the great White Ensign streaming from it almost abeam flapped noisily. 'No, sir. Nor' east is all she'll hold, I'm thinking.'

Bolitho listened, touched by the intimacy between these men. Tyacke's command of small ships had left its mark, or maybe it had always been there.

He shaded his eyes with his hand to observe the ship's slow response, the long jib-boom moving like a pointer until the enemy ships appeared to slide slightly from bow to bow.

'Steady she goes, sir! Course nor' east!'

Bolitho watched the sails buck and shiver, uncomfortable this close to the wind. It was the only way. Only *Indomitable* had the firepower to do it in one attack. *Chivalrous* was too small, the rest too far away. Their chances would come soon enough.

Avery folded his arms close to his body, trying not to shiver. The air was still keen, making a lie of the strengthening sunlight that painted the broken wavelets a dirty gold.

He saw Allday staring around, his eyes searching: a

man who had seen it many times before. He was studying the open quarterdeck, the scarlet-coated marines with their officer, David Merrick. The gun crews and the helmsmen, four of the latter now, with a master's mate close beside them. Tyacke standing apart from the rest, his hands beneath his coattails, and the admiral, who was explaining something to the midshipman, Essex. Something he would remember, if he lived.

Avery swallowed hard, knowing what he had seen. Allday, probably more experienced than any other man aboard, was seeking out the weaknesses and the danger points. Past the tightly-packed hammock nettings and up to the maintop, where more scarlet coats showed above the barricade. Where an enemy's fighting top might be if they were close enough. Thinking of the sharp-shooters, said to be backwoodsmen for the most part, who lived by their skills with a musket. Avery was chilled by the thought. Except that these marksmen would be armed with the new and more accurate rifles.

Was that the source of Allday's worry, then? Because of Bolitho's gesture, the hat with the bright gold lace, and all that it meant, and could mean, at the moment of truth. It was said that Nelson had refused to remove his decorations before his last battle, and had ordered that they should be covered before he was carried below, his backbone shot through, his life already slipping away. Another brave, sad gesture. So that his men should not know their admiral had fallen, had left them before the fight had been decided.

It was plain on Allday's homely features, and when their eyes met across the spray-patterned deck, no words were needed by either man.

'Deck there! The boats is bein' warped alongside!'

Bolitho clenched his fists, his face suddenly unable to conceal his anxiety.

Avery knew, had guessed even from the moment Bolitho had mentioned the primary importance of the boats. Despite the risks and the stark possibility of failure, he had been thinking of the alternative, that *Indomitable* would be forced to fire on boats packed with helpless men, unable to raise a finger to defend themselves. Was this part of the difference in this war? Or was it only one man's humanity?

Tyacke shouted, 'Something's wrong, sir!'

York had a telescope. 'The Yankee's run aground, sir!' He sounded astonished, as if he were over there, sharing the disaster.

Bolitho watched the sunlight catch the reflected glare from falling sails and a complete section of the vessel's mainmast. In the silence and intimacy of the strong lens, he almost imagined he could hear it. A big frigate, gun for gun a match for *Indomitable*, but helpless against the sea and this relentless destruction above and below. The boats were already filled or half-filled with blue uniforms, their weapons and equipment in total disarray as the truth became known to them.

Bolitho said, 'Prepare to engage to starboard, Captain Tyacke.' He barely recognized his own voice. Flat, hard, and unemotional. Somebody else.

Daubeny shouted, 'Starboard battery! *Run out!*'

The long twenty-four pounders rumbled up to and through their ports, their captains making hand signals only to avoid confusion. Like a drill, one of so many. A handspike here, or men straining on tackles to train a muzzle a few more inches.

The other ship had slewed around slightly,

wreckage trailing alongside as the tide continued to drop, to beach her like a wounded whale.

The wheel went over again, while York turned to watch the land, the set of the current, feeling if not seeing the danger to this ship.

'Course nor' by east, sir!'

Bolitho said, 'One chance, Captain Tyacke. Two broadsides, three if you can manage it.' Their eyes met. *Time and distance.*

Midshipman Essex jerked round as if he had been hit, and then shouted, 'Our ships are here, sir!' He waved his hat as distant gunfire rolled across the sea like muffled thunder. Then he realized that he had just shouted at his admiral, and dropped his eyes and flushed.

'On the uproll!'

Bolitho looked along the starboard side, the gun captains with their taut trigger-lines, the emergency slow-matches streaming to the wind like incense in a temple.

Daubeny by the mainmast, his sword across one shoulder, Philip Protheroe, the fourth lieutenant, up forward with the first division of guns. And here on the quarterdeck, the newest lieutenant, Blythe, staring at each crouching seaman as if he was expecting a mutiny. The stranded ship was drawing slowly abeam, the floundering boats suddenly stilled as the reluctant sunlight threw *Indomitable*'s sails across the water in patches of living shadow.

Daubeny raised his sword. 'As you bear!'

Lieutenant Protheroe glanced aft and then yelled, *'Fire!'*

Division by division, the guns roared out across the water, each twenty-four pounder hurling itself inboard to be seized and manhandled like a wild beast.

329

Bolitho thought he saw the shockwave of the broadside rip across the water, carving a passage like some scythe from hell. Even as the first double-shotted charges and their extra packing of grape smashed into the boats and exploded into the helpless ship, Protheroe's men were already sponging out their guns, probing for burning remnants with their worms before ramming home fresh charges and balls.

The quarterdeck guns were the last to fire, and Blythe's voice almost broke in a scream as he yelled. 'A guinea for the first gun, I say! A guinea!'

Bolitho watched it all with a strange numbness. Even his heart seemed to have stopped. Tyacke had trained them well; three rounds every two minutes. There would be time for the third broadside before they came about, to avoid running aground like the stricken American.

Tyacke was also watching, remembering. *Point! Ready! Fire!* The drill, always the drill. Slaves to the guns which were now repaying his hard work.

A whistle shrilled. 'Ready, sir!'

'Fire!'

Boats and fragments of boats, uniformed soldiers thrashing in the water, their screams engulfed as their weapons and packs carried them down into bitter cold. Others who had been able to reach the ship's side were dragging themselves back to a security they could recognize, only to be torn down by the next controlled broadside. The American was burned and scarred by the weight of iron, but mostly it was the blood that was remarkable. On the hull, and down the side, where even the water shone pink in the sunlight.

In a brief lull, Bolitho heard Allday say, 'If they'd

been first, sir, they'd have given no quarter to us.' He was speaking to Avery, but any reply was lost in the next roar of cannon fire.

Outside this pitiless arena of death, another struggle was taking place. Ship to ship, or two to one, if the odds were overwhelming. No line of battle, only ship to ship. Man to man.

York said hoarsely, 'White flag, sir! They're finished!'

True or not, they would never know, for at that moment the third and last broadside smashed into the other ship, shattering forever the scattered remnants of a plan that might have been successful.

As men staggered from *Indomitable*'s guns and ran to the braces and halliards in response to shouted commands to bring the ship about and into the wind, Bolitho took a final glance at the enemy. But even the white flag had vanished into the smoke.

Daubeny sheathed his sword, his eyes red-rimmed and bright.

'*Chivalrous* has signalled, sir. The enemy has broken off the action.' He looked at his hand, as if to see if it were shaking. 'They did what they came to do.'

Tyacke tore his eyes from the flapping sails as his ship turned sedately across the wind, the masthead pendant rivalling Bolitho's Cross of St George as they streamed across the opposite side.

He said harshly, 'And so, Mr Daubeny, did *we*!'

Bolitho handed the telescope to Essex. 'Thank you.' Then to Tyacke, 'General signal, if you please. *Discontinue the action. Report losses and damage.*' He looked across at the tall signals midshipman. 'And, Mr Carleton, mark this well and spell it out in full. *Yours is the gift of courage.*'

Avery hurried across to assist the signals party, but once with them he paused, afraid to miss anything, his head still reeling from the roar of the guns and the immediate silence which had followed.

Bolitho was saying to Tyacke, '*Taciturn* will take command and lead our ships to Halifax. I fear we have lost some good men today.'

He heard Tyacke reply quietly, 'We could have lost far more, Sir Richard.' He tried to lighten his tone. 'At least that damned renegade in his *Retribution* failed to appear.'

Bolitho said nothing. He was staring across the quarter to the distant smoke, like a stain on a painting.

Avery turned away. The gift of courage. Our Nel would have appreciated that. He took the slate and pencil from Carleton's unsteady hands.

'Let me.'

Tyacke said, 'May I change tack and recover the boats, Sir Richard?'

'Not yet, James.' His eyes were bleak. Cold, as that dawn sky had been. He gazed up at the signal for Close Action. 'We are not yet done, I fear.'

CHAPTER SEVENTEEN

THE GREATEST REWARD

Captain Adam Bolitho removed his boatcloak and handed it to an army orderly, who was careful to shake it before carrying it away. It had begun to rain with the abruptness of a squall at sea, and the drops were hard and cold, almost ice.

332

Adam crossed to a window and wiped away the dampness with his hand. Halifax harbour was full of shipping, but he had scarcely glanced at the anchored vessels while he had been pulled ashore in the gig. He could not become accustomed to it, accept that he had to go to the land in order to see his admiral.

Keen had sent word that he needed to speak with him as soon as possible, when, under normal circumstances, they could have met aft in *Valkyrie*'s great cabin.

He thought of John Urquhart, now acting-captain of the ill-fated *Reaper*. Perhaps Keen's summons had come at the right moment. Urquhart had been with him in the cabin, about to take his leave to assume command of *Reaper*, and their farewell and the significance of the moment had moved Adam more than he had believed possible. He knew that he had been seeing himself. although he had been much younger when he had been offered his first ship. But the feelings, gratitude, elation, nervousness, regret, were the same. Urquhart had said, 'I'll not forget what you have done for me, sir. I shall endeavour to make use of my experience to the best of my ability.'

Adam had answered, 'Remember one thing, John. You are the captain, and they will know it. When you go across to her presently to read yourself in, think of the ship, *your* ship, not what she has been or might have become, but what she can be for you. All your officers are new, but most of the warrant ranks are from the original company. They are bound to make comparisons, as is the way with old Jacks.'

Urquhart had looked up at the deckhead, had heard the tramp of boots as the marines took up their positions to see him over the side. It had all been in his face. Wanting to go, to begin: needing to stay where

333

all things were familiar.

Adam had said quietly, 'Don't concern yourself now with *Valkyrie*, John. It will be up to Lieutenant Dyer to fill your shoes. It is his chance, too.' He had gone to the table and opened a drawer. 'Take these.' He had seen the surprise and uncertainty on Urquhart's face, and added abruptly, 'A bit weathered and salt-stained, I fear, but until you find a tailor....'

Urquhart had held the epaulettes to the light, all else forgotten. Adam had said, 'My first. I hope they bring you luck.'

They had gone on deck. Handshakes, quick grins, a few cheers from some of the watching seamen. The twitter of calls, and it was done. Moments later they might hear the calls from *Reaper* across the harbour.

Just before they had parted Urquhart had said, 'I hope we meet again soon, sir.'

'You will be too busy for social events.' He had hesitated. 'In truth, I envy you!'

A door opened, and de Courcey stood waiting for him to turn from the window.

'Rear-Admiral Keen will see you now, sir.'

Adam walked past him without speaking. De Courcey was different in some way, oddly subdued. Because he had shown fear when the two American frigates had hove into view? *Did he really imagine I would run carrying tales to his admiral, as he would have done about me?*

It was the general's room which he had visited with Keen and Bolitho on another occasion, with the same large paintings of battles and dark, heavy furniture, and he realized that this had probably been Keen's idea, rather than ask him to join him at the Massie residence.

He saw that Keen was not alone, and the other man, who was about to leave, was David St Clair.

St Clair shook his hand. 'I am sorry you were kept waiting, Captain Bolitho. It seems I may be needed here in Halifax after all.'

Keen waved him to a chair as the door closed behind his other visitor. Adam studied him with interest. Keen looked strained, and unusually tense.

He said, 'I have received fresh dispatches from the Admiralty, but first I have to tell you that Sir Richard was correct in his belief that control of the lakes was vital.' He glanced around the room, thinking of that day in the summer when the army captain had described the first attack on York. When Gilia had asked about the officer who had been killed. 'The army could not hold the vital line of water communications, and at Lake Erie they were beaten. A retreat was ordered, but it was already too late.' He slapped his hand on the table and said bitterly, 'The army was cut to pieces!'

'What will it mean, sir?' Adam could not recall ever seeing Keen so distressed. So lost.

Keen made an effort to compose himself. 'Mean? It means we will not be able to drive the Americans out of the western frontier districts, especially not now, with winter fast approaching. It will be another stalemate. We, in the fleet, will blockade every American port. They'll feel that as deeply as any bayonet!'

Adam tried to think without emotion. His uncle was at sea, and the brig *Weazle* had brought word that he was investigating the whereabouts of some enemy frigates reported heading north-east. They could be anywhere by now. He thought of Keen's words, *winter fast approaching*. The fierce, bitter rain,

335

the fogs, the damp between decks. Where had the time gone? It was October, by only a day or two, and yet you could feel it.

He roused himself from his thoughts and found that Keen was watching him gravely. 'Sir Richard, your uncle and my dear friend, is to be withdrawn. That was the main point of the dispatches. I shall remain in charge here.'

Adam was on his feet. 'Why, sir?'

'Why, indeed? I am informed that Sir Alexander Cochrane will be taking over the whole station, which will include the Leeward Squadron. A far bigger fleet will be at his disposal, both for blockade duties and for land operations with the army. In Europe. Napoleon's armies are in retreat on every front. It is a land war now. Our blockade has served its purpose.' He turned away, and said with the same soft bitterness, 'And at what a price.'

Adam said, 'I think Sir Richard should be told without delay.'

'I need all available frigates here, Adam. I have scarcely a brig available to retain contact with our patrols, let alone watch over enemy movements.'

'Sir Richard may have been called to action, sir.'

'D'you imagine I've not thought as much? I couldn't sleep because of it. But I cannot spare any more ships.'

Adam said coolly, 'I understand, sir. As your flag captain, I am required to advise, and to present conclusions. My uncle would be the very first to steer away from favouritism, or from encouraging action taken purely out of personal involvement.'

'I hoped you would say that, Adam. If I were free to act....'

Adam turned away as the same orderly entered

336

with a tray and glasses. 'With the General's compliments, sir.'

He said, 'But you are not free, sir, not so long as your flag is flying above this command.'

Keen watched the soldier's steady hand as he poured two large measures of cognac. The general lived well, it seemed.

Adam held the glass to the light from the window. Already it was as grey as winter, like a symbol of time's relentless passage.

Keen swallowed deeply, and coughed to regain his breath. Then he said, 'You may go, thank you.' When they were alone again, he said, 'The warrants for the two mutineers were presented this morning. Have no fear—*I* signed them. Sir Richard will be spared that, at least.' It seemed to spark off another memory. 'John Urquhart took command today, did he not?'

Adam said, 'Yes. The custom will prevail, sir. Both prisoners will be hanged, run up to the main yard by their own ship's company. *Reaper*'s.'

Keen nodded almost absently, as if he had been listening to a stranger.

'I will order *Reaper* to sea immediately. Captain Urquhart can find Sir Richard and carry my dispatches to him. I'll not begin that ship's new life with a damned execution!'

There were voices outside: de Courcey with the next visitors. Keen glanced irritably at the door. 'There is another matter, Adam. If you would prefer to take another appointment, I would understand. It has not been easy.' He looked at him directly, his eyes very still. 'For either of us.'

Adam was surprised that he did not even hesitate. 'I would like to remain with you, sir.' He put down

337

the empty glass. 'I shall return to *Valkyrie* in case I am needed.'

For the first time, Keen smiled. 'You will always be that, Adam. Believe me.'

The same orderly was waiting for him with his cloak. 'Stopped rainin', sir.'

He thought of Urquhart, how he would feel when he was ordered to proceed to sea with all possible despatch. Relieved, probably. And of the mutineer, Harry Ramsay, whom he had tried to help, although he had suspected that he was guilty. At least he would be spared the final degradation of being hanged by his own shipmates.

'A moment, Captain Bolitho!'

He turned, and as if to a secret signal the front doors swung shut again.

She was warmly dressed, her cheeks flushed from the cold air. He waited, seeing her as she had been that day when *Valkyrie*'s powerful broadside had been ready to fire. None of them would have survived, and she would know it.

He removed his hat, and said, 'I trust you are well, Miss St Clair?'

She did not seem to hear. 'Are you remaining as flag captain to Rear-Admiral Keen?'

So Keen had confided in her. He was again surprised, that he did not care.

'I am.'

He glanced down as she laid one hand on his sleeve. 'I am so glad. He needs you.' Her eyes did not falter. 'And, for his sake, so do I.'

Adam studied her. He supposed that she would also know about the battle for Lake Erie, and the regiments involved.

He said, 'You have my good wishes.' He allowed

338

himself to smile, to soften it. 'Both of you.'

She walked with him to the door. Then she said, 'You knew Rear-Admiral Keen's wife, I believe?'

He faced her again. 'I was in love with her.' It was madness; she would tell Keen. Then, he was quite certain that she would not.

She nodded: he did not know whether she was satisfied or relieved. 'Thank you, Captain ... I can understand now why you love your uncle. You are both the same man, in many ways.'

She tugged off her glove, and it dropped to the floor. Adam stooped to recover it, and she did not see the sudden distress in his eyes.

He took her hand, and kissed it. 'You do me too much honour, Miss St Clair.'

She waited until the door had been pulled shut behind him. Her father would be impatient to see her, wanting to tell her about his new appointment here in Halifax. It would be good to see him happy, occupied with his work again.

But all she could think of was the man who had just left her, whose austere face had seemed very young and vulnerable for those few seconds, when he had picked up her glove. Something which even he had been unable to hide. And she was both moved and gladdened by it.

At four bells of the afternoon watch His Majesty's Ship *Reaper* weighed anchor, and under topsails and jib wended her way towards the entrance and the open sea. Many eyes followed her, but no one cheered or wished her well. Captain Adam Bolitho followed her progress until she was lost from view. She was free.

*　　　*　　　*

'Deck there! Boats in the water, dead ahead!'

Tyacke walked to the compass box and then stopped as eight bells chimed out from the forecastle. 'I *was* beginning to wonder, Mr York.'

The sailing-master rubbed his hands. 'By guess and by God, sir. It usually works!'

Tyacke peered along the length of his ship, the guns lashed firmly behind shuttered ports, men working, not certain what to expect. *Indomitable* was steering due west, the wind sweeping over the larboard quarter, the spray as heavy and cold as rain.

He looked aft again and saw Bolitho by the taffrail, not walking but standing, oblivious to the men around him and the marines at the nettings, where they had remained since the attack on the American boats.

York moved closer and murmured, 'What ails the admiral? We prevented the landings, more than most of us dared to hope.'

Tyacke stared at the horizon, hard, hard blue in the noon light. A sun without warmth, a steady wind to fill the topsails, but without life.

Even the casualties amongst the squadron had been less than would have been suffered in a straightforward fight. But the Americans had been eager to stand away, unwilling to risk a running battle for no good purpose. If they had rallied and reformed, it would have been a different story. As it was, the frigate *Attacker* had been dismasted, and the smaller *Wildfire* had been so badly holed by long-range and well-sighted shots that she had been down by the head when she had finally been taken in tow. Most of the casualties had been in those two ships: thirty killed and many others wounded. It had been

340

time to discontinue the action and Bolitho had known it. Tyacke had watched his face when the signals had been read out, giving details of damage and casualties. Some might think that the admiral was relieved because *Indomitable* had not been in the thick of it, and was unmarked. If they believed that they were bloody fools, Tyacke thought.

He swung round. '*What?*'

Lieutenant Daubeny flinched. 'I was wondering, sir, about relighting the galley fire....'

Tyacke controlled his anger with an effort. 'Well, *wonder away*, Mr Daubeny!' He glanced aft again, unable to forget the quiet voice, as if Bolitho had just spoken to him. When he had reported that there were no more boats in the water by the stranded and smoke-shrouded American ship, Bolitho had said, 'It was murder, James. Justified in war, but murder for all that. If that was the price of victory, I don't wish to share a part of it!'

Tyacke said abruptly, 'That was unfair. Pass the word for the purser and arrange an extra tot of rum for all hands. Food too, if there is any, but the galley fire *stays out* until I know what's happening.'

Daubeny said, 'I see, sir.'

Tyacke turned away. 'You do not, Mr Daubeny, but no matter.' To York he said, 'Sir Richard feels it, Isaac. Cares too much. I've not seen him like this before, though.'

York tucked some dishevelled grey hair beneath his hat. 'He's fair troubled, right enough.'

Tyacke walked to the compass box and back again. 'Let me know when you can see the boats from the deck. It will give the hands something to do when we hoist 'em inboard.' He clapped the master on the shoulder. 'A good piece of navigation, Mr York.' He

341

turned as Allday walked aft from the companion. 'You know him best, Allday. What do you think?'

Allday regarded him warily. 'It's not for me to say, sir.' He followed Tyacke's eyes to the figure by the taffrail, the hero others never saw. So completely alone.

He made up his mind. The captain was a friend; it was not merely idle curiosity.

'He knows, sir.' He glanced at the hard, glittering horizon; unlike the admiral, he did not have to shade his eyes. 'It's today, y' see?'

Tyacke said sharply, 'The Yankees are gone, man. They'll not be back, not till they're ready and prepared again. Our ships will reach Halifax and the dock-master will foam at the mouth when he sees all the repairs that need doing!'

But Allday did not respond, nor did he smile.

He said, 'There's always the...' He frowned, searching for the word. 'The scavenger. My wife's brother was a line-soldier—he told me. After a battle, men lying wounded, calling out for help, with only the dead to hear them. And then the scavengers would come. To rob them, to answer a cry for help with a cut-throat blade. *Scum!*'

Tyacke studied his lined face, aware of the strength of the man. The admiral's oak. He heard York's steady breathing beside him. He could feel it too: knew it, the way he read the wind's direction and the set of the current in the painted sea. Tyacke was not superstitious. At least, he believed he was not.

Allday was carrying the old sword, which was part of the legend.

He said quietly, 'We'll fight this day, sir. That's it an' all about it!'

He walked aft, and they saw Bolitho turn toward

him, as if they had just met on a street or in some country lane.

York said uneasily, 'How can that be, sir?'

Allday was saying, 'The hands are going to draw a wet, Sir Richard. Can I fetch you something?'

Bolitho glanced down as he clipped the old sword onto his belt.

'Not now, old friend.' He smiled with an effort, understanding that Allday needed reassurance. 'Afterwards, that would be better.'

He reached out to touch his arm, and then halted.

'Deck there! Sail on th' larboard bow!'

They were all staring round, some at the empty sea, and others aft towards their officers. Avery was here, a telescope in his hands, his eyes darting between them. To miss nothing, to forget nothing.

Bolitho said, 'Aloft with you, George. In my own mind, I can already see her.' He held up one hand. 'Take your time. The people will be watching you.'

Allday took a deep breath, feeling the old pain in his chest. *Scavenger.*

Bolitho knew that Tyacke had turned toward him, and called to him, 'Alter course. Steer west by south. That should suffice for the present.'

He turned away from them, and watched a solitary gull swooping around the quarter gallery. The spirit of some old Jack, Allday thought.

'Deck there!' Avery was a fast climber, and had a good carrying voice: he had told him that he had been in a church choir in his youth. In that other world. 'She's a frigate, sir! I—I think she's *Retribution!*'

Bolitho murmured, 'I know she is, my friend.' He frowned, as Allday's hand went to his chest. 'I'll not have *you* suffer for it!'

He raised his voice. 'You may beat to quarters

again, Captain Tyacke. We have some old scores to settle today!' He laid his hand on the sword's hilt at his hip, and it was cold to the touch. 'So let us pay them in full!'

* * *

Lieutenant George Avery waited for the motion to ease, and knew that more helm had been applied. He raised his telescope, as he had on the first sight of enemy ships only hours ago. It felt like a lifetime. The same marines were still in the foretop, staring at the oncoming American as her sails emptied and filled violently, while she leaned over to the pressure. She was a heavy-looking frigate under a full press of canvas, the spary bursting beneath her beakhead and as high as the gilded figurehead. The gladiator, a short stabbing-sword glinting in the hard glare.

The corporal said, 'The Yankee's crossin' our bows, lads.' But his comment was really intended for the flag lieutenant.

Avery studied the other ship, forcing himself to take his time, not to see only what he expected to see. The corporal was right. The *Retribution* would eventually cross from bow to bow; more importantly, she would find herself to leeward of *Indomitable's* broadside once they were at close quarters. He estimated it carefully. Three miles at the most. Tyacke had reduced sail to topsails and jib, driver and reefed forecourse, and *Indomitable's* progress was steady and unhurried, a floating platform for her twenty-four pounders.

He lowered the glass and looked around at his companions. Somehow, they managed to appear very jaunty and smart in their glazed leather hats with

344

the cockade and plume over the left ear. He noticed also that they had all shaved. They were fastidious about such details in the Corps.

'Won't be long, lads.' He saw the corporal glance at the swivel gun, 'Betsy'. He would know what to expect. They all did.

He nodded to them, and lowered himself quickly onto the ratlines. On deck once more, he strode aft, catching the hurried glances from the gun crews, a half-wave from young Protheroe. On this deck, the gun was god. Nothing else mattered but to fire and keep firing, to shut out the sights and the sounds, even when a friend cried out in agony.

He found Bolitho with Tyacke and the first lieutenant, observing from the quarterdeck. Here, too, the marines had come to life, like scarlet soldiers taken from a box, lining the packed hammock nettings while elsewhere sentries stood guard at hatches or ladders, in case a man's nerve cracked and terror tore discipline apart.

Avery touched his hat. 'She's *Retribution* right enough, Sir Richard. She wears a commodore's broad-pendant. Fifty guns, at a guess. She changed tack.' He thought of the corporal again, the doubt in his voice. 'She'll lose the wind-gage if she remains on that tack.'

York said, 'She steers nor' east, sir.' Unruffled. Patient. Bolitho saw him tap the youngest midshipman's arm as the child reached for the half-hour glass beside the compass box. 'Easy, Mr Campbell, don't warm the glass! *I* have to write the log, not you!'

The twelve-year-old midshipman looked embarrassed, and momentarily forgot the growing menace of the American's tall sails.

Bolitho took a telescope and trained it beyond the bows. *Retribution* had no intention of altering course, not yet. He studied the other frigate: well-built, like so many French vessels, designed to one standard for the convenience of repair and replacement, not at the whim of an individual ship-builder like most British men-of-war. When *Taciturn* and the other damaged ships reached Halifax, they would be hard put to find a mast or a spar that would match any one of them.

He said, 'He is deliberately dropping downwind, James.' He sensed that Daubeny was leaning forward to listen, squinting in concentration.

Tyacke agreed. 'Then he intends to use the extra elevation the wind gives him to fire at full range.' He glanced up at the braced yards, the flag and pendant streaming towards the enemy, and said grimly, 'He'll try for our spars and rigging.'

Avery turned away. The corporal had seen it, but had not fully understood. Both Bolitho and Tyacke must accept it.

Bolitho said, 'Chain-shot, James?'

Tyacke shook his head. 'I did hear they were using langridge, that damnable case-shot. If so...' He swung away as though to consult the compass again.

Bolitho said to Avery, 'It can cripple a ship before she can fight back.' He saw the concern in Avery's tawny eyes, but he did not fully comprehend. *Damnable*, Tyacke had termed it. It was far worse than that. Packed into a thin case, each shot contained bars of jagged iron, loosely linked together so that when they burst into a ship's complex web of rigging they could tear it to pieces in one screaming broadside.

He saw Tyacke gesturing to the gun crews and

346

making some point urgently to Daubeny with each jab of his finger.

That was the advantage of langridge; but against that, it took far longer to sponge and worm out each gun afterwards to avoid a fresh charge exploding in the muzzle as it was rammed home. It took time, and Tyacke would know it.

Bolitho rubbed his damaged eye and felt it ache in response. *If I were James, what would I do?* He was astonished that he could even smile, recalling that almost forgotten admiral who had met his pleading for a command with the withering retort, *Were* a frigate captain, Bolitho....

I would hold my fire and pray that the regular drills hold firm, if all else fails.

Lieutenant Blythe called, 'The enemy's running out, sir!'

Tyacke said, 'Aye, and he'll likely check each gun himself.'

Bolitho saw Allday watching him. Even Tyacke had accepted Aherne, had given him body and personality. A man with so much hatred. Retribution. *And yet if he crossed this very deck, I would not know him*. Perhaps it was the best kind of enemy. Faceless.

Once again, he looked at the sky and the searing reflections beneath it. Two ships with an entire ocean to witness their efforts to kill one another.

He covered his undamaged eye and tested the other. His vision was blurred; he had come to accept that. But the colours remained true, and the enemy was close enough now to show her flag, and the commodore's broad-pendant standing out in the wind like a great banner.

Tyacke said, 'Ready, Sir Richard.'

347

'Very well, James.' So close, so private, as if they shared the deck only with ghosts. 'For what we are about to receive....'

Tyacke waved his fist, and the order echoed along the upper deck.

'Open the ports! Run out!' And from the waist of the ship where the gunner's mates were already passing out cutlasses and axes from the arms chest, Lieutenant Daubeny's voice, very clear and determined.

'Lay for the foremast, gun captains! And fire on the uproll!'

The older hands were already crouching down, as yet unable to see their target.

Tyacke yelled, 'Put your helm down! Off heads'l sheets!'

Indomitable began to turn, using the wind across her quarter to her best advantage. Round and further still, so that the other frigate appeared to be ensnared in the shrouds as *Indomitable's* bowsprit passed over her, to hold her on the larboard side.

The distance was falling away more quickly, and Bolitho saw the topmen darting amongst the thrashing sails like tiny puppets on invisible strings.

The air quivered and then erupted in a drawn-out explosion, smoke billowing from the American's guns which was then driven inboard and away across the water.

It seemed to take an age, an eternity. When the broadside ploughed into *Indomitable's* masts and rigging, it was as if the whole ship was bellowing in agony. Tiny vignettes stood out amidst the smoke and falling wreckage. A seaman torn apart by the jagged iron as it ripped through the piled hammocks, and hurled more men, screaming and kicking, to the

348

opposite side. Midshipman Essex, stockstill, staring with horror at his white breeches, which were splashed with blood and pieces of human skin cut so finely that they could have been the work of a surgeon. Essex opened and closed his mouth but no sound came, until a running seaman punched his arm and yelled something, and ran on to help others who were hacking away fallen cordage.

Avery stared up, ice-cold as the fore topgallant mast splintered apart, stays and halliards flying like severed snakes, before thundering down and over the side. He wiped his eyes and looked again. It was suddenly important, personal. He saw the four scarlet figures in the top, peering up at the broken mast, but otherwise untouched.

'A hand here!'

Avery ran to help as York caught one of his master's mates, who had been impaled on a splinter as big as his wrist.

York stepped into his place, and muttered hoarsely, 'Hold on, Nat!'

Avery lowered the man to the deck. He would hear nothing ever again. When he was able to look up once more, Avery saw the American's topgallant sails standing almost alongside. He knew it was impossible; she was still half a cable away.

He heard Daubeny shout, 'As you bear! *Fire!*'

Down the ship's side from the crouching lion to this place here on the quarterdeck, each gun belched fire and smoke while its crew threw themselves on tackles and handspikes to hasten the reloading. But not double-shotted this time. It would take too many precious minutes.

A marine fell from the nettings without a word; there was not even a telltale scar on the deck planking

349

to mark the shot.

Bolitho said, 'Walk with me, George. Those riflemen are too eager today.'

'*Run out! Ready! Fire!*'

There was a cracked cheer as the *Retribution's* mizzen mast swayed and toppled in its stays and shrouds, before falling with a crash that could be heard even above the merciless roar of cannon fire. York was holding a rag against his bloody cheek, although he had not felt the splinter which had opened it like a knife.

He called, 'Her steering's adrift, sir!'

Bolitho said sharply, 'Helm down, James! Our only chance!'

And then the enemy was here, no longer a distant picture of grace and cruel beauty. She was angled toward them, the water surging and spitting between the two hulls even as *Indomitable's* long jib-boom and then her bowsprit rammed into the enemy's shrouds like some giant tusk.

The force of the impact splintered *Indomitable's* main yard, broken spars, torn rigging and wounded topmen falling on Hockenhull's spread nets like so much rubbish.

Tyacke shouted at his gun crews, 'One more, lads! *Hit 'em!*'

Then he staggered and clapped one hand to his thigh, his teeth bared against the pain. Midshipman Carleton ran to help him, but Tyacke gasped, 'Pike! Give me a pike, damn you!'

The midshipman thrust one towards him and stared at him, unable to move as Tyacke drove the pike into the deck and held himself upright, using it as a prop.

Bolitho felt Allday move closer, Avery too, with a

pistol suddenly in one hand. Across the debris and the wounded he saw Tyacke raise a hand to him, a gesture towards the fallen masts. A bridge, joining them with the enemy.

The guns roared out and recoiled again, the crews leaping aside to pick up their cutlasses, staggering as though with a deadly fatigue while they clambered across to the other ship which had been forced alongside, *Indomitable*'s splintered jib-boom dangling beside the enemy's figurehead.

There was a bang from the swivel gun in the foretop, and a hail of canister raked a group of American seamen even as they ran to repel boarders. The marines were gasping and cheering as they fired, reloaded, and then threw themselves on the hammocks to take aim again. And again. Above it all, Bolitho could hear Tyacke shouting orders and encouragement to his men. He would not give in to anything, not even the wound in his thigh. After what he had already suffered, it was an insult to think that he might.

Lieutenant Protheroe was the first on *Retribution*'s gangway, and the first to fall to a musket which was fired into his body from only a few inches away. He fell, and was trapped between the two grinding hulls. Bolitho saw him drop, and remembered him as the youngster who had welcomed him aboard.

He shouted, 'To me, Indoms! *To me*, lads!'

He was dragging himself across, above the choppy water, aware of flashing pistol fire and heavier calibre shot, and of Allday close behind, croaking, 'Hold back, Sir Richard! We can't fight the whole bloody ship!'

Bolitho was finding it difficult to breathe, his lungs filled with smoke and the stench of death. Then he

351

was aboard the other ship, saw Hockenhull, the squat boatswain, kill a man with his boarding axe and manage to grin afterwards at Allday. He must have saved him from being struck down. In the terrible blood-red rage of battle, the consuming madness, Bolitho could still remember Allday's son, and that Allday had blamed Hockenhull for posting him to the vulnerable quarter-deck, where he had died. Perhaps this would end that festering grievance.

Avery dragged at his arm, and fired point-blank into a crouching figure that had appeared at their feet. Then he, too, staggered, and Bolitho imagined he had been hit.

But Avery was shouting, trying to be heard above the shouts and cries and the clash of steel, blade to blade.

Then Bolitho heard it also. He lurched against a wild-eyed marine, his bloodied bayonet already levelled for a second thrust, his mind still refusing to understand. Faint but certain. Someone was cheering, and for a chilling moment he imagined that the Americans had had more men than he had believed, that they had managed to board *Indomitable* in strength. Then Tyacke must be dead. They would not otherwise get past him.

Avery gripped his arm. 'D' you *hear*, sir?' He was trembling, and almost incoherent. 'It's *Reaper*! She's joined the squadron!'

The explosion was sudden, and so close that Bolitho found himself flung bodily to the deck, his sword dangling from the knot around his wrist. It had felt like a searing wind, the dust and fragments from the blast like hot sand. Hands were pulling him to his feet; Allday, with his back turned, exposed to the enemy as he steadied him amongst the press of

352

dazed and breathless men.

Bolitho gasped, unable to speak, to reassure him, but the agony in his eye was making it impossible.

He said, '*Help me.*'

Allday seemed to understand, and tore his neckerchief from his throat and in two turns had tied it around Bolitho's head, covering his injured eye.

It was like being deaf, with men crawling or kneeling in utter silence beside the wounded, and peering into the faces of the dead.

Retribution's seamen were staring at them, bewildered, shocked, beaten. Their flag had fallen with the broken mizzen mast, but they had not surrendered. They had simply ceased to fight.

The explosion had been confined to the ship's quarterdeck. A bursting cannon, carelessly loaded for a final desperate show of defiance, or perhaps a burning wad from one of Tyacke's guns when they had fired that last broadside with muzzles almost overlapping those of the enemy. A small group of American officers were waiting near the shattered wheel, where helmsmen and others lay in the ugly attitudes of violent death.

One lieutenant held out his sword, and instantly Allday's cutlass and Avery's pistol rose in unison.

Bolitho touched the bandage across his eye, and was grateful for it. He said, 'Where is your commodore?' He stared at the fallen mast, where men were still trapped in the tangled rigging like fish in a net. *Reaper* was closer, and the cheering was still going on; and he wished that he could see her.

The lieutenant stooped, and uncovered the head and shoulders of his commodore.

He handed his sword, hilt first, to Avery, and said, 'Commodore Aherne, sir. He sometimes spoke of you.'

353

Bolitho stared down at the face, angry and contorted, frozen at the instant of death. But a stranger.

He looked beyond them, toward the open sea. Had Aherne heard the cheers, and recognized *Reaper* too?

He turned inboard again. It was right, it was justice, that it should be *Reaper*. Now a witness to victory, and to folly.

He looked around at the breathless, gasping men, the madness gone from them as they dragged the wounded and the dying away from the blood-stained chaos on deck, talking to one another, some without realizing that those who answered were the enemy.

Through the clinging smoke he could see Tyacke facing him across the narrow strip of trapped water, still propped on his pike, with the surgeon on his knees applying a dressing. Tyacke raised one bloodied hand in salute. Perhaps to his ship. To the victor.

Bolitho said, 'Help me back to *Indomitable.*' It was impossible to smile. Had he really cried, *To me, Indoms*, only minutes ago?

Allday took his arm and guided him, watching out for anything that might take him unaware. He had guessed what had happened, and now he was certain of it. He had seen too much to be shocked or awed by the sights on every hand: in his own way, despite the brutal ugliness of death everywhere, he was satisfied.

Once again they had come through, and they were still together. It was more than enough.

Bolitho hesitated, and looked around at the two embattled ships. Men had leaned over to touch his coat as he had passed; some had grinned and spoken his name; a few had openly wept, ashamed, perhaps, that they had survived when so many had fallen.

Now they all fell silent to listen as he looked beyond them and saw *Reaper's* topsails suddenly bright in the hard sunlight. He touched the locket beneath his stained shirt, and knew she was close to him.

'It is a high price to pay, and we have paid it many times before. But we must not forget, for if we do, it will be at our peril!' He raised his head and stared up at his flag at the mainmast truck, so clean, and removed from the suffering and the hate.

'Loyalty is like trust, and must surely reach in both directions.' He looked at the slow-moving topsails again. 'But it is the greatest reward of all.'

It was over.

EPILOGUE

The carriage with the Bolitho crest on its doors, freshly washed that morning, came to a halt by the church. It was cold even for March, but Catherine Somervell did not notice it.

Bryan Ferguson opened the door and lowered the step for her.

'Why not wait in there, my lady? 'Tis warmer, to be sure.' He seemed concerned, anxious that something might go wrong even now. She took his hand and stepped down onto the cobbles, and glanced toward the waterfront.

It was like any other day, and yet it was entirely different. Even the people seemed to be waiting, drawn together as was so often the way in seaports. A rumour, a message, a signal-gun, or a ship in distress. The people of Falmouth had seen it all before.

She adjusted her long green cloak, and the fastening at the throat. She had dressed carefully, taken her time, even though every fibre of her body had screamed at her to leave the house without delay. It still did not seem possible that Richard was coming, that he was probably within a mile of Falmouth at this moment.

She could recall the exact time when the letter had been brought by fast courier from Bethune at the Admiralty. She had already received one from Richard; it had touched on the battle, but he had avoided mentioning the many who had died. Bethune had told her that *Indomitable* was ordered to Plymouth, to be handed over to the care of carpenters and riggers there, eventually. But she was to be paid off upon arrival. A battered ship with her own memories and wounds, and like many of her company, she would wait now, and see if she was needed again.

The church clock at King Charles the Martyr chimed very slowly. Noon. She had been deeply suspicious of Bethune's written suggestion that she await Richard's return in Falmouth, and briefly she had conjured up old or unknown enemies who, even at this last precious opportunity, would attempt to reunite Richard with his wife under some pretext or other.

When she had composed herself and considered it, dismissing her fears, she knew the real reason. *Indomitable* was to be paid off in Plymouth, and Richard would be saying farewell to so many familiar faces. Others had already left, like shadows, carrying

356

memories she could only imagine. He did not want her to see the ship now, but to remember her as she had been when she had climbed aboard, and they had cheered her for it, and Richard's flag had broken out above all of them.

He was alive; he was coming home. It was all that mattered. She had sensed that there were other matters, which Bethune had left unwritten. *I am ready.*

To Ferguson she said, 'I shall be all right. I shall know you are here.' She brushed a strand of dark hair from her eyes, and looked up at Young Matthew on his box, framed against the cold, pale sky. 'Both of you.'

There would be others here today. Unis, waiting for John Allday, although she had not yet seen her: this was a private moment for all who shared it. Perhaps it symbolized, more than anything, the elusive dream of peace, after so many years of sacrifice and separation. Bethune had said that the war was almost over. The allies had scored another crushing victory over Napoleon at Laon, and Wellington had captured Bordeaux: there was even talk of disbanding the local militia, the sea fencibles too. She thought with regret and affection of Lewis Roxby; how proud he would have been on this day. Nancy had visited her often: a sailor's daughter as well as Richard's sister, she was a great comfort to Catherine. And without Roxby's presence filling every room at that great, empty house, it had helped her also. But she would stay away today. She understood, better than most.

She walked on, towards the moored vessels in the harbour, the swaying masts and spars which were now so familiar to her. The smells, too, were a far cry from the slums of her childhood, or the elegant London she had shared with Richard. Fresh bread and fish, tar and oakum, and the salt of the ever-present sea.

She saw people glance at her, some with curiosity, some familiarity, but without hostility. She would always be a stranger here, but never an intruder, and she was grateful for that.

She saw one of the coastguards with his companion, the same pair who had been on the beach as the tide had receded, and she had taken Zenoria's slight, broken body in her arms.

He nodded and removed his hat to her. 'Fine day, m'lady.'

'I hope so, Tom.'

She walked on, until she stood on the very edge of the jetty. And the war in North America? It took second place to most of these people, for whom France had been the enemy for so long. Too long.

Samuel Whitbread, the wealthy and influential brewer, had thundered out in the House of Commons that the war with America should be ended without delay. He had reminded the honourable members of that other occasion when peace had been grudgingly signed after the War of Independence, and Pitt had then remarked, *A defensive war can only end in inevitable defeat.* She lifted her chin. So be it, then.

She heard laughter and noisy voices, and turned to see a group of discharged sailors loitering, watching the harbour. The ones she had heard Allday scornfully denounce as old Jacks who refought their battles every day in the inns and ale-houses, until the parlour lanterns were swinging like those of a ship in Biscay.

But they belonged here today: they were members

358

of what Richard would call the family. One or two of them waved in acknowledgement, privileged to be part of his homecoming. She turned away. There was not one whole man amongst them.

Someone exclaimed, 'There she be, lads!'

Catherine looked across the water, her face like ice in the wind off Falmouth Bay and here in Carrick Roads.

Tom the coastguard said, ''Tis the *Pickle*. Quite right an' proper.'

For my benefit?

She watched the little schooner moving between some moored lighters, distinguished from her merchant sisters only by a large, new White Ensign streaming from her peak.

H.M. Schooner *Pickle. Right and proper*. Her eyes pricked with sudden emotion, but she was determined to miss nothing. *Pickle* was a fairly regular visitor here, as she was at every port and naval station between Plymouth and Spithead. Carrying dispatches and mail, and sometimes passengers, to the port admirals, or to the ships resting from their arduous blockade duties, sheltering in Torbay and protected from the gales by Berry Head.

But here, *Pickle* would always be remembered for her part in a single, greater event. She had run into Falmouth, and from here her commander, Lieutenant John Lapenotiere, had taken a post-chaise non-stop to the Admiralty, a journey of some thirty-seven hours. And all the way the cry had gone with him, of England's greatest victory at Trafalgar, to raise the heart of the nation. And to numb it just as quickly, with the news that Nelson, the people's hero, was dead.

She wondered if Richard had made any comparison, but knew he would not. His memories would be with James Tyacke and the others.

She touched her throat. *And his hopes with me.*

She saw the sails being brought under control, heaving lines snaking ashore to seamen and onlookers alike. *Pickle* had come alongside, her ensign very clear against the grey stones. Lieutenant Avery and Yovell would come by road with Richard's possessions ... She was filling her mind with irrelevant thoughts to control her emotion.

The chair, the wine cooler which she had had made when the other had been lost with his ship. *If it had survived the last action* ... She walked to the end of the jetty, unfastening her cloak so that he should see her, and his fan-shaped pendant resting at her breast.

She saw the blue and white of uniforms, heard people on the jetty raising a cheer, not merely for the hero, but for Falmouth's own son.

The baker's wife was here with her small daughter, the child looking pleased but rather puzzled by the bunch of wild daffodils which she had been given to present as their own welcome.

Then she saw him, straight-backed and tall in his fine gold-laced coat, the old family sword at his side. And close on his heels, turning only to wave to the men on the schooner, was Allday, as she had known he would be.

She stood and watched him, oblivious to the cold. It was so important, too important to ruin in the presence of all these smiling, cheering faces. There were tears, too: there would be many who were not so lucky today. But the tears would not be hers.

The baker's wife gave her little girl a gentle push, and she trotted forward with her daffodils.

Catherine clenched one fist until she felt her nails break the skin, as Richard brushed against the child with his knee.

Allday was there in an instant: she had heard that he was good with children. The puckered face which had been about to burst into tears was all smiles again. The moment was past.

Catherine held out her arms. Richard had not seen the child. *He could not.*

Afterwards, she did not recall speaking, although she must have said something. Allday had grinned, and had made light of it.

Only in the carriage did she hold him, take his hands and press them against her to disperse his uncertainty, and his despair.

It was not a dream, and the ache would be gone until the next time, if it had to be.

Once he kissed her neck, and she heard him say, 'Don't leave me.'

She had answered strongly, for both of them, '*Never.*'

Beyond the harbour, the sea was quieter now. Waiting.